Jacqueline in Paris

ALSO BY ANN MAH

Instantly French!

The Lost Vintage

Mastering the Art of French Eating

Kitchen Chinese

Jacqueline in Paris

A Novel

Ann Mah

HARPER LARGE PRINT

An Imprint of HarperCollins*Publishers*

HarperCollins books may be purchased for educational, business, or sales promotional use. For information, please e-mail the Special Markets Department at SPsales@harpercollins.com.

FIRST HARPER LARGE PRINT EDITION

ISBN: 978-0-06-326622-3

Library of Congress Cataloging-in-Publication Data is available upon request.

22 23 24 25 26 LSC 10 9 8 7 6 5 4 3 2 1

To Arthur, Devorah, Diana, Jérôme, José, Timothy, and all my other French classmates and professors who have given me a priceless gift.

And to everyone who has had the courage and good luck to study overseas.

The American in Paris is the best American.

—F. SCOTT FITZGERALD

Prologue

Afterward I said I would rather not go back for a while. I had lived in Paris for a year and become so enchanted by its pleasures and so despondent when I returned that I felt it would have been better not to go in the first place. I said it partly to appease Mummy, but I meant it too, for when I allowed myself to think of the city—its seasons and moods, the curved shadows cast by wrought-iron grillwork upon limestone walls, the reek of stale cigarettes in the métro, the drizzly rain that softened colors and angles into a Caillebotte painting—I desired it so intensely I felt sick at the thought of losing it again.

It is so different, the feeling you have for a place when you're living there. My first visit to Paris, on the trip with Bow and the other girls from school, I thought the city was all glamour and glitter and rush. Yusha took us to a nightclub on the Champs-Élysées where we stared goggle-eyed at the revue with its full orchestra and satin-voiced siren belting torch songs, the gymnasts and puppeteers and flock of cabaret girls wearing rhinestones, ostrich feathers, and very little else. Miss Shearman, conscious of her duties as our chaperone, feigned shock at the latter, but my darling stepbrother gave her one of his gentle smiles and asked her to dance, leaving us girls to be dazzled in peace. I was eighteen years old and on my first trip to Europe, and I thought everything was marvelous.

When I went to the nightclub again, about a year later, to my surprise it seemed so garish. The orchestra sounded leaden, the torch songs overwrought, the cabaret girls' smiles stretched to a snap, their flimsy costumes glittering like tinsel. By this time I had been studying in Paris for a few months, flying between the Comtesse's apartment and my classes at the Sorbonne and Reid Hall in a lovely, tranquil, misty world. I really liked that quiet, contemplative side of Paris the best.

As time went on, I found my initial school-girl crush deepening into a much more relaxed and healthy affection. Released from a tourist's frenetic pace, I could observe the city and absorb its moods until they reflected my own: the bittersweet nostalgia of a winter afternoon, exiting a matinee to the yellow glow of streetlamps on wet cobblestones, the fizz of early spring when the café *terrasses* filled with people sipping candy-colored drinks. I loved wandering through the Tuileries and dreaming of how it might have looked two hundred years ago, or strolling in an unfamiliar arrondissement searching out street names that sounded like poetry: rue du Roi de Sicile (street of the King of Sicily); rue des Blancs-Manteaux (street of the white coats); rue de l'Arbre-Sec (street of the dry tree). I loved that the most famous avenue in France, the Champs-Élysées, was named after the Elysian Fields, the ancient heroes' paradise of Greek mythology.

I loved all the small theaters dotting the city, their performances as accessible and essential to Parisians as daily bread. The opera, the theater, the ballet—they were all so easy to get to, and so inexpensive. You could go out every night of the season and there would still be new things to see.

My feet have never been so cold as that year, nor have I ever craved coffee and sugar as I did under postwar rationing. Five years after the Liberation, the city was still struggling to recover from the dark days, neglected buildings crumbling and coated with grime, graceful façades pockmarked with bullet holes. Central heating and hot water were rarer than an Akhal-Teke stallion. Threadbare clothes hung off spare frames—everyone was still so thin—and women clattered about in wood-soled clogs left over from the Occupation, when shoe leather had disappeared.

Memories of the war lurked everywhere, as I discovered, but no one would admit it. Even as the mood grew steadily more hopeful—the Marshall Plan fulfilling its promise, fine food in the shops again, and tourists flooding back to the hotels on the Right Bank and Left—the ghosts drifted among us. I tried to ignore them; I wished they would disappear. Sometimes I could lose myself in a gallery at the Louvre, or the wild jazz of an airless basement nightclub in Saint-Germain-des-Prés. But then—a flinch at an unexpected knock on the door; the recoil at the sight of a single boiled potato on a plate; the sobs, quickly stifled, that woke me in the night. Eventually I came to understand that accepting the ghosts was part of loving France too.

But this is not a ghost story. Or, if it is, I am also among the ghosts: me, the reserved girl who arrived in postwar France with an uncertain grasp of the subjunctive tense and a blush for every opinion I expressed. I hadn't known what to expect from a year abroad in Paris, but some of what I'd hoped for came true: freedom from Mummy's critical eye and Daddy's adoring one, the unending wonder of travel in Europe, even a love affair . . .

One morning I woke from a dream: a dinner party in the carved, wood-paneled dining room of a grand château. I was bantering with the heavy-browed Frenchman seated beside me, my voice no longer soft and singsongy but nimble and sure. I was holding my own—in French! As I lay there blinking myself awake in the lustrous chill of a winter dawn, I realized it wasn't a dream but a memory of the night before. I had shed the role of the coy debutante who so often pretended to be empty-headed and become a young woman unashamed of my hunger for knowledge.

I loved it the most of any year of my life.

PART I

L'automne

Chapter One

In all my excitement I had scarcely managed to choke down a hardtack biscuit at dinner. It was September 1949, and I was hanging over the ship's rail with a couple of other Smith girls, hoping to spot the port. After several hours in our lookout spot, we were famished, out of cigarettes, and almost out of patience.

"Are those lights?"

"Where?"

"Over there on the horizon!"

"I think we're still too far."

"Gosh, this is taking ages."

"Can't be much longer now . . ."

"Evening, girls," said a voice behind us, and we turned to find the chief purser regarding us with a twinkle in his dark eyes. "Standing watch?"

"Lloyd!" We giggled and stepped back to gather around him. "We're hoping for land ahoy," said Mary Ann, blinking her round blue eyes. She had blond fringed hair and the placid features of a porcelain doll.

"We're longing to get to France," I added.

"And to get off this ship. No offense," said Martha, who'd been sick for nine days. "I forgot to pack my sea legs," she joked. Even queasy and wan, Martha had a sharpness that sliced across the stodgy, well-bred manner of the other Smith girls. A few days ago, I'd overheard her passionately defending one of my favorite French novels, Colette's *Chéri*, and was left thinking she was someone I'd like to get to know.

"Can't wait to see the back of us, eh?" Lloyd said. "And here I thought you girls've had a swell crossing!"

"Oh, yes, we have!" we chorused. In fact, ever since we boarded the SS *De Grasse* in New York Harbor, we had been showered with attention, feted, and photographed stepping arm in arm across the deck in our best travel suits. The long days at sea held plenty of diversions—screenings of French films and ping-pong tournaments, dances and costume contests. But what I loved most was strolling the promenade deck and staring out at the same vast ocean my French ancestors had crossed to come to America, conscious that I was making my own voyage to meet my fate, albeit in reverse.

Last night at the farewell gala the captain had asked our group to perform *"La Vie en rose"*—we were all crazy for Edith Piaf's sentimental ballad and knew the words by heart—and to my embarrassment he'd insisted that I sing the last verse alone. As the final chorus crested, I had seen more than one passenger blink away tears. Our ship, the *De Grasse*, had been sunk by German troops in defeat, retrieved from a watery grave in Bordeaux, and only recently restored to service as an ocean liner. Our group of about thirty-five young women from Smith College was an anomaly among the diplomats and tourists making the crossing—more than that, we were a sign of hope.

"We should be docking at about twenty-four hundred hours—that's what you girls call midnight," Lloyd said. "Maybe my expert eye can help you find the port." Leaning over the rail, he squinted into the distance. "See those lights?" He pointed. "Bright and still. That's Le Havre."

The lights were mere specks, as faint as distant stars, but I stared at them until my vision blurred. For so long the Normandy coast had existed only as a small square of newsprint map upon which all of us had pinned our hopes during those harrowing days of June 1944, when Allied troops had stormed ashore. Now it was becoming real before my very eyes. Though I wore a coat against the Atlantic's damp summer chill, I shivered a little.

"All right, m'lady?" Lloyd turned to me and proffered a courtly bow. A few days ago someone had told him I'd been named Queen Debutante of 1947, a silly old title invented by one of the New York gossip columns. Lloyd had teasingly addressed me with the chivalrous manners of a Renaissance knight ever since.

"Sure," I said, giving him a sidelong smile. The girls all thought he was dreamy, with his dapper white uniform and cleft chin, and I'd been flattered last night to find his gaze upon me while singing *"La Vie en rose."* Of course, Mummy would rather I perish of the black plague than carry on with an ocean liner's crewman— but my mother wasn't here and a mild flirtation wouldn't hurt anyone. "Isn't this thrilling?" I added in a soft voice. "You must've seen it a thousand times, but I'll never forget it."

"France is darn beautiful, all right. It's the French you have to watch out for." He grinned.

"Oh!" Mary Ann exclaimed. "I can see little boats in the harbor!" I resisted the urge to look. Daddy always told me and Lee that giving a man our complete attention was a girl's most charming lure. "Play hard to get, play hard to get . . . and bam! Turn it on like a lighthouse beam," he had instructed. "Men go wild for that."

"Won't be much longer now," Lloyd said agreeably. "Say, are you girls really going to spend an entire year in this place? I'd have thought a bunch of pretty ladies like you would be settling down with your fellows."

Martha looked askance at the idea. "And miss out on *this*?" she said.

Privately I had to agree with her. I had toured the continent the previous summer, a whirlwind itinerary with three boarding school friends and dear Miss Shearman, our former Latin teacher, as chaperone. But it had been so rushed I felt like I had been allowed only dainty sips of Europe, when I wanted great greedy gulps. Ever since I had first set eyes on Paris, the desire to live there had intoxicated me, making me sick with a longing that felt overwhelming once I returned to the constraints of Vassar's isolated world. Art club. Drama club. The college newspaper. All the while, my soul hungered for experimental theater and modern dance, jazz clubs and art museums, and flirting with a man who could talk about all of it.

And now here I was, sailing to spend my junior year abroad in Paris. I could almost taste the bitter tang of French coffee on my lips, smell the coarse heavy smoke of the tobacco. I tipped my face to the wind, feeling it whip across me with its chill and strength and scent of salt.

"Won't you get homesick?" Lloyd leaned forward to ask. "I can't imagine being away from my mama for so long."

Mary Ann—who had spent the first three days at sea in floods—welled up. "A whole year!" She sighed.

"You'll feel better on dry land," Martha told her.

"Of course I'll miss everyone," I said, so faintly Lloyd had to bend closer to hear me. "But it helps to meet a nice fellow like you."

"But how're you going to talk to people?" he pressed. "Can you speak French?"

"Of course," said Martha, and Mary Ann nodded.

"A little," I said.

"I took French in high school but whenever I try it out, I swear everyone is speaking gobbledygook." Lloyd gave a comic grimace, and we laughed. But a flush crept up his neck, betraying his embarrassment.

"I have that problem too," I said, touching his arm.

Before he could respond, a bell rang. "Excuse me, girls," Lloyd said, springing to attention. "Duty calls. Don't forget to come say goodbye before you disembark, all right?" We agreed, and he stepped briskly away.

An hour later we docked, the *De Grasse* slipping majestically through fog and darkness into the still ravaged port of Le Havre. Above, the midnight sky was choked with clouds of sulfur, beams of light filtering through dense smoke; below, the harbor traffic bustled with shouts and loud noises. "Do let's drink a toast!" cried Mary Ann. "In lemonade," she added hastily. We managed to find three fresh glasses and clinked them together. "To France!" said Mary Ann, and Martha and I echoed her, our faces bright enough to pierce the night.

In our stateroom below, we attempted to sleep before Martha's alarm clock rang at half past four for the pre-dawn passport examination. Despite the early hour, the portside deck was mobbed with what appeared to be the entire ship's manifest of passengers, shouting, shoving, and waving documents as they swarmed around two French officers who seemed more interested in chatting with each other than stamping anyone's papers.

"*Complete* and *typical* French inefficiency," muttered Martha.

"Is this what it's going to be like all year long?" Mary Ann asked, her voice small.

Confronted with the melee, I too felt my spirits beginning to dim.

"What if we miss our train to Paris?" Mary Ann fretted. "How will we find the rest of the group? Do either of you have the address for Reid Hall?"

"Hold on." I seized her arm. "Did you hear that?" Someone was making an announcement, but it was difficult to catch the words above the hum of the crowd.

"Hear what?" Martha froze.

"Wait." I closed my eyes to concentrate on the French: *Visas . . . long séjour . . . à tribord . . .* "Come on," I said, attempting to turn against the crush. "It's on the other side."

"Jackie, no!" Martha pulled my sleeve. "We have to go through passport control."

I shook my head. "Long-stay visas are being processed on the starboard side. Listen, there it is again." Once more I closed my eyes to decipher the words. When I opened them, both girls were staring at me like I'd pulled a kitten from my coat pocket.

"You understood that?" Mary Ann said finally. "It sounded like . . . like . . ."

"Gobbledygook," Martha finished her sentence.

"It took me a few tries," I said as we struggled against the crowd toward the stairs.

"Why did you say you couldn't speak French?" asked Martha when we had reached the starboard deck and joined the queue.

"Did I say that?" Glancing behind us, I spotted a few other girls from our program at the end of the line and lifted a hand to wave at them.

"Earlier, when we were talking with Lloyd . . ." She looked at me sharply. "You don't have to do that, you know. Play dumb."

"I don't know what you're talking about." I turned to rummage in my pocketbook, bristling at the criticism.

I had just checked my passport for the hundredth time when a tiny woman approached us with a brisk step. A long dark braid, threaded with gray, wound in a heavy crown around her head, and she wore a tailored black suit with a delicate pointed collar. In her hands she held a clipboard, which gave her an official air.

"*Bonjour, mesdemoiselles,*" she said. "Smith in Paris, I suppose? I am Jeanne Saleil, the program director." A heavy accent blurred her words, making them almost unintelligible.

"Madáme Saleil!" I exclaimed, almost forgetting my fatigue. "How do you do?"

Her chin tilted up, dark eyes assessing me in a glance, before she shook hands with each of us. "*Bienvenue en France,*" she continued, switching to rapid French. "Let's begin right away, yes? We will speak only French together, and this is how you will progress. Please introduce yourselves," she instructed. "Who will go first?" The three of us stole looks at each other, but no one stepped forward. "Come, girls," she chided. "You'll never learn this way. You must seize the moment!"

Finally, I cleared my throat. "*Bonjour, je suis Mademoiselle Bouvier de* New York." I tried not to wince at the sounds emerging from my mouth, rough and graceless, especially when contrasted with the lilt of her native eloquence.

"Let me see . . ." She ran a finger down the list on her clipboard. "Ah, yes, here you are." She ticked the sheet with a pencil. "Bouvier, Jacqueline."

I started to shake my head. I had been christened Jacqueline after my grandfather Bouvier by parents who hoped it would make me his favorite. But I had always been Jackie—or sometimes Jacks to my sister's Pekes—clipped and boyish, which I'd preferred to the dowdy Anglophone pronunciation of my name. Jack-lyn, my aunts used to say. Jack-lyn, you look peaky. Jack-lyn, your knees are dirty. Jack-lyn, the stables aren't for little ladies.

"Is that correct? Jacqueline?" Madame Saleil repeated. She said it with a swoop—*zhakleen*—all crisp consonants and liquid vowels. It sounded like the name of a novelist who had won the Prix Goncourt, the name of an artist collected in the Louvre—the name of the type of person I longed to be.

I hesitated, but only for an instant. "Yes," I said. "Call me Jacqueline."

Chapter Two

There was Normandy flashing through the windows of our rattletrap little train, its lush green fields a shocking contrast to the battle-scarred villages. There was Paris, chipped and scratched but still magnificent even in the driving rain, the landmarks looming out of the mist as we traipsed by them on an afternoon's sightseeing excursion. How I yearned for the city! But not yet, not yet, for as darkness fell, there was the Gare de Lyon, its cavernous hall quiet after the day's bustle. There we were, all thirty-five of us plus Madame Saleil, boarding the 22h07 to Grenoble, squeezing four by four into our train compartments, preparing for a night of upright sleep as we traveled 575 kilometers—"You should start thinking in the metric system," advised Madame S.—to this university town at the foot of the French Alps.

Sleep seemed impossible as I twisted in my narrow seat, trying to find a comfortable position, my head falling forward every time I drifted off. And yet I must have slept, for I woke to the sight of jagged, snowy peaks set against a rose-streaked sky. "The Alps," I whispered, touching my fingertips to the train window. The mountains' dark and rugged mass emerged from a cloud bank as if from a dream.

A short while later, we were standing in an overlooked corner of the Grenoble train station, suitcases and hatboxes strewn at our feet. *"Mesdemoiselles!"* Madame Saleil clapped lightly, calling our group to attention. "Before I send you to your host families, we have an important task. As you know, Smith respects the most rigorous academic standards. Over the next six weeks here in Grenoble, an intensive language course will prepare you for your studies in Paris. An important part of the program is our *engagement sur l'honneur.*" She held aloft her ever-present clipboard, to which was attached a sheet of lined paper. "By signing this pledge, you promise to speak French, and only French, at all times, with everyone—your professors, friends, host families, and each other. For the entire year."

She handed the clipboard to Mary Ann, who stared at her with huge, blank eyes. "Sign here!" Madame S. urged her, pointing and miming. Mary Ann obediently scrawled her name and passed the clipboard to her neighbor. "Soon you will start thinking in French," Madame S. proclaimed. "Soon you will even be dreaming in French!"

All of this, however, seemed very distant as I stood in my host mother's living room attempting to ask if I could take a bath. Widowed during the war, Madame Laurent lived in the suburb of La Tronche, a few miles from the university. Her rambling cottage, once charming, now appeared dilapidated, with flaking stucco walls and a sunken pitched roof. The surrounding garden had been turned into a vegetable patch, so crammed full it resembled an overflowing market basket. Walking to her front door, I had admired a laden fig tree and a trellis sagging with grapes the size of ping-pong balls. Little did I suspect they'd be the only fruit we'd eat for weeks.

"A bath?" I touched a hand to my chest. "It is possible?" It had been two days since I'd seen a basin of hot water—and a few weeks since I'd taken a real bath in a tub that didn't pitch and tumble with the moods of the Atlantic.

Madame Laurent raised her eyebrows, revealing a web of fine lines across her forehead. "In fact," she began, and then launched into an explanation of which I understood nearly all the verbs and only a few nouns: hot water, kitchen, toilet. Or was it *toilette*? Did she just mention the tramway? Why was she talking about place Victor Hugo? I struggled to make sense of it all, conscious that my face had frozen into a nervous grin.

"Come," she finally said. "I will show you the rest of the house." I followed her up the crooked staircase, averting my eyes from the vivid patches of wallpaper where paintings must have hung, to the second floor. "Here is your bedroom, which you've already seen," she said. "I hope it's suitable."

"It's perfect," I assured her. The room was very simple, almost Spartan, with a narrow white bed, a wooden chair and desk, and an enormous window that offered views of the craggy Alps surrounding us in every direction.

Next to me was the bedroom of the other lodger, Eero, a young Finn studying engineering at the university, our coed housing arrangement the result of postwar shortages. Then came Madame and, at the end of the hall, a closed door. "The bathroom," she said. Peeping inside, I found a bright and airy room furnished with a washstand, pitcher, and bowl—and an uncomfortable truth dawned on me. Was it possible the house didn't have the type of bathroom I took for granted at home, one with shining taps, bright lights for primping, and hot water gushing into a porcelain tub?

Downstairs, Madame Laurent showed me the

dining room—another set of French windows, another exquisite view of the Alps; the kitchen, with its wood-burning stove and antiquated cold-water spigot; and, finally, opening the back door, she gestured toward a small wooden structure a few yards from the house. "The W.C.," she said, and I knew this to mean the water closet, or toilet. At least there was one of those.

As the weeks went on, I learned about the quick, cold sponge bath known as *la toilette succincte*. I learned that hot water was precious, warmed on the stove, and allotted in three-inch increments at the monthly clothes washing. I learned to admire Madame Laurent's thrift. Like all Frenchwomen, and possibly all Europeans, the dark years had given her a flair for using things I would have thrown away: bits of string, laddered nylons, broken buttons. I learned to value the small American luxuries I'd taken for granted: running water, central heating, toilet paper. I learned to carry my own newsprint squares to the privy, in case there were none. And I discovered what Madame Laurent was saying that first day when I so presumptuously asked if I could bathe: Take the tramway to the public bath on place Victor Hugo, where ablutions cost 75 francs.

Grenoble had a way of making you forget about the other places in France you wanted to visit. The enchantment, I think, lay in the mountains circling the town, their presence so commanding you learned to use them for orientation. In the city center, you saw stately stone buildings embellished with ornate wrought-iron balconies, narrow cobblestoned streets lined with cafés, bakeries, and pastry shops. But only a brisk walk away, the countryside slumbered in wild beauty. Peasants clad in traditional Dauphinois dress—men in cropped trousers and white knee socks, women wearing embroidered aprons over rustling skirts—herded cows along twisting footpaths. The mountains concealed vineyards and farms, icy Alpine lakes ringed with birch trees, and even a medieval monastery where the silent devout had produced a sharp yellow-green liqueur called chartreuse for over three hundred years, steeping it with native herbs and flowers.

When Madame Saleil announced that our group would be making a weekend excursion to Provence, I begged her to allow me to visit my ancestral home of Pont Saint-Esprit. I had dreamed of seeing Provence for as long as I could remember, drawn to the bright sun and blazing colors depicted in paintings at the Met and enticed by the tales of Grampy Jack, my Bouvier grandfather, who often told his grandchildren of our noble lineage and lost ancient manor. The truth of the matter was that I was scarcely French, only one eighth on my father's side if I stopped to consider the family tree, which I rarely did because I didn't like to be reminded of it. "We are descended from a house of Pont Saint-Esprit in Provence," Grampy Jack used to say, scattering his lore with royal decrees and aristocratic marriages. "The blood of the nobility courses within your veins." On the worst days of my childhood, when my parents' quarreling rang so loudly in the apartment that I took to hiding in my closet, I would close my eyes and imagine my ancestors gliding along intricate parquet floors and candlelit mirrored halls. It wasn't quite the stuff of fairy tales, but it was enough to make me feel special when Mummy picked and poked at me, when Daddy drank too much and flirted inappropriately.

"Do you have relatives there? I could write to them," Madame Saleil offered when I explained.

"We lost each other many years ago. But my grandfather spoke often of our French family when I was younger."

"The name of a cousin, perhaps? I could ask my sister, who lives in the next village."

I had nothing more than the book Grampy Jack had written and published himself, *Our Forebears*, bound in red leather with gold-tipped pages, which I had tucked at the bottom of my valise despite its leaden weight, then lugged all the way to town to show her. "You see?" I said, as she examined our family coat of arms.

"It's a beautiful history," she said after a lengthy pause. Or had she meant story? In French the word was the same. "I do believe," she said slowly, "one should seize the occasion when it presents itself. What if, while the rest of us visit the Roman theater in Orange, you spent the afternoon in Pont Saint-Esprit?"

"Oh, Madame," I exclaimed. "That would be wonderful!"

"On one condition." She raised a hand. "You must bring a friend."

I tried to hide my dismay. "Really? Must I? I'm sure I'll be perfectly safe, and . . . I wouldn't want to inconvenience anyone. The girls are so excited about the excursion. It would be a shame if anyone missed it."

Madame S. was unmoved. "Before we leave on Friday, please let me know who will be accompanying you."

I spent the next few days thinking about whom I would ask. At this point, most of the girls had drifted into social groups formed by their friendships at Smith, or through residing with the same family in groups of two or three. Living out in La Tronche with Madame Laurent and Eero the Finn, I hadn't made any close relationships—but if I was being honest, I couldn't blame my circumstances alone. Fond though I was of the other girls, I kept my distance, hoping for a more authentic experience rather than one lumped with other Americans. Anyway, I never found it necessary to be part of a crowd. I preferred solitude, especially after long days of lectures on nineteenth-century novels and grammar drills in unheated classrooms. I knew I could have joined them at the nearby Café Anglais, drinking tea or sweet wine, and flirting madly with the other foreign students who gathered there. On Saturday nights, I could have double-dated to the school dance at the Vieux Temple, everyone so fresh faced, friendly, and cheerful, making plans for mountain climbing the next day. But I cherished the moments I spent alone, lost in a book, or, more often, my dreams and imagination. More than anything else, they sustained me.

"Six o'clock," Madame Saleil told us firmly. "That is when we will be back to pick you up. *Au revoir*—and good luck!"

We waved at the bus as it drove away, trailing a stream of exhaust from its rusted tailpipe. "What do you think?" I lifted a hand to shield my eyes against the glare. "Shall we have lunch first, or explore?"

"Let's eat," said Martha. "It's half past two already."

"There's a café open over there." I pointed to a restaurant spilling tables and chairs onto the square.

"Do you think it's suitable?"

"Fine with me," Martha said agreeably, and we started walking.

I had initially considered asking Mary Ann to accompany me, but as she was still too shy to even order a baguette at the bakery, I feared her reticence would dampen my courage, not spur it forward. Martha had proved herself witty and insightful in class—and admirably unembarrassed when she made a mistake (which Madame Saleil said was half the battle of learning a foreign language). Admittedly, her sharp words on the ship still smarted. But we had both been tired from the early hour and long journey, not to mention lack of sleep, and I thought she probably regretted them. How could she not? I wasn't the first girl to bat her eyelashes at a man and I wouldn't be the last.

"*Bonjour.*" A stout, dark-haired woman greeted us from the doorway of the café, wiping her hands on the skirt of her apron. "Two?" We nodded, and she indicated a table set squarely under an olive tree and covered with a worn chintz cloth. At this late hour, there were just a few other customers, but as we sat everyone turned to look at us.

"Guess they don't see too many strangers around here," Martha murmured.

"You want today's special?" Our waitress crossed her arms.

"What is it?" I asked.

"Brandade de morue." She spoke with the rolled *r*'s and singsongy flair of a Provençal accent.

"What is that?" said Martha.

"It's all we have left." She shrugged.

"Two specials," I said.

After our waitress had left, Martha asked me, "What would you like to do this afternoon? Is there something specific you're looking for?"

"Not exactly," I admitted. "My grandfather always talked about our ancestral home of Pont Saint-Esprit, but I don't have any information, except for the family history he wrote when I was a little girl. He spent ages working on it, and when he finally finished, he gave each of us grandchildren our own special copy. I must have read it a hundred times, dreaming about French chevaliers and imagining the court of Versailles. I think that's how I fell in love with France."

Our waitress returned, depositing upon the table a half pitcher of rosé wine, a basket of bread, and a small shallow dish filled with an oily black spread. *"Tapenade,"* she announced.

"Merci," Martha said. "Did we order this?"

"Comes with the special," she said, and retreated inside.

Martha poured wine into our glasses. "Does your grandfather's book mention any places of significance in Pont Saint-Esprit?"

"There aren't too many details," I said. "Lots of descriptions of coats of arms, though. Grampy Jack did love heraldry." I smiled fondly. "He always said that after all this time and neglect the old family château had probably crumbled to bits. I thought the ruins might still be here, though."

"Goodness, your ancestors sound glamorous," Martha said. "Mine were just humble old German carpenters before they emigrated to America."

My ears pricked up. "My great-great-grandfather was a cabinetmaker! He arrived in Philadelphia in 1815." I offered her some bread, then took a piece for myself, spreading upon it some of the black paste. It tasted of brine and earth, with a note of garlic—piquant, if vaguely illicit.

"How about that! A couple of woodworkers." She gestured at the shallow dish. "What is that stuff, by the way?"

"I haven't the faintest idea, but it's delicious. You should try it."

She reached for a piece of bread and scraped on a thin

layer of the oily black stuff, so tentative she reminded me of my stepfather, who had a mortal fear of garlic. "Careful," I teased her. "You don't want to overdo it."

She arranged her knife on the plate, and for a second I was afraid I might have offended her. But when she looked up again, her clear brown eyes were dancing. "I used to be even worse about trying new things," she confessed. "When I was little, I went through a phase where I would only eat white food."

"How did you get over it?"

"I'm still trying." She took a small bite of the bread.

"Well?"

"It's delicious." But I noticed she set the bread on the table and didn't touch it again.

Our waitress reappeared, plunking down two plates heaped with golden-crusted mashed potatoes and a pile of tender salad leaves. *Brandade de morue.* She pointed at the carafe of pale green liquid on our table. "Olive oil." Before we could ask any more questions, she was gone.

"I thought olive oil was medicinal," I said.

"Me too." Martha giggled. "I've seen it at the pharmacy."

"Well"—I reached for the carafe—"when in Provence . . ." I drizzled a thin stream over my food, and she followed suit.

After Grenoble's rustic mountain fare—potatoes, hard cheeses, cured meat, and more potatoes—I was a little disappointed to see even more potatoes. But unlike the starchy tubers of the Dauphiné, which were sliced and baked in cream, these were mashed and mixed with flaked white fish—reminiscent of the plain cod cakes beloved by my stepfather, Hughdie—but threaded through with a fruity, peppery richness that I realized was olive oil and tasted of sunshine. It felt like a holiday to eat something so different. Before I knew it I had finished the plate.

"Did you enjoy your lunch?" our waitress asked when she returned, replacing our empty dishes with one of ripe apricots.

"It was marvelous," I said.

For the first time, she smiled. "Do I hear an accent? Where are you from?"

"We're American," Martha said.

"Americans! So *that* explains the accent. I said to my mother, 'I can barely understand them!' I said, 'They have such thick accents, they must be foreigners!' I thought you were Swedish. She said English. But Americans! I never would've guessed it. Can I get you anything else? A tisane? Chicory? On the house."

"A tisane would be lovely, madame. *Merci*," said Martha. She looked amused but also faintly chagrined.

After all our weeks of studying and speaking French with one another, it would have been nice to have at least been mistaken for Belgian.

"I'll have chicory, please," I said. I had developed a fondness for the wartime substitute for coffee.

She soon returned bearing two steaming cups. "What brings you girls so far from home?" she asked as she set the drinks before us, along with a pot of honey that I knew must be very precious.

"We're university students," Martha said. "Studying in France for a year."

I stirred a polite drop of honey into my drink. "By any chance, madame, do you know of the Bouvier family here in town?"

"Bouvier?" She frowned. "Did you try the place de la République? About ten minutes' walk from here."

My heart skipped a beat. "*Merci*, madame! Will I be able to recognize the property? Is there a landmark I should search for?"

She seemed puzzled, but I assumed it was my accent. "You can't miss it, mademoiselle. There's a sign."

I had imagined bright flowers, sharp light, and all the bounty of a sun-drenched climate. But in the shimmering heat of late afternoon, Pont Saint-Esprit was empty and shuttered, the only signs of life the stray dogs and chickens running past scratched stucco buildings and the occasional drunk sleeping it off in a doorway. Despite its location at the confluence of two major waterways, the Ardèche and Rhône rivers, the town seemed choked with an air of sun-bleached desolation.

Martha and I turned onto the place de la République, and I looked for any signs of the château that had played such a role in Grampy Jack's family legends. But instead of decrepit crenellated walls and a moat, I saw a dusty square lined with shops and cafés, dilapidated shutters closed against the glare—or perhaps closed forever.

"This can't be right," I said. "It looks like the town's shopping area."

Martha touched my arm. "Look over there." She nodded at a storefront of glossy bottle green with a matching awning, its plate-glass windows displaying neat pyramids of canned goods. The sign above the door read:

ÉPICERIE
Antoine Bouvier

"Perhaps these are different Bouviers who are grocers," Martha suggested. "It's a fairly common name, isn't it? Do you know what it means?"

"It means cowherd," I said slowly. A strange feeling

was growing in my chest, but I ignored it as we crossed the street.

"I'll wait here," Martha said, indicating a shaded sidewalk bench. "I have a book—I'll be fine."

The hours posted on the door indicated that the shop had just reopened after the afternoon *sieste*. A bell jingled as I entered, and behind the counter a man glanced up from an accounts ledger. He wore a green apron over a shirt and tie and had dark, wavy hair receding from a prominent forehead. *"Bonjour,"* he greeted me.

"Bonjour," I responded, startled by his resemblance to my cousin John. Turning down an aisle, I pretended to inspect a shelf of dry goods while gathering my wits. Was he one of my distant Bouvier relations? Based on Grampy Jack's stories of grandeur, it seemed unlikely. But why else would we share the same surname? I began to hunt for something to buy so I'd have an excuse to approach him. The shop was tidy, with polished floors and freshly painted walls, the shelves filled with a surprising array of foodstuffs despite the postwar rationing. At the end of an aisle I found a rack of postcards and spun it slowly, selecting a few that pictured the town of Pont Saint-Esprit and its namesake bridge.

"Re-bonjour," the man greeted me again when I went to pay. "Did you find everything you need?"

"Yes, thank you," I said softly, pulling a few coins from my pocketbook.

"Have you had a chance to visit it yet?" he asked, slipping the postcards into a paper sleeve. "Or perhaps you need directions?"

I was startled, but quickly realized he was talking about the town's famous bridge. "Actually," I said, "I'm not here to sightsee. Are you Monsieur Bouvier?"

"I am," he said. The pleasant expression slipped from his face, replaced by a guarded smile.

"*Bonjour,*" I said again, hoping my voice sounded steadier than it felt. "I'm also called Bouvier—Jacqueline Bouvier—from New York. I'm here on a quest, in search of my Bouvier ancestors. I believe they emigrated from this town."

"There are Bouviers in New York?" he asked, surprised. "I remember hearing about a great-uncle who went to America. He was a foot soldier in Napoleon's army, and after the defeat at Waterloo he was forced to flee for his life. He joined Napoleon's exiled brother, Joseph, and became his cabinetmaker. But I was always told he went to—"

"Philadelphia." He and I spoke the word in unison.

"So you know the story too," he said.

"The version I heard was slightly different." I stared down at the tops of my shoes, which were covered in pale dust. "My grandfather spoke often of our ancestor Michel Bouvier, who fought beside Napoleon before emigrating to the United States in 1815. I came to Pont Saint-Esprit hoping to find the remains of our ancestral home. When I saw your shop, I wondered if you might tell me where it once stood."

He raised his eyebrows. "I fear there are no traces of your uncle here, mademoiselle."

"What about the ancient Bouvier château? Surely there must be ruins at least. Do you know where I could find them?"

He gave an embarrassed cough that might have been covering a laugh. "I'm sorry, but . . ."

The odd flutter in my chest had grown to a thundering beat, but still I pressed forward. "Well, how about our role in the American Revolution? My grandfather used to tell us stories about the Bouviers' ardent support of the American cause. Or what about our allegiance to the French monarchy? Long after 1789—"

"Mademoiselle," he broke in, "it gives me no pleasure to disabuse you of these notions, but simply none of this is true. The Bouviers were once but modest cattle herders who became villagers around the time of the Revolution. We have been shopkeepers in Pont Saint-Esprit ever since—and we take pride in our work, humble though it may be."

"Of course," I said. My cheeks felt violently hot. I had been so caught up in my fantasy I had overlooked what was right in front of me. "I am sorry, monsieur," I said. "I suppose I let my imagination get carried away. You have a fine shop."

He bowed his head and jerked it up again, a sharp and perfunctory nod. *"Merci."* He picked up his pencil to dismiss me.

I turned to go, regret slowing my departure. This meeting—this entire day—had not turned out the way I had imagined, and I wished that I could somehow right it. But there were the church bells chiming five o'clock, and there was Monsieur Bouvier frowning at his accounts book, and I knew I had no choice but to leave.

"Papa?" A small voice spoke, and a little boy with dark curls appeared from the back of the shop.

"Simon," said Monsieur. "I thought you were upstairs."

"Can I have a snack? I'm hungry."

"Where is your aunt?"

"It's laundry day."

Monsieur sighed. "My boy," he explained to me. "I'll just fetch him a bit of bread," and he disappeared to the back.

"Bonjour, Simon," I said, crouching down to meet

his gaze. He had a fierce little face and eyes as green and glossy as olives.

"Are you really from New York?" he asked. "I heard you say so."

"Indeed, I am."

"Have you ever met a cowboy? I'm going to be one when I grow up."

"Not a real one, no. But I know they like horses." I pointed to the wooden one in his hand. "Does he have a name?"

"His name is Banjo. Maman gave him to me before she went away."

"He looks terribly valiant," I said. "Do you know I have a horse in America? Her name's Danseuse, but I call her Donny. She's a silly old thing. Definitely not as brave as you and Banjo." *And neither am I*, I thought, as Simon's face turned up to mine, reminding me what we owed the world as Americans, as the victors.

"Can she jump?"

"Danseuse, jump? Oh, boy, can she ever! She'd jump all the way from New York to Paris if she could. Would you like to see a picture?" He nodded, and I reached for my pocketbook to show him the photo I kept inside. "See? She's a chestnut mare with a white star on her forehead. She likes to nuzzle my pockets to see if I've brought her sugar cubes." I handed him the photo, and he examined it.

"Here you are, Simon." Monsieur Bouvier strode toward us and handed the child a slice of bread that had been scraped with something sticky.

"*Merci.*" The boy crammed bread into his mouth with one hand while gazing at the photo in his other. "Banjo likes Danseuse," he announced. "Can he keep her?"

"Simon!" his father admonished. "You can't just ask strangers to give you things."

"Can he keep the picture, *please*?" Simon said dutifully. He set the wooden toy on the shop counter, where it wobbled on thin legs. Something about its worn paint told me his mother had been gone for a while.

Monsieur Bouvier moved to shoo him away, but I touched his arm. "You know, I think that's a fine idea. Danseuse would be pleased to know she's found an admirer."

"What do you say?" his father prompted.

"*Merci!*" he cried, skipping off to play with his new treasure.

"That's kind of you," Monsieur Bouvier said. "He doesn't remember his mother very much, but he knows she loved horses."

He spoke lightly, but my throat tightened at

his words. I wished I knew how to tell him that I understood—that as a child I had also found comfort in animals as a way to fill the emptiness I felt inside. Instead I said, "I loved horses when I was his age too, monsieur."

"Please." He leaned against the counter, his expression softening. "We are almost certainly cousins, are we not? Call me Antoine."

I touched a hand to my chest. "Jacqueline."

"Are you certain you're from America, Jacqueline?" he said gallantly. "Because you speak French like a native."

"You are too kind," I said, blushing, even though I knew he was just being polite. But he seemed genuinely interested, and so I told him about the Smith study-abroad program and how our weekend excursion to Provence had seemed like the perfect opportunity to visit the ancestral village I had dreamed about my entire life. "But now I wonder if I shouldn't have come," I admitted.

"You know, my mother often used to say to me, 'Come back to earth, Antoine, you're living on the moon.' And Simon, I see him doing it too—pretending he's John Wayne crossing the far West and completely ignoring what's in front of him. It is possible that this runs in our family. Just as you were dreaming of your ancestors in France, I used to dream of America. The land of gold, and streets paved with opportunity."

His eyes met mine and I felt a jolt of recognition. Along with our propensity to build castles in the air, we shared the same reluctance to let them drift away. I drew a shaky breath. "It's a bit of a shock to believe one thing and then discover the truth is quite the opposite."

"I take it the land is not actually gold over there?"

Through the plate-glass window, I saw the late afternoon sun had descended incrementally, its fierce light softening into long shadows that had begun to creep across the dusty, desolated street.

I held back a sigh. "Afraid not."

Back outside, the afternoon still blistered with heat. On any other day, I would have been charmed by the climate—so typically Provençal!—but now I couldn't stop brooding over my memories of Grampy Jack, comparing his grandiose tales to the reality of what I had found in Pont Saint-Esprit. Why had he exaggerated so? Was it purely vanity, or had he believed the things he'd written? He had been a stern patriarch, stone deaf and exceedingly loud because of it, although he had a soft spot for me, his namesake granddaughter. He delighted in the verse I penned, introduced me to his favorite poems, challenged me to read with a critical eye.

But he had been vain too, with his bespoke tailored tweeds and waxed mustache, and it didn't surprise me that he might have succumbed to the allure of aristocratic bloodlines—even if he had to invent them.

Had this been his way of protecting us? In the rigid social hierarchy of Park Avenue, the blot of Catholicism or scandal of divorce could forever taint you, and as the child of divorced Catholics, I had firsthand knowledge of both. I had learned to shield myself with my individuality, wearing it like a suit of armor, brandishing my Frenchness as a foil. Tears suddenly stung my eyes. For so long I had believed in my rarefied French heritage as a secret talisman, taking refuge in it, finding strength in it. But now I knew it was a lie.

"We still have time to visit the town's famous bridge before the bus returns," Martha said, glancing at her watch. "If you like."

"Oh, yes, do let's." I tried to inject some enthusiasm into my voice. "After all, how could we come to Pont Saint-Esprit and not visit *the* pont Saint-Esprit? Madame Saleil would give us poor marks for tourism." Examining the map Martha had bought at the newsstand, we turned toward the river.

If Martha was curious about what had happened at the *épicerie*, she kept it to herself. Instead, we chatted about the history of the "bridge of the holy spirit," which she had read while waiting for me. "It's the oldest bridge across the Rhône," she said as we walked. "Almost a kilometer long. Built in the thirteenth century by Alphonse of Poitiers, the brother of Saint Louis."

Once we were standing upon the bridge, however, I failed to see what made it so special. "Why, it's no different from crossing the Key Bridge over the Potomac," I said. "Dirty old river water. And the trees crowd the banks so that you can hardly see a thing."

"The church is quite lovely," said Martha, indicating the Gothic Église Saint-Saturnin along the other side.

"It is," I agreed, but without much ardor.

Martha craned her head in both directions, left, right, and back again. "Hold on," she said, grasping my arm. "We got it wrong! We should be over there"—she pointed at the Église Saint-Saturnin—"looking over here. Not over here looking over there. Don't you see? Come on!" She took off along the bridge, running down a flight of stairs, and I followed close behind. When we reached the quay she came to a stop beside the church, ducking into a patch of shade. "Look!" she said, puffing slightly.

From here we could see the medieval stone bridge as it shone in the afternoon sunlight, stretching across the Rhône in a series of symmetrical arches. At this angle, I could see the length of it, sense the scope—it was an incredible feat of engineering for any era, let alone the thirteenth century. Gazing at its straight, simple lines set against the cloudless Provençal sky, I felt my spirits lift a fraction.

When the bus returned for us at six o'clock, the girls were jolly and sunburned, chattering about the little restaurant where they'd eaten a late lunch and how someone had put a stack of records on the gramophone and they'd all gotten up to dance. "Imagine 'Bongo, Bongo, Bongo' and 'Chattanooga Choo Choo' playing in this tiny village in the middle of nowhere!" Mary Ann exclaimed. "I could scarcely believe my ears!"

I smiled at her earnest astonishment, but I couldn't help wondering how much more of America we would encounter here. I had expected to find France frozen in time—and yet here was our pop music blaring in remote country restaurants, here were small boys idolizing John Wayne and young people ordering Coca-Cola at the café. I had dreamed of traveling back in time—and yet here I was, a witness to European recovery, an envoy of the future.

The past—*my* past—was irrelevant. I would need to summon all my native optimism to see that as a promise.

Chapter Three

I was late, but she was later, and so I waited at a little round table on the café *terrasse*, longing for a cigarette but not wanting to make a bad first impression. Instead, I watched the pedestrians as if they were stage actors: a spidery old lady dressed in black, from her fusty silk hat to her sensible, scuffed shoes; two men in suits greeting each other with double cheek kisses; a group of young people chatting madly as they fanned in and out with the narrowing sidewalk. Were they university students at the nearby Sorbonne—my future classmates, perhaps?

A ray of afternoon sunlight snuck past the striped awning and sparkled on the marble-topped table. Around me the sounds of the café pattered gently—the scrape of rattan chairs upon terra-cotta tile, the clink of thick china punctuating a demure lilt of French voices—and I saw a slight young woman dashing along the sidewalk, a light jacket slung across her shoulders. She paused at the café entrance, scanning the *terrasse* until her eyes landed on me and my red travel skirt.

"Jacqueline?" she said, moving toward me. She wore a crisp white shirt nipped at the waist, a gray pencil skirt, and low heels. Her short dark hair, set in loose waves, was swept back from her forehead, and her straight brows and dark eyes gave her face an intense, serious expression. "I am Claude de Renty," she said. I rose, extending my hand to shake hers, but to my surprise she moved closer and kissed me on both cheeks. "Please excuse me for being late. I was meeting with my history professor and he's a bit verbose." She spoke in quick, colloquial French, slipping immediately into the informal *tu* form of you. "It's all right if we speak French, *n'est-ce pas?*" she asked, sitting in the chair across from me. "I find English sometimes difficult." I was surprised by this as I knew Claude had recently returned from her own year abroad in the United States, studying at Wellesley and Mount Holyoke Colleges. Then again, by requesting that we speak French together, I immediately felt less self-conscious about my own feeble vocabulary and slippery grammar—and perhaps that was her goal.

"Of course French is fine. I'd prefer it, actually."

"*Bon.* Ah—here comes the waiter. Do you know what you'd like?" She tipped her head, inviting me to go first.

"Picon-citron," I said. Madame Saleil always ordered the sharp drink of orange bitters and lemonade at the café, and the Smith girls considered it the height of authenticity. Even though I'd have preferred a soda pop, what was the point of being in Paris and drinking the same old things I drank in New York?

"I'll have a Coca-Cola," Claude said firmly. "With ice." Our waiter bustled away, and she turned to me. "How was your journey? You are not too tired?"

"Not at all." In fact, though I was fresh off the overnight train from Grenoble, I had never felt more alive. "You can't imagine how wonderful it is to be here. And this weather!" I gestured widely, indicating the unseasonable spill of sunshine, the crystalline sky. "It feels tropical after all the rain in Grenoble. I could burst into song!"

A smile flickered across her pale features and quickly disappeared. "We're so pleased to host you this year. My mother especially has been looking forward to meeting you."

"It's awfully kind of you. I don't think my mother would have let me come if the Comtesse hadn't written to assure her she'd look after me." When Mummy had learned some Smith girls were housed at Reid Hall—in drafty cold-water rooms that abutted the men's dormitories—she had moved heaven and earth to find "suitable" lodging for me. Unleashing her social connections like a pack of bloodhounds, she eventually tracked down a summer acquaintance from Newport whose daughter's Parisian mother-in-law knew a widowed countess living in shabby gentility. The Comtesse de Renty was eminently respectable, the matriarch of an aristocratic family that had fallen on lean times, with a rambling apartment in the bourgeois 16th arrondissement. Though she had already committed to hosting two other Smith girls, she agreed to squeeze me in as well. Mummy had been thoroughly pleased (a rare occurrence), and I was thrilled by the prospect of a true immersion with a French family.

"Maman has the apartment all prepared." Claude nodded at our waiter as he placed our drinks on the table. "You will be in the front bedroom by yourself, and Mary Ann and Susan will share the bedroom on the courtyard." She poured from the bottle of Coke, half filling her glass.

"That's so thoughtful—but I don't mind sharing if it's more convenient."

Claude shrugged. "Maman thought this would be

best. Her room is off the kitchen. My sister, Ghislaine, and her little boy are in the *petit salon* next to you. And I'm in a room at the back."

I hid my relief behind a sip of lemonade. I knew Mary Ann from the ship, of course, and recognized Susan as a bright and lively Smithie. But I had feared that in a household of seven, it would be difficult to find the solitude I craved—not to mention forge my own independent social life. At least I would have a place of retreat.

"I do hope we won't be in your way," I said, stirring my drink with a long-handled spoon. "You must let us know if you and your family need time on your own."

"Don't be silly. The apartment is your home. It will be lovely for us to have you there, especially after . . ." Her face closed. "We are delighted."

After what? I wanted to ask—but it wasn't ladylike to pry, as Mummy had told me a thousand times. "Tell me about your classes," I said instead. "You're at Sciences Po?"

She nodded. "I've got geography and economics this semester—and the history of international relations."

I leaned forward, my attention caught by the latter. Growing up during wartime had forged my passion for history—I was twelve when America joined the conflict against the Axis. That was the Christmas

Mummy took Lee and me to Washington D.C. on "a sightseeing tour," she'd said, though I later realized that her true purpose was to introduce us to Hughdie, whom she would marry the following summer; and his son Yusha, who would become my stepbrother and one of my dearest relations. Ten days before our trip the Japanese bombed Pearl Harbor, and we arrived to find the capital crackling with chaotic energy. But still we toured the usual sites: the Washington Monument and Lincoln Memorial; Mount Vernon and the White House, the latter shockingly dreary and quickly forgotten; and ended at Arlington Cemetery, where rows of white graves reached as far as the eye could see. HERE RESTS IN HONORED GLORY AN AMERICAN SOLDIER KNOWN BUT TO GOD, read the inscription on the Tomb of the Unknown Soldier, and suddenly my eyes were burning. The First World War had seemed so abstract, the stuff of dull lessons and grownup talk at the dinner table. But standing on that gently curved hill, the stone markers multiplying in my mind's eye at sickening speed, I finally grasped its devastation. How many more graves would be added here now that America was again at war? How many of my friends' older brothers would be buried here? I had been a precocious child who loved reading history for its tales of flamboyant kings and tragic queens, but that day I understood something else—that history helps us understand the present.

"The class on the history of international relations—will it focus on Europe?" I asked Claude.

"It starts with ancient Mesopotamia, believe it or not. Apparently the Sumerian city-states are considered the first true international system."

"Isn't Sumer utterly fascinating? All those marvelously named kings—Hammurabi and Ur . . ."

"Nebuchadnezzar . . ."

"Oh, yes!" Forgetting my manners, I propped my chin on a hand. "Didn't he build the Hanging Gardens of Babylon for his homesick wife? My sister and I used to swoon over that story."

"Perhaps you could join the course," Claude suggested. "Can you enroll at Sciences Po?"

"I'm not sure. Most of our lectures are at Reid Hall, and we're meant to take the rest at the Sorbonne and École du Louvre. You know—art, literature, theater." Safe subjects, I thought, but didn't say. Predictable. Unthreatening.

From the glint in Claude's eye, I thought she might have understood. "Could you ask the program director?" she suggested.

I considered Madame Saleil and her exhortations to *"profiter du moment présent,"* or seize the day.

She might agree to help me, but Mummy would be displeased if I pursued a special, rigorous academic course. *Men don't like clever girls,* I could almost hear her say. Was it worth risking her ire? "I don't think so," I said.

By this time Claude's glass was empty and I had drunk what I could of the Picon-citron. "Let's take a walk," she proposed. "I'll show you around the neighborhood."

We stepped into the bustle of the boulevard Saint-Michel—*"le boul'mich,"* Claude called it—lined with the universal trappings of student life: cheap restaurants, secondhand clothing shops, stationers, and academic bookstores. I was expecting her to lead me past the Sorbonne, where we would politely admire the famous Baroque chapel, then head toward the Seine, crossing over the pont Saint-Michel to Notre Dame. But Claude's tour of the Latin Quarter was a little different.

"Over there that's *la fac,*" she said, gesturing at an ornate limestone façade. *"La faculté.* The university," she added. "But you'll be spending lots of time there, so we won't stop. Here's my favorite newsstand." She waved at a portly man stacking magazines outside a kiosk. "He's terribly sweet—always saves me a copy of *Les Nouvelles littéraires.*" We turned off the boulevard onto a slender street lined with chestnut trees. "I adore this café," Claude said, indicating an establishment that looked as grimy as all the others we had passed. "They're mean as snakes, but they have the most marvelous *flipper.*" She must have noticed my confusion, because she laughed. "Pinball," she explained in English. "Everyone's wild for it. You'll see."

And thus Claude introduced me to student Paris—frugal Paris—the Paris of turtleneck collars, cold feet, and discounted tickets for all the cultural activities. Her favorite lunch spot, Bouillon Racine: "Meat *and* veg *and* cheese *and* fruit *and* wine—for under 200 francs!" The shabby hotel, the Maison des lettres, where many of her classmates lived: "Not as grim as it looks but some idiot's always playing the saxophone off-key." The tiny box of a nightclub that played *"jazz hot"* on Thursday evenings, and the scruffy experimental theater that staged modernist plays. The cinema on rue Christine that screened undubbed American films. The "essential" (according to Claude) bookshop on the place de la Sorbonne that sold mimeographed copies of university lectures—"so you can skip class, *tu sais?*"

We headed toward Saint-Germain-des-Prés so Claude could collect a book from the library. Because she disliked walking along the Seine—"too many *clochards,*" she said (and thus I learned the word for hobo)—we zigzagged through a tangle of narrow streets lined with ancient buildings, their stone surfaces coated in grime. Tucked at street level was an array of shops—grocers and cobblers, pharmacies and bakeries—the shelves half filled, empty of customers.

We turned a corner, and the river stretched before us, rippling gray and edged by fading trees. "Le pont des Arts," announced Claude, nodding at a wooden pedestrian bridge spanning to the Right Bank. "And here we are."

In front of us stood a veritable Baroque palace, two massive wings arcing toward the river, anchored by a columned portico and topped with a cupola. "*This* is the library?" I said, as we picked our way across a vast cobblestone courtyard.

"Isn't it terrible?" She pulled a face. "It's needed restoration since even before the war."

"Oh," I said, because I couldn't quite tell if this was dry French wit or some innate form of cultural self-criticism.

Inside, the library was as magnificent as its exterior, an immense gallery of wooden bookshelves that were decorated with carved Corinthian columns. Marble busts stood at regular intervals, slim wheeled ladders reached to the top rows, and a bank of windows cast light on the leatherbound volumes. Noting my awestruck silence, Claude explained that this was the oldest public library in France, created by Cardinal Mazarin in the seventeenth century for his personal use. Over the centuries it had grown to house several important collections, including one specializing in French history. "I'm researching a paper on the origins of the French Revolution," she said.

While Claude approached the circulation desk, I explored the reading room. The rare volumes were under lock and key, but I found a shelf of regional French history, pleased to see a book on the folklore of the Alps—I would always think of Grenoble and its environs as my landing spot in France. Against the wall, a wooden stand displayed an oversized tome, which a small brass plate informed me was a replica of the Mazarin Bible, printed by Gutenberg, the original stored in the library's vault. I leafed through a few pages of its uniform Gothic script, trying unsuccessfully to decipher the Latin, before turning toward the windows where a bust of Molière faced the room with a pensive expression.

Through the glass I saw that clouds had begun to gather, dimming the late afternoon light so that my reflection shimmered against the view of moody sky and cobblestones. Without warning a feeling of exhilaration engulfed me, born of the magnificent room, the heady scent of old books, the possibilities of Paris waiting to be plucked like cultured pearls from their oyster beds.

It had started to rain by the time we left the library, the type of sudden, pelting downpour that—I was quickly learning—so often followed an unseasonably warm afternoon in Paris. Claude and I dashed for the métro, but without umbrellas we were soon soaked. "Never mind," she said, after we had squeezed, dripping, onto a rush-hour train. "Once we reach our stop, it's only a few steps to the front door."

Exiting at Jasmin, I had scarcely taken stock of my surroundings before we arrived at a large building located not thirty paces from the station. Claude retrieved a skeleton key from her bag and unlocked the massive door, revealing a spacious foyer decorated in the variegated marble panels and Neo-Classic columns of the Art Nouveau. Ignoring the elevator, we climbed a curved staircase to the second floor, which would have been the third floor back home.

"Maman!" she called, opening the front door. "We're home!"

From the entry hall, the apartment unfurled in an enfilade of rooms and herringbone parquet, smelling of beeswax polish and something delicious cooking on the stove. Sounds of conversation drifted toward us, followed by footsteps.

"Ah, here you are at last!" A tall, slender woman

moved down the hall, the undulating skirts of her sapphire-blue dress almost concealing a limp.

"*Salut, Maman.*" Claude kissed her mother hello. "May I present Jacqueline?"

"*Bonsoir, Jacqueline. Bienvenue,*" said the Comtesse de Renty. She had faded chestnut hair coiffed in artful waves, and a smile that creased the smooth contours of her face. As she moved to exchange cheek kisses with me, I caught the gentle scent of lavender and roses. "It's lovely to meet you, my dear."

"*Enchantée, Madame,*" I echoed. Her eyes resembled Claude's—dark and intelligent—but there was a watchfulness in them that made me feel shy.

"Did you have a pleasant afternoon? I hope Claude hasn't tired you out with one of her beloved long walks." She gestured for my coat and, when I gave it to her, hung it in the front closet.

"I only showed her around the Latin Quarter and we stopped by the Bibliothèque Mazarine," Claude protested. "It wasn't so terribly long."

"I adored it," I assured her. "Especially the library. I wanted to sneak behind the curtains and stay up all night reading books, like when I was a child. My nurse would scold me so terribly, I used to scrub the soles of my feet so she wouldn't know I'd snuck out of bed."

Claude grinned at this tale, but the Comtesse seemed

to regard me with new interest. "I would have done quite the same." She took a step toward the hall. "Now, my dear, you must want to get settled after your train journey, *n'est-ce pas?* We'll have a simple dinner and you can retire early. Claude, can you help in the kitchen while I show Jacqueline the apartment?" Her voice was like birdsong, the French rising and falling with fluid grace, but I sensed that when she issued a request she expected compliance.

Claude nodded, and I followed the Comtesse into a spacious *salon* filled with delicate furniture—spindly-legged sofas and side tables, a carved marble mantelpiece festooned with bibelots, tall windows covered with damask curtains, lofty ceilings accentuating a draft. Tapestry panels adorned the walls, faux-candle electric sconces cast a weak light, and perched on a pair of upright armchairs, I found my fellow lodgers.

"Bonjour!" chirped Susan with a sprightly wave, while Mary Ann exclaimed, "Jackie, hi!" and heaved a relieved sigh. I gave them a polite smile before continuing on the tour.

The dining room was next, the table already set for dinner; then the *petit salon*, now the room of Ghislaine and her son; and then more bedrooms, one, two, three, their doors closed.

At the end of the hall stood the kitchen, dark and

uninviting, with its scuffed linoleum, steamy atmosphere, and multibolted and chained back door leading to the servants' staircase. Claude was here, stirring a pot on the antediluvian stove and looking harried—though she declined our offers of help.

Across the hall was the bathroom, plain with a cracked porcelain sink and antique tub, lit by a dim bulb swinging from the ceiling. "The toilet is here," Madame said, opening the door of a separate chamber. Instead of toilet paper, newsprint squares hung from a hook on the wall. "I'm afraid there's just one for the seven of us," she said. "Parisian plumbing is terribly outdated."

I swallowed my surprise. "It's part of the charm," I said, using my soft little half whisper to hide my discomfiture and noticing for the first time that it sounded strangely saccharine in French.

Walking back down the hall, we arrived again at the front of the apartment. "Here we are at last," Madame said, opening the door of the room next to that of Ghislaine and her little boy. "You're in here."

"Oh!" I exclaimed. "How lovely." And it was, with tall windows facing the street, and a mahogany bed made up in a pale green chintz that repeated in the sweeping curtains. There was a graceful half sink for my toilette, a wooden bookcase semifilled with well-thumbed volumes, a desk with a cane-backed chair, a handsome armoire, and a rug, nobly frayed. Though I hadn't seen the other bedrooms, this one was so well appointed I had the uncomfortable feeling it was the nicest in the apartment, and I suspected Mummy's orchestration.

Madame didn't smile, but she looked pleased. "Would you like to freshen up before dinner? Let me know if you need anything." She closed the door gently behind her, leaving me alone.

My trunk had already arrived—it stood against a wall looking awkwardly sharp and shiny among the rest of the furnishings. Unlocking it, I removed a framed photo of Daddy, placing it on the bedside table, where I always kept it. Then I threw open the windows and leaned over the wrought-iron railing of the half balcony—the type of *balconnet* from which Juliet might have gazed upon Romeo—looking at the small shops dotting the block below. They were starting to close for the evening, tugging down their metal shutters with a rough, grating scrape.

The rain had stopped, leaving behind a fine mist that felt silken against my cheeks after the unexpected chill of the apartment. I half turned to look back at my room, the books winking from their shelves. How I longed to choose one, curl up on the bed, and lose myself in its pages! But no, I still had dinner to get through, hours of polite conversation before I could retreat into my thoughts. And so—even though I knew I shouldn't without asking—I did the next best thing: I lit a cigarette, narrowing my eyes as the heavy French tobacco stung the back of my throat, exhaling deep into the night.

At dinner six of us gathered around the oval table, with Madame at the head. The dining room's delicate crown moldings and furniture echoed the rest of the apartment, but I saw hints of the family's reduced circumstances in a chipped faience soup tureen, waterspotted stemware, and threadbare linen napkins.

"I put Christian to bed a few minutes ago, so if you hear him squawking just ignore him," Ghislaine announced. She was a few years older than me, with the same dark hair and wide brow as her sister, though she spoke more impulsively than Claude. "He's cross because I wouldn't let him spend the night in the car. He thinks it's safe because I found a parking spot right beside the front door."

"He's simply darling," said Mary Ann. "How old is he?"

"He's three. We only recently moved in with Maman, and he's still adjusting." I noticed Ghislaine did not provide an explanation for her son's absent father, nor did she appear embarrassed.

"This soup is delicious, Madame," said Susan from

across the table, changing the subject, like the well-bred Upper East Side girl I remembered from our deb days.

"Thank you, my dear." The Comtesse brightened. "It's just leeks, potatoes, and a touch of butter to finish. Would anyone like some more?"

We shook our heads. Claude said, "Shall I clear the soup plates, Maman?" and began to bustle the dishes away. By this point, I had noticed that, like us lodgers, she and Ghislaine addressed their mother with the formal form of you—*vous*—while Madame called all of us by the informal *tu*—a combination of bourgeois politesse and French grammar that seemed as intricate as an inlaid marquetry credenza.

"We eat lots of soup in this house," Ghislaine said as Claude heaved a covered cast-iron cocotte to the table. "It's one of Maman's great specialties." A playful expression slid across her face.

"It's simple to make, *chérie*," said Madame, unperturbed. "And very forgiving if someone forgets to tell me they'll be home for dinner."

Ghislaine chortled. "*Touché*," she said, and I was struck by their banter, which felt gentle and affectionate, completely unlike the poisonous barbs of my own family.

Susan leaned forward, anxious to please. "How much notice *should* we give for meals?"

Madame replaced the lid of the cocotte and set the serving spoon beside it. "If you're not going to be home for dinner, just a few hours in advance is fine. As for lunch, I'm usually out at midday with my volunteer work, and I suppose you girls will be at school?" We nodded, and she continued: "And breakfast, it's very simple—just baguette, hot chocolate or coffee . . . when we have it. Do you know about the ration cards?"

"Yes," said Susan. "Madame Saleil told us we'd need to go to the *mairie* to collect them."

"That's right," Madame said. "I'm afraid you can't even touch coffee and sugar without them." She took a sip of wine. "Since we're talking about the household, may I ask that, if you smoke, please empty the ashtrays before you retire for the evening."

Along with Mary Ann and Susan, I agreed and hoped no one had smelled my cigarette before dinner.

"Oh, and one last thing," she added. "If you'd like to receive gentlemen callers, they're welcome in the *salon* until ten o'clock." This was unexpected, as we'd been told that most French families wouldn't allow them farther than the front door.

"Golly!" exclaimed Mary Ann. "And here I thought my folks were strict kicking the boys out at eleven," she said in English.

"*Pardon?*" said Madame, who had not understood.

"That's very kind," Susan said, and I added a murmur of appreciation.

"Do let me know if you need anything for your rooms," Madame said, beginning to serve small portions of chicken in red wine sauce. "Extra pillows or blankets? I'm afraid our heater needs repairing." This, then, explained the apartment's pervasive chill.

"Why, the climate here is positively tropical compared to Northampton!" Mary Ann exclaimed. "I'm sure I won't feel the cold one bit this winter."

Claude lifted an eyebrow. "You may be surprised."

They began discussing the winter climate of the Île-de-France versus that of western Massachusetts, but my eye had been caught by a piece of furniture in the corner of the dining room, a glossy cabinet with a curved glass door. From my seat a few feet away, I tried to discern the objects arranged within: a small bird's nest, a silver cup smudged with tarnish, a branch of red coral with arms as sinuous as snakes, a baby's shoe preserved in bronze. Other shelves displayed a disembodied doll's head, an assortment of seashells and stones, the skull of some small animal, a model ship glued with an unsteady hand.

"I see you've noticed my treasures," Madame murmured, as the others debated the merits of mild, rainy days against sunny, sharp ones.

I started. "I was admiring your collection," I said, glancing at her from under my lashes. "It's such a lovely combination of memories and rare objects."

She leveled her gaze at me. "How clever of you to notice, my dear. I've always felt that a *cabinet de curiosités* should display the personal as well as the natural. It adds a sense of surprise . . . an element of wonder."

"In what way?" I asked, intrigued. My parents' homes weren't like this one—not Daddy's poky Manhattan apartment, nor Mummy's manicured houses, which were more a reflection of decorators' tastes than her own. Both my parents were too sensible—or selfish—to nurture a sense of wonder.

"Humans are sentimental creatures, *n'est-ce pas?*" she said. "We gather mementos to help us recall happy occasions, moments of delight—to remind us of the innocence that exists in the world. My husband used to tease me for hoarding all these bits and pieces. But now I find they're like a museum of comfort." Her tone remained light, but I sensed the sorrow underpinning her words. I could only guess at the events that had led her to host three strangers in her home, yet she gave no sign that we were anything but honored guests.

After the chicken appeared a homemade apple tart, and then all three de Rentys insisted we retire for the evening. "Marie will take care of the dishes tomorrow," said Madame. Marie, she explained, was the *bonne*, the maid she shared with the neighbors, who lived on the seventh floor and came in the mornings to clean.

At long last, I found myself alone in my room, physically and emotionally spent and at the same time dizzy with happiness. This day, which had begun on the overnight train from Grenoble, had been long and full of surprises—it was just one day in Paris, and yet it had contained such a multitude of treasures. And now here I was, ensconced in this perfectly eccentric apartment, embraced by this perfect, warmhearted family. Already I found them enchanting: serious Claude, irreverent Ghislaine, and especially the Comtesse, with her quiet dignity, her thoughtful manner of speaking, and her interests, deeply cultivated. She embodied everything I had imagined of Old World aristocracy.

I had hoped to capture all these thoughts in a letter to my stepbrother Yusha. But though it was barely ten o'clock, I was exhausted. Switching off the bedside lamp, I slid under the sheets, which were lavender-scented and icy against my skin. My last thought before falling into a deep and dreamless sleep was how lucky I was to have joined this household at 78 avenue Mozart.

It was a sound that woke me—but what sound? My mouth was dry, and I wished I had brought a glass of water to my room. I turned onto my back, trying to slow my pounding heart, and heard it again—a deep rumble, like the grinding of tectonic plates. An earthquake? I bolted upright. No, nothing was shaking. I peered at my watch, which read half past five. Outside, the sky was as deep and murky as overbrewed coffee. Dawn was still hours away, and with it would come registration at Reid Hall, a trip on the métro . . . and that, I realized, was the sound: the day's first trains rumbling deep below ground, the morning commute already begun. Our building was so close to the station, the subway tracks probably ran directly beneath its foundation.

With a sigh, I twisted onto my side and closed my eyes. But sleep eluded me—I was too uncomfortable—and finally I rose, creeping down the hall to the W.C. In the dark apartment, the parquet floors squeaked mercilessly under my bare feet. I moved as silently as I could, pausing every few meters so as not to wake anyone. I was halfway down the hall, between my bedroom and the bathroom, when I heard the noise. Except this time it wasn't the rumble of a train but a muffled thumping, like someone punching a pillow harder and harder—or perhaps it was someone tangled in the sheets, kicking violently to get free.

I froze, uncertain of what to do. The strange acoustics

of the apartment meant I couldn't tell where the sound was coming from—and I could hardly start knocking on all the bedroom doors at half past five in the morning. And then, as suddenly as the noise had started, it stopped. I strained my ears, holding my breath, but the apartment was silent. Relieved, I made my way to the bathroom and then back to my room, where I closed the door and climbed into bed. I shut my eyes, hoping to capture a few final moments of sleep.

Somewhere far below ground, the métro rumbled. And somewhere deep in the apartment, someone sobbed so discreetly I could scarcely hear the muffled cries.

Chapter Four

After my first trip to Europe last summer, I had been disappointed to learn that my college, Vassar, didn't offer a study-abroad program in France. When I found out that the Smith group in Paris would admit a few other students, I begged my parents to allow me to apply. At first they rejected the idea—as I knew they would—each for their own reasons. Daddy, rattling around his empty Manhattan apartment, said he would miss me too much. "I know I'm being selfish," he wrote to me. "I guess I'll be losing you before I know it to some gink with big ears who you think is so marvelous because he looks romantic in evening clothes and uses his mother's pearl earrings as cufflinks because he adores her so much." In truth, I feared he was too embarrassed to tell me he couldn't afford it.

As for Mummy, she voiced several different objections—the danger ("The war has scarcely ended, darling!"), the weather ("So damp!"), the food ("Not at all slimming!")—before admitting her true concern: She didn't wish to accrue any extra expense to my stepfather. Although Uncle Hugh was generous toward my sister and me—in affection, if not his pocket—he considered parsimony a virtue. ("Did you know," Lee once said, "that Hughdie reuses tea bags? I do suppose that's how he affords all this!" By "all this" she meant the lavish Auchincloss estates—Hammersmith Farm in Newport, Rhode Island; and Merrywood in McLean, Virginia—not to mention his three marriages, five children, three stepchildren, and a seat on the New York Stock Exchange. It was hardly the stuff of tea-bag thrift, but Lee generally spoke in arch hyperbole.)

Mummy had other reasons too: namely, she feared I'd fall in love with an impoverished writer—or, worse, a foreigner with an accent or a beard—and be forced into permanent social exile. The very thought made her nostrils flare. "I hope you know the kind of marriage we are expecting," she never hesitated to remind Lee and me. "After everything we've done for you."

Things came to a head one autumn evening when I was home at Merrywood for the weekend. It was the painful hour before dinner, when Lee and I were expected to join Mummy and Hughdie for "cocktails"—although back then my sister and I hardly even sipped Coca-Cola—always just the four of us, with no sign of our step- or half siblings.

"Oh, there you are," Mummy said when I walked into the drawing room with an armful of magazines. "You look a fright. Where have you been? Your hair's an absolute bird's nest."

"Sorry I'm late," I murmured, and sat down on the davenport next to Lee.

Mummy sighed, crushed her cigarette into a heavy crystal ashtray, and turned to Hughdie. "Yes, do let's invite the Foleys next month. Emily has been so helpful with the committee work, and I'd like to show my appreciation . . ." I picked up a magazine from the pile in my lap and began flipping idly through its pages as Hughdie mumbled his assent.

"What are you doing?" Mummy's glare sliced across Hughdie's plodding tones.

"I'm just reading *Vogue*," I said, in a gentle half whisper. Years of her tutelage had taught me to keep my voice soft and girlish.

"Please don't," she said, leaning forward to light a fresh cigarette.

"But you're talking to Uncle Hugh," I protested.

"When I am speaking, you should be paying attention to me."

"Yes, Mummy," I said, but my lips started to twitch, as they always did when she puffed herself up with such vanity and self-importance. I couldn't control the impish part of me that always wanted to flaunt her rules.

"Don't bite your lip," Mummy added. Her gaze cut to my sister, who was reaching for a salted almond from a silver dish on the coffee table. "No more nuts, Lee. You're practically the size of a house." She tapped her cigarette against the ashtray and returned once again to Hughdie. "Or perhaps we should invite a few more and make it a cocktail reception?"

Though I longed to roll my eyes, I knew better. Instead I counted three ticks from the clock on the mantel, then lowered my gaze to the magazine. But before I could continue reading, a shadow fell across my lap and Mummy was standing in front of me, snatching the magazine from my hands. She opened her mouth, her thin lips a flawless dark red against her pale complexion. "Eyes on me!" she screamed. "I am talking!"

I froze, staring at the mask of fury that had transformed her face. I was familiar—we were, all of us, familiar—with Mummy's episodes, which filled Merrywood with slammed doors, thundering feet, and slapped faces. I understood—as my sister also understood—that her exacting standards were intended to help us attain the most illustrious achievement possible for a young woman of our station: a brilliant marriage. I also knew she could go too far.

"I'm sorry." Did I sound adequately contrite? "I was distracted."

"Dreamy little Jackie," she sneered. "Always with her head in the clouds. What was it this time?" She glanced at the magazine in her hand. "Another article about Paris, *quelle surprise.* Don't tell me you're still indulging that ridiculous fantasy of going to study in France for a year. I assure you it will never happen. Your stepfather and I simply will not allow it."

I resisted the urge to bite my bottom lip. "I don't mind," I bluffed, trying not to let her see how much the words cost me.

"That's fine," she said. "Then we'll have no more sulking about it."

Ultimately it was the accusation of sulking that provoked me. I was disappointed, yes. Defiant, probably. But to accuse me of pouting was unfair, especially since I had always taken great pains to be cheerful and pleasant at Merrywood.

"Have you told your father he can't have you the week after Christmas?" asked Mummy later at dinner, wiping her mouth with a punctilious dabbing motion.

Lee looked distraught. "But Daddy will be all alone!"

"I doubt it." Mummy arched an eyebrow.

"It's all right, Pekes," I told my sister. "It'll only be for a few weeks, and then I'll very likely be there. I've been thinking," I announced to the table in a soft voice, "I could quit Vassar, move to Manhattan, and become a fashion model." In fact, the idea had only just entered my head, but it was taking shape as I spoke.

Mummy's tapered fingers twitched on her knife. "You cannot be serious."

"I am perfectly serious," I said in a tone as airy and sweet as spun sugar.

We faced each other across the table. Mummy had a set to her jaw that I recognized from my childhood when we competed together at summer horse shows in East Hampton. We both liked to win—perhaps more than was considered ladylike. Once when I was eight, my pony threw me midcompetition; I stood up, climbed back on, and continued to the next jump. Daddy was distraught—but Mummy had applauded.

"Who would hire you?" Mummy challenged me.

"I've had loads of offers ever since Cholly's piece." Cholly Knickerbocker was the gossip columnist who had named me Queen Deb of 1947 in the *New York Journal-American*; it was the day Mummy had been most proud of me.

"If only that had led to a husband." She sighed, as she had a thousand times since. "But you'd loathe modeling. You wouldn't last a week," she countered.

"It would certainly pay well. You wouldn't have to worry about me any longer."

At these words Hughdie pushed his chair back. "Enough!" he barked. "Jackie, I agree with your mother. Studying in France is sheer extravagance."

"But, Unk—" I protested.

"As for this ludicrous plan of leaving Vassar and going to live in New York . . ." His face flushed puce. "I've always thought highly of your character, and frankly I'm disappointed."

His words fell like a slap. Though I'd expected Mummy's criticism, my stepfather rarely voiced his disapproval, preferring to let our quarrels burn out while he hovered above the fray. I felt my chin start to tremble, and I clenched my jaw. I hated for anyone to see me cry.

"You've always said there's no shame in earning an honest dollar," I said, hiding my emotion behind a half whisper.

Mummy leaned forward in her chair. "Why on earth would you throw away your future over *this*?" she said, and her tone implied such flightiness on my part—as if I was filled with whims, and studying in Paris was one of them.

I managed to shrug. "Why not?" For what did I have to lose?

Hughdie must have sensed my defiance, for he glanced uncertainly at Mummy. She lit a cigarette, and as she exhaled, I saw her weighing the options. But in this game of chicken, Hughdie was the one who blinked first. Crossing his arms, he gave me a look that froze me to the core. "I will think about it," he said.

I stared at him in disbelief. "Oh, Unk! Do you mean it?" I clasped my hands to my chest, feeling at once ecstatic, grateful, and a little embarrassed. "If you let me go, I'll work so hard while I'm there. I promise I'll come home speaking perfect French, just like a native!"

Mummy had been watching us with an expression of displeasure mixed with relief. Now she lit a fresh cigarette off the tip of the last, and when she spoke her voice was acrid. "There is *always* room for improvement," she said.

Sometimes I had the sensation of missing Paris even while I was living there, the days too fleeting, time slipping from my grasp. On my walks around the city I could rarely admire its beauty without a preemptory twinge for the day when it would no longer be mine. And yet, as I grew to know Paris—its alleyway short-cuts and Roman ruins tucked beside bus stops, its merry little fountains and domed news kiosks—the city's elegance softened into familiarity, like a poem read so many times it becomes a devotion.

My classes took me out of the house each morning to small group seminars at Reid Hall, or vast lectures at the Sorbonne's auditorium, *le grand amphithéâtre*, or various art museums dotting the city. At home we found a rhythm, gathering in the evening to dine on Madame's soups and hearty braises (not all meals were as elaborate as that first one had been, but all were delicious) and adhering to the weekly bath schedule. It wasn't a perfect household, but we tried our best to get along—even Ghislaine's son, Christian, a chatty little three-year-old who proved to be a most demanding phonetics professor. I never did manage to pronounce *grenouille* (frog) to his satisfaction.

As the fall weather turned damp and chilly, the gutters choked with wet brown leaves and the cultural calendar exploded with new exhibits, expositions, and theater pieces. I was happy, and I attributed this happiness to the magic of Paris. But when Ghislaine, distributing the mail, presented me with a letter addressed in Mummy's fastidious looping hand, I felt a familiar throb tighten my neck. Part of my contentment, I realized, had been relief. Here in Paris, I was an ocean away from my mother's hawkish observations—not to mention the seething anger that characterized her relationship with Daddy. Their divorce, and her remarriage to Hughdie, had done nothing to soften their mutual bitterness. Neither could ever allow a mention of the other to pass without some scathing remark.

Everyone at home was well, wrote Mummy; she and Hughdie and the kiddies (my half siblings) were back at Merrywood for the season, and she was looking forward to riding in the point-to-point at the end of the month. Then, having disposed of the pleasantries, she cut to the crux: "I saw Mary Whitehouse last week and she asked if you were planning to call on Paul de Ganay. I thought we agreed that you would introduce yourself as soon as you arrived. You know how important it is to meet the right people, Jackie. That should be your first priority—not some seminar on Talleyrand, or whatever it was that you mentioned in your last letter." I skimmed the rest, biting my bottom lip, and when I came to the end, I was tempted to slip the letter into the kitchen stove and pretend it had sunk to the bottom of the Atlantic.

But Mummy never relented. If she didn't receive a reply to this letter she would send another, and another, until the letters became telegrams, and the telegrams became an actual visit. Sighing, I picked up my pen to write a response—and then I picked up the phone to call Paul de Ganay.

A few days later, we met for lunch at the Brasserie Balzar on the rue des Écoles. I'd purposely suggested a restaurant near the Sorbonne, squeezing our rendezvous in between two lectures so that I'd have no occasion to linger. It wasn't that I had anything against Paul—who was the cousin of Jacques Bemberg, a young Argentinian banker I'd met at the Whitehouses' cottage in Newport last summer—but his connection to Mummy's world robbed him of romance. I hadn't come to Paris to meet another stuffed shirt content to rely on his trust fund.

I arrived at the café from class, my hair wild from the persistent rain. A waiter directed me to a corner table, and I saw Paul was already there, with a newspaper before him and a cigarette between his fingers. They were the hands of a boy, I noticed right away, stubby and blotted with ink. His face too was boyishly round, with lively, light gray eyes set against pale, freckled skin and a mouth hovering on the edge of mischief.

"Jacqueline?" He rose, knocking over his chair, and flushing as he bent to pick it up. Despite my preconceptions, I felt myself softening.

"*Bonjour,*" I said, and we exchanged cheek kisses before sitting down. By this point, I had learned that almost every social interaction began with *les bises,* even between strangers.

"Sorry, I'm afraid I've made a bit of a mess," he said,

pushing aside the newspaper, stubbing out his cigarette, and very nearly upsetting a glass of water in my lap. "I got here early and just sort of colonized this corner. Maman says it's my one true talent." He spoke French with unhurried ease, his vowels long and *r*'s precisely scraped over the back of his throat.

"Are you taking a flyer?" I gestured at the paper, which was open to the racing form.

He grinned. "I was thinking of popping over to Auteuil this afternoon for a bit of a flutter. I've got my eye on a chestnut called Marengo."

"Named after Napoleon's famous steed? 'Loyal, courageous, and steady,'" I quoted. "I've probably read every book ever written about famous horses," I explained at his look of bemusement. "I wanted to call our poodle Marengo, but we all finally agreed on Gaullie, after Général de Gaulle."

"You like horses, then?"

"I miss my horse back home more than anyone else, if that tells you anything."

"Ha!" His laugh, so sudden, lit up his face. "You sound like my mother. I swear she tucks them in and sings them lullabies every night. They all have special blankets embroidered with their names. She's from Argentina, and her papa put her on a horse before she could even walk."

"Do you ride too?" Forgetting my manners, I leaned my elbows on the table.

"The thing I'm really keen on is polo. Now that the war's over, I'm trying to convince my father to build a polo ground at Courances. Wouldn't it be brilliant?"

"Marvelous," I agreed. *And wildly extravagant,* I thought but didn't say. I couldn't tell how much of this idea was impractical youthful exuberance and how much was rooted in reality.

"You must come out and visit our stables," he said, fidgeting with his cigarette lighter. "There's a bang-up horse trail that leads straight through the forest to Fontainebleau. We have this new little Arabian filly who's—" He broke off as a waiter approached our table. "Should we order? You've got a lecture this afternoon, *n'est-ce pas?*"

I nodded and rattled off the first dish that came to mind. "Goat cheese salad."

"And for me a *croque monsieur*," said Paul.

The food arrived quickly, our waiter weaving through the crowded dining room to deposit the plates on our small round table, along with a pot of mustard for Paul's toasted ham-and-cheese sandwich and—with an "*Et, voilà,* for you, monsieur!"—a dish of fried potatoes that Paul hadn't ordered. "You can't have your *croque* without the *frites.*"

Paul laughed and thanked him. After he'd walked away, I said, "Are you a regular here? They seem to know you."

"It's so convenient to the Sorbonne, isn't it? I usually just pop over between classes."

"Hold on, you're there too?"

"I'm doing a year's prep work before I start at the Polytechnique. Actually, I think we're in the same aesthetics course. Tuesdays at eleven? I've seen you in the *grand amphi*'."

"Gosh, I didn't know we were classmates." A blush was creeping across my cheeks. Now I felt doubly embarrassed at my reluctance to contact him.

"Indeed," he said, shrugging off my discomfiture. "We can swap notes."

We ate quickly, the food simple and well prepared. Paul, belying his puppyish clumsiness, proved to be an easy conversationalist, full of questions and impish observations. I became so absorbed in chatting about horses, and Paris, and where one could ride horses in Paris, that by the time he offered me a cigarette from his fresh pack of Gitanes, I had only a quarter of an hour left before class. Glancing at my watch, I felt a little vexed. Why had I boxed myself into this schedule?

"Are you still off to Auteuil this afternoon?" I asked, half hoping he'd invite me to go along. I wasn't exactly attracted to Paul, but he appealed to me in a way that many boys did not, with his earnest enthusiasm. And an impromptu trip to the racetrack sounded like a grand adventure.

"I think I will." He looked through the café window at the sky, which had lightened as we ate. "I should be revising, but it seems to be clearing—and who can resist a fine day at the track?"

"Not I," I said, with an encouraging smile.

But he didn't notice. Or if he did, he ignored it. "All right, it's settled." He pushed his chair back. "I'll place a bet on Marengo just for you."

"If he wins, I expect a cut." I hid my chagrin behind a wink.

"You're on."

We gathered our things and headed to the front to pay. *"Je t'invite,"* he insisted—his treat—and brushed aside my protestations.

Behind the cash register, the café owner's wife beamed when she saw him. "We missed you last week!" she exclaimed.

"You know I can't stay away from your fries, madame," he said, sliding the change back toward her. "They're the best in Paris."

"Oh, you exaggerate, *Monsieur le Comte,*" she said in coquettish tones.

"Don't tell me you're a count along with everything else," I said when we were outside exchanging farewell cheek kisses.

"Just the youngest son," he said cheerfully. "I hardly *count* at all—haha, get it? Yes, that pun was intentional."

I was laughing as he waved goodbye and bounded off in one direction—to the métro—while I headed in the other, toward the Sorbonne, wondering when we would meet again.

"You didn't say your lunch was with *Paul de Ganay!"* Claude's eyes widened to the size of sunflowers. "From *the* de Ganay family?"

"Do you know them? I meant to ask before, but I forgot."

"I certainly know *of* them." She fastened her wet umbrella and hung it in the crook of her arm, where it dripped onto the métro platform.

It was another rainy morning and we were waiting for the train to take us to our respective *facultés* for class. Claude wore rubber boots, but my shoes were already soaked from the brief walk to the station, a damp chill penetrating my feet. At home, the apartment's heater was still broken, and while no one had complained, I noticed we'd all started wearing scarves in the evening. Thankfully, Madame had informed us at breakfast that the repairman was coming at the beginning of next week: "And not a minute too soon! Winter in Paris can be vicious." At this, Mary Ann—her blood thick from a Chicago childhood plus two years in western Massachusetts—had laughed.

"They're one of the extended names," Claude said now, adjusting the book bag on her shoulder.

"I'm sorry, what?" Though my French had improved dramatically in the past few weeks, Claude spoke so quickly and without context that I often had no idea what she was talking about.

"A *nom à rallonge.*" She arched an eyebrow, mildly amused at my bewilderment. "It's a sarcastic term for surnames that use the particle *de*—the aristocratic names," she explained. "Such as de Ganay, de Biron, de Noailles . . ."

"And you—de Renty."

"Ye-es." She fingered the strap of her bag. "But these families are still connected to their estates. They've got vast parcels of land in the country, and Parisian townhouses in the Faubourg Saint-Germain—that's the aristocratic part of the 7th arrondissement. The de Ganays have a *hôtel particulier* on the rue Saint-Dominique, and a château outside of Paris with many hectares. Not to mention their other properties in France and South

America . . . Argentina, I believe? Our family is . . . different."

These were the families of privilege, I surmised from her tone. Later I learned that while they owed their current fortunes to modern French industry—sugar and rubber plantations, chocolate factories and printing presses, banks, insurance, and a myriad of other avenues—in truth the money had been theirs for several centuries. They were the names in the *Bottin mondain*, the French social register, which listed their titles (*prince, duc, comte*), their club memberships (Jockey, Racing, Automobile), their family seats in the country, and their Paris mansions (labeled H.P. for *hôtel particulier*).

I knew the American version of this world from my boarding schools, debutante balls, and Newport summers, from Mummy's aspirations for her daughters to marry into the kind of wealth that she had almost—but not quite—attained with Hughdie. And from this world, I knew to anticipate the belief that a woman could be a wit or a beauty, but not both; that she could nurture her intellect or she could marry, but not both. From a very young age, I had been made aware of the role expected of me. I thought I had escaped it for a while by coming to Paris, but it had found me, even here.

"If you're invited to Courances, you must go."

Claude raised her voice over the roar of the approaching train. "By all accounts it's magnificent."

"Is that their château? Yes, Paul mentioned it."

We boarded the subway, leaning against the fold-up seats near the door.

"You would adore it," she said, and I expected her to extol its formal gardens or art collection, its antique carved woodwork or tapestry carpets—which were all things I did adore, although not necessarily at the price of tedious conversation. But Claude already understood me better than I knew. "I've heard it's like stepping into the eighteenth century," she said, shifting her weight against the train's turn. "A living museum."

"That does sound rather spectacular," I admitted.

But before I was asked to Courances, I received an invitation to the home of Jessie Hunt, a friend from Vassar. Jessie was half American and half French, and though she was stuck in Poughkeepsie (heaven help her), she had asked her mother to invite me for afternoon tea. Lulu lived just outside of Paris, and she was a poet and satirical novelist, twice married and divorced, with who knew how many lovers since. She was exactly the type of person that would horrify Mummy, and I was thrilled to meet her.

But what did one wear to tea with a libertine? The

morning of the gathering none of my clothes seemed right.

"Why not your gray suit?" Claude suggested when I solicited her opinion. "And the velvet hat with the veil?"

I wrinkled my nose. "It seems so churchy."

"The sleeveless plaid dress and black turtleneck blouse then?"

"You don't think it's too square?"

"For tea with your friend's mother?"

"She's eccentric." I reached for my cigarettes and lit one. "She writes poetry and smokes cigars."

"Golly." Claude was urbane, but she looked slightly taken aback at this last bit of information. "Where does she live?"

"Somewhere south of Paris. Hold on, I have her letter." I rummaged through the papers on my desk, finally unearthing it from the bottom of the pile. "Verrières-le-Buisson."

She inspected the address. "Château de Vilmorin?" She emitted a kind of disbelieving gasp. "Are you meeting Louise de Vilmorin?"

"Is she called Lulu?"

"Possibly."

"I thought her last name was Hunt, but that must

have been her ex-husband." I inspected her signature, which was just a loopy scrawl that read "Lulu." "I suppose de Vilmorin is one of the extended names. And she lives in the family château . . ." Suddenly this outing seemed considerably less outrageous than I'd hoped.

"Don't look so glum. I don't think it's what you're expecting. Despite her name, Louise de Vilmorin is not at all stuffy and bourgeois. She's famous for her madcap parties with, say, film directors and morally bankrupt minor Hungarian royalty."

I brightened. Unconventional intellectuals and corrupt Mitteleuropa counts sounded more along the lines of what I'd been hoping to find. Reaching into the armoire, I pulled out an orange taffeta skirt. "Will this do? With the black turtleneck blouse?"

Claude tilted her head and gazed at the clothes. *"Pas mal,"* she said eventually, "not bad."

I'd been in France long enough to know that this was generous praise.

The Comtesse Louise de Vilmorin—"Call me Lulu, darling"—was wearing denim jeans and a tatty sweater. Between her thumb and index finger she held a cigar, a curl of smoke rising from one end, while the other appeared damp and vaguely fleshy. A pack of terriers yapped at our ankles, their fur matted with mud.

"Don't mind them. Sit. Sit!" Her thin mouth dropped into a frown. The dogs ignored her. Or was she speaking to me? I glanced behind me, uncertain.

We were standing amid a crowd in the château's main *salon*, a bright, oval-shaped room filled with furniture arranged in small clusters. Louis XVI–style chairs mingled with upholstered bergères, a swirling three-person conversation seat stood before the rust-colored marble fireplace, chintz sofas were wedged between tall windows, and small round tables displayed chinoiserie vases. On the far wall hung a portrait of a plump, pink-faced man clad in a red military jacket sitting awkwardly astride a rearing white horse.

"I'm delighted to meet you," I said primly. "Thank you for having me."

"A pleasure, my dear girl, a pleasure. Remind me who you are?"

"I'm Jessie's friend. From Vassar," I added, as her eyebrows rose in perfect arches. "Your daughter."

"Oh! *That* Jessie. Yes, I remember you now . . . Josephine? Jemima?"

"Jacqueline Bouvier."

"Oh yes, of course!" She leaned across me to ash her cigar. "Jacqueline, the herder of cows."

Unsure of how to respond, I took refuge in the banal. "This is a lovely room."

Lulu removed the cigar from her mouth and looked around. "Is it?" she said doubtfully. "I'd like to redecorate but can't decide how. Which would you choose—lavish blue and white? Or terribly austere Empire?"

I had the oddest sensation of understanding every word yet not having the faintest clue what she meant. "Empire?" I repeated.

"Hmmm. Yes, I could see that." She seemed on the verge of laughter but trapped it, waving a hand toward a drinks table. "Do have some champagne, darling. Or tea, if you prefer. *Fais comme chez toi*—make yourself at home. Lovely to meet you." With a vague smile, she drifted away.

On the pretext of fetching a drink, I crept to the wall and observed the room, which was filled with people in groups of two or three, chatting in low voices with their heads bent together. It struck me that though everyone in the crowd knew each other, none of them seemed to go together. A slick-haired man in a flannel suit spoke with a smooth-faced kid wearing a black turtleneck. A girl in a full-skirted New Look frock, her hair pinned into a chignon, eyed a woman wearing a boilersuit with diamonds and red lipstick. I felt their gazes slide over me, and suddenly I was filled with such discomfort that

I wondered if I should slip out of the house without saying goodbye.

But it had taken me almost two hours to get here: first the métro, then the commuter train, and then a taxi from the station. And what type of person would sneak away without meeting anyone besides the hostess? Certainly not a daughter of Janet Lee Auchincloss. For if Mummy had taught us anything it was that etiquette was to be observed at all times, and that there was no greater gift than a social connection—and though I chafed under her rigid expectations, I had to admit that in this particular credo she was correct.

Straightening my shoulders, I gulped some champagne, lit a cigarette, and marched over to the nearest pair: a slim, bespectacled man wearing a three-piece suit and a tall, heavy-eyed woman with a wild nest of dark hair, blood-colored lips stark against her powdered face.

"*Bonjour*," I greeted them with my best debutante smile.

Their conversation interrupted, they turned to stare at me. The man blinked with an encouraging expression, but the woman held still, eyebrows fixed upon her high forehead. She wore a wide-skirted peasant-style dress belted so tightly she resembled a cinched pillow and, instead of a handbag, carried a wicker basket that covered her middle.

"And who might you be?" she said.

"Jacqueline Bouvier," I said softly, willing myself not to blush.

The man stepped forward. "Jacqueline, I am Jean. *Enchanté*." He proffered his cheek and we exchanged kisses. "And this is Marie-Laure—"

"The Vicomtesse de Noailles." She pronounced each syllable with precision. I extended a hand, from which she recoiled as if I'd offered her a dead goldfish. A full five seconds passed before she spoke again. "And how do you come to be here?"

"I took the train," I said, and Jean gave a chortle.

"What a charming accent," he said gallantly. "English?"

"I'm from New York," I said, exhaling a band of smoke. "I know Jessie—Lulu's daughter"—he nodded, though I doubted either of them knew who Jessie was— "and I'm studying in Paris for a year."

"Junior year abroad?" Jean said in English, his accent nearly impenetrable. "I just read an article about American students returning to Paris," he continued in French. "You are living with a family?"

"Yes, in the 16th," I said. "Do you know the Comtesse de Renty?" It wasn't like me to name-drop, but under Marie-Laure de Noailles's continued cold stare, I felt permitted.

"Oh, are you staying with Germaine?" A glimmer of interest sharpened her hooked features. She turned to Jean. "Have you seen her since the Mass for Robert?" she asked.

"I haven't seen her for ages, poor thing."

"I can't believe she's in this position, after everything she suffered during the war."

"What happened during the war?" I asked.

A look passed between them. "I suppose it's not a secret," said Jean eventually. "She's very active with the ADIR."

"What is that?"

"L'Association de déportées et internées de la Résistance," he explained. "It's an organization for French women who were deported and imprisoned for their work with the Resistance."

Though I'd understood him perfectly, I struggled to process the words. Imprisoned? Resistance? *Madame?*

Marie-Laure de Noailles found a cigarette and lit it. "Germaine and her husband were part of a spy ring called Alliance," she said, blowing smoke past my shoulder. "They were rounded up just before the Liberation of Paris and spent the rest of the war in German prison camps. Robert died at Ellrich. But Germaine managed to survive."

"She was sent to Ravensbrück," Jean said.

He spoke with great solemnity, but I hadn't the faintest clue what he meant. A fine thread of sweat began prickling the back of my neck, and I pushed my sleeves to my elbows.

"Surely you've heard of the women's concentration camp?" Marie-Laure narrowed her heavy-lidded eyes as if I was very stupid. "In northern Germany? Ghastly conditions—very few survived. You must have read about it in the newspaper?"

"Of course," I said, the fib sticking in my throat. It was impossible to imagine Madame in such a place: Madame with her gentle voice and simple dresses in clear, bright colors. Madame, who every morning paraded her grandson's toy soldiers across his bedside table. Madame, who remembered our favorite foods and the way we drank our coffee.

But then I recalled the sobs I'd heard in the small hours of the morning. They'd happened again twice, and I'd decided it was Christian crying after a nightmare. Now I wondered if they might have come from Madame.

"I knew she was widowed, but I had no idea about . . . any of this." I swallowed, instinctively moving my cigarette to my lips. But my stomach had begun churning so violently I instead reached toward the ashtray to extinguish it.

A shadow crossed Jean's face. "If I may paraphrase Tolstoy," he said, "we all lived through the same war, but each of us suffered in our own way."

Marie-Laure de Noailles blinked. "Turned out all right, though, didn't it?" A waiter presented a mirrored tray of canapés and she popped a tiny, perfect vol-au-vent in her mouth. "Oh, I don't mean the camps, you imbecile," she said, taking in my expression of reviled shock. "They were abhorrent and so typical of Hitler—such a revolting little man. But when that fascist de Gaulle took power everything went to shit. We made so much progress during the war, and now here we are in bed with the Americans. Look at the ludicrous NATO treaty we just signed."

"We call Marie-Laure the Red Vicomtesse," Jean said. "She's passionately leftist."

I sputtered on a sip of champagne. Back home the color red signified danger, and the far left spelled subversion. Everyone was skittish about communists, especially after the events of last summer when Whittaker Chambers accused the government lawyer Alger Hiss of spying for the Soviets. Thwarting the invisible enemy was all anyone could talk about, the newspapers were filled with ominous editorials, and even Yusha had toyed with the idea of meeting the CIA recruiters who were making the rounds of all the Ivy League campuses. Before I left for France, my starched-collar Republican stepfather had taken me aside for a serious talk. "Watch out for that dangerous socialist element of Europe, Jackie," he'd commanded. "Whatever you do, don't let them sell it to you. It's the thin end of the wedge." I had laughed and waved away his vehemence, because of course I had no intention of befriending anyone involved with leftist liberal circles. I could never have dreamed I'd come across any such person like that here, in this rarefied Parisian *salon*, let alone a vicomtesse gleefully spouting radical political views while everyone looked on in mild amusement.

"De Gaulle's a *cagoulard*, Jean. All the evidence points to it," she insisted.

"I'm not saying you're wrong. Only that I'm not completely convinced," Jean said calmly.

"Why else would they have joined him in London? Fourcaud, Passy, Duclos." She enumerated the names on her fingers. "What do *you* think?" She turned to me. "Aren't you Americans full of opinions? If, that is"—an insolent smile twitched the corners of her lips—"you've managed to follow along."

I took my time lighting another cigarette. I'd never

heard the word *cagoulard*, not in the newspapers I'd read at home, nor from my classes in Paris. I'd certainly never attempted to discuss world affairs, having been told from an early age that a lady never aired her opinions in public. As Madame de Noailles's disdain grew icy, I opened my mouth and prayed for a miracle.

"You offer such a fascinating perspective," I said in a half whisper, so that they had to lean close to hear me. "I'll have to—" I was going to say, think about it, but before the words left my mouth, I heard someone calling my name.

"Jacqueline!" It was Paul de Ganay, moving toward me at a clip. A small woman trailed closely behind, her dark, bobbed hair bouncing silkily against her slender neck. He kissed my cheeks. "May I present my mother? The Vicomtesse de Ganay."

Her gray eyes gleamed. "A pleasure," she said. "Paul was just telling me about you." In her words, I caught the warm trill of a Spanish accent.

"I didn't know you'd be here," Paul said, as his mother greeted the others, whom she seemed to already know. "I can't believe these two haven't yet eaten you alive," he added in an undertone.

"You arrived in the nick of time," I said, puffing on my cigarette with relief.

"Dear little Paul," Marie-Laure de Noailles drawled.

"Last time I saw you, you were a little boy of about two piddling in a corner of the garden. But you've developed a burliness that's really quite erotic. A bit too beefy for my tastes, true, but I wouldn't turn my nose up."

I gasped and tried to hide it behind a cough, but the others appeared unfazed.

"Oh, Marie-Laure, really," the Vicomtesse sighed. "You're embarrassing him." Paul had flushed to the roots of his hair.

"If that's true, Maria—which I doubt—then he's far too sheltered." She swallowed a yawn, glancing toward the windows, her posture stiffening. "Who's that with Oscar?" she demanded, so that we all turned to stare at a leather-skinned man chatting with a young woman whose hair rippled like a wheat field. Without another word, she stomped over to them.

"So she's still with the Spanish surrealist," the Vicomtesse observed.

"Who knows?" Jean said. "Is she a stark modernist or simply stark raving mad?" Out of the corner of my eye, I saw Madame de Noailles pawing at her lover while staring at the young woman with a challenging smile. "Perhaps I should try to deter her," Jean murmured, moving toward them.

A waiter circled nearby and Paul flagged him down,

thanking him with elaborate courtesy once our glasses were refilled.

"She simply adores shocking people," the Vicomtesse said, taking quick, dainty sips of champagne. "I suppose because she can." From the note of resignation in her voice, I gathered that Marie-Laure de Noailles was both impressively titled and extravagantly wealthy and thus felt permitted to flaunt her ill-mannered malice. "You're not a young lady who shocks, are you, Jacqueline?" the Vicomtesse asked.

"Only if there's electricity, Madame la Vicomtesse."

She gave a fleeting smile that didn't quite reach her eyes. "Paul tells me you're fond of horses," she said. "Did you enjoy your visit to Auteuil?"

"Sorry? I haven't been to Auteuil." I turned to Paul, puzzled. "I thought you—"

"It's all right, Jacqueline," he interjected with rapid precision. "Maman knows about our trip to the track last week. I promised not to skip class again, and she's not cross anymore." His eye caught mine.

"Oh, well . . ." I thought quickly. "We had a lovely time. Except that my horse didn't place." Paul laughed a little too hard.

"But I thought you'd won." The Vicomtesse turned to Paul, bewildered.

"She's joking, Maman," he said. "It was Jacqueline who convinced me to bet on Marengo. I owe her."

"Don't be silly." I found a cigarette and accepted a light from Paul, allowing my fingers to brush his sleeve. "It was just a lucky guess."

The Vicomtesse finished her champagne and set her empty glass on a small round table where it blended into an arrangement of Venetian vases. She touched my arm with her gloved hand. "You must come see us at Courances, my dear. Paul will take you riding."

"I would love that," I said sincerely.

"He'll call you next week to fix a date." She shot a glance at her son. "Isn't that right, *chéri*?"

"Hm?" He had been staring over my shoulder, but at her voice he startled to attention. "Yes, absolutely, next week."

After they had left, I turned to see what he'd been looking at. But there was only the waiter moving soiled glasses onto a tray.

All the way home, and for the rest of the night, scenes from the afternoon swirled in my head, clamoring for attention, so that just as I began to examine one, another loomed with all its confusion, embarrassment, and peculiar exhilaration. I felt like I had experienced more in the past few hours than in the last five years. There was Madame's tragic wartime history and also the remarkable discovery that she had been a Resistance spy. Lulu de Vilmorin and Marie-Laure de Noailles with their ancient family fortunes, flaunting their privilege with radical views, shabby clothes, and even shabbier manners. Paul and the confusing fib he'd told his mother. And me, fumbling my way through a strange new culture, all my notions of propriety and possibility turned suddenly upside down.

For days afterward—years afterward—I cringed whenever I thought of that afternoon. I had set out for the château de Vilmorin feeling quite sure of myself, but a few short hours had revealed the limits of beauty and good breeding—had shown me that everything so admired by Newport and New York high society was but a frippery in a Paris *salon*. They had proved that Mummy was wrong in her belief that a dazzling marriage was the pinnacle of female achievement. For I had glimpsed the possibility of another kind of life—not merely married to someone distinguished, but a person of distinction myself—and I understood that if I was to attain it, my fate depended on my wits. I would need to cultivate my curiosity, read more widely, expand my coursework beyond the boundaries of suitability.

Mummy would not approve. But Mummy wasn't here.

Chapter Five

The class was the History between the World Wars, and at this point in the semester, it was the only one at l'Institut d'études politiques with room for a Smith girl.

"The professor has a reputation for being rigorous, which will mean a considerable amount of additional work. Are you prepared for that?" Madame Saleil regarded me over the tops of her spectacles.

I nodded and spoke with a confidence I didn't quite feel inside. "My host sister is a student at Sciences Po so I'm familiar with the expectations."

She straightened a pencil on her desk. "I'm pleased to see you applying yourself more forcefully into your studies, Jacqueline. You could be a stellar academic if you put your heart in it."

My cheeks grew warm, for I couldn't tell if she was being sincere or trying to encourage me. Thus far, my grades had been merely satisfactory. "It can take me some time to find a rhythm," I said.

Madame Saleil gave me a reassuring smile. "Fear not. We'll make a real French intellectual out of you yet."

"*Merci*, Madame. I'll do my best." Even as I thanked her, the flush remained high on my face. For someone like Jeanne Saleil, so steeped in French academia, intellectualism was the goal, the summit—it was the extreme opposite of the *beau monde.* All my life I had been taught to turn my nose up at bluestockings, but the afternoon at Lulu's *salon* had spurred me to challenge myself.

The class met on Thursday mornings in an overcrowded lecture hall on the rue Saint-Guillaume. The professor—whom we called *le Maître*—was the esteemed lecturer Pierre Renouvin, a veteran who had lost an arm in the Great War. I sat at the back of the hall, the better to avoid unexpected questions, because at the slightest hint of uncertainty—a quiver in your voice, a hesitating pause—a forest of arms would shoot up to answer in your stead. Over the bowed heads of my classmates I had a clear view of Maître Renouvin's angular figure, his left sleeve empty and pinned upon itself, and I often wondered if his true opinions of Germany were as impartial as those he expressed.

Maître Renouvin was a political theorist, an expert on international conflict who believed that a country's social, economic, and geographic situations defined its policy and diplomacy. His lectures were like a butcher's knife, sharp and sure, carving his philosophy into concise language. I scribbled notes, the ink of my hurried pen smearing across the page, and when he used vocabulary I didn't recognize, I wrote down the phonetic sounds, puzzling out the words later with my dictionary. "Is everything understood?" he asked at the end of every class. It was a rhetorical question, for of course we hadn't understood everything. We were meant to steep ourselves in his ideas, reflect upon them, puzzle over them for days, weeks, months, or even years. Our goal was to refine our critical thinking so that we were constantly questioning the world, examining and judging. It was a marked contrast to the rote memorization of my American education, and though I dreaded the lectures, I couldn't deny the exhilaration of answering the Maître's rapid-fire questions in front of the class, of being pushed and prodded into examining everything from every angle until we fully understood.

The Théâtre de la Madeleine was a sea of crimson, the color repeating in the seats, the carpets, the walls, the curtain drawn across the stage. If I leaned over the balcony rail and craned my head, I could just glimpse the evening's guest of honor, the writer Colette, her corona of gray curls as fine and flighty as dandelion fluff.

I had first read Colette the summer I turned fifteen, devouring a copy of *Chéri*, which I was sure Mummy would have forbidden had she known about it. I read constantly when I was younger, much of it too old for me, taking care to hide the books of which she disapproved. From the very first page, the novel absorbed me, a tale of a dissolute young man and the older woman who is his lover; awash in sensuality, loss, and sorrow; and, above all, callow youth contrasted with aging beauty. I read the novel over and over again that summer, reveling in the sumptuous descriptions of decor and fashion, the splendid meals, and Colette's biting commentary on the ways in which people adapt to change. Now I was here to see *Chéri* come to life, and Colette herself—French literary icon, first woman president of the Académie Goncourt—was sitting in a stage box only meters away. It was the play's opening night, the type of glittering literary event I had dreamed about all last winter in Poughkeepsie, and I kept reminding myself to observe the details and absorb them so that I could retreat into this memory whenever I needed an escape.

"I can't tell you how thrilled I am to be here," I murmured to Ghislaine. "Thank you so much for inviting me." I gave her arm a squeeze.

"It's a treat for me too." She patted my hand in return. "When you told me how much you loved *Chéri*, I knew I simply had to move heaven and earth to find tickets."

"Oh, dear, I hope it wasn't too much trouble." I bit my bottom lip. "I thought your boss had a pair he didn't want." This was the problem with living in a foreign language—I often missed social nuance, and sometimes I misheard conversations altogether.

"Hmmm? Yes, that's how I got them in the end." She lifted a pair of mother-of-pearl opera glasses and peered down on the seats in the orchestra section. "Look at this crowd! I don't think I've ever seen so many artists and writers in one place. And a lot of government bigwigs too, of course." I assumed she recognized the latter from her work as a secretary at the Ministry of Defense.

Of the three de Renty women, Ghislaine remained the one I knew the least. At home she was so preoccupied she often answered questions she thought we'd asked instead of the ones we actually had: "I think it's going to rain," she once said, when I'd inquired if we could trade bath times; or "Sorry, I'm trying to quit smoking," when Mary Ann, searching everywhere for her address book, had asked if she'd seen it. In the mornings, she rushed around the apartment, bundling Christian into his coat, hurrying to drop him off at the crèche before she went to work. Many evenings, hollow with fatigue, she ate an early kitchen supper with her son instead of joining our more formal repasts in the dining room. All of us in the household kept an eye on Christian—who, according to his mother's warnings, was as acquisitive as a young fox, stealing any little object that caught his fancy—but Ghislaine made it clear that the responsibility for his care rested on her shoulders. Tonight, however, Madame was watching over her grandson.

"Simone de Beauvoir. Over there in the aisle," Ghislaine said now, handing me the binoculars. "And Sartre behind her."

I peered through the lenses to see a tall, graceful figure whip around to exchange words with Sartre and shake his hand off her arm. "I think they must be quarreling," I whispered, watching him storm down the row to his seat.

"He reminds me of my ex-husband." Ghislaine accepted the opera glasses and placed them in her lap. "He liked to pick a fight at the worst possible moments, in the worst possible places. I suppose I should have known from the way we met." She spoke casually, as if the memories had ceased to trouble her.

I had a thousand questions about Ghislaine's past, but I felt sheepish about revealing my curiosity. "How did you meet?" I finally asked.

"He worked with my father during the war." She fiddled with the binoculars, folding them into their case. "You know about my parents' war efforts?"

"Yes," I admitted, and her face cleared.

"I never know what Maman wants me to say. It feels wrong not to talk about it, as if it never happened. But of course it still causes her a great deal of pain. She was reluctant to join Alliance at first—afraid something would happen to Papa. *Et voilà* . . ." She shrugged, a Gallic shrug that conveyed a multitude of emotions.

"I'm so sorry," I said in a low voice. "You must miss him terribly."

"We all do. Even André—that's my ex-husband. It's why we eventually split up—all the speculation. Wondering who had informed on my parents, and why. Someone had a grudge against Maman and Papa, I'm certain of it. Why else were they arrested after the Normandy landings? André swore it wasn't anyone in his circuit, and of course I believed him. Why wouldn't I? Back then I thought we were all on the same side."

"What do you mean?" But the house lights were dimming, the audience settling. In the dark silence a stick pounded three times upon the wooden stage: *les trois coups*, signaling the beginning of the performance. The spotlights flared, and there was Jean Marais as Chéri, dressed in pajamas and a patterned silk robe, his thick honeyed locks swept back from sculpted features; there beside him was Valentine Tessier as the fading courtesan, Léa, wearing a low-cut gown with a rope of pearls wound round her neck.

I tried to lose myself in the play, but the Chéri and Léa of the stage felt flat compared to the characters of the novel I knew so well, the dialogue stilted, the story forced into three acts. Ghislaine too seemed fidgety, shifting awkwardly in her seat. I glanced over to see her head jerk forward and realized she was struggling to stay awake. Onstage the banter turned bitter and my thoughts lingered on the conversation we'd just had. Though I had only known the de Rentys for a few weeks, I had already grown fond of them, especially Madame, with her gentle manner and the value she placed on daily rituals, lighting candles each evening at dinner, or buying fresh flowers on Saturdays for the apartment. She rarely spoke of her husband but kept a nosegay next to his portrait on the mantelpiece, a silent tribute.

So it was true, I thought: The Comte and Comtesse de Renty had been Resistance spies during the war, someone had turned them in, and they had been deported to concentration camps. But Ghislaine's confirmation of their wartime history only raised more questions. How had her ex-husband known her parents? Why would Ghislaine suspect his circuit of betraying them? And what did she mean about everyone being on the same side—*back then*? I resolved to ask her after the play.

But when the cast had taken their final bows, the spotlight found the author in her stage box and the audience rose en masse, bursting into thunderous applause. Colette stood upon arthritic knees to acknowledge us, her adoring fans. Her expression mordant with wit despite sagging jowls, she beamed as we paid homage to her life's work. It was a moment of literary grandiosity that entranced even the most caustic Parisian critics, leaving the audience hushed as we exited the theater. Despite her earlier fatigue, Ghislaine also seemed moved, reaching into her pocketbook and discretely blowing her nose.

We walked to the métro in silence. I wanted to return to our earlier conversation, but it felt incongruous to raise the subject now. As well, Ghislaine had lapsed into one of her preoccupied reveries, her distant expression precluding questions. We were nearly home when she roused herself.

"Claude mentioned that you're taking a course at Sciences Po," she said.

I nodded. "I'm hoping I won't regret it. Your sister makes it look easy, but already there's so much work, I'm studying with inky fingers half the night."

She laughed, and I noticed that for the first time tonight she seemed alert and animated, like she was really listening. "If you ever need someone to edit your school essays, I'm happy to take a look," she said. "I used to be quite a grammar whiz back in the day. I do so admire all you college girls. You know, I dreamed of studying at Sciences Po, but now I realize I don't have the discipline. It seems terribly glamorous, though. I keep asking Claude if she'll take me on a tour, but she claims she spends her lunch hour in the library."

"Yes, you must come! I could show you around," I said, surprising myself with the offer. It wasn't like me to mix acquaintances—I had always preferred to compartmentalize my relationships, keeping my worlds separate so that no one knew every side of me. It was an impulse left over from when Mummy and Daddy divorced and the New York press splashed the sordid details across the gossip pages. I could never forget the humiliation at school, my classmates falling silent whenever I entered a room, their eyes upon me. I knew some people judged me as aloof and snobbish because of the way I drew my circles close, and yet to share too much of myself made me feel exposed and vulnerable. I couldn't help it.

But with their tragic circumstances, their dignified sadness, the de Rentys had endeared themselves to me. Perhaps it was because I recognized their reserve—reticence born of past sorrow—that I felt akin to them. Though I couldn't fathom the depths of their suffering, I understood their silence.

"I do hope you'll stop by Sciences Po sometime. It would be a pleasure," I said to Ghislaine as we climbed the métro stairs at Jasmin and walked the thirty steps to the front door. "I'd love to invite you for tea or lunch. It's the least I can do after this evening."

"All right then, it's a date." She flashed me a smile, her eyes bright.

I had questions, but who could answer them? Usually I asked Claude to help me navigate the choppy waters of French history, culture, politics, politesse, and, well, everything. But I could hardly interrogate her about her own family. Meanwhile, Mummy's admonitions kept floating through my mind—"It's not ladylike to pry, Jackie"—except lately I'd found my-self silently challenging her. Why was female deco-rum the principle that defined all situations? Why was it inappropriate to express interest in a friend? Ever since the soirée at the château de Vilmorin I had wondered how many of Mummy's rules I could defy without her finding out.

"You're looking very dapper," I called, as Paul strode up to me outside the newsstand.

"Gosh, really? Thanks." He looked down at his sweater vest, which was the color of daffodils, a flash against the dark afternoon. "My old nanny knitted this for me."

Above our heads, the train status board began changing information, the letters and numbers clatter-ing as they shuffled and settled. "Track 15," Paul said. "Come on, I'll take your case." He shifted his carryall to a shoulder, grasping my valise with one hand and my hatbox in the other.

"Maman is thrilled you're coming down for the week-end," he said, once we had settled into our train seats. "I honestly think she might have repainted the stables."

"I hope you're joking. I'd be mortified if she went to any trouble."

"She's been snatching sugar off the black market like a pirate pillaging gold bullion."

"Who else will be there, may I ask?"

"Don't worry. It won't be like that dreadful party at Lulu's. Half that crowd would never stoop to visit us—we're far too boring." He lit a cigarette, turning his head to exhale. "It's just a group of friends I've known for ages, and with any luck we'll be able to join the *chasse à courre* at Fontainebleau. You do hunt, *n'est-ce pas?*"

My spirits, which had deflated at the word boring, began to brighten. "Oh, yes. I adore it."

"My brother Jean-Louis and his wife will be there too. They moved back home a few months ago. They just got married and won't let anyone forget it."

The train swerved around a curve, and I fell against him, allowing the side of my leg to brush his. "Is that so bad?"

"Just wait. You'll see." He gently straightened himself, inching away to give me more space.

I crossed my arms. "Say, I've been thinking about what you told your mother about the racetrack. Should we get our story straight?" The incident had flashed into my mind a few times over the past days. I wasn't upset he had lied to his mother—after all, I often tiptoed around my own—but I wondered why he'd done it.

Paul ran a hand through his hair until it bristled. "Thanks awfully for covering for me. It was bad form to spring that on you—sorry."

I shrugged away his apology. "It's fine—it was un-expected, that's all. Does she disapprove of the track? Or is it something else?"

He frowned at the cigarette in his hand, the ash growing so long it trembled. "She doesn't like me to gamble." He crushed the butt in the ashtray between our seats. "She was terribly cross when she suspected how much I'd lost at Auteuil that day. I suppose she thinks I'll throw everything away on a foolish bet."

"But didn't you win?" Wasn't that what he'd said at Lulu's? Perhaps I'd misunderstood.

"I wagered more than I thought," he said. I waited for him to elaborate, but he merely lifted his eyebrows and offered me a cigarette before lighting another for himself.

A pale blue car met us at the station, all gloss and shine against the midautumn gloom. A young man climbed from the driver's seat and kissed Paul on both cheeks.

"Jacqueline, my brother, Jean-Louis," Paul introduced us. I found myself looking into a face that resembled his, except that it was leaner, tanned instead of freckled, with a mustache, darkly debonair, and eyes of sharp blue instead of lively gray.

"His *favorite* brother," Jean-Louis said with a wink, stooping to kiss me hello. "Lovely to meet you,

Jacqueline. I've heard so much about *la petite améri-caine.*" He tossed our bags into the trunk, gesturing for me to sit in the front while Paul folded his lanky frame into the back. "Come on, Maman will unleash the hounds if we're not home in time for tea."

"Where's Philippine?" Paul raised his voice against the wind rushing in from the open windows. "I thought you two were joined together."

"She's feeling a bit poorly." Jean-Louis met his eye in the mirror. "Don't worry, nothing's wrong. It's just that we're . . . expecting a happy event."

I had no idea what he meant, but suddenly Paul launched himself at Jean-Louis from the rear, so that the car lurched to the side of the road. "I'm going to be an uncle?" he croaked, planting an enormous kiss on his brother's cheek.

"Yes, well, try not to kill us, all right?" Jean-Louis chided him, though he'd puffed with pride.

"Congratulations," I said softly, feeling shy in the face of their emotion.

"*Merci.*" Jean-Louis glanced over with a smile, en-snaring me in the blue flash of his gaze.

We turned down a long *allée* lined with chestnut trees, their branches reaching up and interlocking to form a tunnel. This was always the worst moment of a house party—not knowing if the other guests would be nice or nasty, likewise the food, and, here in postwar France, wondering if the rooms would be heated. At least there would be horses, I thought.

We rounded a curve, and the château loomed before us in Classical lines of brick and pale stone, a formidable double staircase jutting from the façade in twin semicircles that curved to form a horseshoe. The surrounding moat was laid out in precise right angles, lengthening at one end into a rectangular pond. Acres of manicured lawn unfurled to a forest that stretched as far as my eye could see. Later I would discover the intersecting paths that led to a series of gardens, each one as precisely planned and detailed as a Renaissance painting.

"Leave the bags. Someone will fetch them," Jean-Louis said, pulling into the driveway with a spray of gravel.

A slight figure emerged from a side door. "Jacqueline!" the Vicomtesse de Ganay called. "So lovely to see you again." She kissed me hello, trailing a scent of geraniums and roses.

"I'm here too, Maman," Paul teased, and she rapped him on the arm before stretching on tiptoe to embrace him.

"You're just in time for *goûter*," she chattered, as we entered the house through a dark vestibule. "Nanny insisted on making scones for you, Paul. I had to ransack the pantry to find a jar of strawberry jam she deemed acceptable. Will you run up to the nursery and thank her, *chéri?* She's missed you so."

"Of course." He started up a back staircase but not before Jean-Louis cut him off with a flourish.

"Nanny actually made the scones for *me*," he said with a grin, elbowing Paul in the side. They raced up the stairs, jostling each other.

The Vicomtesse continued down the hall, unruffled. "Let me show you to your room," she said.

Even as I saw Courances for the first time, I knew it would remain one of the most extraordinary houses I would ever visit, an enfilade of rooms adorned with carved wood paneling and gilt-embellished frescoes, walls of variegated marble—a gallery spanning the length of the château lined with portraits dating back five hundred years, a *grand salon* crammed with marquetry furniture and paintings that I longed to examine—it was all light and shadow, parquet floors and thick silk carpets, antique majesty and discreet modern comfort.

My bedroom, in the north tower, had windows on all sides and—miracle of miracles—a bathroom of my very own, gleaming white with a deep, claw-footed tub. I spent a long time soaking in it the next evening before dinner, refreshing the hot water and reflecting on the house party.

The other guests were not the ruddy, middle-aged country set I had anticipated, but a group of friends who had grown up with the de Ganay brothers, young, light-hearted, and unexpectedly wholesome. They hadn't all fought in the war (though a few of the older boys had joined the Free French in London), nor did they all have extended names (some were double-barreled), but they all carried themselves with the careless confidence born of wealth and privilege.

As Paul's mother made the introductions, I soon realized everyone paired off quite neatly into couples, either newlywed, engaged, or understood: Jean-Louis and his wife, Philippine. Her sister, Sabine, with Nicolas. The Vicomte's goddaughter, Hélène, and her fiancé, François. Paul's school friend Henri and his sweetheart, Florence, whose mousy hair matched her demeanor. The only two left were Paul and me. Was the Vicomtesse playing at Cupid? Or perhaps it was the Vicomte? Or had I misinterpreted Paul's cues on the train? Maybe he'd invited me to avoid playing goose-berry for the entire weekend.

None of it mattered once the hounds had the scent

of wild boar in their noses and my horse, Cocotte, was flying across fields and fences. I abandoned myself to the thrill of speed and power, the rush of wind against my face, the intensity of the exercise. For a few hours I was conscious only of the crisp air and barking dogs, the smell of wet leaves, the steady clip of horses' hooves, the fluid motion of Cocotte as she cantered, the dip of her head when she snatched at a passing bush.

We lost the scent, but it didn't matter. I'd always hated the brutal part of the hunt anyway—for me the exhilaration was in the risk and chase, the show of strength and skill. We returned to Courances flushed and high-spirited, chattering about the morning's exploits—even the Vicomtesse had lost her usual demure demeanor and was teasing Paul about leaping the fences instead of passing through the gates. "You don't have to jump every one, *chéri*," she said.

"I see *la petite américaine* has been on a horse before." Jean-Louis trotted up beside me as we entered the courtyard. The grooms appeared to help us dismount and lead away the horses, but he swung himself down before handing off the reins.

"Oh, just a few times," I said, basking a little in his admiration.

He offered a hand to help me dismount, his eyes

glinting impossibly blue in the noon sun. I hesitated, not wishing to offend his pride, yet conscious of flirting with a married man in front of his entire family. Finally, I tossed my head and jumped down by myself, ignoring his laugh.

Everyone trooped inside to the morning room, which was laid for an early buffet lunch with great platters of charcuterie, rows of sturdy country pâtés encased in ornate pastry crusts, and cups of hot consommé laced with sherry in case anyone needed warming up, which no one did—our blood was already running high. Philippine appeared, her cheeks wan beside Jean-Louis's glowing complexion, but managed only a nibble of bread before she abruptly stood, knocked over her chair, and fled the table. Jean-Louis excused himself to follow her.

"Nature is ruthless, *n'est-ce pas?*" On my other side, Paul poured wine into our glasses.

"Have they been married long?"

"About a year—just after he returned from Indochine."

"He spent the war in Southeast Asia?" Paul and I were the same age—we had been children during the war—but I'd assumed Jean-Louis had not fought, like many of his social sphere.

"Not the duration, no. At first he worked under-cover here in France, and then he went to London for a bit."

"With the Free French?"

"With the charming Général de Gaulle himself." He winked and reached for his glass of wine.

Was Paul joking? I assumed so—for there was little about de Gaulle's rigid, upright posture that seemed particularly charming—and yet I couldn't be sure. Once again I felt the conversation slipping away from me, just as at Lulu's tea party, leaving behind an un-pleasant feeling of being tested and not measuring up. Though I'd never lacked a witty riposte in English, in French I could feel as callow as any dime-store stereo-type of my compatriots.

"Is it true de Gaulle's a *cagoulard*?" I asked, mostly to prove that I wasn't in over my head. The word had come to me suddenly, though I still had only a vague notion of what it meant: Madame Saleil had briefly explained that La Cagoule was a nickname for the Comité secret d'action révolutionnaire, a secret anti-communist group active before the war that leaned so far to the right it nearly tipped into fascism. Its mem-bers were nicknamed *cagoulards*—the hooded ones—after the menacing, face-covering hoods they wore at their meetings.

Paul lifted his eyebrows and subtly dropped his voice. "Some people think so, but as much as the Général dislikes the communists it seems farfetched to think he'd condone the Cagoule's kind of violence— assassinations, bombings, sabotage . . ." As he listed the group's activities, I tried to absorb my shock. The *cagoulards* sounded like veritable terrorists.

"On the other hand," Paul continued, "the Général did recruit a couple of known *cagoulards* to join him in London. And after Georges Loustaunau-Lacau was arrested by the Gestapo, there were always whispers that de Gaulle was giving Marie-Madeleine special help for Alliance."

I had been trying to keep track of all the unfamiliar names and details. But at the mention of the de Rentys' spy ring, my heart gave an involuntary jump. "Who is she?"

Marie-Madeleine Fourcade, Paul explained, had worked at a far-right magazine started by Georges Loustaunau-Lacau, a former military aide and acknowledged *cagoulard*. When the war broke out, she helped him form an unusual spy ring, neither communist nor Gaullist, but extremely right wing and anti-Vichy. After his arrest, Marie-Madeleine took over Alliance, expanding the network across France with support from the Free French and the British government. "She recruited widely among her set," Paul said. "I suppose that's why so many of them were arrested. Our crowd is laughably bad at subterfuge."

On the surface, at least, this explained the fate of the Comte and Comtesse de Renty. But what else had Ghislaine said? I blinked and heard her words again: "Back then I thought we were all on the same side."

With more confidence than I felt, I said, "What a miracle that all those groups agreed to work together—communists and socialists, liberals and conservatives, the right, the left, and everything in between."

He shrugged. "They had a common enemy. But it didn't take long after D-Day for the alliances to splinter."

"The old disagreements didn't vanish with the war?"

"What was there before is still there," he agreed. "Except it's even more pronounced. The old grudges have become more bitter, and the desire for revenge more bloodthirsty. The communists haven't forgotten the plots against them, and the conservatives have grown more convinced there's a Soviet master plan to take over the West. Especially now that the numbers are strong—30 percent of French are communists, you know—they see conspiracies everywhere. In fact"—he paused to spear the last piece of ham on his plate—"I hear Marie-Mad has started working for the government again."

"Spying?" The word emerged in a hiss, even though I hadn't meant it to.

"Indeed." He picked up a piece of bread, breaking it cleanly in half. "I was going to say the communists have become the new enemy. But I guess for some they've always been the enemy."

I dressed carefully for dinner, taking extra time with my makeup, powdering my face and lips, applying lipstick in raven red, blotting, powdering, and finally touching up with lipstick again. I had noticed the appraising glances of my chic French counterparts and I was determined they would not outshine me.

Downstairs, I found the *grand salon* empty, even though I was fifteen minutes late by the antique clock on the mantelpiece. A fire crackled behind an intricate screen, and beside the piano a table stood ready for the *apéritif* with rows of clean glasses, small bowls of nuts and olives, and bottles of iced champagne waiting to be popped. I hesitated, unsure if I should sit and wait for the others, unwilling to be the maladroit first, yet also reluctant to make the long trek back to my tower room. Finally, I pulled my evening stole around my shoulders, opened one of the tall windowed doors, and stepped into the night.

I hadn't come outside to smoke, but of course I lit a cigarette, the heavy odor mingling pleasantly with the cold air stinging my face and neck. I strolled along a little gravel path, relishing the sound of my crunching heels against the rural calm, and as I walked I thought about Paul and his family. Initially I'd assumed the de Ganays were like other distinguished families I had known, their home bearing the familiar trappings of luxury: fleets of cars and horses, servants who unpacked your bags upon arrival, hothouse fruits and flowers on the table. But now I realized my error. For in the château's *grand salon*, set into the wall above the fireplace, was a bas-relief portrait of Louis XIII, former king of France, his strong features and curly locks depicted in profile. When I'd admired it, Philippine told me he was the family's benefactor, having offered the château to a forefather, Jehan de Ganay, in the midsixteenth century, "in grateful recognition of his service," she said. From her words I surmised that the de Ganays had been entwined with royalty for generations, both as counselors and consorts, their name evoking a fortune and privilege untouched by the vagaries of revolutionary zeal, or world wars, or Napoleonic inheritance laws.

For all that Mummy wanted me to make a good

match, I knew she wouldn't approve of Paul. She would feel intimidated by the de Ganays, by their foreign elegance and poise, their peculiar elongated syllables and deep, rasping r's. She would turn cold and critical and pretend to be unimpressed, when really she felt inadequate.

An easterly wind was kicking up, teasing the remaining leaves from balding branches. I drew my wrap closer, but it was just a gesture, for I was conscious of the ancient château behind me, its windows glowing with warmth and light. In its shelter I felt impervious to the cold.

By the time I returned inside, everyone had gathered and all were looking longingly at the bottles of champagne. Before my cheeks had lost their chill, the corks were dislodged, the wine was poured, and a housemaid began circling the room with the filled glasses.

"Gosh, was everyone waiting for me?" I turned to Henri and Florence, who were standing by the windows.

"Of course—*comme il faut.*" Florence shrugged. She was wearing a pastel frock of chiffon and lace that made my black satin gown seem macabre.

"Don't worry, you couldn't have known." Henri gave me a look that made me feel like, nevertheless, I should have, somehow.

I accepted a glass and sought out Paul, who was in

the corner frowning and eating almonds. "Hello, Comrade," I said with a wink. "Champagne drinkers of the world unite."

He laughed and touched his glass to mine. The wine's effervescence fizzed at the back of my throat, and I began to relax into the party's ambience. Paul and I were almost exactly the same height, which made it difficult to look up into his eyes, but I tilted my head and focused my attention on him completely, a bit of flirtation that I had never known not to flatter a man.

"Listen, Jacqueline," he began, then stopped and flushed.

"Yes?" I said softly, so that he moved closer to me.

He spoke in a low voice. "It's fine around me, of course, but you shouldn't joke about communists. It's not appropriate for mixed company."

"Oh." I fell back, stung. "I was only teasing."

"I know. But these things could easily fall on the wrong ears." He gulped from his glass. "I thought you'd want to know."

"Thought she'd want to know what?"

Turning, I found Jean-Louis, dashing in evening clothes, his mustache neatly groomed for the occasion. "Santé!" He raised his glass, and we followed suit. "Wait, wait, look me in the eye," he instructed me, his gaze meeting mine in a sharp blue flash. "And, whoops, don't cross glasses." His hand shot out to grasp my arm, preventing me from colliding with Paul. "Or else you know what happens!"

"What happens?" I asked.

"Seven years of bad luck," said Paul.

"Something like that," Jean-Louis agreed, elbowing his younger brother. Paul began blushing again, and I guessed some racy innuendo was being referenced.

"Now, now, it's not nice to tease *la petite américaine*," I said with mock severity. "You wouldn't want us to cut off the cigarettes and chocolate bars, would you?"

"But is it not an honor to be teased?" asked Jean-Louis with a twinkle. "After all, we only make fun of the people we really like." He inclined his head with a courtly gesture.

"You flatter me, monsieur."

"Is it working?"

I laughed and moved toward the fire. Though I enjoyed flirting with Jean-Louis, I felt surprised that a married man would play at this game with his younger brother's date, while his own wife stood not three feet away. What's more, no one appeared to care. Paul lit a cigarette and drifted toward the phonograph, where Henri was selecting records. Philippine—whose spirits seemed revived—sipped a glass of champagne with rosy cheeks and giggled with her sister over an old photo album.

At dinner I found myself seated beside the Vicomte, who needed only a little encouragement to launch into his opinions on modernizing the estate. As he talked about tenant farmers and government subsidies, we ate roasted venison in a ruby-colored wine sauce, and I admired the Rococo frescoes adorning the walls and ceiling of the dining room. My mind had wandered so far from the table that when Jean-Louis addressed me I gave a little start. "Tell us, Jacqueline," he began, his eyes snaring mine. "How does the horse riding in France compare with the United States?"

I sipped from my glass of wine, trying to find the right words in French. "This morning was marvelous, of course," I said. "But my stepfather's stables in Virginia are a bit more informal." I hesitated before attempting a quick translation. *"Je monte à poil,"* I said, meaning, I ride bareback.

A thick silence blanketed the room. Across from me, Jean-Louis twitched and brought a napkin to his mouth. Paul's face turned scarlet, like he was struggling to contain a sneeze, and Philippine had frozen with her cutlery in midair. Finally Madame la Vicomtesse spoke from the other end of the table. "I think you mean *'je monte à cru,'*" she said. "*'Je monte à poil'* means . . ."

Her gentle expression cracked into a shriek of mirth. "It means . . ." she gasped, "I ride naked."

Everyone erupted, shouting with hilarity until the tears streamed down their cheeks. I began to laugh too, feeling a little hysterical at making such a ribald linguistic faux pas in front of my elegant French hosts. For years afterward, I regaled my friends with this story of my most mortifying French error. But I never made that particular mistake again in my life.

Chapter Six

I noticed immediately when I returned from Courances how drafty the apartment on avenue Mozart
suddenly felt. Perhaps winter had taken hold over the
weekend—or maybe a few days of central heating had
spoiled me—but an insistent chill was creeping past
the edges of the unsealed doors and window frames,
hovering in the high-ceilinged rooms. I hated to complain to Madame, so I spread an extra blanket across
my bed and donned another sweater, ignoring the cold
to admire the pure, pale light falling through the thin
panes of glass.

At breakfast the next morning, Susan and Mary Ann
told me about the heater repairman's last visit. "He
kept saying, '*Ohhhh, c'est pas possible, madame.*'"
Susan pulled a long face and made her voice comically

deep. "But Madame said he should ignore his innate cultural pessimism and finally he agreed to go look for parts." She glanced toward the door, even though the de Rentys had already left for the day. "I do hope he comes back soon. Even this one has started to feel the cold." She jerked a thumb at Mary Ann.

"I only mentioned it once!" Mary Ann protested. But when she rose from the table to bring her dishes to the kitchen, I saw she was wearing two pairs of white ankle socks with her wool-lined slippers.

It must have been the cold, or the damp—or both—that caused me to wake with a tickle at the back of my throat a few days later. I lay in bed, reluctant to leave its warmth, half wondering if I should stay there for the day. But it was only a faint scratch—and my art history class had planned a visit to the Musée de l'Orangerie that I hated to miss. After sipping a tisane with honey at breakfast, I decided not to mention it and wrapped a wool scarf around my neck before venturing out into the mist that felt like needles on my skin.

The paintings at the Orangerie dazzled me with their deft color palettes and quick brushstrokes. Our speaker, a renowned curator and expert on Impressionism, urged us to stand daringly close to the canvases. "Closer . . . closer! Inspect it! So near you could smell it!" he exhorted us.

I was studying a Corot—all summer sky and bur-geoning trees, dappled shade splashed across a dusty road—when the daubs of paint begin spinning. Stag-gering backward, I tumbled into Martha, who stood directly behind me.

"*Désolée,*" I apologized, struggling to regain my balance.

She held my elbow steady. "Are you all right?"

"Fine," I assured her, and felt her grip relax. "I guess I was wishing a little too hard that I was in the painting."

She turned to look at the canvas. "It makes you want to shade your eyes, doesn't it? All that hot sun."

"Especially on a day like today," I said, with a shiver that was meant to be theatrical but quickly turned involuntary.

"Are you sure you're all right?" Martha frowned, her gaze sharpening. "You're awfully pale."

I swallowed against the knives in my throat. "I'm feel-ing a bit poorly," I admitted. "Maybe I should go home."

"I'll tell *le Maître*. Go on, don't worry about class— you can borrow my notes later."

In the métro station, a train waited on the platform, but I couldn't muster the energy to skip down the stairs to catch it. The next train took an age to arrive, and then, as I trudged up the stairs at Jasmin, I spotted the pharmacy and decided to stop for more aspirin. By the time I had finished waiting in line—only to learn they were out of aspirin—a strange ache had begun radiating through my body. Inside our building, I sagged against the elevator wall as it creaked to the second floor.

I could think only of bed, of curling up under the quilts and sleeping for a thousand years. That must explain why I didn't hear the voices as I fumbled for my key on the landing, why I didn't notice that anyone was in the apartment until I was halfway to my room.

"Jacqueline!" Madame called from the hallway, startling me so that I jumped. She caught sight of my pale face and moved toward me, her plum-colored dress rustling. "Is everything all right, my dear?"

"I'm feeling pretty rotten," I admitted. "I came home to rest."

"*Oh, ma pauvre petite,*" she clucked. "Can I bring you anything? Something to eat? A cup of tea?" From the *salon,* a swell of women's voices rose in merriment. Madame glanced toward the sound, flushing slightly. "I invited some friends to lunch today. I didn't realize . . ."

I shook my head. "I'm sorry I've interrupted you. Please, I'll be fine. I'm going to take some aspirin and go to bed."

"I'll come check on you later. Rest well, my dear."

In my room, I found my dwindling supply of aspirin

and swallowed two tablets before crawling into bed. Closing my eyes, I tried to still my mind. Voices from the *salon* seeped through the closed door of my room, murmurs giving way to shouts of laughter—or were they sobs? I'd never met any of Madame's friends—in fact, I didn't even know she *had* friends. I knew she spent her days volunteering at the ADIR headquarters, a modest building on the rue de Guynemer, bordering the jardin du Luxembourg. But aside from the vague objective of assisting former deportees, I wasn't sure exactly what she did there. I had a feeling she preferred it that way.

I tried to sleep, shifting uncomfortably from side to side, but their words reached me, jagged sentences and phrases puncturing my rest:

"Do you remember the day La Vachère kicked over the soup pot?"

"Fat yellow-haired German cow."

"If I'd had the strength I would've ripped the coat from her body and forced *her* to crawl in the snow."

"Do you remember how we licked the soup from the ground? We were so desperate to catch those drops before they disappeared through the cracks of the floor."

"The floor was filthy."

"And covered in frost."

"She did it on purpose."

"That's what Jeannie said when she tried to defend us."

"Yes, before they beat her."

I shouldn't have been listening—I didn't want to be listening. I pulled a pillow over my head and tried to muffle the words. But they kept coming. Lice. Guard dogs. Dysentery. Typhoid. Tuberculosis. Barracks like hovels. Hovels that were infirmaries. The hunger, the emaciation, the punishments. The unending threat of the gas chamber. The words became images and the images flickered in an endless looping nightmare. Heaps of bodies stacked in shallow graves.

I must have cried out in my sleep for I woke with the sound in my ear. The voices had disappeared, and in their place I heard piano music playing on the Victrola— Satie's *Trois Gymnopédies*—the pure notes lingering in the calm. Madame was moving about the apartment—I recognized the limping shuffle of her gait—and a pale wash of yellow light tinged the sky. I had slept the afternoon away and now the sun was setting.

There was a soft knock at my door. "Come in," I croaked, my throat raw.

Madame entered, a steaming mug in her hands. "How are you feeling, my dear?" she asked gently. "I brought you a tisane."

"*Merci.*" I swallowed with effort. "Sorry to trouble you," I said, although what I wanted to say was, I'm sorry I intruded on your gathering. I'm sorry I overheard your conversation. I'm sorry—so dreadfully sorry—those things happened to anyone, and especially you.

She set the mug of tea on the bedside table and hovered beside the bed. "It's no trouble at all. I hope we didn't disturb you this afternoon." In the lightness of her tone, I sensed a defense—one I sometimes employed myself: a presumption that no well-mannered person would attempt to pry behind a pleasant façade. And though I had a thousand questions, she had given me a cue, and my respect for her forced me to obey it.

"Not at all," I whispered. "I slept like a stone."

"Good." Her face cleared. "I'll let you rest." With a reassuring smile she closed the door quietly behind her, leaving me alone with my thoughts.

After that day, it became difficult for me to talk to Madame as I had before. Though I'd known she had been imprisoned at Ravensbrück—though I'd read about the slave labor camp in the newspapers—connecting such brutal Nazi violence with the serene matriarch of our household had shaken me to the core. I felt embarrassed by my luck, that my life thus far had been virtually untouched by death or grief. All our usual conversation topics seemed so trivial—our classwork and meals, the pompous professor of nineteenth-century literature whose twanging Midi accent I imitated at dinner to make everyone laugh. All of it embarrassed me.

How could I have wondered how many more times Madame would serve leek and potato soup when she had once scrambled in the snow for spilled drops of larvae-infested gruel? How could I complain about the draft in the dining room when she had been hosed down each winter morning, forced to stand outside while the water froze on her naked body? How could I fret over poor exam marks when she had once led a work-camp boycott refusing to allow her slave labor to benefit the Nazi war machine? The things I'd heard were unbearable—and I felt like a coward because I hadn't had to bear them at all.

I didn't tell the others what I'd learned. Madame's suffering was too profound for three American girls to discuss it like something out of a penny horror novel. Though I longed to ask Claude about it, I wasn't sure what she and Ghislaine knew—how much their mother had told them and what she had omitted. And so I kept everything to myself, striving for the discretion Madame prized, even as I flinched whenever I recalled what she had endured. Above all, I knew Madame wouldn't want our pity.

As the weeks went by, to my relief, I began to see Madame as a whole person again: not only a victim of tragedy, but a grandmother who invented little songs for her grandson; a stylish woman who loved to dress in rich colors—never widow's black or gray, but vibrant hues of blue, and green, and purple; a Parisienne nurturing a passionate love affair with her city. Perhaps sensing my reticence, she made an extra effort to chat about new art exhibits, and useful bus routes, and how to identify bits of antique porcelain at the flea market, as if these were the most important things in the world. It was clear she had put the past behind her—or so I thought.

For it was around this time that I began hearing odd sounds again in the small hours, thumps and muffled cries. They were similar to the noises I'd heard my first night at avenue Mozart, and at first I dismissed them as the restless sleep of little Christian—Ghislaine always said he woke up with half the bedclothes on the floor. And so, I said nothing, not wanting to make a fuss, until one wet night in mid-November.

A storm had broken while we slept, half waking me with bursts of pelting rain and tree branches scratching the windows like sharp fingernails. The sounds were ghostly but by this time I was used to them—my room faced the street and was exposed to the elements, unlike those sheltered on the courtyard—and I turned on my side to go back to sleep. I had just drifted off when there came a shriek so sharp and sudden it shattered any residual drowsiness. I froze, my ears straining past the howling gale for more clues. *"Please, please, please,"* I thought I heard a woman implore. *"Help me."*

Terrified that something was wrong, I slipped from bed, tiptoed to the door, and opened it, steeling myself for what I'd find in the hall.

Darkness. Silence, broken by the tick of the dining-room clock. A rush of water running through the pipes. I moved quietly, wincing at the chill against my bare feet, stepping carefully to avoid the creaky spots in the floorboards, pausing outside each bedroom door but hearing nothing within. By the time I reached the end of the hall, my heart had returned to its normal rhythm and I was convinced I'd imagined the sounds. After using the bathroom, I turned to go back to bed, creeping down the hallway. "Oh!" I gasped, as I half collided with a figure dressed in flowing white. In the gloom it was difficult to discern if it was ghost or human, friend or intruder. "Who is it?" I managed to hiss past the lump in my throat.

The figure reached out and grasped my bare arm with rough, cold fingers. Before I could scream, I heard a voice whispering clumsily: "Jacqueline, shhh. It's me, Germaine."

Germaine? Who was that? I stiffened, ready to snatch away my arm and flee, when I caught a familiar scent of lavender. It was Madame's perfume, and, peering closer, I saw that, yes, it was Madame standing before me, her hair loose and wraithlike around her shoulders, her lips sunken without the dentures I hadn't realized she wore.

"Oh, Madame," I whispered, sagging with relief. "I didn't see it was you. It's so dark my eyes are playing tricks on me."

"Did you hear something?" She peered past me as if expecting someone else to appear.

"I did, just now," I said. "I thought it was someone crying. But it could have been the wind. The storm." I gestured at the windows. "Or perhaps little Christian . . ."

"It was me."

"What?"

"Just a bit of dyspepsia. It happens at my age, I'm afraid. Oh, but my dear, you are shivering! You must return to bed." She placed a hand on my back, her work-rough palm catching on the fabric of my nightgown. "I was afraid I'd woken someone, but there's no need to be frightened." With gentle pressure, she guided me back to my room and ushered me inside. "Don't worry," she whispered before closing the door. "There are no ghosts here tonight."

For a long while I lay awake, puzzling over her words, and sleep, when it finally came again, was heavy. I star-

tled awake to the call of voices and milky light streaming through a gap in the curtains. Madame, Claude, and
Susan were leaving—I heard the front door slam—and
everyone else was in a flurry as they rushed to get ready.
In the hall, Ghislaine stood before the mirror snatching
curlers from her hair, while Mary Ann stomped to and
fro, looking for her loafers. "You'd better hurry if you
want to make it to class," she called as I brushed past her
from the bathroom. "Didn't you set an alarm?"

"I slept straight through it." I patted my damp face
with a towel. "Something woke me around three and I
had the darnedest time drifting off again."

"Golly, I didn't hear a thing," said Mary Ann.
"What was it?"

I hesitated, not wishing to betray Madame's privacy.

"Sorry, it was Christian." Ghislaine spun from the
mirror, dark curls bouncing. "He had a bad dream and
woke up crying."

"Poor little fellow," Mary Ann clucked.

Ghislaine nodded and turned back to the mirror to
finish brushing her hair. Our eyes met in the reflection, her gaze darting away.

"I used to get awful nightmares when I was a kid,"
Mary Ann was saying. "My big brother would hide in
my wardrobe and pop out just as I was drifting off to
sleep. It used to frighten me to bits."

"I'm sure Christian will outgrow them soon," Ghislaine said, snapping her lipstick shut.

"Outgrow what, Maman?" Drawn to the sound of his name, Christian popped out of the hall closet with a pair of loafers flapping on his feet and a tattered book in his sticky hands.

"My shoes!" exclaimed Mary Ann, kneeling to pry them away. "And what's this?" She snatched the book from him. "My address book! Good golly, I've been looking for it for ages!"

He ignored her, frowning up at Ghislaine. "What will I outgrow?"

"It's time to go. Get your coat on," she instructed.

"Tell me! What is it? What? What?" With each word Christian tugged at Ghislaine's skirt.

She bent to thread his arms through the sleeves of a shapeless wool garment. "Your nightmares, *chéri*."

"I don't have nightmares," he said.

She smiled at him patiently. "You had one last night, remember?"

"No, I didn't."

"You did, *mon grand*. You woke up in the middle of the night crying."

"I didn't!"

"You've just forgotten because you're so little. Now get your shoes on. We're already late."

"I'm not little!" he protested, his face crumpling. "That's not nice!" He began to howl as Ghislaine thrust shoes upon his feet, bundled him into several more layers, and pulled him out the door.

Mary Ann heaved a groan into the calm. "I can't believe he had my address book this whole time, the little terror."

The clock chimed the quarter hour, reminding me of my tardiness. I ran to get dressed, in such a rush to leave that it wasn't until later in the day that I noticed the thread of misgiving running through my thoughts, pulling them into a pucker that refused to smooth. Madame had said it was she who had cried out in the night, and I'd accepted her explanation. But why had Ghislaine told me it was Christian? One of them— Ghislaine or Madame—was lying to me. But why?

Over the next few days I tried to brush away my concerns, but instead of dispersing they dug into my subconscious. Of course I trusted Madame and Ghislaine—indeed, I had begun to think of the de Rentys as my French family—but I couldn't understand why they would deceive me about something so inconsequential. Didn't we all have indigestion, or bad dreams, or worries that woke us in the night? Their secrecy made no sense—unless Madame had something terrible to hide, something worse than her lingering scars of war.

———

"**Table for two?**" The waiter pinched his lips. "Did you reserve?"

"No, but—"

"*Désolé*, mademoiselle. We are full."

I tipped my head to one side, gazing at him through my lashes. "Are you sure? We're tiny—we can squeeze in any old corner."

He shrugged and turned to another customer. Sighing, I stood on tiptoe to peer above the crowd, hoping Claude would arrive, fretting about how we'd find a table at any of the other cafés on the street, which were all heaving with customers.

"Mademoiselle, *bonjour!*" It was the waiter, suddenly beaming, and there was Claude standing beside me. "Come with me!" he cried. We followed him to the back of the room, where he installed us at a wobbly table with a flourish. "Anything for Mademoiselle Olivia," he said with a wink.

"Olivia?" I asked when we were seated and smoking. "Is that your pseudonym?"

"He thinks I look like Olivia de Havilland," she said, exhaling out of the corner of her mouth. "*C'est ridicule.*" But despite her eye roll, I could tell she was pleased.

Around us the restaurant crackled with voices, the

clank of thick crockery, and chairs scraping across tile. The *bouillon* was a dim, sticky-floored relic of a previous era, once a working-class canteen, now a cheap student bistro with a daily set menu where regulars stored their napkin and cutlery in pigeonholes along a wall. Claude dutifully retrieved hers, while I made do with a battered fork, a dessert spoon, and a knife so dull I doubted it could slice camembert.

Across the table, Claude arranged her silverware with painstaking precision. I had invited her to lunch under the pretext of celebrating the end of our midterm exams, but really I was hoping to learn more about Madame, Ghislaine, and the strange sounds I'd been hearing in the night. Though I didn't want to pry, my concerns had begun invading my sleep, waking me with a peculiar foreboding that left me straining for clues.

"Oh, good, here comes the waiter. I'm famished, aren't you?" Claude unfolded her napkin with such a cheerful flourish that I felt slightly abashed.

"*Et voilà, mesdemoiselles!*" He set down a basket of sliced baguette and plates of soup floating with limp *lardons* and rough chunks of cabbage. Claude seized her spoon, drank a mouthful of the thin, drab liquid, and abandoned it. "How I adore this restaurant," she said without irony. "They truly do not care."

I sampled the soup, which tasted like stewed socks. "It's slimming, at least."

"Did you know malnutrition is the main cause of ill health among Parisian students? It's true!" she insisted when I laughed. "It's a tradition for French students to live like paupers. Sort of a reverse chic."

She began describing the lodgings of one of her classmates who lived in a shabby Latin Quarter hotel: "broken furniture, leaky toilet down the hall, the smell of grease everywhere . . . It's terribly romantic." As she talked, I racked my mind for a way to broach the delicate topic of her mother and sister, resisting the urge to fidget. Finally, I reached for my pocketbook and withdrew a fresh cigarette, lighting it off the old one, ignoring Mummy's scolding voice in my head telling me it was unseemly to chain-smoke. Our waiter appeared, whisking away the soup plates and replacing them with a main course of veal and a sodden gray heap that Claude identified as braised endive.

"How curious!" I said, unfolding my slice of roast. It was as thin as fine silk and riddled with tiny holes, as if the chef had pierced the meat with nails. "Is this some sort of French cookery technique?"

Claude stopped chewing and looked more closely at the food. "Damn it. I was hungry too."

"What's wrong with it?"

"Nothing, I suppose—it's cooked. But when the war ended, I swore I wouldn't eat wormy meat again."

"Worms?" I stared at the plate. "Oh, Claude, that's atrocious. I had no idea . . ." Her eyes, when she lifted them, were dark and stony.

"Never mind." She pushed her plate away and took a piece of bread. "A bit of a regimen never hurt anyone."

I set down my cutlery, my thoughts suddenly racing as I arranged the fork and knife across the plate of food. "Is it something you can talk about?" I said eventually, so softly I wondered if she'd heard me above the din. In her silence, I held my breath, hoping I hadn't upset her.

"I can't complain. I was luckier than most," she said. "My parents sent me away to Normandy to stay with some friends. We could get fresh milk and vegetables, and there was a large garden where we raised rabbits. It was heaps better than Paris, where there was absolutely nothing."

"I didn't know you were in the countryside." I frowned, gazing down at my plate. "Did Ghislaine go too?"

She drew a deep breath. "They wanted her to, but she refused. She's three years older than me, you know, and by that time she had a boyfriend, and an apartment, and war work of her own . . ." A strange expression flickered across her face and then disappeared. "It was Ghislaine who wrote me a few weeks after the Liberation and said to come home. I assumed we would all be together again, finally. When I arrived at avenue Mozart, she told me that Papa and Maman had been deported, accused of being enemies of the state. Our apartment was completely deserted—the beds unmade, dirty dishes in the sink—it was as if they'd been snatched out of thin air. Ghislaine said they'd been taken weeks ago in the middle of the night. No one had a clue."

The shock was still livid in her face, the bone-rattling jolt of returning home expecting to celebrate the Liberation, only to find her parents had vanished. Claude and I were the same age, so I knew she had been just sixteen at the end of the war, a mere schoolgirl.

"Papa didn't survive Ellrich," she continued slowly. "We knew the odds were slim, yet still I hoped. But, no." The Comte Robert de Renty had been buried in a mass grave, she said, the family unable to recover his remains. "He managed to scribble a message on a métro ticket and throw it out the window of the truck deporting him to Germany. A woman found it on the street and sent it to us. They were the last words we ever heard from him. 'See you again, I hope, my dears. Pray for me, for I will surely need it.'"

"And your mother?" I asked, unable to contain my curiosity.

"She was rescued by the Swedish Red Cross just before the end of the war. They took her to the sanatorium at Malmö to recover, but still, several months later, when we were finally reunited, she was all skin and bones. When she first got home she slept on the floor next to her bed—it was as if even her lumpy old mattress was too luxurious. But her sleep was broken, and she would wake me sometimes, gasping and shaking in her dreams. When I tried to comfort her, she didn't want to speak of what happened there, and I didn't dare ask questions. Even now, four years later, she doesn't talk about it. Most of what I know, I learned from snatches of telephone conversations, or meetings—like the one a few weeks ago." She found a cigarette and lit it, her eyes meeting mine and glancing away.

"I couldn't help overhearing," I admitted. "I got the sense they rely on each other very much, even now."

She exhaled a plume of smoke that might have been a sigh. "I think she's closer to them than her own daughters. They're so glamorous and beautiful, so discreet about their Resistance work. You know they *se tutoient* each other, and she and I do not," she said, meaning that they called each other the informal form of you.

"Oh, Claude." I spoke more carefully this time, for I understood how that would wound her. "They experienced something unimaginable together. You and your mother have a different bond."

"I suppose."

I wanted to tell her how sorry I was, but I knew she wouldn't like it—Claude avoided displays of emotion—and I wanted to tell her how I admired her strength, but I knew her French character would squirm beneath such an American celebration of her suffering. "I'm glad you told me," I said finally, conscious that she had shared something very precious—that which she wanted to forget but couldn't.

For a while we sat and smoked, each of us lost in our own thoughts but content to be silent with one another. Eventually our waiter appeared, and Claude smoothed her expression. He took away our laden plates without a glimmer of interest, exchanging them for a dish of apples and cheese that we greeted with quiet cheers. "At long last, sustenance!" Claude exclaimed, and from her lopsided little smile I surmised she was relieved to have left the subject of the war behind. And yet, now that I knew her better, I understood that her thoughts never left it, that though her sorrow had softened with time, it hadn't faded. Beneath her serious, capable façade was a young girl still reeling from grief.

Later that afternoon, after Claude had gone to class and I was at the library studying (but actually leafing through the glossy pages of *Paris Match*), I found my thoughts returning to our conversation. For though I felt relieved to have an explanation for those strange sounds in the night, another part of me regretted asking Claude to talk about the war. The details of the de Renty family's suffering were so much more wretched than anything I could have imagined—uniquely terrible; and yet, I now realized, also universal, for the war had touched everyone in France, each person I met hiding their sorrow behind a fine veneer. I had imagined this a joyful time of hope and rebirth, yet I was discovering a nation still raw with anguish. How would they ever turn the page?

Chapter Seven

Many years later I read that the French thought of 1949 as the first "prewar Christmas since the war," and I felt so fortunate to have witnessed their return to bounty—shopping without rationing, the shelves once again crammed with foods that had been absent for nearly a decade (except for coffee, of course, but that was always available on the black market). Everyone seemed caught up in the spirit of indulgence—smoked salmon for breakfast at Courances, a shockingly delicious sliver of foie gras terrine at the *bouillon*—and at nearly every meal someone was exclaiming about being *gourmand*. The word, I learned, meant greedy—but greedy in the best sense, greedy with appreciation of the finest foods.

"Oh, look! Roasted chestnuts!" Martha darted

toward a vendor standing beside a rough metal stove that smelled of singed paper.

"*Deux fois*," I said when I'd caught up to her, ordering my own paper cone, then closing my fingers around the warmth. Martha and I had been strolling around Saint-Germain-des-Prés for less than half an hour, but already the cold had asserted itself.

It was the first Sunday in December—the first Sunday of Advent, as a good little Catholic, I knew—and the first day of the *marchés de Noël*, the Christmas markets that had sprung up in the same spots in Paris for hundreds of years. Thanksgiving had been the week previous, a regular school day like all the others, which had made me more homesick than I'd anticipated, but here amid the festive atmosphere I sensed the seasons returning to their familiar rhythms. The air stinging my cheeks was heady with fir trees and coal smoke, sausages and mulling spices. I pulled a chestnut from the bag and pressed the glossy shell to crack it, slipping the kernel in my mouth, sweet and floury.

A large shiny car pulled up to the square, dispelling a group that descended upon the market with a great clamor, their flat American accents distinct even from a distance.

"I thought they would've gone away by now, yet

here they are—great roving packs of them," Martha muttered.

I glanced at the group. "See that tall woman in the fur coat? I think I saw her last night at the Ritz." I cocked my head. "Yes, it's her. I recognize the swooping voice and that sweet little husband gazing up at her adoringly."

"Are they following us, or are we following them? That is the question." Martha tugged at her gloves.

"Or perhaps we all have the same checklist of places?"

Paris was small, but it never felt smaller than when you were hoping to avoid other Americans. The city was crawling with them, young and shiny and flush off the black market exchange rate—not just tourists, but diplomats and newsmen, aspiring novelists and students on the G.I. Bill, and lost souls struck with wanderlust and blessed with trust funds. They clung together in great expat flocks, drinking at the same cafés on the boulevard Saint-Germain, shopping together at *les grands magasins*, dancing at the same nightclubs, talking, talking, talking in bad French and loud voices. There had been not one, not two, but five tables of them at the Ritz Bar last night, all of them flashing their broad smiles and hale complexions, their sharp new clothes marking them out as foreigners. They had seemed so happy and unencumbered by the past—and their high spirits contrasted so starkly against the memories I knew most French people wanted to forget. With only a sliver of shame, I had shied from them, tucking myself into the corner of the banquette among Paul, Sabine, Henri, Florence, and a few of the others I'd met at Courances. Pretending to be French.

Martha and I wandered among little market stalls admiring glass ornaments that sparkled in the dim light, hand-painted cards decorated with scraps of ribbon and lace, bits of brocante china and antique linens, great feathery bunches of evergreens, and flower bulbs to force into bright fragrant blooms. A street musician played the accordion, and little lights twinkled in the gathering dusk, pushing away the heavy sky so that it felt like we were nestled inside a brilliant bubble. Even the nuns looked festive as they sailed up the abbey steps for vespers, their dark habits fluttering in the breeze.

I bought a few Christmas cards to send home, and then an extravagant Advent wreath made of pine cones and elaborately twisted fir boughs, spiked with four candles, one for each Sunday preceding Christmas. I hoped its fresh perfume and lush alpine branches would please Madame, because I so wanted to cheer her during this season of memories. As the child of divorced parents, I knew too well how the holidays could echo with hollow longing.

"Are you going to the dance next weekend?" Martha asked. By this time, we had surrendered to our frozen limbs and found a spot next to the bonfire in the *place*, standing close to the flames while sipping mugs of *vin chaud*, the warm, sweet wine tracing a molten path down my throat. Across from us stood the Église Saint-Germain, its Romanesque tower looming over the square as it had for almost a thousand years.

I hesitated. "I wish I could. It sounds marvelous." Madame Saleil had organized a dance for us Smithies at Reid Hall the following Saturday, inviting a group of military students from l'Institut polytechnique. "Wait till you see them in their formal dress, ladies," she'd said with a twinkle. "White gloves and cape, bicorne hat and sword . . . it is, shall we say, immensely rewarding."

Sensing Martha's disappointment, I added: "I'm meant to be away for the weekend."

"Again?" She arched her brows. "Someday you must tell me where you go on these weekends of yours."

I heard the affection in her voice, but despite my fondness for Martha, I felt my defenses rise. "Just visiting some friends." In truth, I was going back to Courances, but it was the Vicomtesse de Ganay—not Paul—who had sent me a note of invitation.

"I guess there's no special fellow then?"

I shook my head, for though Paul and I frequently went riding together in the bois de Boulogne, our relationship hadn't progressed beyond friendship, nor did I expect it to. Despite all my flirting, he still teased me like a sister, and our dates were often group outings. In fact, last night at the Ritz Bar he had spent most of the evening arguing with Henri about whether or not Victor Hugo should have exiled himself on the isle of Guernsey a century ago. "The government considered him a traitor," Paul had insisted. "He would have been executed if he'd returned to France."

"Yes, well, he should have kept his opinions about the Second Empire to himself in the first place," Henri retorted.

"He felt he had a moral duty."

"Not everything has to be a public fight."

"He was courageous. He had principles." Paul's voice frayed at the edges.

"He was a fool." Henri drained his glass of scotch and signaled to the barman for another, shaking off the cautionary hand Florence placed on his arm. When the drink didn't come fast enough, he rose to fetch it from the bar himself. A few seconds later Paul joined him, and though I couldn't hear them, their expansive gestures and frowns indicated that they were still quarreling.

I had witnessed it before, this intense French passion for culture, and it never ceased to thrill me: the vigor of their debates over literature, and painting, and dance. A couple of weeks ago I had attended an absurdist play and watched in open-mouthed astonishment as two men in the audience broke into fisticuffs over the meaning of the piece, slugging each other right there in the aisle at intermission. It was unlike anything I'd ever experienced in a Broadway theater, and it made me terribly sad when I considered how we Americans so often dismissed the arts as a frivolity.

"Do you have plans for Christmas?" I asked Martha now, attempting to change the subject.

"I'm traveling. Austria first, then Germany."

The sip of wine I'd just taken slid down the wrong way. "By yourself?" I said, when I had managed to stop coughing. By all accounts, Austria and Germany were ghostly, bomb-ravaged husks still under Allied occupation, their cities in a state of semi-ruin.

"I'll spend Christmas in Vienna with friends of my parents. Pop says half their building was blown to bits in an air raid, but the section with their apartment is perfectly unharmed—apparently that's quite common. After that, I'll continue on to Munich by myself."

"Gosh, that sounds intrepid." Then again, if there ever was a girl with the nerve to travel alone, midwinter, to the war-scarred former Axis powers, it was Martha.

"It'll be interesting," she said slowly. "And also probably quite uncomfortable. My mother thinks it's too risky for a young girl on her own. But what kind of history student would I be if I didn't seize this opportunity to see what it's like? Especially now, after everything we know that's happened. It feels almost as if something's pulling me there—like I have a responsibility."

I thought of Madame, of all the terrible things she had seen and experienced in Germany, wrought by German malice, and decided in that instant that I could never set foot there.

"I think you're awfully brave," I told Martha, and I meant it.

"Reckless, more likely." She drained her mug and set it on the ground. "How about you? Off somewhere fun?"

"Yes, to London for Christmas with friends of my father. And then back here, I suppose. Or I'll take another trip, perhaps somewhere sunny. The days are awfully short and dark this time of year." We had three weeks off for the Christmas break, three weeks that I secretly wanted to spend exploring Paris by foot. But Madame Saleil had hinted that we should absent ourselves over the holidays, if possible, to allow our host families some privacy. Susan and her friend Peggy were going to Italy—Rome, Florence, and Venice—and though they'd invited me to accompany them, I'd declined because of my trip to England. But perhaps I'd meet them somewhere in Tuscany, or I could join Mary Ann and her cousins for skiing in Courchevel, or maybe I'd be asked back to Courances for the New Year's hunt. All the possibilities were appealing, though none of them made me feel the way Martha so clearly felt about her trip.

I swallowed the last drops of mulled wine, cradling the cup between my hands. I was just about to propose that we return our mugs and head toward the métro when someone approached us, a tall young man wearing a handsome tweed overcoat and a ready smile.

"*Excusez-moi.*" He lifted his hat and ducked slightly, revealing thick sandy hair combed so neatly I could see the teeth marks. "Didn't I see you last night?" He spoke in French, but I recognized his accent immediately, the vowels flat and ordinary and American.

"I'm not sure, did you?" I responded in French, unwilling to give anything away.

"At the Bar Ritz? You and your friends had a table near the window. You were wearing a green dress and drinking a champagne cocktail," he said, as I blinked at him slowly. He frowned. "Listen, I'm not a creep.

It's just that you look awfully familiar, and I spent half the night trying to figure out why, and now here you are again."

His French was better than I thought it would be, and maybe that's why I relented. "You're American, right?" I said in English. "Us too."

"Is that so?" Even in the firelight, I could see a flush rising upon his even features. He moved with the confidence born of good looks, and it struck me that he wasn't used to being wrong footed. "Well, you certainly had me fooled," he added, recovering himself with a graceful smile. "Your French is excellent, Miss . . ."

"Bouvier. And this is Miss Rusk." I gestured at Martha.

"John Marquand Jr. Pleased to meet you." He thrust a hand forward to shake ours, the gesture oddly foreign after all the months of cheek kisses.

"How do you do, Mr. Marquand?" I offered him a demure smile.

"Please, call me Jack," he said. "Bouvier . . . where do I know that name?"

I bit my lip and hoped Martha wouldn't mention the Queen Deb article, which was the one thing most people knew about me. Suddenly he snapped his fingers. "I've got it: You graduated from Miss Porter's a few years back, right? My kid sister went there. What was that funny entry you had in the yearbook? Your life's ambition was—"

"Never to be a housewife." I gave him a rueful smile. "I'm afraid I horrified everyone."

"It's a good line."

"It wasn't just a line."

Jack raised an eyebrow. "You're not in Paris for the shopping, then, I take it."

"We're students," I informed him. "And we're very serious. In fact, we're not even supposed to be speaking English right now."

"It's true," Martha chimed in. "We signed a language pledge."

He held up his hands in mock supplication. "Please don't make me speak French with you girls again—it's too intimidating."

"We'll make an exception for you." I glanced at him through my lashes. "If you promise not to rat us out."

"Only if you have a drink with me," he said. "You too, Miss Rusk. I have a pal who would love to meet you."

"Maybe," I said. But I gave him my number all the same, and he promised to call to fix a date.

"*Alors!*" Martha said, once we were heading toward the métro. Now that we were alone again, we'd loyally reverted back to speaking French. "That was unexpected."

"Wasn't it?" I concentrated on walking as briskly as I could with an enormous bushy wreath cradled in my arms. "It's funny how you can go halfway around the world and meet someone from practically next door." I had discovered that Jack used to live eight blocks from Daddy's apartment on the Upper East Side.

"Hm." She dug into her pocketbook as we approached the métro station. "Actually, I didn't mean him."

It was only much later, when I was home and getting ready for bed, that I wondered if she had been talking about me.

One evening about a week before Christmas, Madame surprised us, reaching into the wrought-iron *cage* that hung outside the kitchen window, where the eggs, milk, and other perishables were stored, and producing five dozen oysters she'd bought at the market that morning. Marie, the *bonne*, shucked them for dinner, her hands moving with the dexterity born of a Breton childhood. We gathered in the dining room, where the Advent wreath's candles glowed at the center of the table as they had every night since I'd brought it home, because Madame liked to flaunt tradition and light all four at once, every morning and every evening.

"I thought this would be a nice change from soup." She smiled warmly around the table. "And since we won't be together at *le réveillon*, I wanted to organize something festive for my girls before we all break up for the holidays."

Le réveillon was Christmas Eve, which Madame, Claude, Ghislaine, and Christian would be spending with the oldest de Renty son and his family in Lyon. I felt as touched that she had planned something special for us as I was that she thought of us as her girls.

"I've never had a raw oyster," Mary Ann said, looking doubtfully at the platters before us.

I hadn't either, though I didn't like to admit it. But Madame showed us how to squeeze lemon over the quivering flesh so that it flinched, before bringing the shell to our lips and slurping up the sweet brininess. It tasted fresh and wild and almost savage—just as I imagined the rocky coast of western France.

"Did anyone else get caught in the *manif* today?" Susan asked, after we had swallowed a good portion of the oysters and washed them down with a flinty Muscadet wine. Rough piles of overturned shells had replaced the shimmering pearly faces. "I was at place de la Concorde, and the protesters had completely blocked the bridge leading to the parliament."

"Oh, *that* must be why I waited so long for the bus!" Mary Ann broke a piece of rye bread in two and spread salted butter on half. "I finally gave up and got on the métro."

"Are there usually protests so close to the holidays?" I asked.

"They happen anytime," Claude said. "They never stop."

Indeed, it occurred to me that I couldn't remember a week that autumn without a *manifestation.* They must have been announced or had a schedule printed somewhere, but I always seemed to run across them unexpectedly, the traffic stopped on the boulevard Saint-Michel as bands of marchers chanted, waved signs, and expressed their support of—or disagreement with—the North Atlantic Pact, or the Radical-Socialist Party, or American imperialism, or any other number of issues. Even when I disagreed with the protesters' opinions, I admired their civic commitment, so passionately engaged—so typically and romantically French. I had never happened upon a demonstration in New York City.

"Was it another one of those horrible anti-American rallies?" asked Mary Ann. "Their propaganda posters are so hateful, I just shiver every time I walk past."

"No, it was something about giving amnesty to wartime collaborators," Susan replied, using her fork to fish a lemon seed out of an oyster shell. "I couldn't quite grasp the details."

I froze, concentrating on my plate, aware that Susan had veered unwittingly close to a sensitive topic.

Claude spoke before I could say anything. "A bill just passed in the Cabinet." She explained that it proposed granting amnesty for low-level collabora- tors sentenced to "national untrustworthiness" or "national degradation." "Parliament will vote next week," she added, "and if it passes, eight thousand of them will be freed."

"Well, *I* don't think they should be forgiven," Mary Ann said, with the confidence of someone whose life had been untouched by the Occupation. "They col- laborated with the enemy! Why should they get any special treatment just because the government wants to move on from the war?"

Ghislaine barked a laugh. "And eleven million French communists would agree with you," she said. "They'll exploit every one of those petty little crimes to settle old scores and burnish their propaganda— anything to insist *they're* the only ones who risked it all in the Resistance. Oh, the anti-communist neighbor sold butter on the black market? By all *means*, sentence him to ten years of prison! They'll do whatever it takes to protect their political agenda."

"Oh, Ghislaine, honestly." Claude rolled her eyes. "I know plenty of communists at school who would do no such thing. You think there's some Soviet master plot but that's sheer paranoia."

Ghislaine's eyes flashed at her younger sister. "*Paranoia*? How can you say that when China just went red a few weeks ago? If we're not careful, Korea will be next. What about the atom bomb? Did you forget the Soviets tested it last summer? They don't care about innocent human life or—or women, or children—they'll kill us all given half the chance. Why do you think the Americans created the Marshall Plan?"

"To prevent the spread of communism in Europe, yes, I know." Claude sighed, as if they'd had this discussion a thousand times before. "But aren't you being a bit melodramatic? A lot of communists are simply young idealists hoping to create a more just and equal world." She spoke with clear precision, her words calm and reasonable. "They're not all radical subversives."

"Trust me"—Ghislaine's face was ablaze—"if you knew even half of what goes on in the Soviet Union, you wouldn't be so flippant."

"How would *you* know?"

"I assure you," Ghislaine said, and her voice shook before she managed to control it. "I know far better than you."

"Now, girls," Madame interrupted. "Don't dabble in extremes. I'm not saying one of you is right, or wrong," she added, as her daughters opened their mouths to argue. "But it's easy to condemn people you don't know—especially if you don't know how they live. Don't you remember how we felt about the Germans before we went to visit after the war?"

"Oh!" I gasped, before I could check myself. "You went to Germany *after*?" I could scarcely believe my ears. Why on earth would she return there, after everything she had endured?

"Claude and I went in the summer of '46, yes, just after she passed *le bac*," Madame said. "My late husband's cousin was there. He invited us to the French-occupied zone and we spent several weeks touring around."

"It was utter devastation," Claude said. "Towns completely decimated, streets deserted, and when you did meet someone they were almost always maimed or injured. Nearly all the women clad in black . . ."

"The worst was the children—do you remember?" Madame's face tightened. "The terrible, stoic look on their faces, as if they were constantly bracing themselves for the worst."

"How awful," breathed Mary Ann. "I don't think I could bear it." Though I stayed silent, I agreed.

"It was painful, yes," Madame admitted. "I thought I hated the Germans after everything they did. But seeing those ordinary lives so completely destroyed, I couldn't bring myself to be angry anymore. They suffered from the Nazis too."

She spoke simply, but knowing what I did about her past, the force of her forgiveness made me reel. Glancing around the table, I saw the others were equally moved, even Susan and Mary Ann, who knew nothing of Madame's history.

"Our classmate Martha is going to Vienna and Munich over the winter break," I said to the table. "I told her she's awfully intrepid, but she said she feels like she has a responsibility."

"Perhaps we all do," Madame said mildly. "Two wars in twenty-five years—it's enough. Can you imagine what Europe could achieve if France and Germany worked together?" She spread her hands wide toward me, Susan, and Mary Ann. "And we need you too, *mes petites américaines*, to go and see, and feel, and help us remember so we can move forward."

As she spoke, it began to dawn on me what it meant to be in Europe at this moment. We weren't merely witnesses to the continent's recovery, but also to its past, our collective memory ensuring that the truth wouldn't disappear or be distorted as long as we continued to tell it. Though I had followed the war as assiduously as any other American teen, until now it had been abstract to me—words on a page, news on the radio, the older brothers of friends missing or dead. A tragedy that happened to other people. But here among this French family that had suffered so deeply, among these ladies I had grown to love and admire, my comprehension of the war had found a form, and it was vicious, and throbbing, and real. I hadn't felt a responsibility before now, but sitting in this candlelit dining room amid the de Rentys' gentle voices, I accepted it: a commitment to understand their suffering and forgiveness, to help Europe become whole and prosperous, to recognize their sacrifice.

I wanted to know more. I wanted to see.

Chapter Eight

27 December 1949

Dearest Daddy,

It was such a treat to hear from you before I left for London—and happy New Year to you too. I can't quite believe we're on the cusp of 1950—halfway through the 20th century—isn't it thrilling? We toasted your good health on Christmas Day, all of us, even Ann's little twins, who are an utterly enchanting pair of five-year-olds. They are complete opposites: the girl, Gale, with delicate fair curls like a Renaissance cherub; while the boy, Greville, has thick black locks and a devilish gleam in his eye, exactly like someone I know . . . Truly, he is your spitting image and I believe your suspicions must be dead right. Ann was in fine spirits and asked after you several times. She sends her love . . .

I paused, pressing the sheet of paper against the blotter. It had been a splendid holiday with the Plugges in London, an old-fashioned English Christmas of roast beef and crispy potatoes, cracker riddles and parlor games, and a brandy-soaked plum pudding alight in a halo of violet-tinged flames. Most of all it had been heavenly to see Ann again, still as beautiful and gay as when I'd known her in New York nearly eight years ago.

Ann was married then, as now, to Captain Leonard Plugge, a plummy-voiced British politician twenty years her senior. When the Blitz began, she had come to New York with their four-year-old son, Frank. The first time I saw her was in the lobby of Daddy's apartment building on East 74th Street, looking as slender as an exclamation point in a dove-gray suit that offset her lustrous red hair. She was laughing with the doorman as he showed her how to hail a taxi, her English accent so crisp and pure my eleven-year-old self longed to record and study it. In fact, Ann had many different accents for many different occasions, and her prior life as an actress and model had taught her exactly when to use them.

A beautiful and flirtatious new neighbor, a recently divorced Daddy—need I say more? Before long, Lee and I were being asked to take little Frank on our outings to Central Park, the three of us spinning on the carousel while our parents were occupied at home. A few months later, when we arrived in East Hampton for the summer—we always spent several weeks at Grampy Jack's estate, Lasata—it wasn't much of a surprise to find Ann and Frank renting a sweet little clapboard cottage a short walk away.

Daddy fell madly in love with Ann that summer—we all did, she was so fun and lighthearted, so generous with her empathy. She spent hours on the shore with Lee and me, hunting for beach glass to add to our collections, while Daddy taught Frank how to swim. At my horse shows she sat at the front of the stands, twisting a handkerchief so tightly around her fingers the tips drained white. She never minded about dirty knees, or unbrushed hair, or crumbs on the floor, or if the lunch dishes sat in the sink because we'd decided to go out and pick wildflowers. By the end of the season, Ann had charmed all our extended Bouvier family, even Grampy Jack, who declared her "a sparkplug" and assigned her and Frank dedicated spots at the Sunday luncheon table.

Labor Day arrived, and Lee and I returned to Merrywood happy. Daddy was drinking less and the puffiness around his eyes and jowls had receded. Ann had promised to teach us to speak in a spotless English accent and said she'd take us for ice cream sundaes the next time we were in Manhattan. There were even signs she and Daddy had begun talking of the future—

whispered conversations late into the night, drafts of long letters shared between them, and the appearance of a pretty pearl ring (she wore it on her right hand, to be sure, but she never took it off). Lee and I spent hours speculating about what their wedding would be like—the clothes, flowers, and food—squabbling over which of us Ann would ask to be her maid of honor.

Our parents' marriage had collapsed so slowly and spectacularly, Lee and I didn't know romance could end in other ways. In any case, we hadn't seen signs of discord because there hadn't been any—Ann was always there when we visited Daddy on the weekends, lovely and cheerful and full of plans. And then, one day, she wasn't.

"'E came and took 'er away," Daddy said when we managed to rouse him. He was drunker than I'd ever seen him, unwashed and unshaven, on a bender of who knew how many days. After enquiring discreetly with the housekeeper and doorman, Lee and I managed to piece the story together. It seemed that Ann's husband, Leonard Plugge, had flown to New York City and persuaded her to return to England with Frank. It would have been terribly romantic if not for Captain Plugge's conviction that divorce would derail his political career—or the armfuls of girls he was rumored to keep in London, or his threats of a custody battle if

Ann insisted on leaving him. Ann hinted at some of this in a letter written to Lee and me on her trans-Atlantic crossing—and she explained all of it eight years later, during our week together at Christmas.

Over the holiday I came to understand that Ann viewed her marriage as one of convenience, turning a blind eye to her husband's indiscretions. He basically lived at his club, coming home for the occasional meal. The one thing they both cared about was the children: Frank, now a cricket-mad twelve-year-old; and the twins, born roughly five years ago, soon after their parents' reconciliation. So soon, in fact, one couldn't help but wonder about their lineage.

Daddy swore it was impossible. But Daddy had sunk after Ann's departure, drinking too much, swearing too much, writing us long letters that often unraveled into an unintelligible scrawl. He'd lost interest in his usual pleasures—dating, sports, the stock market—claiming all of them had turned rotten. Not only was Ann gone, but Lee and I had also left New York, moving to Merrywood when Mummy married Hughdie. Though Daddy didn't say it, I sensed the dead weight of loneliness threatening to pull him under. I fretted over the questions he avoided. Why had he sold our rambling family apartment for a modest two-bedroom? Why were his cupboards filled with tins of baked beans when he said he dined at the 21 Club every night? Why had he disappeared to Florida for three weeks without sending us word? Every time we saw him, I resolved to ask, and every time he distracted us with a trip to the racetrack, or lunch at Schrafft's, or a charge account at Saks, and I felt ashamed to pry because he so clearly adored us.

I hated to think of Daddy alone at Christmas in his New York apartment, shuffling the deck for another game of solitaire, the heavy clink of a bottle hitting the rim of a glass, followed by the lapping sound of whiskey tumbling within. And maybe that's why I wrote what I did about the Plugge twins, even if I wasn't totally convinced it was true. I knew it would please him to think his love affair with Ann had left a legacy.

Biting my lip, I rummaged through my desk, wanting to read Daddy's last letter to me again, but it was such a jumble I finally gave up—Christian must have searched the drawer for scrap paper while I was away. The yellow light of the lamp cast a circle around me, creating the illusion of warmth as I sat wrapped in two sweaters and a pair of earmuffs. A sudden, fierce rain pelted the windows, and the empty apartment creaked and settled in the afternoon gloom. A few hours ago, I had returned to avenue Mozart, hastily wringing out some laundry, which I hoped would dry before I left again the next morning. The de Rentys were in Lyon,

Susan and Mary Ann still on their European travels, and before dawn I would board a train, bound for Austria and then Germany. Daddy would be aghast at this plan, which meant I had to tread carefully. I briefly rubbed my hands together and then picked up my pen again.

Tomorrow morning I'm setting off on a trip to Vienna and Munich—doesn't that sound terribly romantic? My classmate Martha (Rusk) invited me to join her and I truly can't imagine a more suitable place to usher in the new decade. Martha is lovely and sensible and speaks excellent German, so there's absolutely no reason to worry. It'll be such an adventure to travel like regular folks, sitting up all night on the train and chatting with strangers—such a change from the last time I crossed the continent with Bow and the girls, which was so luxurious we scarcely saw a thing. I'll take lots of photos to share with you, dear Daddy. Won't it be fun to stay up late and look through them together when I'm back?

With love,
Jackie

There. I had probably hinted at too much adventure, but it would do. Folding the thin sheets of paper,

I slipped them into an envelope and sealed the flap, finding a stamp—and Daddy's last letter—in the drawer of my bedside table. By the time he read this, I'd be safely back in Paris, which was exactly why I'd told him now, and not before. I planned to write Mummy a similar letter on the train and post it once I got to Austria. My parents might be cross with me, but they couldn't stop me.

I lit a cigarette and considered cooking an egg or something simple for dinner. But the thought of tangling with the stove, the matches and kindling and tricky flue that needed cleaning, held little appeal. I thought of the phone message Ghislaine had left on my pillow—*M. Marquand called again, 21 décembre, 17h15*—along with his number. But I didn't feel much like getting dressed and dining out with someone I hardly knew, even someone as attractive as Jack Marquand. And besides, it was better to keep a man waiting. I thought of the stack of novels I'd bought in London, and the *croissant aux amandes* I'd purchased for tomorrow's breakfast, and suddenly there was nothing I wanted more than to eat pastry for supper and curl up in bed with a new book. I reached out and felt my laundry, which was almost dry. It would be ready in the morning, and so would I.

Martha had been skeptical when I'd asked if I could join her. "Are you sure you don't mind traveling third class?" she said, with a look that indicated she didn't think I could manage it. But I reassured her, and we quickly made plans to meet in Vienna, then continue on to Munich, where some friends of Yusha's had promised to take us dancing on New Year's Eve. "Forget your vanity. Bring your warmest things," she told me. "They say the cold is worse than here."

I had thought of proving myself to Martha by staying in Vienna at a simple inn. But by the time I stumbled off the train at the Wien Westbahnhof, my limbs were so stiff and frozen from the overnight journey that I impulsively took a taxi straight to the Hotel Imperial. I'd heard about it from my school friend Bow, whose mother had extolled her stay there last year—and if anyone recognized a fine hotel it was Mrs. Emily Foley. I wanted hot coffee, hot buttered toast, and a long, hot bath—and after living in Europe for a few months, I knew I couldn't count on finding those things just anywhere.

"*This* is how you rough it?" Martha said when we met in the early evening. Her foot tapped the variegated marble floor, while overhead a massive crystal chandelier cast the lobby in lustrous brilliance.

"I heard there's a café around the corner that has the most delicious chocolate cake," I said, after we had kissed hello. "Shall we go there first?" I led her out the revolving doors and down the block to a coffee shop with marble-topped tables and bentwood chairs. Most of the customers were British and American—military men wooing Austrian girls with cigarettes and sweets, each pretending the other didn't have an ulterior motive—a hint at the occupying forces still governing the country.

After Martha and I had eaten our fill of *pâtisserie*, we walked around the historic center, the evening sky as thick as a blackout curtain. Devastation was everywhere, but scattered in patches, so that piles of snow-dusted bricks stood next to pristine buildings, and elegant façades gave way to heaped desolation. I had expected to find signs of recovery but they seemed more like a dream than a promise. On the street, men and women bore sallow complexions and an unmistakable gauntness that spoke of deprivation. At the Stephansplatz, a fretwork of scaffolding sheltered the roofless cathedral, while a few meters away a group of grubby children begged for scraps from a brightly lit sausage stand. The cold was a dagger slicing through my fur coat, punishing my gloved hands when I withdrew them from my pockets to photograph the illuminated buildings: the State Opera House, the Hofburg Palace, the Parliament.

"Oy!" shouted a voice, so close I jumped. My camera had blinkered me, but lowering it, I saw three guards wearing sheepskin hats and uniforms of olive drab. They had appeared from nowhere and were now charging toward us with sullen expressions. As they drew close, I saw the red star in the center of their hats and my heart began to pound—they were Soviet soldiers. Martha moved next to me, linking her arm with mine—either in solidarity or fear, I couldn't tell.

"Hello," I said, forcing a bland smile. "Is something the matter?"

The largest soldier snarled something in Russian. His eyes, bulging slightly from his face, were like chunks of glacial ice.

"Do you speak English?" I asked, keeping my voice soft.

"*Nyet.*" He shook his head.

The three men circled us now, their bodies forming an enclosure so that we couldn't escape even if we had been foolish enough to ignore the handguns hanging from their belts. Glacier Eyes yanked at the camera around my neck, causing me to lose my balance and fall against Martha. He pointed at a nearby building, an imposing brick structure filling the entire corner, its arched windows and portico adorned with bas-relief statues. I could scarcely breathe as he gestured and shouted at me, great clouds of condensation billowing from his mouth.

"I'm so sorry," I faltered. My heart was thudding with a sick, uneven rhythm. "I don't understand."

Glacier Eyes continued barking a stream of sharp, angry consonants, pointing at the camera and then the building.

Martha squeezed my arm. "I think he's saying that it's forbidden to take photos here," she said quietly. "Look around the corner." Craning my head, I saw two massive portraits hanging from the building's façade, and my stomach dropped as I recognized the stern faces of Lenin and Stalin, and between them an enormous red star.

"I guess this is Soviet headquarters," I muttered to her, and turned to Glacier Eyes, holding up my hands. "It is very beautiful, that is all."

His eyes bored straight through me, so that I couldn't help but blink. When he spoke again, he managed to summon up an English word. "Spy."

"No, no, no," Martha said.

"We're American," I said with a nervous grin, gesturing widely with my hands as if to indicate a bridge between us. "Allies."

The severe expression on his face changed to one of absolute contempt. He barked at the two other men, and they tightened their circle, moving to grasp Martha and me by the arm. "What are you doing?" she cried. "We're not—we can't go with you."

"We're Americans—we're students," I protested, my mind whirling. How had this afternoon gone so terribly wrong? A few minutes ago I'd been entranced by Vienna's ravaged beauty, and now a Soviet soldier was gripping my arm so hard I feared he would snap it clean in two.

"We're just two silly little tourists!" Martha insisted. A passing couple glanced over briefly, then burrowed into their scarves, unwilling to meet my eyes.

The guards began to pull us toward the building. "Wait," I gasped as we passed under a streetlamp. "Wait, please!" Lifting the camera from my neck, I quickly unclasped the back and tore out the film so that it unspooled to the ground, exposed to the light. "All right? It was only a few snapshots, I swear. They're gone." I crushed the strip of film under my heel to illustrate my point.

Glacier Eyes looked down at me and I swear I caught the flicker of a smile. Then, to my relief, he uttered a tangle of words and released me. I stumbled back, scarcely able to stand on my own, my legs were shaking so. Beside me Martha also stepped free, crossing her arms against her chest.

"Goodbye, ladies," Glacier Eyes said in flawless English. "You may go now." The three men bowed in unison and walked away—but not before I heard them sniggering at the shock on our faces.

"Those bastards," I said several seconds later, when I trusted myself to speak without bursting into tears. "They knew we were just a couple of kids."

Martha shoved her fists into her pockets, mute with rage.

Across the square, I spotted a café glowing against the dark sky. "Come on," I said. "Let's warm up for a minute."

We found a table and ordered coffee and schnapps and little sugar-dusted cookies filled with jam that neither of us could eat. The plum-flavored liqueur spread warmth through my body, reaching my fingers and toes. For a long time we drank silently, alternating sips of coffee and schnapps, lost in our thoughts. How often during the war had I shuddered at the news reports from Austria and Germany? Boots tramping against cobblestone streets, the shattering of shop windows, families rounded up and herded onto trucks by soldiers too powerful, and brutal, and ruthless to oppose. It was one of the reasons I had avoided coming here in the first place, the possibility that there was some indomitable streak of cruelty in the Teutonic soul. Now that I was here, I saw these people were beaten, bombed into submission, hollow with defeat. They had become the victims, subject to the whims of the occupying forces—American, British, French, and Soviet troops—and the latter seemed to operate under a different code of honor. I hadn't fully grasped the significance of the Berlin blockade last year, when the Soviet Union had tried to oust the United States, France, and Britain from the city with a show of brute force, cutting off ground traffic and causing malicious shortages of food and other supplies. Nor had I taken seriously Ghislaine's warnings about Soviet aggression, dismissing them as the paranoia of a lonely, overworked young parent. But after today I had no trouble believing that the Soviets would happily swallow Europe and subjugate it to rules set by Moscow, if given half the chance.

The world order had shifted, revealing a new menace.

Martha, ever savvy in the ways of budget travel, liked night trains because they helped save on hotel fare. And thus we found ourselves on the 22h51 bound for Munich, settling into a third-class carriage for the seven-hour journey.

Our second day in Vienna had passed more gently than the first, eased in part by the city's cultivated beauty. Vienna had endured over fifty air raids, yet its elegance lingered, and I found myself sinking into centuries of Habsburg glory as we explored the treasures of the Kunsthistorisches Museum, attended a Mozart concert, and admired the prancing Lipizzaner horses with their satiny, compact bodies. In the evening, Martha brought me to the home of her parents' friends, Herr Doktor and Frau Wagner, who lived in a half-ravaged building with a slanting staircase leading to their perfectly intact apartment. They gave us pear schnapps, schnitzel with potato salad, and apple strudel heaped with thick cream as Strauss waltzes played on the phonograph.

"You girls must eat more!" urged Frau Wagner. "You're much too thin."

I accepted another piece of her delicate strudel, though I hated to think what the meal must have cost them.

Her husband refilled our tiny glasses with schnapps. "This will encourage the appetite," he said with a smile.

They were so delighted to speak English with us, so eager to share their culture and to hear about ours, peppering us with questions about Paris and America, asking our impressions of Vienna.

"You have been to stroll the historic center, ja?" the

Herr Doktor asked me. "Seen the Stephansplatz and the opera house?"

"It's magnificent." I sighed. "Even despite the rubble, the city's beauty is captivating. Vienna will flourish again soon, I feel certain."

"First we must rid ourselves of these Soviet ogres, and then the work can begin," he agreed.

"Heinrich . . ." Frau Wagner lifted a cautionary eyebrow.

"It's fine, Frieda. No one is listening anymore. The war is over—and these young ladies are intelligent enough to recognize that our Soviet occupiers are brutal, greedy pigs."

"They certainly frightened us half to death yesterday," Martha said, before launching into the tale of our encounter with the three Soviet soldiers.

"The bloody cheek of them," said Frau Wagner, once Martha had finished. She puffed her cheeks. "They ought to be boxed on the ears."

But the Herr Doktor was deeply troubled by our story. "This is not what we expected when the occupation started," he said with a frown. "We thought the Allies would work together. But it seems like the Soviets are pressing their advantage in the most brutal ways, and upon even the most innocent people."

"Communism does seem ghastly," I said. "Malicious

and ruthless. I never thought I'd say this, but I suppose deep down I really am just a contented little capitalist."

At this the Wagners laughed, as I had meant them to, but then a wistful expression stole over the Herr Doktor's face. "I'm inclined to agree with you at this point," he said. "Capitalism does have some good aspects—reward for personal initiative, for one. But there's a dark side too. How is it fair for only a lucky few to derive so much profit from the muscle and hard labor of the working class?" He stroked his beard. "No, we can't dismiss communism just because of the abuses of Stalin and others of his ilk. The ideals at its foundation are admirable: a classless society where money does not drive everything, where people are treated equally; a brave new world without hunger or racism. Is this not a beautiful dream?"

"A workers' utopia, eh, Heinrich?" Frau Wagner teased. "I'm not sure that's going to happen." She bestowed an indulgent smile upon her husband. "He was quite left leaning in his youth," she told us.

"I still am, my *Liebling*," he said, patting his pockets and producing a pipe. "Still am. But now I'm wise enough to see the dream has been corrupted. Or perhaps it was always impossible." He filled the pipe with loose tobacco, pressing it down with his thumb before striking a match to light it.

I watched the smoke curl through the air, considering his words. Back home everyone had become so fervently anti-communist, especially since last summer, when newspapers were buzzing with opinions about Alger Hiss's guilt and the Soviet Union's existential threat to the West—and men like my father and stepfather denounced reds over their double scotches, blustering about a third world war. Without really thinking about it, I had accepted and adopted these beliefs. But here in Europe I kept finding myself confronted with new political points of view, ones that clashed with my own and forced me to consider the validity of what I'd always believed was correct. I had never thought of communism except as a threat, but now that the Herr Doktor had revealed its idealism I finally grasped the appeal. To be sure, communism wasn't for me—I was too fond of a chic hat—but I could imagine the freedom of a society that prized people over profit margin, where artists didn't fret about the value of their masterpieces, and girls like me could marry for love. I knew the Herr Doktor was right—it was an illusion. But it was a lovely one.

Around ten o'clock, we left for the train station, pressing upon the Wagners the little gifts we'd brought—chocolate and cigarettes, bars of soap, and packets of dried fruit—exchanging addresses and promising to write even though we knew we wouldn't. It was one of the great joys of travel, these fleeting exchanges and ephemeral friendships, the way people you met abroad would forever linger in your memories of a place.

Now on the train, Martha and I settled into the window seats of a bank of four, facing each other. She pulled her coat over her lap to serve as a blanket before rolling up a sweater and attempting to wedge it between her head and the window.

"Hmph." She stretched cautiously. "I have a feeling I'm going to regret this tomorrow."

"We can take turns switching places," I suggested. "That way we won't get a crick in the neck."

"Good idea."

Our seatmates appeared one after the other: a small woman with brittle features, her gray hair twisted into a bun, settling next to Martha; and then a man, too fleshy and florid to be suffering much from rationing, wedged himself beside me with some effort. *"Guten Abend,"* the woman greeted us, and we echoed her with smiles. The man said nothing, unfolding his newspaper.

I read my book for a while and, when the train lights dimmed, closed my eyes. The carriage wasn't cold, but a chill seeped through the window so that I arranged my coat over my body, burrowing within its folds. My head grew heavy, but just as I began to drift off, the fur slipped from my shoulders and slid down to my lap. Again and again it happened, so that I must have adjusted it half a dozen times before I felt something—or, rather, someone—tweaking the coat away, stealthy but sure. I froze as thick fingers moved past my arm, inching closer to my breast . . . I snatched the coat up and the hand withdrew.

So, my neighbor was a groper. Shifting in my seat, I surreptitiously removed a hatpin from my pocketbook. Then I rearranged my coat over myself, closed my eyes, and waited. Sure enough, a minute or two later, I felt a movement—at my thigh this time, the old lecher—drawing closer, closer . . . Grasping the pin between my fingers, I thrust blindly in his direction and was rewarded with a yelp. The hand disappeared, and I heard grumbling in German. Opening my eyes, I found the man clutching his arm and glaring at me.

"Oh no, did you drop something?" I cooed. At the sound of my voice, Martha and her seatmate awoke and stared at us.

"*Bitte*," the man muttered, then turned away from me.

I fell into a light doze after that, undisturbed. In the middle of the night, Martha and I rose to trade places. "Here, you'll need this," I whispered, slipping the hatpin into her hand. She seemed baffled but took it, and we settled down to continue sleeping.

Several minutes passed, and then I heard a yelp, followed by more German swearing. Peeping over the edge of my coat collar, I saw the man scowling at Martha. "Are you certain it wasn't a wasp?" she asked innocently. Her eyes met mine and we burst into giggles that grew louder and louder as the man gathered his things and huffed off to another compartment.

We arrived in München—Munich—a little after six o'clock in the morning. Dawn was still hours away, the night sky ebbing to leaden gray over the ruined city. I thought Vienna had prepared me, but the devastation here was vast and complete, a wasteland of tumbled bricks, twisted metal girders, and disintegrating buildings, black and hollow. The Altstadt—the old town— was in shreds, and what the air raids hadn't destroyed the freezing rain and snow were now gently eroding.

"I read that 90 percent of the historic center was destroyed in '44," said Martha, as we picked our way through muddy paths that might have once been streets. "I knew I was being sentimental bringing Pop's old Baedeker guide. But why didn't I realize it would be completely obsolete?"

"I'm not sure anyone would be capable of imagining this," I said, gritting my teeth to keep from shivering.

Grimy puffs of smoke rose from caved-in basements where scavenging children darted in and out, dressed in cast-offs inadequate for the weather. Bundles of rags lay heaped in the shallow shelter of doorways, occasionally moving when we passed so that I nearly jumped out of my skin. There were people in those piles of cloth, huddling, trying to stay warm, but I didn't know how they could bear it: The wind bit through my coat, my gloves, my boots, turning my hands and feet to aching stumps, bringing tears that rained down my cheeks in icy tracks.

We reached the Marienplatz, and the atmosphere shifted. The town hall—called "new" but built in the 1860s—had sustained minimal bombing damage. Its elaborate Neo-Gothic façade appeared like a mirage amid the ruins, an American flag flying from the balcony, military personnel streaming in and out. Many of the buildings around the square also appeared remarkably intact, some with solid new roofs and fresh coats of paint, others boasting the first scaffolding I'd seen in the city. I couldn't quite put my finger on it, but the mood seemed more energetic here, charged and full of purpose.

"Miss Bouvier?"

I turned to find the strong, square features of Jack Marquand. "And Miss Rusk!" he exclaimed, as Martha walked up, waving a stack of prewar postcards. "What are you two doing here?"

"*Guten Tag!*" I greeted him, unable to suppress a smile of surprise. Yes, Europe was small—and the number of places Americans congregated in Europe was even smaller—but it was quite a coincidence to run into him here. Still, I tried not to look too pleased. Men like Jack Marquand enjoyed the chase.

"Oh dear, please don't tell me you girls are here on another language exchange," he teased. "My German is even worse than my French."

"Don't worry, we're just sightseeing," Martha reassured him. "Although Jacqueline may have other motives—at least, according to the Russkis," she said with a wink.

He raised his eyebrows. "I'm intrigued."

"It's a long story," I said with a little shrug, though secretly pleased by his interest.

"Well, how about we go have a long lunch and you can tell me." He flashed a smile. "Aw, come on," he pressed when I hesitated. "You haven't returned my calls—and then I find you here in Munich, right next to American headquarters looking like some kind of miracle . . . What's a fellow got to do to spend time with the elusive Miss Bouvier?"

"Well . . ." I glanced over at Martha, who was leafing through a tourist booklet, pretending not to listen. "Maybe just a sandwich."

"Don't mind me," said Martha. "I'm going to see *The Third Man* dubbed into German. J.B., I'll meet you back at the Frau's." Frau Becker owned the rooms where we were lodging, her establishment popular among Reid Hall students for its central location and generous breakfasts.

"Isn't this place swell?" Jack said, after we had made our way to a nearby beer hall. A brass band played merry tunes with a steady drum, and American soldiers twirled pretty German girls dressed in dirndls, the laced bodices and full skirts hiding their gaunt figures and bright smiles transforming their thin faces. Waitresses, also in dirndls, rushed about carrying enormous steins of pilsner—I counted ten, eleven, twelve glasses at a go—baskets of thick pretzels, plates of bratwurst and potato salad, while behind the polished wood bar, a man clad in lederhosen dispensed beer from shining taps.

"It's just like the Germany I used to imagine before . . ." My voice trailed off as I remembered the frozen wasteland only a few meters from here.

"I suppose they're hoping to move on," Jack observed gently. "Like everyone."

He ordered for us—delicate white veal sausages and

local beer, bitter and yeasty, the only thing on offer—
and as we ate, he talked about the service friends he'd
spent Christmas with in Munich, and I told him about
getting detained in Vienna by Soviet soldiers, embel-
lishing the tale so that by the time I finished, he was on
the edge of his seat.

"Holy cow, I'm sweating just listening to this!"
he exclaimed. "You and Miss Rusk have sure got
some—"

"I hope you're not going to say pluck," I teased, test-
ing his wit.

"Backbone," he said with mock indignation. "Please.
I would never use a two-penny word like plucky to de-
scribe someone like you. What kind of writer would
that make me?"

"You're a writer?" I withdrew my case of cigarettes,
surprised. With his earnest manner, he had struck me
as a bureaucrat—State Department, perhaps—but this
was far more intriguing. "Is that what brought you to
Paris?"

"Sure, just like every other kid who read Hemingway and Fitzgerald, and dreamed of Montparnasse and
Saint-Germain-des-Prés. Talk about two-penny." He
shot me a wry smile. "I wrote for the *Lampoon* at Harvard, and then I was an editor at *Cosmopolitan* for a bit.
Now I'm working on some short stories and a novel.

It's more fun having my stuff rejected in Paris than in New York, that's for sure."

"Wait a second." I leaned toward him so he could light my cigarette. "John Marquand . . . I thought your name was familiar. The spy novels with the Japanese agent? Mr. Moto—is that you?"

"No. That's my father. Would you like coffee?" He waved at a waitress. "Two, please. Now, Miss Bouvier—"

"Please." I fluttered my hand past his sleeve. *"Jacqueline."*

"Jacqueline." He grinned. "I'd like to know more about *you.*"

"Oh, I'm terribly dull, I'm afraid." I turned to exhale smoke, steeling myself for tedious questions about where I'd gone to school and who we knew in common.

"Are you listening? Because this is extremely important." He leaned close, and I caught a scent of pine and fresh snow. "If you were stranded on a desert island, would you rather have a cup of hot coffee or a hot bath?"

I began to laugh. "Bath, definitely."

"Whiskey or gin?"

"Champagne."

"Darn it, I should have guessed that. *Pain au chocolat* or *pain aux raisins?*"

"*Croissant aux amandes*—but they're harder to find."

"Ingres or Courbet?"

"Is it terribly démodé to say Ingres? I adore Neo-Classicism."

"Not at all! I've always found Courbet rather messy, to be honest. All those short brushstrokes." The waitress delivered our coffee and we nodded our thanks. "Marie Antoinette or Josephine Bonaparte?" he continued.

"Madame de Pompadour." I held my breath.

He whistled. "Mistress to Louis XV?"

"*Chief* mistress," I corrected him. "And an influential patron of literature and the arts."

"Marx Brothers or the Three Stooges?"

"Oh, Marx Brothers, definitely. Is there any question?"

He leaned back in his chair. "You impress me, Miss Bouvier."

I shrugged away his praise, even though it pleased me. "I could say the same about you, Mr. Marquand," I said, gazing at him through my lashes. The air between us fairly crackled, and I tried to regain my composure. "Would you mind passing the sugar?" I asked. Daddy's voice was in my ear: "Play hard to get, Jackie; all men are rats."

As he handed it to me, our fingers touched—a quick

brush, but enough to make my stomach flip. With some effort, I drew myself up and crossed my arms.

"You're not heading back to Paris tomorrow night, are you?" Jack looked hopeful. "We could see in the new year on the train."

I crushed my cigarette in the ashtray and reached for my cup of coffee. "I'm in Munich for a few more days."

"Too bad," he said. "I guess our next date will have to wait until we're back in Paris."

"I'll try to squeeze it in," I said, flashing him a little grin.

"I'll take that as a yes." His dark blue eyes lingered on me until I looked away.

On New Year's Eve, Martha and I had plans for cocktails, dinner, and dancing at a nightclub with some service friends of my stepbrother Yusha. In the meantime, our day was free, and it was lovely with the first true sunshine I'd seen since leaving Paris.

"Anything you'd like to see this morning?" I asked Martha as we breakfasted at Frau Becker's on poppyseed rolls and hard-boiled eggs, smoked cured meats and liverwurst spread, yogurt and muesli, butter and soft cheese, and an array of jams representing every fruit in Bavaria.

"If you're thinking of sloping off again with the

devastating Mr. Marquand, of course I don't mind," she teased, spooning red currant jelly on her plate.

Despite myself, I blushed. Jack had occupied many of my thoughts since yesterday, but I hadn't thought it so obvious. "He's on his way back to Paris, so I'm afraid you're stuck with me," I said lightly. "Shall we take a stroll in the English Garden? The weather is beautiful."

"Actually, I was thinking . . ." She paused, uncharacteristically hesitant. Reaching for the milk pitcher, she poured some into her coffee. "I'd like to visit Dachau," she said quietly.

A chill touched the base of my spine. "The concentration camp?"

She nodded. "After the movie yesterday, I started talking with some French students, and they encouraged me to go."

"It's close to Munich?"

"Only ten miles from the city limits. Apparently you can take the tramway." Martha gulped coffee, as if for strength. "I made up my mind this morning, when I saw the fine weather. But if you'd rather give it a miss, I understand. Obviously it's not the jolliest outing."

"No, I'd like to go," I said slowly. Along with almost everyone I knew, I'd been glued to the radio as the U.S. Army liberated the camps back in 1945, the news reports leaving me limp with shock. I thought of the Comtesse de Renty and the silent vow of responsibility I had taken at her table. "It feels important to see, if we're allowed."

The tram was open to the elements, and the ticket system more complicated than we'd anticipated so that the conductor had to repeat himself several times before giving up and letting us ride for free. We sat near the back, flustered with the embarrassment of miscommunication.

"Aw, I wouldn't worry about it if I were you," said a broad accent. Behind us we found a young G.I. with cropped red hair and a grin on his freckled face. "Americans, right?" he added.

"What gave it away?" I said, and he laughed.

"You two are a sight for sore eyes, let me tell you," he said. "A fellow likes to have a chat, you know?" His name was Tommy; he was nineteen years old and on his first deployment. "They didn't waste any time getting me over here," he said. Tommy missed his kid sisters, his mom's boiled dinner, and the Red Sox. "Gosh, I hope I'm home for opening day," he said. "I've gotta see the Splendid Splintah back in action."

By the time he asked where we were going, we were halfway to Dachau. "Never heard of it. What's there?" he asked with genuine curiosity.

I swallowed my astonishment and began describing what had happened there, the unspeakable horror and suffering, the cruelty and death. The sparkle faded from his face. "But—why?" he asked in disbelief. "Listen, if you girls want to see Munich, I'd be happy to show you around."

"You're awfully sweet," I said. "We're going as observers."

"The site's been threatened," Martha said, explaining that the local Bavarian government had proposed bulldozing the Leitenberg, the camp's mass grave, where over twenty thousand people were buried. "They claimed it was a landscaping project, but of course people accused them of a cover-up." In quick, clipped sentences, she told us about the French team of observers who had visited the camp a few months ago. Instead of a memorial or informational panels, they found signs that prohibited the public from visiting. ENTRY FORBIDDEN. AREA INFESTED, they read, while others warned against DANGER OF INFECTION. An uproar in the press ensued—the French accusing the Germans of erasing history, the Germans claiming the French were communist agitators—the two sides arguing for weeks before finally the Germans capitulated. "Earlier this month, Dachau was rededicated as a site of memory," Martha concluded. "I guess that's why I wanted to visit today."

I felt shaken by her explanation. But glancing over at Tommy, I found him flushed with emotion, his hands balled into fists.

"I've gotta go with you girls," he said suddenly. "I can't believe I've never heard of this place until now. Do you mind if I tag along?"

"Of course not," I said, surprised.

"Strength in numbers," Martha murmured.

Afterward, what I remembered most was the vastness. No place before or since has felt as immense and empty as Dachau on that last day of December 1949. The barren sweep of graveled yards, the barracks lined up like harvested logs, the way the elements punished, sharp and merciless, unhampered by trees or shrubs that might have blocked the wind, or rain, or sun, or the gaze of Nazi guards. On and on we crunched across the gravel, and with each audible step I became slowly aware that everything about the place was designed to make it impossible to escape.

American troops had liberated Dachau four years ago, but parts of the camp were still in use. Some buildings were used to imprison Nazis and conduct war-crime trials, while the barracks housed refugees from Eastern Europe. These sections were behind barbed-wire-trimmed fences, so that we sensed, rather than saw, the squalor of the camp—heard its howling babies, smelled the stewing cabbage and basic lavatories. France had sheltered me from the war's displaced persons, but now here they were—teachers and bakers, doctors and housewives, librarians and everyone else forced to keep moving because they had no home to return to. What would happen to them? I had no idea and, worse, I didn't think anyone else did either.

We walked and walked without signs to inform us, nor escorts to guide us, the bright cold burning against our skin. The French students Martha had met the day before had given her a rough idea of what to look for, and it was obvious when we found it because the atmosphere shifted, becoming thick and silent.

It was a brick building, low and thin, with a gently sloping roof and a square cement chimney soaring meters above. We entered through one of several doors, blinking as our eyes adjusted to the dim light. The room was long and narrow, with plain whitewashed walls and a rough cement floor punctured by drains, the space echoing and empty—except for four red-brick furnaces paired off at opposite ends.

Four ample furnaces. Four gaping furnace mouths. I blinked and saw guards plucking wasted corpses from a heaping pile, shoving them into the flames. I heard the fire's roar and snap, felt its raging heat, smelled the burning flesh. Over forty thousand people had been murdered at Dachau, over forty thousand different deaths—caused by disease, overwork or malnourishment, brutal medical experiments, executions for petty infractions, or gassed in off-site chambers, their bodies burned to ashes here in this crematorium. I had never known death like this, death in the multitudes, death caused by malice, so many deaths that it was impossible to value and honor each one. My stomach pitched, nausea rising to my throat, and I fled outside, struggling to breathe as I gagged.

I was wiping my eyes with a handkerchief when I heard crunching footsteps, and then Tommy appeared. "You all right, miss?" he asked.

I drew a shaky breath and shook my head.

"I never could've imagined something like this," Tommy was saying. "Never in a million years. Christ almighty." His face had drained of color so that his copper freckles stood stark against pale skin. "Pardon my language, miss. But Jesus Christ, those fucking monsters."

More footsteps announced Martha, looking equally ashen. "I can't," she whispered, before her hand flew to her mouth. What had she wanted to say? Can't talk? Can't believe it? Can't bear it? I felt all those things too.

It was just past four o'clock, but already the shadows

were growing long. "Sun goes down like a cannonball around here," Tommy observed. "I wouldn't want to get caught out after dark."

Retracing our steps, we found the station, bought tickets, and sat at the back of the tram. We'd be in Munich in under an hour—all that horror occurring a stone's throw away, a morning's commute to work, barely enough time to read the newspaper. Tens of thousands of people murdered next door.

"What were they thinking?" Martha asked. I didn't know how to answer. When she spoke again, it was only to repeat the question.

Tommy bid us farewell at the Marienplatz, scribbling down his address and promising to write. "Today was somethin' else. You better believe I'm going to remember you girls," he said. "But you won't catch me going back there anytime soon." We all managed weak smiles. It occurred to me that I'd probably never see him again, yet his snub nose and freckles would remain forever entwined with my memories of Dachau. "Let me know if you're ever in Boston, okay? I'll take you to a Sox game!" he called, before jogging off to meet his pals at the commissary.

Back at Frau Becker's, Martha and I prepared for

a night out that felt incongruous to the day's events. I sat at the dressing table, staring at my same square face and dark hair, same wide-set eyes, strong brows, and mouth that alternated between impish and wistful. But I didn't feel the same.

Martha stepped into her evening frock, adjusted the shawl collar, looked in the mirror, and frowned. "This dress feels all wrong," she said.

"You look lovely," I said, but I knew she wasn't talking about her appearance. In fact, I myself had half a mind to plead a headache and cancel on Yusha's friends. But I certainly had no desire to be in this room all night, staring at embroidered throw cushions and fussy china figurines as images of skeletal horror played across my imagination. For once in my life, I was desperate to be at a party that was loud, hot, crowded, and bright—and to stay there for a week if possible.

We finished getting ready in silence, dusting powder across our noses, gathering items for our evening bags, slipping on high heels.

"Come on," I said, sliding my fur coat over my dress of midnight-blue silk. "The boys will be here soon."

Their names were Fisher, George, and Mac, and we found them in the living room joking with Frau Becker in broken German while she poured them thimbles of schnapps. While not exactly handsome, together they were crisply dressed, broad shouldered, and so full of health their freshly shaved faces glowed.

"You girls ready? We've got a jeep outside," said Mac, who seemed to be in charge. "*Danke schön* for the schnapps, Fraulein," he said to Frau Becker, who beamed at him. Stooping slightly, he kissed her on both cheeks.

"I bet she doesn't wash her face until 1951," I whispered as we stepped out of the apartment.

"Poor thing," he said. "Of course she definitely dabbles in the black market, and I'm willing to bet her denazification is dubious. But it's got to be a grim life for her now."

"Sure," I said, knowing he was right. Mac's hand touched my elbow as we walked downstairs to the lobby, and the knot in my neck began to loosen, my jaw unclench. Behind me, Martha was joking about frost-bitten fingers, and a feeling of calm surged through me, so relieved was I to be among these young Americans with their familiar dispositions and rational points of view.

"Your chariot, ladies." Fisher opened the door of a jeep that was parked on the sidewalk right outside the apartment building.

"How convenient!" Martha raised an eyebrow.

He had the grace to flush. "To the victor goes the parking?"

"In this cold, I'm not complaining," Martha assured him.

"You girls hungry?" said George, the quietest of the three.

"Famished." I climbed into the backseat, squeezing between Martha and Fisher. "I just realized we forgot to eat lunch."

Mac, behind the wheel, glanced at us in the rearview mirror. "What on earth were you girls doing today that you forgot to eat?"

Beside me, I felt Martha tense and thought I understood. We were having such a nice time, after all. But I was still floating with relief, disarmed by their familiarity. "We went to Dachau," I said. "Have you been?"

Silence. And then: "Gosh, no."

"That place gives me the creeps."

"You girls are darn brave, that's for sure."

I shoved my hands into my coat pockets to warm them. For several seconds no one spoke, and the silence felt like criticism. "Where are we going for dinner?" I finally asked in a soft little voice.

Mac glanced back with a smile. "Thought we'd go to the Hofbräuhaus. It's a beer hall that's like a miniature Munich. You girls will love it."

"That sounds marvelous," I murmured.

"Emphasis on the *bräu*, I hope," Fisher said, and the boys all laughed.

A few minutes later, we parked outside the same half-timbered beer hall where I'd lunched with Jack Marquand. A noisy crowd had gathered on the sidewalk, and light and music spilled from the windows. We sailed past the waiting people directly into the restaurant, then headed straight to a table off the dance floor, where a waiter whisked away our coats, popped a bottle of sekt, and poured five sparkling glasses, all before I had lit a cigarette.

"Not too shabby, eh?" Mac looked pleased.

"It's exactly how I always imagined Munich," I said automatically, because that was what I'd said to Jack the day before. The truth was, my head had begun to ache again, a knot twisting from the base of my skull into my shoulders.

"*Prost!*" Fisher raised his glass to the table, and we drank, the sparkling wine making my stomach churn.

"Goodness, this is going straight to my head," Martha said with an uncertain smile. She looked as pale and uneasy as I felt.

"Have one of these." George proffered a plate of little toasts spread thickly with whitish butter. Martha declined, but I popped one in my mouth, tasting salt and smoke, and a film of fat that thickened when I sipped the chilled wine. "It's pork *Schmalz*," he explained at my expression. "Seasoned lard."

"Delicious," I said with forced enthusiasm, knowing the grease would cling to me all evening.

The band had taken a break, but now they struck up again, a country polka enticing couples to the floor. I watched the dancers bob and skip and spin, the dirndl skirts of the German girls twirling, their braids flying. The room heaved with heat and noise, and everywhere there were flushed faces and tapping feet, voices booming with high spirits, heads thrown back in laughter, while the music played on and on. And I felt nothing except my heart pounding with a cold, sick beat.

PART II

L'hiver

Chapter Nine

For the entire journey back to Paris, I could think of little else than what I had witnessed in Germany. The bleak wretchedness of Dachau, the crumpled wasteland of Munich, the merrymaking at the Hofbräuhaus—all of it haunted me, filling me with a profound horror that seeped into my dreams. On the night train, I woke again and again with a jolt so violent I feared jostling Martha next to me. Sometimes she roused me, crying out in her sleep. But we didn't discuss what we had seen—it was enough to have seen it.

It was a relief to return to the regal Beaux-Arts beauty of Paris and to the gentle calm of avenue Mozart. France had its own ghosts, to be sure, but at least I could trust the de Rentys, whose stance regarding the war I didn't have to question. Especially now that I had a clearer idea of the nightmare Madame had endured, her silence and forgiveness stunned me. I had failed to forgive far less, even of my own parents.

Paris in midwinter was moody, the days short, the skies changeable. The lovely soft autumn mistiness had been replaced by hard bursts of wind and rain that rattled the windows and turned umbrellas inside out. Bright days brought a sharp, dry crackle to the air. The cold was the great equalizer of France that winter, for no one—rich or poor—was warm enough at home, and everyone sought comfort in public spaces. On a visit to the Louvre, I was puzzled to see a crowd gathering around a small landscape by a minor Baroque artist, wondering if I'd missed its significance—until I moved closer and saw they were all grouped around a vent blowing hot air. Martha told me that the little girl who lived next to her host family asked if the rumor could possibly be true: "Can Americans *really* sit in their drawing rooms without wearing coats?"

At avenue Mozart we resembled hibernating bears, dressed in our sweaters and shawls and earmuffs, padding through the cold parlor in layered socks, our breath emerging in great puffed clouds. Even Mary Ann had ceased to boast about her hardy Midwestern blood, humbly donning an unflattering wool hat and thick hand-knit stockings that she'd unearthed from the bottom of her trunk. I had always loved winter, with its crisp, purifying cold and thrilling possibility of snow, but that year in Paris taught me that what I actually loved was winter with the luxury of central heating. In my coddled little life I had never lived without it, just as I had never known hunger, or fear, or living under the enemy's thumb. It was a realization that came with its own particular twist of shame.

Sometimes I would go to a café for an hour, just to warm my feet. But mostly I studied in bed under a pile of blankets, swaddled in wool sweaters and fingerless gloves, scribbling madly with a leaky fountain pen. For as soon as January had begun, our professors assigned a pile of papers that would decide our grades for the semester—so many *dissertations*, on such varied topics: Compare the tragedies of Racine and Shakespeare. Discuss the role of tradition and innovation in the work of Ingres. And from our philosophy professor, the most archetypal French question of all: *A-t-on le droit de se suicider?* Does one have the right to commit suicide?

Four months ago I would have been paralyzed by any of these essays. But when I bent my head to work, I was surprised to find my thoughts fluent and organized, the sentences shaped with new eloquence. And it wasn't only my written French that had improved.

In shops, I no longer pointed mutely at what I wanted but asked questions in great detail. In restaurants, I no longer ordered the few dishes I knew but thoroughly perused the menu. In my mind, a map of Paris had sprung up, so that whenever someone mentioned an arrondissement, I pictured how to get there by métro. The city had ceased to be a web of unfamiliar streets and had become a place of preference and memory, scattered with landmarks like the café where Claude and I first met, the *tabac* near Reid Hall where I bought cigarettes before class, the spot where I boarded the métro each morning that left me exactly at the station exit when I got off the train. Four months ago, I would have been astonished to know any of these things, astonished that tourists stopped me for directions, or that a waiter would ever presume I was Belgian, or that I could hold my own in a classroom debate about existentialism. But I was a different girl from the one who had arrived four months ago.

"**So *this*** is student life!" Ghislaine lit a cigarette and gazed avidly at the little tables occupied by groups of two or three.

"I hope it's not too disappointing," I said, for the café was not a particularly nice one, the floors scuffed and ashtrays overflowing, tables littered with rumpled copies of *Libération* and *L'Humanité*, the favored newspapers of the left, which evidently included many of my classmates.

"I'm interested in everything. Like I said, I dreamed of going to university, but the war cut that short."

"Such a pity," I said, suddenly self-conscious. "You would have been brilliant."

"Yes, it's too bad." She returned to observing the room, swiveling her head as if memorizing the details to re-create them later.

It was early January and we were in the study period between semesters, two weeks of exams and essays that would determine our grades for the term. Ghislaine and I had finally found time to meet at Sciences Po— I'd suggested a chintz-swathed *salon de thé* that served homemade tarts and cakes—but she had insisted on this grubby student café, which was popular because it was cheap. I opened my schoolbag and extracted a sheaf of loose pages, handing them to her. "Thanks again for looking over my history paper. I just hope it's not too deadly dull. Our writing must seem awfully stilted."

"Nonsense." She shrugged away my concern. "I'm delighted to read anything you give me."

"You've saved me from so many silly mistakes. I know Mary Ann and Susan feel the same way. We're awfully grateful." The three of us had started showing

Ghislaine rough drafts of all our school essays, relying on her keen eye to catch misspelled words and grammatical errors.

"I'm happy to help," she assured me. "As I told you, this is one of the few things I'm good at."

Our waiter appeared, depositing teapots and cups on the table with a clatter.

"Have you met many French students?" Ghislaine asked, as we busied ourselves pouring tea and adding honey. She was dressed casually, wearing low heels and a touch of lipstick, her dark hair soft and waving around her face. With a heavy satchel over her shoulder, she looked like a college student herself.

I hesitated, considering her question. Generally my classmates clung to their own groups, so tight-knit I suspected their friendships had formed in the womb. As well, I acknowledged with a twinge of guilt, I hadn't made much of an effort to meet new people. Especially between lectures, when everyone rushed off to eat a cheap and cheerful lunch together at the *foyer*, I preferred to take solitary walks, snapping photographs or browsing the book stalls of the *bouquinistes* along the Seine. Mummy would have called this behavior selfish, and though I didn't agree, I knew it wasn't socially enriching.

"Does Claude count?" I asked, and she smiled tolerantly. "I also see Paul de Ganay and some of his friends. But that's outside of school, I suppose."

"What about clubs? Societies? Associations? I'd think this place would be hopping with political groups . . . Students organizing protests . . . All those handsome idealists . . ." She gave a coy shrug.

"Oh, is that how you meet them?" I teased. But Ghislaine remained silent, and I worried she thought I was being too frivolous. It hadn't occurred to me to join a political club, but now I wondered what I could learn from one. Was I taking advantage of my time here in Paris?

"It's such an important moment to be more active, don't you think?" Ghislaine sipped her tea and frowned. "The future of Europe is literally hanging in the balance. Women here in France, we only got the vote five years ago. So many of us are longing to do something for our country."

"Like during the war," I said, thinking of Madame.

"Yes, of course during the war." She pushed a strand of hair away from her face. "But I'm talking about now—the new threat we're facing. *On veut s'engager.*" We want to engage.

I lit a cigarette, unsure of how to respond. I had the uneasy feeling I was being tested somehow, and failing.

Ghislaine leaned forward in her seat. "How about your Smith friends? Are any of them politically active?"

I blew a little smoke over my shoulder. "My friend Martha went out last week with a fellow who said he can't decide between communism and democracy. Believe it or not."

"What did she say?"

"Oh, she thinks he's adorable—terribly young and naïve and dazzled by everything in the city."

Ghislaine smiled thinly. "Yes, but which *side* is she on?"

I laughed. "Is there any choice? Democracy, of course!"

"So there's no one in your Smith group who follows politics?"

"Well, we all read the newspapers, of course. But no, I can't think of anyone who's especially involved." As far as I knew, the Smithies in my program filled the hours outside of school with ballet classes, drawing ateliers, or music lessons.

"And you're definitely not in any clubs?"

I shook my head, and she began extinguishing her cigarette with a stabbing motion. "I have to get back to the office," she said, scraping back her chair. "We have a conference beginning tomorrow. Lots of bigwigs—everyone's in a frenzy."

"Oh!" I blinked, surprised by this abrupt change in plans. "Would you still like to visit the campus? There's not much to see, but I can give you a quick tour."

"Sorry, *chérie*, I must fly." She reached into her pocketbook and brought out a thick roll of banknotes.

"No, no, *je t'invite*—I'll take care of the check." I stood to kiss her cheeks. "You go ahead. I'll stay to finish my tea." Having planned on a chat and stroll with Ghislaine, I now had almost two hours to fill until my next lecture, but no matter. I could study—or start reading the slim little biography of Sergei Diaghilev and the Ballets Russes that I'd found in a Latin Quarter bookshop a day earlier.

"You're a darling—*merci*." She threw on her coat and dashed out the door, moving briskly down the block. It was only when she reached the corner and turned that I realized she was heading in the exact opposite direction of the métro that went to her office at the Ministry of Defense. I puzzled over this mystery for a moment before deciding that Ghislaine's affairs were really none of my business.

Reaching for one of the crumpled newspapers, I began to leaf through it, scanning the articles. One editorial warned against the threat of "Coca-colonization," declaring that if Coca-Cola was widely distributed in France as proposed, its delivery system would double as an anti-communist spy network. Another called for the prohibition of *"les bombes atomiques,"* urging the "five great powers"—China, France, Russia, the United Kingdom, and the United States—to form a pact to strengthen the peace. "The new movement has even gained the support of the artist Pablo Picasso, who has created an international logo for peace, a lithograph of a dove," concluded the article. "'I stand for life against death; I stand for peace against war,' Picasso declared."

Without warning, a flutter rose in my chest like swiftly beating bird wings. It was the same disquiet I'd felt in Vienna at the Wagners' table, that sensation of being confronted and challenged to look at my preconceived ideas from a new perspective. I had been so quick to dismiss communism as crackpot leftist extremism—and clearly some of their ideas were ridiculous, like this paranoid Coca-Cola spy ring—but there were others, like world peace, that didn't sound so outlandish. I had no stomach for another war and neither did anyone else I knew—certainly not now, less than five years after our victory, and especially not all-out nuclear destruction.

Tossing the paper aside, I stared at the lipstick print on Ghislaine's teacup, considering our conversation. "The fate of Europe is hanging in the balance. We're facing a new threat," she'd said. I supposed she was talking about Russia and her fear that a Soviet master plot would soon take over the continent. And yes, after meeting those Soviet soldiers on that cold night last month in Vienna, with their mocking smiles and brute force, their disregard for international law, the idea of a master plot didn't seem that ludicrous after all. But maybe communism wasn't as clear and sharp and defined as I'd always believed. Maybe it was a thousand tones of gray, with as many streaks and smudges and subtleties as a charcoal line drawing.

Perhaps Ghislaine was right—perhaps this was the time to become political. I thought of Claude, who was a member of the Union des femmes françaises, a women's rights group formed soon after the Liberation. But that was Claude—so passionate about equality that I wouldn't be surprised if she ran for office one day. The war had given her and Ghislaine—and Madame, as well—a new independence, one born of loss, and I saw they had no choice but to forge their own path in this era that granted them the right to vote and serve on juries.

My choices were different. I'd been born with the vote, though I hadn't yet exercised it. Political activism wasn't the type of thing nice debutante girls participated in—and honestly I didn't feel I'd developed my views enough to defend them. And yet, there was an idea that wouldn't let go, a word Ghislaine had used during our conversation: *s'engager*. In my mind, I had translated it as to engage, but now I remembered that it meant something else: to commit.

On veut s'engager, Ghislaine had said about French women—we want to commit. She meant women like her mother—who hadn't been able to join the army or vote, but who had seen their country so damaged, they'd found their own way to resist. The war had altered Madame's life in terrible ways, but it had left her with a commitment to her fellow female resistants that I deeply admired. I couldn't think of a weekday that Madame hadn't volunteered at the ADIR, the advocacy group for women who had been deported and imprisoned during the war. It was the type of devotion not often seen in the drawing rooms of Mummy and her friends.

I wasn't certain about any of the isms I'd seen floating around Paris—communism, socialism, conservatism, feminism—all of them blinking with their own peculiar signal. None of that moved me particularly. And yet I felt something stirring within me, an indefinable hunger to do more. Paris was awakening me, giving me an energy I hadn't felt before, challenging me to commit to something larger than myself. But what?

"Can I get you another?" Jack bellowed, gesturing at my empty glass. We were sitting inches from each other, but I could barely hear him over the music.

I smiled and nodded, and when he rose to fetch the drinks from the bar, I snatched up a cocktail menu and tried to surreptitiously fan myself. My face was so damp with sweat I felt my lashes clinging stickily when I blinked, and I cringed, thinking of my makeup.

Across the table sat George and Jimmy, two of Jack's friends from college—or were they also writers? The club was loud, and I hadn't heard what Jack said as he introduced them. When we arrived after dinner, they were already there, listening raptly to the quartet on-stage. I had seen their eyes slide over me, dismissing me in a glance. With Jack's arm around my shoulders, I hadn't really minded.

Between my essays for school and Jack's deadline for an article he was writing for a literary journal, we hadn't seen each other for a couple of weeks, not since Munich. And perhaps I had been avoiding him—for whenever I remembered the way his dark blue eyes had lingered upon me, I felt my body respond in a way that half terrified me. In all my relationships I was most comfortable when I could conceal my emotions so that no one ever knew what I was thinking. But something about Jack made it hard for me to remain elusive.

By ten o'clock the Rose Rouge was so filled with smoke, I could scarcely see three feet in front of me. It was a tiny club, housed in a dim, shabby basement near

Saint-Germain-des-Prés, but with its wild music—*"le jazz hot,"* as the French called it—and young, sinuous crowd, the decor was hardly the point. The place was steamy, packed, and thrumming with energy, and it felt like the center of the universe.

Jack returned with our drinks, handing round glasses of amber liquid, no ice. "Is this okay?" he shouted at me. "It's all they've got left."

"It's fine, thanks!" I said and took a sip, trying not to grimace as the alcohol traced a line of fire down my throat. It was the first time I'd drunk whiskey, on a night filled with firsts: first Saturday night out with Jack, first visit to this Left Bank *boîte*, first time in mixed company. The Rose Rouge was what we called a "Black and tan" back home, a nightclub where Blacks and whites freely mingled. Here in Paris, where segregation—legal or otherwise—didn't exist like it did in the States, this distinction hardly mattered. But after my teenage years in suburban Virginia, being here felt daring—even though I would rather have died than admit it. Jack's friend Jimmy was the first Black man I'd ever sat and had a drink with, but since the others didn't act like this was a big deal, I didn't either, and after a while I realized it wasn't.

The band took a break and the boys began talking about something Jimmy was working on, a novel about a Harlem teenager unfolding over a single day. "He's a boy who's backslid from his family, his church, his community," Jimmy was saying. "And he's got this father who's a preacher who hates his guts. His mother gives him some money to explore the city for the day, and when he sees all these places that are so splendid and untouchable, he's filled with conflicting emotions. And then he ends up back in Harlem at his father's church, and then . . . I don't know." Jimmy threw himself back in his chair. "I'm afraid I might never finish it."

As I listened to Jimmy list all the things he was trying to avoid in this novel—cheap emotion, facile morality, an overly tidy plot—I wondered what it would be like to have the discipline and perception to write something that would challenge and explore our understanding of the world. Daddy was always encouraging me to write a book—"All you need to do is make an effort and I know you'd land a bestseller," he'd said in his last letter—but though I enjoyed writing, I had no illusions that I had anything meaningful to say.

A stack of records dropped onto the phonograph, and at the unmistakable strains of Claude Luter's clarinet, couples rose to dance. Jack grabbed my hand, but before we could head to the area in the center of the room that served as a dance floor, someone touched my shoulder from behind. *"Coucou!"* Claude greeted me when I turned. Beside her stood a slender young man with elfin features who kept casting shy glances her way. "This is Bernard," she said, touching his sleeve.

"You came!" I exclaimed, popping up to greet them. Claude and I hadn't planned to meet tonight, but as we were getting ready for our dates, she'd mentioned that the evening might bring her here too, and we'd agreed to look out for each other.

I introduced her to the boys and everyone exchanged cheek kisses. It was the first time I'd ever heard Claude speak English, and, despite her previous protestations, it was flawless. Somehow I wasn't surprised.

"You look awfully familiar," Jack was saying to her. "Have we met before?"

Her head tilted up as she scanned his face. "I don't believe so," she said. "I'm sure I'd remember you."

"She has a sister who looks just like her," I interjected.

He frowned, puzzling it over. "Does she go to readings at the Compagnon de voyage?"

"Where?"

"The communist bookstore in the Latin Quarter."

"Good heavens, no," I said with a laugh. "She wouldn't set foot in a place like that." *And what*, I wondered, *were you doing there?*

"I stop by sometimes for my book research," he said, answering my unasked question. "Geneviève." He snapped his fingers. "That's her name. She lives in the suburbs—Saint-Denis, I think? She usually sits at the back."

"Oh well, then, it's definitely not her. Claude's sister is named Ghislaine."

Glancing at Claude, I saw a strange expression fly across her fine features, one that looked almost like alarm. I blinked and it was gone.

"Let's go powder our noses," she suggested.

"We'll be right back," I told the boys. Bernard sat in my chair and I heard Jack offering to get him a drink from the bar.

"How do you know Jack?" Claude asked as we waited in line for the W.C. The rear door of the club was propped open, letting in a draft of winter air that cooled my neck but did little to dispel the dank odors.

"We met on the street," I admitted. "But we have mutual acquaintances." As soon as I'd learned that Jack had graduated from Harvard, I'd sent a letter to my stepbrother. Yusha reported back that his boarding-school roommate had worked with Jack on the *Lampoon* and confirmed he'd moved to Paris. "He was there back in August '44," Yusha wrote. "Marquand's division was among the early wave to reach the city."

This last part I only assumed to be true, since Jack was too modest to boast about his war record, let alone his participation in the Liberation.

"Oh good." Claude looked relieved. "When he mentioned that bookshop, I wondered if he might be a fellow traveler."

"What do you mean?"

"Someone who sympathizes with communist ideology but isn't a full-fledged party member," she explained as we inched to the front of the queue.

"A Harvard man like Jack? I doubt it. Anyway, Yusha would have told me something like that." I had full confidence in my stepbrother's judgment.

"I'm sure you're right."

I gave her a sidelong glance. "Bernard seems awfully sweet on you," I teased. "He just keeps *gazing* at you. And when you started speaking English with the boys I thought he might burst his buttons."

"Oh, you're exaggerating . . ." she protested. But a flush was rising across her cheeks, and I suddenly wondered if the relationship was more serious than she'd let on.

The door of the W.C. swung open, releasing a smell that made me recoil. A girl stepped out looking ashen despite her fresh lipstick.

"You don't have any tissues, do you?" Claude asked, rummaging through her pocketbook.

"I have a handkerchief." I pulled it from my bag and offered it to her. "It's clean."

She winced and shook her head. "Do you want to go first?"

Glancing into the W.C., I saw a flat porcelain basin set into the tiled floor. For a second I was tempted to run away, but I knew I couldn't last the night. "All right."

"I'll watch the door," Claude said. Then, noting my reluctance, she murmured, "Stand as far back as possible when you flush."

I stepped into the small, dim space, attempting to breathe shallowly through my mouth. I'd heard the Smithies joke about *les toilettes à la turque*, though I'd somehow managed to avoid them thus far. But now here it was, a ceramic hole in the ground bordered by two flat footpads. You were meant to pull up your skirt and squat over the hole, a maneuver requiring balance, skill, and strength that I thankfully possessed from all those years of horseback riding. Still, I cringed as cold air brushed parts of me that I preferred to remain covered, and little droplets splashed my ankles. I grabbed a newspaper square from the stack on the nearby ledge, glimpsing a headline from last week's *France-Soir,* and gritted my teeth.

BAM! BAM! BAM! A sudden pounding on the door made me jump and lose balance, my heels scrambling for purchase on the slick porcelain surface. I hastily gripped the walls on either side of me, my dropped skirt swinging perilously close to the murky puddle below.

"C'est occupé!" I heard Claude say crossly. And then: *"Ça va, Jacqueline?"*

"Ça va!" I said brightly, though my heart threatened to burst from my chest. I reached for the flush chain and pulled, remembering a fraction of a second too late to keep my distance. Lurching from the revolting spray, I managed to claw open the door and tumble outside.

The queue of people snaked down the hall. "Finally!" muttered a stocky young man in a roll-neck sweater.

"Everything all right?" Claude asked.

"I think I just aged ten years."

"Keep moving, girls!" shouted the roll-neck sweater.

Claude shot him a haughty look and then stepped into the W.C. *"Félicitations,* you are a true Parisienne now," she told me and closed the door behind her.

I washed my hands at the cold-water sink in the hall,

peering into the grimy mirror hanging above it and marveling that my makeup hadn't smudged. Claude emerged from the toilet, unruffled, and we returned to the table.

The boys were nursing whiskey and talking, but when Jack spotted me he sprang to his feet. "How about that dance?" At my nod his fingers entwined with mine, cool and dry. The band, now returned, had launched into a jitterbug, lively notes skipping through the thick air as couples twisted and bobbed. Jack held me tentatively and for an awkward moment I thought he might not know how to dance. But as I began to move, he broke into the swing, limbs akimbo, and I realized he'd feared the same of me.

The band was on a tear and everyone could feel it, the room alive with our energy, the music popping with an exhilarating beat. Of course I'd been to night-clubs before, but never anything like this, so scruffy and cramped I could smell the sweat rising. Swept up in the music, feet and arms flashing, we danced until breathless, and for the first time in a long time I didn't care about my wild hair or sticky face. I was conscious only of my body, strong and nimble; and Jack, moving with fluid ease nearby; and the feeling of his hand on mine as I spun, unaware of the time until I glanced at my watch and stopped dead.

"You all right?" Jack's hand cupped my shoulder. "You want something to drink? I'm a bit parched."

"I'd love it." I reached up to wipe my forehead with the back of my hand but then thought better of it. "But it's almost midnight."

"Ahh. The pumpkin hour."

"My host mother is an angel, but I don't dare miss the last métro."

We found our coats and said goodbye to George and Jimmy. "What about Claude?" Jack held my coat so I could slide my arms through the sleeves.

"She and Bernard left a bit ago." She hadn't said goodbye, only caught my eye from the door and waved before slipping out. "You're stuck with just me, I'm afraid."

"Lucky me." He set a hand against my back and we stepped into the night.

After a mad dash for the métro, we squeezed onto the last train, which was filled with late-night revelers. In the harsh light of the crowded subway car, our hands gripping the greasy pole, I felt extra aware of Jack's presence, his height and broad shoulders looming above the wiry French boys beside us. He was telling me about his apartment near Saint-Germain-des-Prés—"perfumed with my neighbor's *eau de* cooking grease," he joked— but I was having trouble focusing my attention, and it wasn't just because of the whiskey I'd sipped at the club. I kept staring at his mouth, wondering what it would be like to kiss him, and then glancing away when he looked at me.

I knew some people thought I was a flirt, but the truth was I'd only ever kissed two boys. The summer I was sixteen there was Charlie Whitehouse, whose parents owned a cottage up the road from Hughdie's in Newport. He was eight years older than me, just back from the war, terribly dashing on a horse, and my crush on him was so fatal I blushed just seeing his helmet hanging in our stables. All summer long we went riding and played tennis, and sometimes after parties he'd come back to Hammersmith Farm with me and Yusha to eat scrambled eggs at midnight and play records on the Victrola. He kissed me there on the porch one night at the end of the season, smooth and practiced. For weeks I had longed for him to do this very thing, but once he did—his hands stroking my shoulders, his whiskeyed breath on my lips—he ceased to be glamorous and mature and became simply old.

I came out the next summer in Newport wearing a long dress of white satin and gauze, ruffles at my neck, gloves reaching to my elbows. The dance floor of the Clambake Club was a burst of swirling skirts and light feet, the orchestra playing waltzes, candlelight glittering against jeweled necks and wrists and fingers and ears, and the heavy scent of hothouse flowers casting a spell of such enchantment that I ended the evening by kissing Bev Corbin at the ninth hole of the golf course. Bev was a dear childhood friend, with a crooked grin and a love of puns, and the kiss was sweet, the fairy-tale ending to a fairy-tale evening. But by the time the night had dissolved into dawn, I realized it was the champagne, not his charm; the summer breeze, not his smile. I still regretted it, for I'd always been fond of Bev and didn't mean to wound his pride. I was sorry our friendship never recovered.

Since then, there had been plenty of first dates but not many that I cared to follow up. There had been little flirtations—men I met on the train, friends I knew through Yusha—but no one who had ever enchanted, or enthralled, or excited me. Mummy thought I was irresponsible—"Your bloom is fading, Jackie," she warned me—but though I did dream of a husband, and a home, and babies to fill the loneliness inside of me, it wasn't everything I wanted. I had seen how marriage could shrink a girl's life into a series of concentric circles, leaving no room for living in the thrill of possibility. For as long as I could remember, I'd desired something more—something big. The problem was, I didn't know what it was or how to find it. Of one thing, however, I was certain: A marriage like my mother's, a marriage of convenience, would drown me.

Eventually Jack and I arrived back at avenue Mozart, drawing up beside my front door, the streetlamps reflecting off the limestone building and casting our faces in a yellow glow. Now that we were alone, I felt uncharacteristically awkward, and fought the urge to light a cigarette.

"Do you need to get upstairs before your clothes turn to rags?" Jack smiled down at me.

"I still have a minute," I said softly. "But gosh, it's chilly." I exaggerated a shiver so that he wound an arm around me.

"You're quite the dancer, Miss Bouvier." He gave my shoulders a squeeze. "I could barely keep up with you out there."

"You cut a pretty fine rug yourself, Mr. Marquand." I tipped my head to one side, feeling my senses flood with his presence, the fresh juniper of his cologne mingling with the heady scent of sweat, the rumble of his voice against my ear, a subtle darkening along his jaw that left me imagining it rough against my cheek. I leaned into the steady warmth of him, and when his face turned to mine, I felt my reserve melting into an unfamiliar molten puddle that both thrilled and terrified me. I moved my head and now we were kissing, our lips and tongues slipping together, all my thoughts disappearing, except for this single moment hovering crystal clear, time standing still.

Later, much later, after we had kissed for a few seconds—or maybe it was an eternity—after I had bid Jack farewell and he said he'd call me tomorrow, I crept upstairs and collapsed across my bed, rumpled and exhilarated. It had been the best of nights, and not just because of the kiss, but also the Rose Rouge, the music, Jack's friends, all of it adding up to Jack himself—the ease, and wit, and confidence of him; the quiet, sure-footed way he moved through every situation.

Nowhere except in Paris, I thought, as the adrenaline began to seep from me, nowhere except in Paris could I have experienced a night like this. I changed into my pajamas, cleaned my face and teeth, and climbed into bed, curling underneath a heavy pile of blankets. Even as I closed my eyes to sleep, my whole entire self felt electric.

I woke late the next morning, past nine o'clock, to a spill of sunlight across my pillow. I'd forgotten to close the curtains, and through the window I saw a flash of blue streaked with wisps of clouds, the first clear sky we'd had in several days. Lingering beneath the covers, I relished the rare sensation of being fully and completely warm, while the events of the previous night raced through my head. Being with Jack, kissing him, had made me feel alive and charged with a wild force. But now in the bright wash of sun, I saw clearly how much I liked him, and I heard clearly Mummy's objections—"Who are his people, Jackie?"—and I recognized clearly my vulnerability. In the light of morning, I wanted to shy away.

Outside, the church bells began to chime the hour. It was Sunday, the first of the term—our new courses would begin tomorrow—and the first day in months that I was free of studying and could do whatever I liked. The sound of Christian's little socked feet came pounding across the creaky parquet floors, followed by voices in the hallway. The de Rentys were leaving to spend the day at a friends' house in the country, driving there in Ghislaine's car and returning in the evening. As Ghislaine and Claude bickered about the best route to take, Christian complained about his itchy scarf, and Madame's calm tones rose above everyone, ushering them out the door.

Susan departed next, dashing off to her singing lesson with a quick, sure step. That left Mary Ann—Mary Ann of the thick Midwestern blood and outspoken opinions, Mary Ann who had a habit of forgetting the language pledge, Mary Ann who was so often at a loose end. She was terribly generous, but her extravagance could feel overwhelming, like the afternoon she'd brought home an enormous *filet de bœuf* and deposited it on the kitchen table. "I've been pining for a great juicy slab of roast beef, haven't you?" she'd said cheerfully, tremendously pleased with herself, not noticing the mortified expression that had replaced Madame's usually gentle countenance. That evening Madame roasted the cut beautifully rare, and we ate it over two meals, exclaiming over Mary Ann's largess. But secretly, I'd thought of it as the meat of shame.

The morning sun was starting to slant past my windows, and my stomach rumbled, hungry for breakfast. Yet if I left my room now, there was a good chance Mary Ann would find me, ask about my plans for the day, and angle to tag along. For several moments I wrestled with my conscience, knowing what politeness demanded, yet desiring to spend the day alone.

Before I could decide what to do, the phone rang and footsteps galloped to the front hall to answer it. "*Allô?*" came Mary Ann's voice, loud and eager. "*Oui? Comment . . . ? Désolée . . .* Oh, blast." And then, a few seconds later: "Oh, thank heavens, you speak English . . . Yes, but I think she's still sleeping. I'll just tap on her door, shall I? May I tell her who's calling? Just a moment. JACKIE!"

I popped my head out. *"Coucou!"* I smiled, hoping to coax her back into speaking French.

"Someone named Jack is on the phone for you and"—she clamped a hand over the receiver—"he sounds dishy!"

Jack was calling *now*? I wanted to hear from him, of course—but hardly so soon, less than twelve hours since we'd parted. I hesitated for a fraction too long.

"Shall I take a message?" Mary Ann hissed in a stage whisper.

"No, it's fine." I moved to take the phone. "Thanks, though." I gave her a distracted smile.

"Jackie!" Jack cried after I said hello. In the background, I heard the bustle of voices and clanking crockery and assumed that, lacking a line in his flat, he was ringing from his local café. "May I call you that?"

"You may not," I said with mock severity.

"Jacqueline," he said humbly, with a grin in his voice. "I don't suppose I can convince you to lunch with me on this fine day? I know this terrific little bistro at Ménilmontant, and afterward I thought we could poke around Père Lachaise."

"The cemetery? You certainly know how to sweep a girl off her feet," I teased.

"Not just any cemetery!" he protested. "The final resting spot of Molière! Oscar Wilde! Proust! I could go on and on. Surely this is catnip to a literary aficionado like you."

"Well, it is on my list . . ." I wavered despite myself. Still, I sensed it was too soon—and not just because of Daddy's admonitions about playing hard to get. Being with Jack Marquand felt as thrilling and precarious as the first ice skate of winter, the smooth gliding accelerating to barely controlled speed, the shaky turns, the threat of a spill. I needed to regain my balance before I saw him again. "I wish I could, but I'm just dashing out the door to meet a friend," I said, the fib slipping off my tongue. I glanced in the hall mirror at my pajama-clad self, hair rumpled, face unwashed, and nearly jumped out of my skin when I saw Mary Ann hunting for something in the coat closet behind me.

"Aww." Jack's disappointment seeped across the line. "Lucky friend."

"How about a rain check?" I said, slightly regretting my decision.

"You bet," he said warmly, and after a bit of banter we said goodbye.

"So I take it Jack's a wet noodle?" Mary Ann emerged from the coat closet and shot me a solicitous smile. "Too bad."

"It's not that," I said, annoyed she'd been eavesdropping but not wanting to show it. "He caught me off guard, that's all."

"Don't you just hate it when they call up and ask you out at the last minute? I always say no on principle. I want to tell them: Hey, I'm not your beck and call girl."

"As you should," I agreed, edging toward my room as my stomach emitted an audible growl.

"Say!" Her pale blue eyes lit up. "Are you hungry? You want to go down to the café for an early lunch and have a good gripe about men?"

I tried not to wince. Mary Ann was lonely, and I sympathized—on Sundays especially, the rituals of home seemed very distant. But I also didn't want to go to lunch with her, or anyone. "I wish I could," I said as gently as possible, "but I'm already late to meet someone . . ."

This time the fib was not so smooth. Mary Ann flushed to the tips of her blond fringe. "All right."

"How about another time?" I suggested in a soft little half whisper.

"Sure." She shrugged and disappeared into the *salon*.

I bit my bottom lip against a pang of guilt. Clearly I'd offended her and would need to somehow smooth things over. Later tonight I'd invite her to do something. The winter season was full of enticing new theater productions, even for someone who scarcely spoke French . . . or we could go to the ballet, which demanded no foreign language skills at all. Reassured, I quickly washed and dressed, ran a brush through my hair, patted my nose with a perfunctory dusting of powder, and slipped out the front door.

Many years later, after I had been married and widowed and forced to become someone else entirely, I learned that Mary Ann had described me to a biographer as "secretive and aloof"—and when I heard it, I immediately thought of that day. "Jackie kept herself apart from most of us," the book quoted her as saying. "We may have been roommates, but that year in Paris she led a privileged and distant life."

The criticism was unfair, but it stung because it held an edge of truth. Yes, I was privileged, but it was a fragile privilege, dependent on the conditions set by Mummy and Hughdie, who had made it clear his stepchildren would inherit no more than his good will. Yes, I protected my solitude, but it was a form of self-protection, born of self-awareness and past sorrow. And, yes, there were times when I probably went too far—including with Mary Ann, I acknowledged—but I never meant to exclude, or keep myself snobbishly apart, or any of the other things they said about me. I wished I could make people understand that when I said I had plans, it was genuine: I had plans with myself.

In the jardin du Luxembourg, the day's warmth and light were like a drug and Parisians were intoxicated, stripping off overcoats and lifting their faces to the sky. I ate a sandwich and then opened my book, the cigarette between my fingers floating a lazy curl of smoke over my head. Around me people sat in groups of two or three, chatting or reading, waving away the pigeons with a half-hearted flap. The park resembled a *grand salon*, a great outdoor drawing room with metal garden chairs as rigid and formal as Baroque furniture, and plantings as precisely designed as rare tapestries. Like many spaces of elite Parisians, it was devised more for beauty than comfort.

Too soon the sun began to fade, leaving behind a familiar chill—a reminder from Dame Nature that it was still winter, and the day's warmth had been a gift. Leaving the park, I walked south along the rue d'Assas in search of number 100bis, which turned out to be a narrow sliver of a passage leading to a garden court-yard. A house stood nestled at the back, a charming little structure with wide casement windows, a sloping roof, and whitewashed walls half covered in vines. This was the atelier of Ossip Zadkine, the Russian-born French sculptor who held an open house every Sunday afternoon. Martha had attended one a few weeks ago and proclaimed it one of the most eccentric experiences of her life.

Inside, the studio was spacious and bright, wooden stands and tables displaying tall, blocky sculptures in various stages of completion. Great hunks of raw wood and stone were scattered around the room, fragments of ebony and marble crunched underfoot, and rough sketches hung pinned from the scuffed walls. A few visitors milled about the studio, sipping wine the color of pale straw, speaking in hushed voices, and inspecting the œuvres, which were massive in size and heavily abstract.

Zadkine himself sat perched upon a stool in the corner. I recognized his white floppy hair and puckish features from a *Vogue* article I'd read last year. He was surrounded by a throng of friends and acolytes, identifiable by their paint-spattered clothes and deferential laughter, the jealous manner with which they closed their circle tight against curious onlookers like me. I hovered on the edge of the group, and as I listened to Zadkine present his work, holding forth on form and shape, and whether convex and concave lines and parallel planes could achieve a sort of visual rhythm, a thrill shot through me. I had dreamed of a moment just like this one, ensconced in the French avant-garde, surrounded by abstract ideas. "Out of chaos can come a multidimensional unity," Zadkine said with a wave of his hands, and I pulled out a scrap of paper to scribble down his words so I could puzzle over them later. My pencil scratched in the silence, and it took a moment before I noticed that everyone had turned to look at me.

"*Bonjour, mademoiselle,*" Zadkine called with a lopsided smile. "I don't believe I've had the pleasure."

Flushing under their collective gaze, I gave an awkward little wave. "*Bonjour,*" I murmured, hoping I could hide behind brevity.

"You are an artist, perhaps?"

"Me? No, only a student."

"Now, now, Zad. She's a little young for you, hey?" A ruddy-faced man gave a sloppy chortle that made me suspect he'd drunk more than his share of the wine on offer.

Zadkine ignored him. "Do I hear an accent? Where are you from?"

"New York."

"Ah, New York City." His expression grew doleful. "I was there during the war—rented a little hovel in Greenwich Village, tried to sculpt. The news from

France was so bad, my heart just wasn't in it. As soon as I could, I came back to Paris."

"Of course you did!" cried the drunken man. "Americans are so vulgar it's shocking." He turned to me, leering. "Tell me, mademoiselle: What's it like to come from a country that has no real culture of its own?"

"I don't think that's true," I protested feebly.

"No art, no literature, no music . . ."

"What about jazz?"

"Oh, sure, *le jazz*—if you consider that music." He guffawed, and the rest of the group joined in—all except Zadkine, who smiled thinly but remained silent.

I drew a breath, conscious that I was being teased in that typical French manner meant to provoke and incite debate. I suspected old Monsieur Blotto over there didn't give two shakes about American culture, but he enjoyed seeing me flustered. I ducked my head, prepared to defer and diffuse the situation, as I'd been trained to do my whole life. "I'm sure you know far more about music than I do, monsieur," I murmured, blinking slowly in a manner that was meant to encourage his ego to swell. Such flattery had always worked with men in the past—but to my surprise, instead of an indulgent smile, he snorted.

"Vapid as chewing gum and Coca-Cola," he muttered, turning his back to me. It was the gesture of dismissal that nettled me more than the words.

"You know," I called before the group had closed their circle, "my country may not date back to ancient Gaul, but we most certainly do have a culture of our own. Artists like Winslow Homer are every bit as original as French realists like Rousseau or Millet. As for literature, what about Mark Twain? Edith Wharton? Their novels are as insightful as anything by Balzac or Flaubert. Perhaps, monsieur"—I raised an eyebrow—"you think we Americans have no culture because you yourself have no knowledge of it." I smiled at him sweetly.

The group snickered, and I knew I'd landed a blow. But before I could savor my triumph, old Monsieur Blotto clapped his hands in mock applause.

"*Bravo, mademoiselle!*" he cried. "How refreshing it is to meet a young foreigner who knows something about history and the arts! No one would even guess you were American—if not for that smile." He flashed a simpering look that left me speechless.

My face was aflame as the group dispersed to refill their glasses. For months I had been forming my perceptions of the French—but never had I stopped to consider how the French perceived Americans. Now I knew they thought us uncultured and boorish, sugary and insipid, arrogant victors dominating Europe with our fat wallets and phony smiles. It was a cutting opinion with a kernel of truth, as the best criticism always was. Lighting a cigarette, I tried to regain my composure, but smoking didn't bring its usual calm.

I had come to France to discover the place that had existed for so long in my imagination—and in many ways, I had. But I hadn't understood there were other lessons to be learned so far from home: that overseas I was not only a visitor but a guest; not only a student but an envoy; not only an observer but also the observed. I had come to France to avoid my future—the hunt for the elusive "brilliant match" that Mummy spoke of with increasingly pointed frustration—if only for a while. And yet here was my future confronting me with all the possibilities I hadn't known to dream of back home. I had finally discovered a world of art and passion, and it stirred my soul far more than anything I had ever experienced in a Park Avenue drawing room. I dreaded the thought of losing it. But I knew I could never completely belong in France either. Who did I want to be? I didn't know, but I suspected that if I didn't figure it out soon, the world would decide for me.

Glancing outside, I saw that full darkness had descended, turning the windowpanes into mirrors that reflected the room behind me. A steady trickle of people continued to enter and leave the studio—friends, students, and admirers of Zadkine—and I had the feeling that the gathering would go on for hours, growing no larger or smaller but constantly depleted and refreshed by new arrivals. With a frown, I extinguished my cigarette in a nearby ashtray and buttoned up my coat. It was past seven o'clock and I'd need to hurry to be home in time for dinner.

"Leaving already, mademoiselle?" Zadkine materialized before me, stepping out of a door that blended so perfectly with the wall I hadn't noticed it.

"I'm afraid so," I said, pasting on my best debutante's smile. "Thank you for a lovely afternoon."

He ran a rough hand through his tousle of silver hair. "You did not find us too difficult, I hope? Fabrice, for example—he likes to tease *les américains* but sometimes it comes off as a bit . . . critical."

Critical? More like hostile. But no, I assured Zadkine that old Monsieur Blotto had been interesting, even enlightening. *"Au revoir, monsieur."* I spoke in my clearest tones, holding out my hand. "It has been a most memorable occasion."

To my surprise, instead of grasping my fingers, Zadkine bent suddenly to the floor. When he stood again, he was holding an ebony chip from one of his works in progress, which he pressed into my hand. "For *la petite américaine*, a souvenir," he said, his rubbery features falling into unfamiliar serious lines. He must have noted my expression, for he added: "I didn't leave France by choice, you must have guessed. I was a refugee, like many others, a dark period. But here I am." He shrugged. *"Merci, alors."*

It took me a moment to absorb his words, and before I could stammer out a response, or even say farewell, he had waved and returned to the party. For a minute I watched his silver head bobbing through the crowd, and when it slowed, surrounded by admirers, I stepped out into the night, holding the door open for a thin-faced young man who rushed inside with a stack of pamphlets clutched to his chest.

On the métro home, I sat in a corner seat, feeling a little shaky. It had been a shock to be pigeonholed, criticized, and dismissed for something beyond my control—my nationality—and my cheeks still burned with the unfairness of it. Despite the anti-American protests I'd witnessed in Paris—despite the bright yellow posters I'd seen plastering the walls near school, with their shrill denunciations of American imperialists—*"LAISSEZ NOUS TRANQUILLE!"* (Leave us alone!), *"LA FRANCE NE SERA PAS UN PAYS COLONISÉ!"* (France will not be colonized!)—I had never for a moment suspected any of it was directed at *me*. Now I felt it, as swift and sharp as a kick to the shin, and it didn't matter if I deserved it or not because here, overseas, I represented more than just myself.

It all made me feel more alone and lost than I'd imagined possible in a place I loved so much. I shoved my bare hands into my coat pockets, pausing as something cold and sharp grazed my knuckles. Drawing it out, I found the shard of ebony that Zadkine had given me, gleaming dully in the overhead lights of the train. Later, I would wrap it in a handkerchief and place it in the top drawer of my bureau. For now, my fingers closed around it, a memory to keep.

Chapter Ten

Jack lived in a distinguished-looking building on the boulevard Saint-Germain that, like almost every other in Paris, had a pale stone façade stained with soot and neglect. But the mansard roof glowed shiny in the rain, and the warm light spilling through the apartment windows allowed glimpses of high ceilings and antique mirrors hanging above marble mantelpieces. The heavy front door opened with a click and I passed through to the lobby, where a graceful staircase curved to the floors above, edged by a wrought-iron railing of loops and curls. Beside the stairs stood an elevator, its cage doors bearing a neatly written sign that read HORS SERVICE.

Aside from the broken lift, it was all quite a bit grander than I'd expected, especially for a young writer of limited means. Perhaps Jack was more accomplished than he'd let on—or his father more generous. I climbed the stairs, my fingers gripping the polished banister, heading toward the buzz of voices that grew louder as I neared the second floor.

The apartment door was ajar. I stepped inside and was immediately swallowed by the party: the smell of cigarettes and scent, the damp heat of people pressed together on a winter night, the uneven notes of a jazz record bobbing above the hum of conversation. I found my way down a hall lined with doors, all closed, to a bedroom lit by a soft lamp. On the bed tilted a towering pile of garments, and I deposited my fur on top, hoping and failing to recognize any of the other coats. Claude and Bernard were supposed to be here, and Martha too—not to mention our host.

Back in the living room, I felt around in my pocketbook for my cigarette case, taking my time lighting a smoke. A young man stood by the fireplace, and I approached him just to have someone to talk to.

"*Bonsoir,*" I said. With his dark looks, he reminded me of Daddy, except for his stature, which was short and stout, like a bulldog. "I'm Jacqueline." I offered him my hand, which he pressed with a soft grip.

"Charlie." He grinned at me. "You are one of Jacques's American friends?"

"Jacques? Oh, you mean *Jack*. What gave it away?"

"The handshake, instead of *les bises*, of course."

I flushed, for I sometimes still confused when to clasp hands or kiss cheeks.

"Never mind," he said gallantly. "I find it very charming."

"And you? How do you know Jack—I mean, Jacques?"

"We met at the shop."

"What shop?"

"The bookshop—Le Compagnon de voyage," he added, at my look of confusion. "On the place Monge. Do you know it?"

"I'm afraid I don't." But I frowned at the glowing tip of my cigarette, for it did sound familiar.

"At first I was surprised, because obviously I didn't expect to see an American there. But we started talking after one of our democratic youth meetings, and he had some interesting things to say about the manifesto."

"What manifesto?

Charlie chuckled like I'd made a joke. "*The Communist Manifesto*, of course."

Perhaps I looked more shocked than I thought, because his smile started to slip. "Have you read it?"

"Er, no, I haven't." I raised my cigarette to my lips. Of course: Le Compagnon de voyage was the communist bookshop Jack had said he sometimes visited for research. "I'd love to hear more about these meetings," I said, wondering where Charlie fell on the leftist political spectrum.

Before he could respond, I felt a hand upon my shoulder, and there were Claude and Bernard greeting me and then, to my surprise, turning to embrace Charlie with gigantic grins. "You know him?" I said to Claude as the boys went off in search of drinks.

"Charlie? Sure. Nice guy. He let me borrow his lecture notes when I caught bronchitis last year."

"Watch out," I murmured. "I think he's one of them."

"One of what?"

"You know." I lifted my brows. "A red."

"Oh, yes, that's no secret. Charlie heads up one of the communist student groups at school." She looked amused. "You sound like Ghislaine."

"Is that so bad?"

"Listen, don't pay any attention to her. Communism's not taboo here like it is in the States. For most French people, it's just another political opinion. We have communist ministers in the government, don't forget."

"But how can you be friends with someone whose beliefs are so opposed to your own? Don't you argue?"

"Of course we do. Vehemently." She shrugged. "But we are French. We disagree, but we also celebrate our political differences."

I inhaled the last vestige of my cigarette and crushed it in the ashtray. "You know, back home, if someone even *suggests* you're a communist, you get shunned. You can lose your friends, your job . . ."

"Oh, sure, in America everything's black and white—even when it comes to the reds. But things are different here in France, you'll see. They're not all raving fanatics. Some of them are quite charming."

"Are my ears burning?" Jack appeared with two glasses of wine and handed one to each of us. "I was sent to deliver these."

My pulse began fluttering at the sight of him, but I greeted him with a chaste kiss on each cheek.

"We were just talking about some of Sciences Po's student groups," Claude said.

"I met Charlie," I added.

Jack beamed. "Isn't he a great kid? Did he tell you his parents named him after Karl Marx?"

"No, but he told me he met you at a *Communist Manifesto* book club."

He gave an easy shrug. "Part of my book research."

"One day you're going to have to let me read this novel of yours," I said, half joking.

"Gosh, would you?" he said eagerly. "I'd love your thoughts but haven't dared impose on your time."

I darted a glance his way but found no guile there. "I'd be honored," I said, flattered to see an uncharacteristic flush creeping across his cheeks.

"I'll give you some chapters later. Don't leave without them, okay?" He touched my arm, and a spark shot through me.

By this point the apartment had gotten so crowded we were nearly standing on top of each other. Jack seemed to have invited everyone he knew in Paris, from the waiter at the café downstairs to his writers' group—a trio of Yalies who looked like they bled blue—to his sister-in-law's cousin, who was a Norwegian soprano engaged by the Opéra de Paris. I saw Jimmy across the room, looking dapper in a white shirt and string tie, his brow creased with that deep intelligent furrow, and Martha chatting with a wild-haired bearded fellow everyone called Doc who said he was starting a magazine for expats. Susan, who had come with Martha, thanked Jack for the invitation and exclaimed that she knew she must have met him somewhere, he looked so familiar. Claude, Bernard, and Charlie were spiritedly debating which landmark café served the worst food: the Flore, the Deux Magots, or the Brasserie Lipp. I'd never been at a party like this, with so many disparate people flung together—it could have been a disaster but for Jack's moving effortlessly between languages and conversations, pouring drinks and making introductions. The room crackled with his presence so that even as I chattered gaily I found it difficult to keep myself from staring at him.

It wasn't like me to moon over a man, especially someone as unsuitable as Jack. For as much as I liked him, I knew Mummy and Daddy would disapprove—even though he'd gone to the right schools, even though his father had won the Pulitzer Prize, he was still an impoverished writer with poor prospects. Which was pure snobbery, I thought, glancing around the spacious *salon*, taking in the heavy oak furniture and richly patterned carpets. Jack clearly managed to live perfectly well. Of course, as Mummy would no doubt point out, here in Paris the dollar was strong.

Twisting toward the ashtray, I snuck another glance. He was standing in the doorway to the kitchen chatting with his downstairs neighbor, a *dame d'un certain âge* wearing an enviable velvet pantsuit. As he ran a hand through his hair, I wondered what would happen if I crossed the apartment with swift steps, threw my arms around his neck, and kissed him. He must have sensed my thoughts, for in that instant he turned and his eyes caught mine.

Suddenly it all seemed so trivial—Mummy's expectations, Daddy's possessiveness, Lee's rivalry, the pressure on me to make a brilliant match. I didn't want to think of any of that, or any of them, not tonight, not at this party. I could flirt with a waiter if I chose, or dance with a communist, or make eyes across the room at a handsome man of limited means. There was no one to accuse me of being selfish, or hiss at me about my future. Maybe in Paris the future didn't even exist.

If anyone asked, I could say I'd drunk too much wine. But I was perfectly clearheaded as I walked toward Jack, made my excuses to his neighbor, and caught his fingers between mine. I had never felt more lucid than when I pulled him out of the apartment into the cool calm of the landing. Finally I could smell the smoky pine scent of him, absorb his heat. Finally we were kissing, his lips moving along my cheek to my ear as he whispered, "I've been wanting to do this all night."

I pressed my face against his chest and felt his heart beating madly. "Are you nervous, Mr. Marquand?" I reached up and touched his hair, which was just as soft as I'd anticipated.

"Only that you'll disappear." In the murky light, he looked suddenly young and vulnerable.

"I'm here," I promised, stretching up on tiptoe to kiss him again and again.

The day after the party I carried Jack's book around the apartment looking for a quiet spot to read. But every time I settled into a chair, something began to distract me. First it was the ringing telephone, then the itchy scratch of my wool stockings. My ears were cold, my neck was hot, Mary Ann was asking if she could borrow my fountain pen, Madame was calling us for lunch. When, finally, I curled up on the sofa—only to open the manuscript box upside down, upending the pages in a disorderly heap—I had to wonder if I was subconsciously avoiding the novel. For better or worse, what I read there would alter my opinion of its author.

"*Partisans in Love*, by John Phillips," Ghislaine said, stooping to retrieve the title page from the floor and handing it to me. "Who's that?"

"Hm? Oh, just a friend," I said, examining the sheet of paper. Jack had told me he'd used a pen name in an attempt to distinguish himself from his famous father.

"Sounds intriguing." She finished stacking the pages, placing them neatly in my lap. "Let me know what you think."

Jack's novel was about a Bolshevik named Vlad who

finds himself exiled in the "foul hole" of Belle Epoque Paris. When he meets Inès, a beautiful French communist, his passion for the cause is reignited, but the conflict between his mistress and wife portends heartbreak. Jack had given me about half the book, and when I finished the chapters, I sat still and quiet for a long time. The story needed polishing but the voice was strong and insistent, a disillusioned man striving to reconcile emotion, duty, and political ideals. On the last page, he had scribbled a note: "Based on the true story of Vladimir Lenin and Inès Armand who met in Paris in 1909 and corresponded until her death in 1920." My breath caught in my throat: Jack had succeeded in humanizing Lenin.

I began arranging the manuscript pages back into their cardboard box. Across from me, Claude looked up from the letter she was writing. "That was quick," she said. "How was it?"

I reached for a cigarette and took my time lighting it. "It was . . . surprising." I turned my head and exhaled a ribbon of smoke. I couldn't explain it, but I felt shy about sharing my opinion with her.

"Does he write well?"

I pressed my lips together. "He does." In fact, I found myself slightly dazzled and unnerved by his skill. If he had been less of a writer, it would have dampened his attraction, offering an excuse a part of me still hoped to find.

She looked at me steadily. "You like him."

I shrugged. "Sure, but what does it matter? He's not someone I'd bring home to Mummy or Daddy."

"*Alors?* They are not in Paris."

"Yes, but they have certain expectations about the type of man I should marry. Doesn't your mother feel the same way?"

"Maman?" Claude's eyebrows rose. "No, she doesn't care about any of that anymore. She survived the worst and now she feels she can live however she wants."

I sighed. "Unfortunately my mother still cares very deeply about all of it. Especially whom I marry."

"Who said anything about marriage?"

I fumbled with my cigarette. When I looked up again, Claude had a coquettish glint in her eye. "Do I shock you? I remember from my time in Massachusetts that you Americans have a different view of these things. You are more . . ."

"Puritanical?"

"Conservative, perhaps." She shrugged. "It is another point of view, that is all."

"You and Bernard—have you—" I stopped short, blushing deeply.

"He's lovely, isn't he?" She breathed a dreamy sigh.

"Does your mother know?"

"I'm not sure. Possibly. But like I said, she no longer cares what people think. She only wants us to be happy."

I balanced my cigarette along the edge of the ashtray and watched the smoke snake through the air. Madame was a deeply private person, but if I thought about it carefully, there were hints that what Claude was saying was true. The clothes she wore, for example: not the respectable fusty black of widow's weeds but elegant dresses in bright, clear colors. The hours she spent volunteering at the ADIR rather than hobnobbing with society ladies. Even the home she kept, with never a word of censure about her older daughter's divorce or the fatherless grandson in her care. Madame was wise enough to remain discreet, but she lived on her own terms.

Over the next few days and weeks I found my thoughts turning again and again to the conversation I'd had with Claude. I wasn't shocked that she and Bernard had been intimate, but I was surprised she'd talked about it so openly. That kind of behavior could get a girl kicked out of college in the States, and I was more familiar with the whispers and giggles of the Vassar dorms, girls hinting at the topic with arch innuendo, their curiosity only barely outstripping their embarrassment. Claude made it clear that here in France such taboos were viewed as silly and affected.

It all made me feel a little shy around Jack, and I hoped he couldn't guess the thoughts running through my head. We saw a lot of each other that winter, sharing our favorite parts of Paris. Walking across the Champ de Mars sheltered beneath a single umbrella. Celebrating Martha's birthday at a nightclub on the Champs-Élysées; drinking bottle after bottle of champagne that Jack snuck away to pay for though he swore it wasn't him but some mysterious benefactor. Saturday nights at the Rose Rouge, pressed together on the dance floor, not caring about the sweat filming my clothes, and hands, and face. Sunday afternoons at the café, drinking *chocolat chaud*, leafing through a stack of newspapers, and talking about his novel.

"You're certain I'm not boring you?" he asked one day, after I'd helped him iron out a particularly tricky plot point. "Your edits are as sharp as anything I ever got at Harvard."

"Not at all," I assured him, his praise glowing within me. I loved thinking about writing this way, refining, trimming, and tightening the story in the right direction, his words challenging me to consider a different perspective.

When we weren't together, I saved newspaper articles for him, clipping the quirky human interest stories that I knew his writer's sensibility would savor. When we weren't together, I caught myself wondering what would happen if I allowed things to go further, if I suggested we meet at his apartment one afternoon after class; if I tugged the starched shirt from his trousers and ran my hands along the smooth skin of his back as his fingers pulled at the zipper of my dress. Sometimes, alone in my room, I found myself blushing wildly. I'd never before entertained such thoughts, not about anyone.

Of course I would never act upon my impulses. I'd seen what happened to girls who got caught out and, anyway, it wasn't in my nature to lose control. But after that conversation with Claude I began to notice just how often couples met after class and disappeared, or slipped away at parties, and I realized that the behavior I'd considered risqué and illicit was, here in France, something natural and accepted, a pleasure of life that wasn't talked about in whispers. There was even a slang term—*le cinq à sept*—that referred to the early evening period, from five to seven o'clock, when such trysts occurred. As a daughter of Black Jack Bouvier, I'd grown up worldly enough to know some women were freer with their bodies than I'd been taught to believe was moral—but now I began to question the idea of morality itself. If a young couple loved each other, why should they have to wait for marriage?

All these questions preoccupied me more than I would have admitted. But my musings were largely philosophical, for I wasn't in love with Jack—and the reason I knew was because I refused to allow it to happen. Martha liked to tease me about it—"For someone who says she doesn't care a fig, you sure spend an awful lot of time with him," she twinkled—but I assured her our relationship wasn't serious.

"He knows as well as I do that the romance is more about being in Paris than with each other," I said. This didn't quite explain why I enjoyed chatting with him more than anyone—or the expression I sometimes caught on his face when he thought I wasn't looking, half longing, half wonder—but I brushed those details aside. Sometimes Jack mentioned the future—"One day I'll take you to this marvelous little restaurant in the south of France where all the artists used to pay with their paintings before they were ever famous. Just imagine, Picassos plastering the walls like movie posters!"—and I'd give an inconsequential little murmur and make sure to avoid his calls for a few days.

One Saturday evening in late February, Jack came to avenue Mozart to pick me up for a date. I was feeling a trifle blue, for I had seen tight clusters of forsythia buds while walking in the park that afternoon and noticed the days were growing subtly longer and brighter. It was almost spring: I had only a few months left in Paris, then some weeks of summer travel, before I'd sail back to New York, my grand adventure finished. I was brooding when the doorbell rang—and not ready in the least, my hair in curlers and nail varnish still sticky. But that was the natural order of our dates: Jack always punctual, waiting patiently for my entrance.

Tonight, however, Jack had procured tickets for the Opéra Garnier, and I knew I couldn't dawdle too outrageously. Claude and Mary Ann were at the cinema and Madame was giving Christian a bath while Ghislaine nursed a bad toothache in bed. So it was Susan who opened the door and invited Jack to wait in the *salon*, where she and Martha were knitting socks for Polish refugee children. Hearing his voice, I sprang to action, flapping my hands to dry my nails and wincing as one of them smudged. My stockings laddered, first one, then another, I discovered a cigarette burn on the right thumb of my second-best pair of gloves, then spent ages searching my room for Jack's manuscript, which I had finished annotating the night before and wanted to return to him. Sounds of laughter drifted from the *salon* as I hastily powdered my nose and stepped into an unpressed frock, hoping the wrinkles didn't show. By the time I was ready, I was decidedly out of sorts.

They were chatting so gaily they didn't hear my step, and for a moment I felt grateful to the girls for entertaining Jack so handily. In the *salon*, shaded table lamps cast a soft glow, and a small fire crackled in the hearth. Martha sat on a low stool beside the mantelpiece, frowning over the tangled knitting in her hands. Jack was on the davenport, leaning forward with an earnest expression that I knew so well it made my heart swell. I hovered in the doorway, waiting for him to look up and beam at me as he had a hundred times before.

Finally, he did smile. But not at me. No, all of Jack's attention was focused on Susan, who sat across from him, perched on the edge of an armchair, her blond curls gleaming in the firelight like a Botticelli angel. She was telling a story, eyebrows arching and furrowing with comedic exaggeration, throwing out her slender hands as she reached the punch line. Just as I came into the room, the three of them burst into laughter, their mirth fading when they saw me.

"Jacqueline!" Jack leaped to greet me, kissing me on both cheeks. "Gosh, don't you look lovely."

"Sorry about the wait," I said softly. "Though it

looks like the girls have been keeping you busy." I threw a sideways glance at Susan.

"Sue was just telling us about the time she and her brother brought home a baby squirrel from Central Park," Martha said, looking up from her knitting.

Susan sat up straight so that a ball of yarn rolled from her lap. "We tried to feed it with a fountain pen and, well . . . I guess if you don't know Bobby it's not that funny . . ."

"Bob and I rowed crew together at school," Jack added.

"And here I am, their most loyal supporter—the girl who attended every single meet—and this one didn't even recognize me." She jerked her head in Jack's direction.

"That was before I heard you cheer! I would've known that great galumphing voice of yours anywhere." He shot her a teasing grin.

"*ALLEZ* CRIMSON!" Susan shouted, throwing her arms into the air. Jack let out a laugh that reverberated around the room.

"Should we go, Jack?" I half whispered into the silence that followed. "I wouldn't want to miss the curtain."

"Hm? Oh, yes, certainly, if you like." He slid his hat on his head as I went into the hall to fetch my coat.

"Did you leave this for me?" he called. In the mirror, I saw him pick up a familiar battered manuscript box from a side table.

I frowned, for I didn't remember leaving it in the *salon*. Marie the *bonne* must have moved it when she was cleaning. "I finished going through it last night," I said, but no one heard me. In the reflection, I saw Jack asking Susan something, and then I saw her scribbling on a scrap of paper. She handed it to him and he slipped it in his coat pocket. ". . . would love to hear from you anytime," I barely caught her words before the blood rushed to my face, its heat catching me by surprise.

Martha appeared at my shoulder. "You all right?" she said quietly, taking my evening bag so I could adjust my hat.

"Fine." I pulled my gloves on with a jerk.

She looked at me with a shrewd expression. "Are you still sure you don't care a fig?"

Before I could respond, Jack was in the hall, holding the front door open. Madame and Christian came out of the bathroom to wave goodnight, and Susan wished us a lovely time. And there was Martha grinning and grinning as the door shut behind us.

"You're awfully quiet tonight." Jack twisted in his seat to look at me. "Everything all right?"

"I'm just a little tired." I raised my eyes to the swirling Classical frescoes adorning the domed ceiling of the Opéra Garnier.

"If you get too sleepy, you can put your head right here and take a nap." He patted his shoulder. "No one will mind."

"I'm not sure the performers would agree," I said dryly, but nevertheless I tucked my hand into his arm and gave it a squeeze. The lights dimmed and into the darkness came the sound of three blows upon the stage, and then the orchestra surging into the romantic strains of *La Traviata*.

I had already been to the Palais Garnier twice this season, once to see *Madama Butterfly*, the other for the ballet *Le Corsaire*, both times sitting high in the fifth loge and peering through my opera glasses at the tiny figures on the stage below. Tonight our seats were so close I could see the flounces and ruffles of the performers' costumes, absorb their expressions, feel the vibration of their voices. It was a magnificent production, and I should have been captivated—except I couldn't stop thinking about the interaction I'd just witnessed between Susan and Jack.

It wasn't that they were flirting. They hadn't been— not technically—and even if they were, a bit of banter wouldn't have bothered me. No, I'd sensed something else, a familiarity even though they scarcely knew each other, a kinship of the sort that took me months to develop, a crackle between them quick and instinctive. Onstage, Violetta sang of possible love and misfortune, and I folded my arms across my chest, pressing hard against a hot discomfort. When the curtain fell at intermission, I felt snappish and irritable, even more so because I knew it would be unladylike to show it.

As the house lights rose, Jack turned to me. "Champagne?"

"Gosh, yes, that sounds wonderful," I cooed, shooting him a dazzling smile. He looked at me a little strangely but placed his hand on my elbow to guide me into the aisle.

There was a crush at the bar, but at a nod from Jack two coupes magically appeared. "*Santé, Monsieur Jacques,*" said the barman with a wink.

"You *know* him?" In my incredulity, I briefly forgot my pique.

Jack touched his glass to mine before squinting in the man's direction. "He does look familiar. We might have chatted at the bookshop sometime."

"Or perhaps he was at a Harvard crew meet," I said before I could stop myself.

He laughed. "Now that was a heck of a coincidence, wasn't it? I had no idea Bob Coward's kid sister was in

Paris. You must be glad to have Sue as your roommate. She seems like a great girl."

I took a large sip of champagne. "What is that supposed to mean?"

"Nothing! I thought she was a hoot, that's all."

"Sure, but you haven't seen the way she hangs her wet laundry on the radiators. They're stone cold half the time, but there are Susan's blouses dripping all over the living-room floor."

He grinned. "That does sound rather . . . damp. I'll keep that in mind the next time I remove my shoes in the Comtesse de Renty's *salon*." Something about his dry amusement made me so cross I was tempted to kick him.

"Don't say I didn't warn you," I snapped.

He drew back in surprise. "Are you sore with me?"

"Should I be?"

"I don't think so," he said slowly.

"So you think it's perfectly acceptable to flirt with one of my roommates—and even ask for her address?"

"Ask for her address?" he repeated, bewildered. "I didn't—"

"I saw her write it down and give it to you."

He looked down at me, frowning, and then suddenly his face cleared. "That was her brother's address! I asked Sue where I could write to Bob. See for yourself." He fished the scrap of paper from his pocket and showed it to me. It read ROBERT COWARD, followed by a Midtown address in Susan's scrawl.

My heart had been thumping, but now it started racing. "Gosh, I guess I just assumed . . ." I bit my lip, blushing furiously. Jack was looking at me with an expression of such delight and astonishment that I realized I'd revealed more than I'd intended—more, in fact, than I'd admitted to myself.

"Jacqueline." He reached down and caught my hand in his. "Surely you must have guessed by now, I—" He swallowed hard. "I'm not interested in flirting with any other girls. It's *you* I care about—you, and only you. I love how much you know about eccentric things, like Napoleon's favorite horses and dogs, or the official royal mistresses of the kings of France. I love the way you choose your words so precisely. I love the way you can link just about any current political scandal to the court of Versailles. I love the ruthless way you edit a manuscript, slicing away all the pretension and posturing until there's just the clean curve of a story. I love your sly sense of humor, and how you speak French with just the whisper of an accent. I love the way you keep people at arm's length because you're shy; but once someone has won your trust, you have the truest, most loyal heart I've ever known. I even love that when

I ran into you in Munich you told me you only had time for a sandwich."

I laughed, partly because I was embarrassed he had seen through my ruse in Germany, but also because I was confused to find myself in this moment. All my life I'd been taught that men were prey to be captured with flattery and pretty smiles: "For goodness' sake, don't let on that you have a brain," Mummy so often declared. "It intimidates them, darling." But Jack was different. I wasn't sure if it was because I hadn't considered him a serious suitor, or because I was so far from home, or because I had absorbed some French lesson about a woman's wit elevating her beauty, but with him I hadn't felt the need to compromise any part of myself.

I could feel Jack's eyes upon me, but I couldn't turn my head to look at him. The truth was, I had shied from a moment like this, believing I couldn't reciprocate his feelings. But I could never have guessed that all this time he had seen me so clearly, that he had understood my truest and most private self—or that this recognition would make me feel so shaky, like some part of me was dissolving. Without thinking, I leaned over and kissed him, tentatively at first and then more deeply, until I was conscious only of his lips and hands, my trembling limbs.

"We should go," Jack said into my ear, sending a wild chill down my spine.

For a second, I didn't know what he meant, and I was prepared to follow him anywhere. But then I became aware of the blinking lobby lights, signaling us to retake our seats, the ushers shooing everyone back inside the theater. We followed the other stragglers down the aisle and sat as the house lights began dimming, the audience settling with a last restless cough.

Jack reached for my hand and linked our fingers together. "I love you," he murmured. At that moment, the orchestra struck up again so that I was unable to reply. But I felt it.

Chapter Eleven

The Musée Nissim de Camondo was overlooked by most tourists. It didn't have the iconic paintings and sculptures of the Louvre, or the Impressionists of the Orangerie, or the decayed splendor of the Rodin Museum. But as I followed Madame through an enfilade of rooms, each one more beautifully appointed than the last, I understood why she had called it the most exquisite museum in Paris.

It was a Wednesday afternoon in late February, and as on most Wednesday afternoons, Madame and I were out together. She had taken to planning little weekly cultural excursions, sharing with me the antique ceramics, furniture, and textiles that she adored. At first Mary Ann and Susan had come too, but they soon discovered they had limited enthusiasm for Aubusson carpets or Rococo ornamentation. "It's all so fussy, it makes me want to sneeze," Susan explained. Mary Ann was keener, but she preferred a lightning tour that whirled from Gothic altarpieces to Neo-Renaissance clocks in an hour, rather than a minute examination of a single era. And so Madame and I were left to our own particular pace.

Madame told me that her passion for the decorative arts had been born of childhood visits to bourgeois relatives and burnished by a lifetime of poking around museums and flea markets. Being with her was like a seminar in the history of French design, and I loved listening to her musical voice as she described the characteristics of a particular master craftsman, pointed out the parquetry designs fashioned from varied wood grains, or shared the principles of ideal beauty, *le beau idéal*, that dictated the Empire style. I could never have suspected how her lessons would endure, how I would rely on them when called to restore the White House, how they would influence me to devote time and study to creating a museum that celebrated the American decorative arts, one comparable to the stately homes I saw in Europe, accessible to all.

Our outings usually brought us to the Musée des arts décoratifs adjacent to the Louvre. But today we had come to the Musée Nissim de Camondo, an imposing double-winged *hôtel particulier* on the parc Monceau. I had been in fine homes before, of course, dozens of them. I had waltzed in re-created Renaissance ballrooms, lunched beneath Rembrandts, slept in the ornate beds of deposed Italian royalty. Unlike those houses, however, this one was decorated with a collector's meticulous eye. As Madame explained, almost every item originated from the France of the second half of the eighteenth century.

"Isn't it extraordinary?" She spoke into the rarefied silence of the salon des Huet, an oval room designed to display seven Rococo panels of the artist Jean-Baptiste Huet. "The furniture, and paintings, and sculptures, and objets d'art . . . all of it from the same period. The Comte de Camondo once told me that his goal was to create a museum honoring the Age of Enlightenment, the epitome of Neo-Classical beauty, and a modern home—with central heating."

"You knew him?"

"I knew his daughter, Béatrice. She used to have the most marvelous parties when we were little girls— fantastical ice sculptures, pony rides in the garden, simply magical. And then as a teenager I had a devastating crush on her brother, Nissim. We all did, he was so dashing."

"Neither of them lived here after the Comte passed?"

Madame had bent to examine a silvered console table, and at first I thought she hadn't heard me. "No," she said eventually, straightening. "Nissim died in the Great War, like so many young men of my generation. He was barely in his twenties. It was a terrible tragedy for the entire family, but the Comte especially took it very hard. Afterward, he buried himself in his collection, scarcely seeing a soul, hardly ever going out. And when he died, he left this house and all its contents to France. A museum dedicated to the memory of his son."

"And Béatrice?"

"She died as well, I'm afraid. Along with her husband and their two children—they were killed at Auschwitz. The family no longer exists."

All the air left my chest. "None of them?" I managed to say.

Madame turned toward a carved gilt screen. "Béatrice insisted France would never arrest her, a Frenchwoman from one of the great French families. Not after everything her father had done for the country. Not after her brother had died for the République. But in the end, the Milice cared only that she was Jewish. When Robert and I first heard they had been deported we were devastated. It was an alarm bell for both of us. That was when Robert decided we had to do something."

She moved toward the fireplace to regard the mantel

clock, festooned with gilded palm trees and a Chinese figurine. I waited for her to continue, but as the silence lengthened I realized she was not going to share anything more. "Come." She gestured toward the hall. "I want to show you my favorite room."

I followed her through another drawing room, as grand as the first, then a study, a second smaller study, a gallery lined with intricate tapestries, and the dining room with its paneled walls of mint green, finally ending up in a small room with glass-fronted cabinets on all sides. From the shelves, a collection of china glowed in the interior lighting.

I glanced around the dim space, which was both windowless and airless. "*This* is your favorite room?"

"You are surprised?" She tilted her head. "I suppose, yes, it lacks the grandeur of the other rooms. But though this house has many treasures, I've always believed the porcelain room to be the heart of the collection. The Comte adored it too—he used to take his meals here when he dined alone."

I looked more closely at the gilt-edged dishes on display—plates and bowls, platters and tureens, egg cups and teacups, jam pots and coffee pots and chocolate pots, and a hundred other odd-shaped pieces that I couldn't identify—each one depicting a bird against a field of white, rimmed by a border of pale green.

"They are magnificent, no?" Madame stooped to examine a sugar bowl.

"Very pretty," I said, though, truthfully, the china appeared no different from other fine porcelain, delicate and rather fussy.

"It's called the Buffon service, named after the Comte de Buffon, the French naturalist of the late eighteenth century," Madame said. "The birds are taken from his great work, *L'Histoire naturelle des oiseaux*. Look closely—each one is different."

I peered into a cabinet. Indeed, the creatures were as accurately depicted as an Audubon engraving, each with its own peculiar set of the head, angle of talon, and backdrop of natural habitat. A bright-beaked toucan sat on an ice bucket, a tiny parrot on a shell-shaped compotier, a partridge on a punch bowl. There were large birds and tiny birds, dull-feathered birds from the French countryside and dazzling ones from the colonies, preening, pecking, and posing. The dishes filled the shelves, the shelves filled the cabinets, and the cabinets filled the room.

"It's a wonder they didn't run out of birds to paint," I said.

"Ah, but they had thousands to choose from. The Comte de Buffon's work spans several volumes. It's truly encyclopedic."

I later visited the workshop at Sèvres and learned that the Buffon service was made in 1784, the pieces hand-painted and gilded by master craftsmen who left their marks upon the backs. Only five years later, the French Revolution smashed such trappings of luxury to bits—but the Buffon service was spared, albeit scattered across Europe. Its survival, and subsequent reunion by the Comte de Camondo, was a veritable miracle.

"I suppose it's a sort of *cabinet de curiosités*, isn't it?" Madame said. "A different kind of collection, yes, but one still celebrating the natural world."

All this time I had been imagining the Comte alone in his splendid home, eating solitary meals in this room that was more like a closet, trying to subdue his grief by seeking solace in the beautiful things around him. It seemed impossibly sad. But at Madame's words, I remembered something she'd once said about her own *cabinet de curiosités*, the collection of personal treasures gathered in her dining room. What had she called it? "A museum of comfort," I repeated softly.

"Oh, my dear. You remember." She said no more, but she was pleased, I could tell.

We descended the curved staircase to the first floor. The family's personal apartments were here, dressed in antique wood paneling, Savonnerie carpets, and fine paintings celebrating the hunt; an alcove bed with three exquisitely carved headboards; a bronze equestrian statuette; tiled bathrooms with claw-footed tubs and vaulted ceilings.

The Comte de Camondo's dressing room had been turned into a family gallery with photographs covering the walls—Béatrice on horseback, Nissim and the Comte lounging in garden chairs, the Comte with his grandchildren, Béatrice and Nissim with their arms thrown round one another. They were the kind of photos everyone had in their albums, a captured moment, fleeting and forgotten. In the Camondos' absence they made my heart twist. Surely the Fates had made a terrible mistake. For how could they have spared this house full of fragile objects but murdered the family that had cherished them?

We moved into the garden, a formal space with orderly paths and tightly clipped ornamental hedges. Another museum visitor was here, a slender woman wearing a tailored gray coat, sitting on a bench smoking a cigarette. My eyes would have slid past her if Madame hadn't stiffened.

"Is that you, Marie-Madeleine?" she called across the parterre.

The woman gave no indication she'd heard, lifting the cigarette to her lips and inhaling until the tip glowed.

"*Coucou*, Marie-Mad! Over here!" Madame persisted.

With a visible sigh of displeasure, the woman stood and walked toward us, her heels crunching on the fine dirt path. "For heaven's sake, Germaine," she said when she reached us. "Didn't you learn anything from working with me?"

But Madame made no retort, merely stooping to kiss her cheeks. "I assumed you wouldn't want me calling you Hedgehog," she said with a little smile.

Marie-Madeleine rolled her eyes. She had pale, delicate features and the calm, unblinking demeanor of a cat. "You really are terrible at it, aren't you?" But there was a note of affection tempering her exasperation. She turned her gaze upon me, her blue eyes so penetrating I wanted to shield myself. "Let me guess—you're one of the American girls living with Germaine this year."

"*Oui, madame*," I faltered. "I'm Jacqueline."

"Marie-Madeleine Fourcade, *enchantée*." The name was familiar, but I couldn't place it. As she stretched to kiss my cheeks, I caught the scent of her perfume, dark and sinuous. "You are enjoying your time in Paris?"

"*Oui, madame.*" I ducked my head, aware that I was repeating myself but unable to think of anything clever to say.

"I was just showing Jacqueline the porcelain room," Madame said.

"Isn't it frightful?" Marie-Madeleine pulled a face. "All those beady little eyes."

A flicker of amusement twitched the corners of Madame's mouth. "It's considered one of the great masterpieces of the decorative arts, Marie-Mad."

She shrugged. "*A chacun son goût!*" Dropping her cigarette, she crushed it with the toe of her shoe. The butt lay on the ground, pink lipstick staining one end. Madame lifted an eyebrow, but Marie-Madeleine apparently had no scruples about littering. I stole another glance at her. She was younger than I'd first assumed, somewhere between Madame and me. They seemed so different in age, attitude, and interests, I couldn't guess how they knew each other. "And Ghislaine?" Marie-Madeleine asked. "How was her dentist's appointment?"

"What do you mean?"

"Her tooth. Wasn't it bothering her?"

"Yes, but when did you see Ghislaine? I thought you'd stopped working."

"Ah, but the work is never finished. Remember?" Marie-Madeleine smiled sweetly.

Madame opened her mouth and shut it again, looking so discomfited that I began to feel uncomfortable on her behalf. Reaching into my pocketbook, I extracted a cigarette and lit it.

Marie-Madeleine recoiled. "Excuse me, dear. Would you mind smoking that over there?" She nodded at the bench where she'd been sitting. "I'm allergic to Gitanes."

I assumed this was a joke, for the butt of her cigarette lay two inches from my shoe. She stared at me with a small, expectant smile. It took a moment to realize that she was completely serious.

"I'll just be a minute, Jacqueline," Madame said.

I made my way to the other side of the parterre and sat on the bench, the chilled stone seeping through my coat. From here, their voices faded to a murmur, so that I sensed the cadence of their conversation rather than heard it. Tapping my cigarette, I tried to recall how I knew the name Marie-Madeleine Fourcade. One of my professors? No. Claude? No. A newspaper article? No. As I stared at the ground, the wind shifted, carrying with it Marie-Madeleine's odd clipped drawl.

"Like I said before, she was helping me with something at the Ministry."

"What?" pressed Madame.

"It was nothing. Just one of Charles's little projects. As I told you, there's no need to—" The wind changed again and I lost the thread.

So Marie-Madeleine must work at the Ministry of Defense with Ghislaine. Was that who had mentioned her? No, that didn't seem right either. I frowned at the cigarette in my hand, watching specks of ash scatter from the tip. Then the wind shifted again, so that I caught Marie-Madeleine speaking in more conciliatory tones.

"I must say you're looking awfully well, Germaine. I have to congratulate you on the way you've overcome all that unpleasant business of a few years ago."

"What do you mean?"

"Only that you look so elegant—so full of vitality. No one would ever guess that you'd been at Ravens-brück."

Madame did not respond, and, risking a glance in her direction, I saw that she had drawn herself up to her full height.

"Of course, I have heard," Marie-Madeleine continued, "that things weren't *quite* as bad there as they say. I suppose people like to exaggerate."

"I assure you," Madame said glacially, "none of it is an exaggeration."

I dropped my gaze to my lap. Before I caught Marie-

Madeleine's response, the wind changed, making their conversation once again indistinguishable. I finished my cigarette, carefully snuffed it, and collected the remains in a small tin case I kept in my pocketbook for that very purpose. Eventually, crunching footsteps alerted me to Madame's approach.

"Ready?" Her expression betrayed no emotion, but her cheeks were pinker than usual.

I sprang to my feet, following her back toward the house. Marie-Madeleine was gone, but as we passed the spot where she'd been standing, Madame bent to collect her cigarette butt, pinching it between her gloved fingers before depositing it in a nearby trash bin. "So inconsiderate," she muttered.

We were halfway home on the métro when I remembered. It was Paul de Ganay who had mentioned Marie-Madeleine Fourcade and her Resistance spy ring, all those months ago at Courances. During the war, she had been the head of Alliance, which made her Madame's spymaster. And what else had Paul said? I frowned, remembering his lowered voice as he told me: "I hear Marie-Mad has started working for the government again."

Postwar penury and the high price of coal meant that we were each allotted one bath a week at avenue Mozart, a hasty, shivery event punctuated by feet pounding up and down the hallway, knocks on the bathroom door, and calls of "Are you done yet?"

Such ablutions were adequate but hardly enjoyable. As I sat in my semiotics of poetry class, shifting against the rigid back of a wooden chair, I found myself longing for the deep peace of a scalding tub. A day earlier I had gone riding with Paul de Ganay in the bois de Boulogne and, along with a good gallop, I'd been hoping to ask him more about Marie-Madeleine Fourcade. But when a stray dog spooked my horse and I got thrown—provoking an old back injury—we had cut the outing short.

Daddy had warned me against riding in France, fearful I'd redamage a disc. And now here I was, stiff and scarcely able to walk. As Professeur Lefebvre unspooled yet another meandering sentence about Voltaire's shaded symbolism, my back ached with the dull throb of regret. I would go home immediately to rest, I decided, treat it with aspirin, and sneak in an extra hot bath. At the break, I swept my notebook into my satchel and hobbled to the métro.

The apartment was still littered with the morning's flotsam—shoes jumbled by the front closet, breakfast dishes on the table. It felt slightly illicit to be here without anyone's knowledge, especially in the late afternoon, the hour of cat burglars and secret assignations. The hall clock ticked so loudly in the silent rooms, it seemed to follow me.

In the bathroom, a rare shaft of sunlight pierced the frosted window, revealing scuffs, cracks, and scrubbed linoleum worn so thin I felt a competing twinge of guilt alongside the pain. Eventually I decided that Madame would understand, and I drew the bath as deep and hot as I dared. Gritting my teeth, I maneuvered myself into the tub, holding my breath until the scorching water became bearable. I leaned back, closed my eyes, and allowed myself to drift.

The sound of voices in the apartment made me startle up with a splash. I must have fallen asleep, for the bathwater had cooled considerably, my fingertips felt as wrinkled and rubbery as fresh walnuts, and the angled sunbeam had moved past the window, leaving the room gray and dim. The voices were growing louder, moving down the hallway—it was Madame and Ghislaine, walking past the bathroom door. I held my breath as they passed, cringing as I imagined what would happen if they found me here in the tub when I was supposed to be in class—and when I had taken a bath only two days ago.

To my relief, they crossed the hall and went into the kitchen. "Are there any apples?" asked Ghislaine.

"Look in the drawer," Madame said. "I'll make him a jam sandwich."

They were preparing a snack for Christian, I guessed, who would soon be home from the crèche. I gazed down at my legs, pale and distorted in the bathwater. As long as I remained motionless they had no idea I was in here. But the light was fading, the water turning cold—I couldn't stay here all evening. At some point, someone would come in to take a bath. I cast my mind over the schedule and winced. It was Monday—Mary Ann's day.

Ghislaine's voice broke my thoughts. "*Mais, non, Maman!* Don't start fussing with that chicken now. We have to leave in five minutes!"

My ears pricked up. They were going out again? Perhaps there was a chance I could escape unnoticed after all.

"I just need two seconds, *chérie.* If I don't start dinner now, it'll get too late when I'm back."

"It's fine, Maman. No one minds eating a little late."

"That's easy for you to say," Madame said mildly. "Since you're not going to be here."

Silence. "Actually . . . my plans changed. I'm not going out after all."

"Honestly, Ghislaine! How many times have I asked

you to tell me right away if you're going to be home for dinner?"

"Sorry! I forgot."

"These meals don't appear out of thin air, you know. I put a significant amount of time and effort into planning them. Is it too much to expect a little consideration?"

"I said I was sorry!" Ghislaine snapped. "If it's that much trouble, I can eat bread and cheese with Christian in the kitchen."

"You might have to," Madame retorted. "This chicken is smaller than I thought."

I had never heard her so irritated, and it caught me by surprise. I shrank back from her sharp tone, inadvertently splashing bathwater over the side of the tub.

"Did you hear something?" said Ghislaine.

I froze.

"What?"

"I don't know. It sounded like . . . splashing? Could there be someone in the bathroom?"

"I think it's more likely your imagination is playing tricks on you," Madame said tartly.

I held my breath for several seconds until Ghislaine spoke again. "We should leave to get Christian. If you're still coming with me."

"I said I would, didn't I?"

Dishes clattered into the sink.

"Is something wrong?" ventured Ghislaine. "You seem upset."

"You want to know what's wrong? I'll tell you." Madame raised her voice over the running tap. "I ran into Marie-Madeleine Fourcade, and she told me you'd been working for her again."

"What do you mean?"

"You know exactly what I mean."

"It was nothing, Maman," Ghislaine said glibly. "I was only helping her with something small."

"What?"

"I can't tell you."

They were silent for a moment. "You promised you wouldn't get involved again," Madame said.

"Yes, but our entire future is at stake! Do you know what will happen if the communists take over? Have you forgotten the Berlin blockade? The Soviets would have let them starve to death to gain control. That could be us—we could be the next Soviet satellite. Everything we have—everything we fought for—it'll be completely destroyed. We'll all be subjugated to—"

"There are other ways," Madame broke in, her voice calm. "You can help in other ways."

"You're burying your head in the sand!" Ghislaine

insisted. "Just like you and Papa did at the start of the war. If it wasn't for Marie-Mad, we'd all be eating sauerkraut right now. I'm not sure you understand how much she's sacrificed."

"I'm quite aware of what it means to sacrifice, thank you," Madame said crisply. "And I would prefer not to sacrifice my daughter. Marie-Mad has lofty ideals, but she can be careless. I learned that the hard way." There was a long, tense pause, and then Madame spoke again. "I understand this is important to you," she said. "But try to keep a cool head. Think of your family. Think of your son."

"I'm doing this for him!" Emotion seeped through Ghislaine's voice. "You wouldn't believe some of the things André says. The way he mocks me—or threatens me when I don't agree with him. It seems impossible we were ever on the same side about anything, let alone married."

"He *threatens* you?"

"Only to stop giving me money for Christian. But I can handle him. Don't worry, Marie-Mad and I have a plan."

"Ghislaine." There was a warning note in Madame's voice.

"I know what I'm doing."

"Just promise me." Madame's tone turned insistent.

"Promise you won't get our lodgers involved—our American girls. If there's even a suspicion they're being cultivated, or mined for information, it would be a scandal of epic proportions. And I'm the one responsible for them."

"Don't be silly, Maman," Ghislaine demurred. "I wouldn't dream of it."

By this time I was shivering, whether from the tepid bathwater or what I'd overheard, I couldn't tell. I had begun to fear they'd forgotten about fetching Christian, but then just as suddenly as they had appeared, they left. When the front door closed behind them, I extracted myself from the tub and shuffled to my room, pulling clothes on with effort. As I grew warmer, the pain in my back receded to a dull throb, and my thoughts began to clear.

Ghislaine said she'd helped Marie-Madeleine with one small thing. That could mean anything. Except I knew that Marie-Madeleine was a spy. I cracked the window and lit a cigarette, feeling my jaw unclench as the smoke filled my senses. By the time I finished, I had managed to convince myself that the conversation I'd overheard was perfectly reasonable. Obviously Ghislaine was anti-communist—she had made that clear from the outset—and, especially after my experience in Vienna, I understood her position. I too had sensed a Soviet menace hovering in the air, a fear un-expressed but expansive. But surely Ghislaine wouldn't involve herself in something so dangerous as spying, would she? This family had risked enough during the war—they had risked enough for a lifetime.

I emptied my ashtray into a little paper bag, which I would take out to the garbage can before dinner. Then, switching on the lamps in my room, I picked up the book I was reading and arranged myself flat on the floor. There were still a few hours to rest my back and lose myself in the pages of *La Condition humaine*, André Malraux's prize-winning novel that was one of Jack's favorites.

I began to read but my eyes kept skimming the smooth printed lines without sense. It was drafty on the floor and I felt jumpy, my mind unable to stop dis-secting my recent interactions with Ghislaine. What did I really know about her? Mostly I thought of her as Christian's *maman*, a divorced mother worn out by juggling her job with the care of her small son. I had no real knowledge of her work, her tastes, her history, or her interests (outside of French grammar), and it occurred to me that the cloak of motherhood was an excellent cover for someone who had something to hide.

Suddenly I was remembering the day we'd had tea

at Sciences Po, the day Ghislaine had asked so many questions about political groups, and student protests, and whether I belonged to any clubs. She had seemed awfully disappointed by my responses, even cutting our meeting short. At the time, I'd thought it was her eccentric way of teasing me about my love life—but was it possible she'd been probing for something else? I sat up, gasping at the pain twisting through my back.

Was Ghislaine using me as a source? Had her interest been a façade, a way to extract information about my friends, my classmates, and my professors? It was a ridiculous notion because I was no one—a mere student—and I knew nothing. Or did I? Had I unwittingly told her something useful? I closed my eyes, combing my memory more carefully but coming up blank. I should have felt relieved, but as I pried myself from the floor and moved to the edge of the bed, my skin began to prickle. Odd-shaped pieces were suddenly clicking together, unexplained incidents now making sense.

There was the night she'd invited me to the premiere of Colette's *Chéri*. I'd thought she was being kind, but now I saw she might have been cultivating me. Was she truly interested in my friends, or trying to discern if they could be useful to her cause? What about the displaced letters in my room, or Jack's disappearing and reappearing manuscript, or even Mary Ann's missing address book: Had they really been moved by Marie the *bonne*, or squirreled away by little Christian—or had there been another curious hand? And then there was Ghislaine's self-proclaimed love of French grammar—which gave her the perfect excuse to read all of our schoolwork.

I glanced around my bedroom. Had Ghislaine been here while I was out? Had she rifled through my desk, read my letters? This had been my refuge, sunny and serene, with its heavy furniture and chintz curtains of pale green. But now everywhere I saw deceit, the flowers staring from the drapes like unblinking eyes, the rich mahogany wood as dark as dried blood. I had thought we were friends, but now my instinct told me that Ghislaine had been stringing me along. It was the same feeling I remembered from childhood, of being secretly watched and scrutinized, my classmates eyeing me, judging me, trying to pry out the details of my parents' divorce. And, just as when I was a child, it left me feeling betrayed and angry, with no safe place.

Ghislaine had lied to me about nearly everything. And for what? She should have gone to Claude instead—although Claude would sooner bite her sister's head off than feed her information about any of her classmates. Unless—the thought hit me—was it possible Claude also knew? Claude, my dearest friend in Paris, the French person I trusted the most—was she spying on me too? It seemed impossible.

A hot sensation was expanding in my chest, filling my lungs, threatening to explode. Footsteps began trudging up the stairs, causing my heart to hammer, and suddenly I knew I couldn't stay here in this apartment another minute. I needed air; I needed movement; I needed to escape the feeling that everyone everywhere was watching me. I grabbed my coat and bolted.

The day, which had appeared so bright and dappled from my window, lost its shine as the sun set, a snappy wind rattling the barren tree branches and whipping against my face. I thrust my hands in my coat pockets and walked as quickly as my sore back allowed, in the direction opposite to Christian's crèche. The pain had sharpened, but I gritted my teeth—I'd tolerated worse on horseback—and quickened my pace.

My heels clicked up the quiet residential streets of the 16th, past stately apartment buildings and convenience shops, along boulevards rushing with pedestrians, cars, and donkey carts delivering the evening milk. Eventually, the tangle of streets gave way to the Seine, the sky here a sullen sweep of clouds reflected in the water. Boats moved swiftly in the current, flat-bottomed barges and tourist vessels maneuvering past colorful *péniches* anchored on the quay. I crossed at the pont de l'Alma, weaving through a gaggle of Americans who had stopped to gape at the Eiffel Tower rising in deceptive delicacy from the other side of the river. Men in business suits brushed past them with impatient frowns, but I couldn't muster any disdain. Even after all these months it still dazzled me too.

By this time the sky was growing dark—it was a good point to turn back—but I wasn't ready to head home. I didn't have a destination in mind but my feet found their own direction, carrying me toward the center of town, the streets becoming familiar as I neared the university. There was the *tabac* where I bought cigarettes after class, the antique print gallery whose windows I regularly admired. There, shuttered for the day, was the student café where Ghislaine and I had met a few weeks ago.

My breath grew short, forcing me to slow and stop. Sweat was beading my hairline, and, searching for a handkerchief, my heart sank as I realized I'd left the house without my pocketbook. I was stranded in the center of town, without a *sou* to take the métro home or even make a phone call.

I ducked into a doorway, trying to find my bearings. Night had fallen but the corner was bright, light streaming from the streetlamps and café windows, the dueling cinema marquees, the stall hawking rewarmed crepes and desiccated bonbons. Even with my eyes closed I would have known the carrefour de l'Odéon, its rich sugary smell making my stomach growl, for this was where Jack lived, in one of the handsome buildings lining the boulevard.

At the thought of him, my pulse began to slow. Of course this was where my feet had brought me—to Jack, who had stolen my heart with his calm logic and steady resourcefulness. He would know what to do; he would help me navigate this strange and uncomfortable situation.

I walked toward his building, looking up at his windows. The curtains were tightly drawn without any chinks of light escaping from the edges, and for a fleeting moment I felt a glimmer of misgiving. I didn't want to disturb the concierge—and I knew it was rude to show up unexpected—but when a stooped couple exited the building and shuffled off arm in arm, I didn't hesitate, slipping through the door before it swung shut. The lobby was as I remembered it, including the handwritten sign on the broken elevator, and I gingerly made my way up the stairs to his apartment on the second floor.

I rang the bell, wincing at its trill, which was louder than I expected. Faint sounds of domesticity were emanating from the other apartments—dishes clanking, voices scolding, the chime of the radio news marking the quarter hour—but behind Jack's door there was silence. I combed my hair with my fingers, suddenly conscious of disturbing his evening. A minute passed, and then another. I rang the bell again, uncertainty beginning to creep through my veins. If Jack wasn't home, what would I do? I could go to Reid Hall and find Martha but I didn't think she'd have a solution either. I pressed the bell again.

Heavy footsteps pounded across the floor and the door flew open. *"Oui?"* Jack stood before me, his face severe. He was wearing a polo-neck sweater and gray flannel trousers, his hair sticking up like he'd been running his hands through it. At the sight of me, his eyes widened. "Jacqueline! I didn't expect—What are you—?" He scanned my face, stepping closer. "Is everything all right?"

I launched myself at him, breathing in his scent of fir trees and brushed leather mixed with thick cashmere. "I'm sorry to turn up like this," I said.

"Are you kidding? I was hoping you'd drop by," he said lightly.

"You were waiting right by the door, I suppose," I said with a fleeting smile, relieved to sink into our old banter.

"I had to doll myself up first! Couldn't let you see me in my old house rags." Gently, he touched my arm. "Would you like to come in?"

A few minutes later, I was sitting on the sofa sipping a cup of tea to which Jack had added a generous tot of cognac. He knelt at the hearth, building up a blaze to warm my frozen limbs. When the flames began to spark and crackle, he sat beside me, stretching an arm across the back of the sofa, the soft wool of his sweater touching the nape of my neck. As my hands and feet warmed, they began to burn, adding to the confusion clouding my thoughts.

"How about something to eat?" Jack asked. "Have you had dinner?"

"Oh gosh, dinner!" I started, hot liquid splashing in my lap. "What time is it? Half past seven? I should ring home or they'll worry. Is the café still open?" I set my teacup down on the low table and began struggling to my feet, trying not to grimace at the prospect of walking all the way downstairs to make the call and then all the way back up again.

Jack jumped up to offer me a hand. "Are you all right?"

"I went riding yesterday and pulled my back, that's all."

"You want an aspirin or something?"

"I'm fine." I offered him a thin smile, straightening myself with difficulty.

"Say"—he shoved his hands in his pockets—"maybe you should use the phone in my study. It's probably easier, with the elevator still out."

"You have a line?" I couldn't keep the surprise out of my voice. "Why didn't you say?" He'd always called me from the café downstairs, and I also rang there to leave him messages.

"Honestly, I get so caught up in work, I need an excuse to leave the house." He half turned, looking a little shamefaced. I wondered if he was trying to save money by not using the phone too much.

"Well, if you're sure you don't mind . . ."

"Of course not." He led the way down the hall, opening a door that I had assumed was a closet. "Here we are," he said, switching on the lamp. "My hideout."

"Golly," I said, looking around the room, which was as spacious and well furnished as the rest of the apartment. "This is some hideout." A green velvet armchair sat in the corner, surrounded by shelves filled with books, and before the window was a large desk, Jack's typewriter rising from it like an island amid a sea of papers. "Are there any other rooms in this place you've been keeping secret?"

"Only the ballroom," he said with a wink, freeing the telephone from a pile of newspapers and setting it before me. "I'll leave you to it."

I had a hunch Ghislaine would answer the phone, and of course she did. The sound of her drowsy drawl made me wince—but it was easier to fib to her than the others. I made my apologies, telling her I'd gone for a drink at the café with some friends, lost track of time, and would eat dinner with them at Reid Hall.

After I hung up, I sat for a moment in the calm of Jack's study, waiting for my heart to steady. The room was darker than the others, the shutters closed over the windows, a well-placed lamp casting a pool of light on the typewriter and the papers splayed across the desk. Amid the jumble of newsprint clippings and scribbled-over manuscript pages peeped the bold green masthead of the leftist highbrow literary journal *Les Lettres françaises*.

Jack popped his head through the doorway. "Did you get through?"

I drew a deep breath and nodded. "Shall we finish our tea? I'm awfully thirsty."

He came and switched off the desk light, offering me a hand to guide me from the dark room, closing the door behind us with the other. Back on the sofa, I curled up beside him. If only I could stay here forever, in the warm bright sanctuary of his apartment, instead of returning to the cold watchful parlor of avenue Mozart. Even though I agreed with Ghislaine's political opinions, I still found myself flinching at her prying, my anger hissing to the surface, making my cheeks hot.

"Are you sure you're all right?" Jack looked at me, alarmed. "You look like you swallowed a wasps' nest."

And so, with the help of more cognac-laced tea, I related the conversation I'd overheard that afternoon, telling him of my suspicions about Ghislaine and the puzzling incidents of the past few months. Jack listened carefully, nodding and making occasional sounds of encouragement. When I finished, he leaned forward to refill our cups.

"Drink that," he said. "It'll help."

I took a sip, closing my eyes against its warmth.

"Why would"—he frowned—"why would Ghislaine try to use you for information?"

I shook my head. "I wish I knew. I've been racking my brain all afternoon, and it makes no sense."

"Was she trying to learn more about one of your classmates? Or a professor? Do you know anyone who might be a fellow traveler?"

"Well . . ." I shot him a look under my lashes. "There's you . . ."

Jack looked positively affronted. "Me?"

"You spend an awful lot of time at that bookstore."

"For research!" he insisted. "I swear to you, Jacqueline, I have never been a communist in the past, and I'm not one now." His eyes met mine, clear and steady, and I knew he was telling the truth.

I rested my head briefly against him. "I've never even read Karl Marx."

"Ah, but you should." He stretched an arm around my shoulders, drawing me closer. "Know thy enemy and all that."

"The only explanation I can think of is that Ghislaine was trying all of us, hoping to find something. Scattershot approach."

"Would she really be so disorganized? I know I haven't met her yet, but this makes her sound as daft as a brush."

"Yes, well—" I remembered something Paul de Ganay had told me. "I suppose her crowd isn't so skilled at subterfuge."

He smiled faintly. "You're probably right."

"What do I do now?" I reached for my teacup and swallowed a gulp. "I'm so angry I could kick something. I can scarcely bear to go back there—even though I've loved it so much. I feel like something precious has been snatched from me. The thought of being watched all the time, knowing she's been rifling through my things—" I pressed a hand against my mouth, remembering something else. "What if Claude's involved too?"

Jack frowned, his fingers on my sleeve. "No," he said after a moment. "I don't think so."

"Why not?"

"Claude's smart and engaged—but she's no ideologue. She's too reasonable to stake her relationships on politics." He stared into the dregs of his cup. "The thing is," he said eventually, "you are who you say you are. Ghislaine can look through your belongings all she likes but there's nothing to discover. Eventually she'll figure that out if she hasn't already—and she'll lose interest."

As I considered his words, so plain and sensible, they calmed me, even more than the strong spirits I'd been drinking. Of course he was right—I had nothing to hide. My political opinions were an open book—still unformed, perhaps, but never a secret. And though Ghislaine's snooping had come as a shock, when I considered her motives, I found it difficult to begrudge her passion—especially when I remembered my confrontation with the Soviet soldiers in Vienna, the way everyone on the street had averted their gaze. I knew the threat was real and fearsome. I too shuddered to think of France under Moscow's thumb.

I drew a deep breath and let it out slowly, feeling my anger loosen its grip on my reason. Here in this warm room, tucked into the solid semicircle of Jack's arm, our teacups half full on the low table before us and the fire flickering on the hearth, it occurred to me that maybe, just maybe, I had been irrational. Yes, Ghislaine had overstepped a boundary, and in so doing provoked my temper, but in the end no harm had befallen either of us. And though I still wasn't sure how I could go home and face her without flinching, I sensed the heat of my emotions ebbing into embarrassment. Without warning, my face flooded, and I leaned over to hide in Jack's shoulder.

"You must think me an awful little fool," I said, my voice muffled against the soft nap of his sweater.

"What? Why?" He stroked my back.

"Just turning up like this, out of the blue. Full of funny ideas and getting so worked up about them." I covered my cheeks with my hands. "I feel ridiculous."

"Oh, sweetheart, no!" He pulled away to meet my eyes, his hands gripping my shoulders. "It means the world to me that you came here tonight—that you trusted me." He swallowed hard. "You know I'm in love with you," he added quietly.

He had said it before, at the opera, but this time I felt the words land somewhere deep inside of me. Maybe I hadn't really believed him then—or maybe I simply hadn't wanted to. But now I heard something in his voice that made me feel calm and steady, sure of myself—accepted for who I was, not the girl he thought I should be. The edges of my reserve began to soften and dissolve.

"I want to make you happy, Jacqueline." His voice dropped so low it felt like a caress.

"I'm happy now," I whispered, and as I said it, an ineffable lightness lifted my heart. I could forget any ambitions—mine and everyone else's—and allow him to make me happy.

I leaned over and kissed him, closing my eyes at the pressure of his mouth, the roughness of his cheeks, the sensation that time was standing still. My hands stroked his sweater, and then his skin, hot and smooth beneath the layer of wool, his lips touching my face, my neck, his fingers tangling in my hair. I pulled at his clothes, wanting to be as close to him as possible, to feel my bare chest upon his, to feel everything recklessly and indelibly.

"Jacqueline," he whispered, his mouth at my ear causing me to shiver. "Are you sure?" He pulled away, his expression tender, and instead of being shy as I'd always imagined this moment, I felt flushed, and desired, and confident.

"Yes." I nodded, my eyes not leaving his face. "Yes," I said again, reaching forward to lift the edge of his sweater, pulling it over his head and revealing the lean contours of his torso. He eased me back on the sofa and began unbuttoning my blouse with agonizing care, trailing a finger over the outline of my brassiere, across my stomach, and hips, and thighs, slipping farther and farther until I gasped and trembled against him.

I know what they said about me later. The speculation, the innuendo. The whispers that I drank too many grasshopper cocktails one night and lost my virtue to Jack in the elevator of his building. For the record, I've always found crème de menthe revolting. I never found out who started the rumors, but I have an idea who spread them: George Plimpton and Thomas Guinzburg, those swaggering boys who worked on the *Paris Review* with Jack and who, decades later, loved to gossip about me as though our paths had ever crossed that year. And then too there was Gore Vidal—my ersatz stepbrother, relic of Uncle Hugh's second marriage and inventor of stories that ensured he was the center of attention.

The one thing I know is that Jack never said those things about me. That evening remained precious for us both, a memory I've returned to again and again, like a long cool drink of water reviving me during the parched seasons of my life. And even though things didn't work out between us—even though we broke each other's hearts—I know the story didn't come from him, because once upon a time we loved each other. And also because that story always got one key element wrong: The elevator was out of service.

Afterward, I lay in Jack's arms, listening to the snap and crackle of the fire and thinking about all the things that mattered so much back home and how they felt so distant and inconsequential here in Paris. I imagined the life Jack and I could have together, and it sparkled with fun, and sophistication, and adventure. We would sunbathe on Mediterranean beaches, and visit ancient Silk Road outposts, and invite friends over to eat raclette on cold winter nights. Jack would write important books, and we would surround ourselves with other authors and artists, musicians, actors, and all the eclectic folk who lived and thrived in Paris—see the latest exhibitions, plays, and ballets for a song. And if I couldn't afford to keep a stable or a yacht, or dress in the latest season of Dior, it wouldn't matter because I'd be part of something infinitely richer, the cultural zeitgeist. Together with Jack, I could create the kind of life I'd dreamed about.

It was around ten o'clock when we left Jack's apartment. He asked if he could accompany me home in a taxi, and I agreed, mainly because I wanted to prolong our time together. We sped across Paris, the car following the curve of the Seine, and the lights shimmered in the river, and his hand was solid on my knee, and we were chatting a mile a minute, and when we swept by the pont Alexandre III, I saw its gold winged horses shining like angels in the night sky, and my heart caught in my throat. And I knew that it was impossible to be any happier than I was in that moment with Jack by my side.

I could never have guessed how he would betray me.

PART III

Le printemps

Chapter Twelve

By the time mid-March arrived, it felt like winter was dragging on like a ham and two people, as Dorothy Parker might have said, with gusts of rain, sleet, and wind punctuated by sunlight too harsh without the shade the leafless trees could not provide. Everyone cast longing glances at the café *terrasses*, which in warmer weather spilled onto the sidewalks with all the color and costume of a theater production. But only the boldest folk sat there now, huddled deep beneath the awnings, their laps covered with blankets. The rest of us trudged inside with ravaged hair and dripping umbrellas, to nurse cups of tea and wish they were tall glasses of lemonade.

It was on such an evening that I pulled a black satin evening gown from the back of my wardrobe, donning it with a three-strand collar of pearls. Inspecting myself in the mirror, I thought I looked pretty nice, the strapless lines of the dress emphasizing my long neck and shoulders, and hiding the wide hips that Mummy found so physically abhorrent. I didn't have a sensational figure, but with the right clothes I could look slim. My rough, dark hair had been smoothed into sleek waves, and my skin was lustrous thanks to all the Parisian rain. My eyes stared back at me, planted so far apart that it took an optician three weeks to make a pair of glasses with a bridge wide enough to fit over my nose. All my life I had hated my eyes—until now, until Jack had confessed how they bewitched him, as serene and knowing as a sphinx.

Jack. At the thought of him my pulse quickened. We had met twice since that evening last week, but our time together had been too short, only a few stolen moments between classes. I was busy preparing for another round of final exams and essays, and he was working long hours on an article for the *Atlantic*, an analysis of the upcoming French elections in June. A day earlier, he'd left on a research trip to Marseille, attending the annual congress of the Partisans of Peace, a communist youth group. Before he returned, I would depart for spring break with Martha and a couple of other girls from school. We'd visit Madrid and Toledo, and all the

Spanish towns along the way to Valencia, and though I would miss Jack, I was excited about the trip. In any case, Jack had assured me that he'd be working flat out on his article, which he hoped would help establish him as a serious journalist.

Tonight was in honor of Paul de Ganay and his twenty-first birthday, which his parents were celebrating in grand style. The Vicomtesse de Ganay had planned a ball at the Pavillon Ledoyen, the storied restaurant near the Champs-Élysées, inviting her friends and their children, a few dozen or so of the young set I'd gotten to know through Paul. There would be champagne, and a dance orchestra, and Madame had granted me special permission to stay out until three, which meant that after the party I could go with the others to Les Halles, to eat *soupe à l'oignon* at Au Pied de Cochon amid the rowdy bustle of the central food market before dawn.

"*Ohhhhh la la la la!*" cooed Claude when I stepped into the *salon*.

"*Magnifique*," agreed Madame, circling me to admire the entire ensemble. "You'll be the loveliest girl at the party, *chérie*."

"I'm just glad this dress still fits after all the croissants I've been eating," I said, embarrassed by their admiration. The room seemed awfully bright and quiet, especially compared to the lavish candlelit world I was about to enter.

I joined them in the sitting room, perching on the edge of an armchair. Madame was writing letters by the fireplace, and Claude was studying for an exam, her notes and books spread on the sofa. Aside from Christian, who was mercifully asleep in his room, they were home alone for the evening. Susan and Mary Ann were at Reid Hall attending a lecture by Janet Flanner, the *New Yorker* journalist who wrote under the pen name Genêt. Ghislaine was away for the weekend, visiting friends in the country. I'd made a point of avoiding her the past few days, though I didn't think she'd noticed, and her absence now was a relief.

Paul was late to pick me up—so late I began to fear he'd forgotten me, even though we had confirmed by phone the day before. When he finally arrived, he leaned long and heavy on the doorbell, so that it was practically still ringing when Madame answered it. Right away I saw that he was drunk. He hid it well, but there was a vacant, glassy look in his eyes that I wasn't accustomed to seeing. Madame fussed over him, wishing him a happy birthday and asking after his mother, whom Madame had met once through a distant cousin. I fidgeted throughout this conversation for, cultivated as they were, the de Rentys ranked several rungs below the de Ganays, if not in name then definitely in fortune, and my experiences with Mummy had taught me that such social interactions were rarely benign. Madame and Claude, however, were as warm and natural as ever, shooing us out the door with smiles and double cheek kisses.

Outside, a Rolls-Royce idled at the curb. The uniformed driver closed the doors behind us with a quiet, heavy thump, the same sound Hughdie's cars made, the sound of money. In the backseat, I drew a wool blanket over my knees, and with my fur coat around my shoulders, and hot air gusting from the vents, I felt more comfortable than I had in months. Paul usually traveled around the city by métro, but tonight his parents had indulged him with the chauffeured car, and I had to admit it was exceedingly pleasant.

Paul slid down, slumping against the back of the seat. "Thanks for coming tonight."

"I wouldn't have missed it for the world," I assured him. "It's a very special evening."

"Is it?" He closed his eyes. "I don't know. This party. These people. The *haut monde* of the Faubourg Saint-Germain," he said, referring to the aristocratic quartier of his birth with its intricate rules of politesse. "Everyone posturing and preening, and marrying each other, only to start having affairs with each other. And the same for their children, and their children's children. It all seems so . . . futile."

"Do you wish to break free?" I asked, lightly, so that he could make a joke if he wished.

His eyes opened, and they were devoid of the boyish merriment I had grown to expect. "Yes." He swallowed hard, and for a terrible moment I thought he might cry. "Have you ever been in love, Jacqueline?" he asked.

His words caught me off guard. Paul and I never spoke of topics like love, or grief, or existentialism. Our conversations were always as light and inconsequential as meringue, a puff of sweetness melting on the tongue; and honestly, I had long ago ceased to take him too seriously.

I stared at my hands in my lap. "I imagine I know how it feels," I said slowly. "Are you . . . in love?"

His head dropped. "Yes."

"I guess your parents don't approve?"

"They don't know." He cleared his throat. "It's someone . . . unsuitable."

Glancing over at him, I saw a look of such utter wretchedness flash across his features that my heart broke for him.

"She comes from the wrong sort of family? She's part sea monster?" I joked, hoping to coax a smile.

He shook his head. "It's just . . . someone inappropriate. I can't explain." He retrieved a silver flask from his coat pocket. "Do you want some marc?"

"All right." I surprised us both by taking a swig, the harsh alcohol burning a path down my chest. I handed him back the flask and he drank deeply, his Adam's apple working in his throat.

"Do you know why this birthday is supposed to be so special?" Paul concentrated on screwing the cap back on the flask. "In the Middle Ages, the stages of knighthood were in multiples of seven. A boy became a page at age seven. A page became a squire at age fourteen. And a squire became a knight at age twenty-one."

"So tonight you become a chevalier!" I clasped my hands together. "Shall I dub thee Sir Paul?"

He inclined his head gravely. "I do hereby swear to honor the chivalric code, milady."

The car was slowing, turning into the driveway of a Neo-Classical pavilion with a crowd on its steps and golden light streaming from the windows. "We're here." Paul drew a sharp breath. "Oh, Jacqueline, I'm so unhappy."

Impulsively, I leaned over and kissed his cheek, squeezing his hand as he helped me out of the car. "It will pass," I whispered. "It always does."

The first person I saw was the Vicomtesse de Ganay,

her bare shoulders rising from a magnificent full-skirted gown embellished with sequins, rhinestones, and pearls. She glided toward us with an expression of forced calm. "Where have you been?" she demanded of her son, after greeting us with double cheek kisses. "Everyone's been asking. Your father is livid."

"I'm here now," Paul said.

She tilted her head up to examine him. "Is that lipstick?" She rubbed at his cheek with her thumb, her eyes darting toward me. I guessed at the conclusion she had drawn, blushing deeply. To my surprise, her face softened. "Never mind, *mes chéris.* Come, let's join the party."

We followed her upstairs to a long glass *salon* overlooking the park. Elaborate crystal chandeliers cast the room in a honeyed glow that reflected in the long mirrors covering the walls. The party swirled with gowns of floating lace and chiffon, scents of perfume and hothouse flowers mingling with cigarette smoke. Waiters circled with champagne, which I accepted, and hors d'oeuvres, which I did not. The little toasts heaped with gleaming caviar looked delicious, but I was wary of eating at parties. Instead, I lit a cigarette and drifted toward Sabine and Hélène, who were standing by the bank of windows. By now I'd grown accustomed to their sly observations, and while I wouldn't have called them friends, we'd formed a delicate acquaintance-ship over cocktail hours at the Ritz Bar, and dancing at l'Éléphant Blanc, the group's preferred jazz club in Montparnasse.

"Coucou, les filles!" I greeted them.

Their heads flew apart. *"Ça va, Jacqueline?"* They dutifully kissed me, but with reluctance. I guessed I had interrupted some gossip.

"Did you just arrive? Did you come with Paul?" Hélène arched an eyebrow. She was wearing a pale pink strapless dress with a tulle overskirt, more school-girl than soignée.

"No one's seen him all night!" added Sabine, her dark eyes widening. "Can you imagine missing your own birthday party?"

"I just got here," I said, feeling an instinctive need to protect my friend. "Is that Henri over there?" I caught his eye and waved. He gave me a nod, and the cool blonde by his side turned to gaze at me. "Who's he with?" I asked the girls.

They exchanged a look. "That's Sonia," said Hélène.

"He split up with Florence?" I risked another glance in their direction, smoothing my expression when I found Sonia still staring at me.

Sabine leaned closer. "She's Swedish. Her family has an estate outside of Gothenburg."

"They met skiing in Zermatt last month," whispered Hélène. "And now they're engaged!"

In my surprise, I swallowed a sip of champagne too hastily. "Golly!" I said, barely managing to recover my composure. "That's wonderful. I hope they're very happy."

The girls exchanged another glance, one I couldn't decipher. Before I could probe, a hush dampened the room.

"Oh, look!" Sabine clapped her hands together. "Paul's here."

He was by the stairs, making slow progress across the room, stopping to greet every guest with double cheek kisses, his mother circling him forward like a sheepdog with an errant member of her flock. His face was pale—I suspected Madame la Vicomtesse had been force-feeding him black coffee in the kitchen—but he moved with the natural grace of his station. If he hadn't spoken to me so frankly in the car, I wouldn't have guessed his unhappiness.

It might have been my imagination, but as Paul drew near to Henri and Sonia, I sensed the girls oozing with prurience. Were they holding their breath as he and Sonia exchanged a formal greeting? Did they crane their heads, trying to overhear the conversation? Perhaps it was her Swedish reserve, but I did not see Sonia smile.

Paul had just turned to his friend, leaning forward to touch his cheeks, when Henri swept him into a rough embrace, slapping him on the shoulder and nearly throwing him off balance. Paul, who had been so wan, flushed deeply and stepped back, ending the moment as quickly as it had begun. When his mother touched his arm, he moved forward to greet the next pair of guests, his eyebrows raised with an air of pleased anticipation.

Beside me, Sabine and Hélène exhaled and pretended to admire a huge arrangement of white roses and lilies as if they hadn't been watching Paul like lions stalking an antelope. A few seconds later, Sabine murmured something about powdering her nose, and the pair floated toward the ladies' room—to continue gossiping, I presumed.

I stood alone by the windows, observing the other guests chatting in little groups with their lilting cadences and arch smiles. Mummy's voice in my ear prodded me to start mingling, but I was too startled to make light conversation, too stunned by what I had just seen, my mind too busy skipping over the past months, seeing with new eyes the clues that had been hiding in plain sight. Paul was indeed in love with someone as unsuitable as he had avowed. For his sake, I hoped no one else had noticed. The buzz in the room told me otherwise.

I had seen such men in New York City, our nanny avoiding a certain stretch of the East 50s, refusing to explain why, no matter how we pestered. My real education came from Gore, my almost stepbrother, who turned up at Merrywood from time to time. Daddy called him a fairy and referred to him with a curled lip of disgust, but I had a soft spot for Gore, who found Hughdie as dull and timid as I did. Gore lived on his own terms, without shame, though I sensed his acid tongue hid some dark demons. His stories often pushed the boundaries of decorum too far, but he also disabused me of any foolish naïveté, leaving me with a pretty clear idea of the subjects Mummy and Hughdie forbade us children to discuss. He spared no one in his gossip, talking airily of men who were light in their loafers, confirmed bachelors, husbands with double lives, the limp wristed, the friends of Dorothy, the sissies, the pansies, always spoken of with a self-mocking shudder or jeer so that I knew exactly what other people would think, how aberrant they would judge them, how scandalous.

Gore would have adored the little tableau playing out in front of me now. It was the type of atmosphere I remembered from my childhood, when my parents' divorce was splashed across the tabloids—my photo in print alongside sordid details about Daddy's affairs and financial failures, Mummy's temper and the violent ways she exorcised it—my classmates eyeing me avidly, waiting to see if I would crack. Even after the documents were signed, it didn't end, Mummy moving us to a dingy little apartment where she paced, and chain-smoked, and bit her nails to the quick, scheming to save herself from social ignominy in the only way she knew—by marrying for money—finally succeeding with Hughdie, love and passion be damned. It had all affected me more than I cared to admit, leaving me with the unpleasant insight that the only thing that could keep you safe was money.

I suspected Paul also knew there were stark consequences for those who broke the rules of our social sphere. Everyone and everything could disappear if you dared to test the limits of respectability. I recognized his humble acquiescence to his mother's will, his stoic bonhomie, the skill with which he sidestepped questions he deemed too personal. Whereas I used solitude to protect myself, he used humor, always deflecting with a joke.

That night I ate filet of beef with spring peas and artichokes, and frozen pistachio parfait garnished with imported Sicilian strawberries. Afterward, we danced beneath Ledoyen's ornate coffered ceiling, the waltzes and foxtrots giving way to old-fashioned reels that left everyone breathless and high-spirited. By the end of the night, the judgmental atmosphere had softened into a mood that seemed almost sentimental. I tried to shift along with it, but my thoughts lingered on Paul. It wasn't that he wore a mask that surprised me, but rather that I hadn't perceived it—I, who prided myself on my sensitivity and powers of observation. It had happened with Ghislaine too, this strange shifting of belief and reality, leaving me shaken and alienated. For the first time since arriving in France, I felt a dart of homesickness. America had seemed like an increasingly distant and dreamlike place, and I hadn't missed it until now—but it turned out to be harder to shed than I'd thought. Maybe it would always be that way.

Sometime in the small hours we gathered on the front stairs for a last photograph, our fine clothes crumpled, hair mussed, cheeks flushed. The boys were joking as they jostled into position on the back steps, the girls settling among them, giggling at their antics. I stood at the front, angling my shoulders toward the camera in the most flattering pose I knew, my beaded evening bag in my hands and a serene smile on my lips.

When I look at that photo now, so many years later, it all comes flooding back. The smell of cigarettes and faded perfume in the hall, the wisp of cold air floating in from the front door left ajar, the ache in my feet from standing all night in heels. I'm hungry and a little shivery, but in a few minutes we'll pile into the heated cars and head to Les Halles, to eat onion soup with strands of melted cheese flying as fine as cobwebs. Paul, his mask now firmly back in place, is telling a joke that I don't quite understand. The others guffaw, their big, goofy grins captured forever with a click of the camera. Their laughter is a declaration of their familiarity, their particular humor, their relationships intertwined for generations. It reminds me that I'm different, that I'll never truly be a part of their world, despite my fluency and Francophilia. I am right here with them, but I am not one of them.

Two days later I went to Spain with Martha and the other girls, reveling in the warmth and sun-drenched colors, and delicious bits of food they gave you when you ordered a glass of wine. It was a trip so unbelievably jammed that every night we collapsed into bed and then got up the next morning ready to start again. For a week we visited museums and old churches, walked through streets dripping with bougainvillea blossoms, ate dry-cured ham and sharp sheep's-milk cheeses, went to little bootleg nightclubs that stayed open until seven in the morning, and met some awfully nice English and Spanish boys. It was funny how much alike people from different countries were.

When we got back to Paris, the city felt still and monochrome compared to Spain's warmth and dazzle. But exiting the métro at Jasmin, I breathed in the familiar scent of morning newsprint from the kiosk on the corner, and heard the steady sweep of our *gardienne*'s broom upon the wet sidewalk before our apartment. All of a sudden I was gripped with nostalgia for a moment that was still happening, this feeling of leaving and coming home again to Paris.

Upstairs, I found Ghislaine and Christian in the *salon* reading a picture book. Or, rather, I found Christian howling as he waved the page he had just ripped from the book, while Ghislaine scolded him with a pinched expression. Her hair looked lank, like she hadn't had time to wash it, and the top button of her blouse dangled from a loose thread. All this time I had been dreading seeing her, afraid my anger would spill over, but suddenly I felt myself softening. I couldn't imagine what it was like to be completely responsible for a child, knowing his happiness and well-being depended solely on my resourcefulness. Even though Ghislaine had her mother and siblings, the family's reduced circumstances meant they could never truly feel secure. Anything could derail them—an illness, an accident, even just plain old age. It was the type of uncertainty that could drive you to desperate measures, like a marriage of convenience, or trading on the black market. Or spying.

Christian continued wailing, his face wet and red, his mouth a dark circle of toddler fury. Ghislaine sighed and shut her eyes for a long moment, looking like she might start crying too.

"Hey, Christian. Hey." I knelt on the floor, trying to distract him. "Do you want to go to the park? Let's give your *maman* some time to rest, what do you think?"

His mouth closed with a gulp. "Can we go on the seesaw?"

"Yes," I said, pulling a handkerchief from my pocket and wiping his cheeks. He loved to pretend the long, narrow board was a horse leaping up to jump fences. "Come on, *mon brave*." I held out my hand and he took it, his fingers hot and sticky.

"Are you sure, Jacqueline?" Ghislaine asked. "You really don't have to."

"Don't be silly. I'd like to stretch my legs after the train ride, and Christian can introduce me to his trusty steed." I rose from the floor. "Let's see who can get their coat on first, shall we?" As Christian ran to the hall, I added: "We'll be home in time for lunch, all right?"

She sighed. "*Merci*, Jacqueline. I've been at my wits' end all morning. His father was supposed to take him for the day, but I have no idea what happened to him. Typical," she added under her breath.

I remembered thinking as we left that she looked utterly exhausted.

The day was gray, but a trifling gray, the sky covered with ragged clouds that looked like they might disperse with a few strong gusts of wind. As we turned the corner to the park, Christian raced ahead, leaping into the sandbox to join a group of little boys who were digging an enormous trench with their heels. I sat on a nearby bench and lit a cigarette, my thoughts drifting, as they often did, to Jack.

It had been over a week since I'd last seen him— or, to be precise, ten days and a handful of hours. The entire time I was in Spain I had imagined us there together, a holiday just for the two of us, no talk of work or school or future plans, but instead art, and wine, and sun, and the rapid-fire banter that never failed to electrify me. I'd written him two postcards, and we had plans to meet for dinner tonight, whether or not he had managed to finish his article. I couldn't wait to tell him about everything I'd seen and everyone I'd met, and I longed to hear the same from him.

So absorbed was I in my reverie that I didn't see the man until he was crouched beside Christian in the sandbox. He wore a belted tweed coat and had the type of handsome, heavy features that could quickly turn puffy and dissipate.

"*Non,*" I heard Christian say. "Don't want to."

I snatched my pocketbook from the bench and dashed over to them. "Excuse me," I demanded. "What are you doing?"

"Who are you?"

"I might ask the same of you," I said, even though now I had a pretty good inkling.

He grasped Christian by the shoulder. "He's coming with me."

"He most certainly is not, monsieur. His mother left him with me and I don't know who you are."

His lip curled. "I'm his father. And it's not my problem if his mother is too busy skulking around Marseille to look after her son."

"What on earth are you talking about? Ghislaine isn't in Marseille. She's at home."

"Ask her yourself then," he said with a smirk. Other than his looks, it was difficult to understand what Ghislaine saw in him. Then again, I had witnessed enough of Mummy and Daddy's divorce to know how far things could unravel in a marriage, until everyone and everything associated with the other person became repugnant.

Christian's father shifted his weight. "Come on, son,"

he said. "You know better than to keep your grandparents waiting." Grasping the little boy by his armpits, he hauled him to his feet. Glancing down at Christian, I saw his face frozen into a blank stare. Ultimately that was what frightened me, for normally he would be thrashing and screeching like a wild fox caught in a trap. Quickly I moved to grab his other hand, feeling him grip my fingers so tightly they cracked.

"I'm sorry, I can't let him go with you," I said. "I need to check with his mother first."

His face hardened. "Listen, girl, if I were you, I wouldn't make things so difficult. You won't like the consequences."

It was a threat, and not even a veiled one. I shot a look at his sulky, sculpted features, unsure of how to proceed. He was bigger and stronger than I, with a brutish demeanor that boded ill. Though I didn't think he'd harm me, I couldn't be sure of what he'd do to Christian once he was alone with him.

"We'll walk back to the apartment and ask Ghislaine," I said with more confidence than I felt, and Christian's grip on my hand loosened a fraction at these words. "Let's go find Maman, *d'accord*?" I asked him, but he remained mute and withdrawn.

"See? He doesn't want to," said his father.

He's terrified of you! I wanted to say. Instead, I dug

up the sweet, breathy voice I used on occasions like this. "I'd hate for Ghislaine to be cross with me," I half whispered, glancing at him through my lashes. "I'm sure you understand."

He raised his eyebrows, his posture softening almost imperceptibly, and I allowed myself a discreet glimmer of triumph. Few men were able to resist the vulnerable charm of the helpless—how could I have forgotten? I lowered my eyes, waiting for him to bend to my will, but to my surprise he gave a grunt of scorn. "Americans," he snorted. "Are you really that facile? And here I thought it was a stereotype. Time to go," he told his son. "We're late."

But before they could leave, I heard the rapid crunch of running feet on the fine dirt path and Ghislaine appeared before us breathing heavily, her face red with exertion. "I saw you from the apartment coming out of the métro," she said to her ex-husband, without a word of greeting. "Where the devil have you been?"

At the sight of her, his scowl deepened. "Perhaps *you* would like to tell *me* exactly why I came across my son in the park with this—this—*American imperialist* looking after him." He threw a look of disgust in my direction.

"We haven't heard from you for weeks, and now you turn up expecting us to fall in line with the snap of your fingers? No, sorry, André. It doesn't work that way."

"How would you know if I've been here or not? It sounds like you've been plenty busy with your own little projects. Gallivanting hither and yon." He leered at her.

"What is that supposed to mean?"

"I know you were in Marseille last week, Ghislaine."

"I don't know what you're talking about," she snapped, the blood still high in her face.

"Do you think I'm a fool? Léon saw you at the congress for the Partisans of Peace. He told me he didn't know you cared so much about the future of the party. Scribbling notes constantly, apparently."

My ears pricked up. Jack had also attended the Partisans of Peace congress last week in Marseille—but I knew better than to mention that now.

"It's none of your business what I do, or where I go." Ghislaine's face remained impassive, but through her coat pocket, I thought I glimpsed the bulge of a clenched fist.

André moved closer to her, so close I could scarcely hear the words when he spoke. "You better not be digging around and using it against us," he breathed, and somehow his quiet tone was even more menacing than before. "Consider this a warning."

To my surprise, Ghislaine barked a laugh. "Or what? You'll pull out my fingernails? Burn me with a hot poker? Please, these idle threats are so tedious."

It was his turn to flush. "It's not coming from me. And it's not idle. I suggest you take it seriously."

"That's what you said last time. And the time before that." She rolled her eyes theatrically. "Haven't you heard of the boy who cried wolf? I suggest you mind your own business, and I'll mind mine."

"*Maman.*" Christian, his hand long ago released by his father, tugged at his mother's sleeve.

"Yes, what is it, *mon cœur?*"

"I have to make *caca.*"

André emitted an exasperated sigh. "Can you hold it until we get to your grandparents'?"

Christian gave a short, sharp shake of his head. It occurred to me that this was why he'd turned so pale and mute, with that vacant look of distress. Perhaps he wasn't so afraid of his father after all.

"All right, come on, let's go home." Ghislaine turned toward the park gate.

Again, Christian shook his head, his face starting to crumple. "Too far . . ." he whimpered.

"The café, then." She pointed across the street. "Papa will take you."

André grimaced. "*Me?* Why can't you do it?"

She sucked in a sharp breath, her lips pressed together. "Fine. I'll do it. As usual." She bent to retrieve Christian's hand. "Come on, *mon cœur.* Papa will wait outside the café and then take you to see Papi and Mémé, *d'accord?*" As they walked away, she turned briefly to glare at André.

He waited thirty seconds before following them out of the park. *"Au revoir,"* I called after him, but he made no acknowledgment, nor did he notice me watching as he crossed the street. It was strange: When he thought no one was looking, his expression changed from belligerence to fear.

The cork slid out with a muffled thump, our waiter holding the bottle at a precise angle so that the wine trickled into the sparkling coupes, leaving only a whisper of mousse around the edges. He nestled the bottle into a silver bucket, gave a deep nod, and disappeared.

"Cheers!" Jack said. He stretched to pick up a glass from the low table in front of us, handing it to me before taking the other.

"Here's to your article—your book—everything!" I shifted on the red velvet sofa, raising my drink and meeting his eyes. When our glasses touched, they chimed with the high, clear note of fine crystal. "Tell me again about the telegrams," I urged, taking a sip.

"Oh, gosh, you don't want to hear all that again," he protested, but with a lopsided shrug that told me he was pleased by my interest.

"I most certainly do! The first time was so exciting I missed half the details. Now I want to hear it again from the beginning, slowly, so I can savor every word."

And so Jack told me about how he returned home from Marseille to find not one but two telegrams from New York. The first was from none other than Harold Ober, renowned literary agent to Fitzgerald, Faulkner, and other greats, asking—nay, imploring—to represent Jack's novel. The second telegram came from his editor at the *Atlantic*, urging him to file his article on the upcoming French elections as soon as possible. "MORE WORK TO COME STOP," it added.

"I still can't believe it." Jack swallowed half his champagne in a gulp. "Harold Ober and the *Atlantic* all in the same day, and they both want *me*? It's finally happening, just like I always dreamed."

"Of course it is. And it has nothing to do with a dream. Think of all those Sunday afternoons you spent meeting folks for your research, all the late nights revising. You've earned this, darling."

He felt around for his cigarette case, offering me a smoke and striking a match to light it before touching the flame to his own. "You've been incredible, you know that? I'm certain Ober wouldn't have been interested in the manuscript without your edits. I just hope this means I can finally—" He broke off, swearing as the

flame touched his fingertips. "Sorry, I wasn't paying attention." He shook out the match, dropped the scorched
stub into the ashtray, and examined his thumb. "I better
go rinse this in some cold water. Be back in a second."

I leaned against the velveteen sofa, watching the
smoke from my cigarette swirl in a lazy haze against the
bar's scarlet furnishings. Tonight Jack had surprised
me twice: first with his news of literary triumph, then
by whisking me to the Hôtel Continental, marching
straight to the bar and ordering their finest bottle of
vintage champagne. "We're celebrating," he'd told the
lugubrious barman, whose countenance did not flicker
at this information.

Though I'd never been there before, I knew the Hôtel
Continental was once considered the most luxurious in
Paris. Glancing around the room, I saw that its Belle
Epoque chandeliers, frescoes, and pilasters looked a little
shabby after four years of Nazi occupation. In the corner,
a group of English tourists swigged whiskeys without ice
and talked loudly about the next morning's bus departure. A stout bespectacled man wandered in from the
lobby, shrugging off his soft tan coat. He ordered a glass
of pastis and sank into a large armchair by the window,
disappearing behind the pages of Le Figaro.

Jack dropped back onto the sofa beside me, brushing my cheek with his lips. "Now I want to hear every-

thing about you. Tell me all about your trip to Spain. Did you go to Botín in Madrid and eat the roast suckling pig, just like Hemingway?"

And so I told him about our holiday, describing the warmth and flowers, the glittering Mediterranean light, the glasses of orange juice that glowed like captured sunshine, the embassy reception we'd gone to with a delegation of visiting American senators, who kept asking if they could procure us any cigarettes, lend us any money, or introduce any nice boys to take us out.

Jack roared at this last anecdote and said I should use it in a short story one day. "You should try your hand at fiction, sweetheart. I imagine you as an American Nancy Mitford, all sly observation and skewering wit."

"Sounds like a good way to make enemies." I gave him a little smile.

"People rarely recognize their true selves," he said, gazing at the champagne bottle as a bead of condensation slid down its side. The waiter appeared to refill our glasses, and after he moved away, Jack took my hand in his. "How are things at avenue Mozart?" he asked in a low voice. "I know you just got back, but have you seen Ghislaine?"

I nodded. "It's funny. The whole time I was in Spain, I was dreading seeing her again. But then this morning when I got home, Christian was being such a holy terror, I felt sorry for her. She seemed utterly wrung out."

"Does she have no one to help her?"

"Sure, we all do, her mother and Claude especially. Even so . . ." I lifted my hands in the air.

"What about her ex-husband?"

I brought my cigarette to my lips, exhaling slowly. "I met him at the park today. Let's just say I understand why they divorced. He's the type who likes to get his way."

His eyebrows shot up. "He better not have given you any trouble."

"Me? No, Ghislaine would've ground him into fine dust. That's the odd thing—he talks awfully tough, but she doesn't give a fig. If anything, *he* seems terrified of *her.*" I tapped my cigarette against the ashtray, remembering the hunted look on André's face when he thought no one was looking.

"Sounds like she's better off without him."

"Yes, I think so—Oh!" I grabbed Jack's arm. "I almost forgot to tell you—she was also at that meeting in Marseille!"

His smile froze. "No, I—Golly! Are you sure? The congress for the Partisans of Peace? How did you—? Who told you—?"

"Ghislaine's ex was trying to pin her down about it.

He even accused her of snooping around and using the information against 'us'—whoever that is. She denied everything, of course, but I assume she was there gathering intelligence."

"Is he a pinko?"

"He sounded more like a card-carrying party member. Would you believe he had the gall to call me an American imperialist?"

"What did you say?"

"Ghislaine was in such a fury, I didn't dare breathe a word. She accused him of threatening her—which he was—but she wasn't the least bit frightened. Then they started bickering over who would take Christian to the café to use the toilet, and then they left."

Jack was silent for a moment, his thumb rubbing my shoulder. "And he didn't ask your name? Or anything else about you?"

"No, but I'm sure he could find out if he wanted to. He knows where I live, for one thing. Why?" I turned to look him in the eye. "Do you think he's dangerous?"

"I doubt it, sweetheart. He sounds like a spiteful man trying to even the score against his former wife. Did you tell Ghislaine I was in Marseille?"

I shook my head. "Should I have? I figured Ghislaine would think I was interfering when really it was just a funny coincidence."

"Quite right." But Jack seemed distracted, shifting in his seat and edging closer to me. He picked up his glass, holding it up to contemplate the effervescent liquid before draining it. "You know, I'm suddenly famished. What do you say we head over to the restaurant and see if they can seat us early?"

"But the champagne!" There were at least two glasses left in the bottle.

"We'll leave it for our waiter. Perhaps it'll improve his mood." Jack winked and pulled out a sheaf of franc notes, leaving them on the table. "Come on."

I took a final regretful sip, the taste of citrus zest lingering on my lips as I followed him outside. "Where are we going?" I asked, matching my stride to his, our heels echoing beneath the covered arcade that lined this stretch of the rue de Rivoli.

"I booked a table at Roger La Grenouille." At the street corner, he glanced around and proceeded to cross without breaking pace.

"That's my favorite bistro!"

"Is that so?" He grinned, a flash of even teeth gleaming in the streetlight.

He'd remembered. I must have mentioned it at some point, so casually even I had forgotten. But he had listened, and remembered, and thought to take me there even though it was his special news we were celebrating, and suddenly I felt like my heart might burst. I gave a running skip and caught his hand, pulling him into the shadowed depths of a portico, reaching my arms around his neck and kissing him until I half forgot where I was—until the sound of footsteps drawing closer brought me back with a start. I broke from Jack, burying my face in his shoulder. His hat hid his eyes, but he was watchful, his fingers twitching against the belt of my coat. When the clicking heels finally faded, I peered out to see the broad back of a portly little man, plain camelhair coat, ordinary trilby. No one who knew us. No one who cared that we'd been necking on the street where anyone could have seen.

Jack too seemed relieved. He grabbed my hand and we snaked through a tangle of streets off the rue Saint-Honoré, pausing in darkened doorways to kiss, before dashing down the next narrow alley, the next hidden passage. We reached the pont des Arts and crossed the Seine at brisk speed before diving into the twisting little streets of the Left Bank. I was leading him now, past familiar shops, around sharp corners, dodging pedestrians on the bright boulevard, drawing to a stop beside a pair of towering oak doors that I sometimes saw in my dreams.

"Do you think dinner might wait?" I gave him a

quick, bold glance, holding it long enough to see his pupils widen before I started blushing.

"Let's forget the bistro. I make a mean plate of scrambled eggs."

Inside his apartment, Jack took my face in his hands and kissed me tenderly, slowly. We had all the time in the world for each other, here in these rooms that smelled of laundry starch and wood polish, all the time in the world to tangle our half-clothed bodies together, all the time to close the curtains before we lit the lamps, so that not a sliver of light spilled into the night.

Chapter Thirteen

And so another term began, our third and final trimester of the academic year, and if I thought time had been moving quickly before, now it was bolting away in great galloping strides. All the Smith girls were buzzing about their plans for the summer—either traveling around Europe or returning home to get married—and every day at Reid Hall one of them would ask me, "What are *you* doing, Jackie?" until I wanted to scream.

I hadn't the faintest idea what I was doing—not now and certainly not three months from now. I had a ticket home, of course—on the *Liberté*, which would sail in late August—but lately Mummy had been pressuring me to come home two months earlier, in time for the season in Newport. Meanwhile, the summer in Europe beckoned with its promise of sharp light and dry heat, its white nights and pebbly beaches, its long, late lunches and chilled pink wine and lazy hilltop villages baking in the afternoon sun. I ached to experience it all, but Mummy's letter had suggested that ten months was more than enough time for me to spend abroad. "Why not come home and focus on your future?" she had written in her smooth, even script.

Of course I hadn't told her about Jack. I knew that the mere hint of him would prompt her to launch an investigation worthy of a Pinkerton detective, examining Jack's lineage, his prospects, and his politics, finding fault with all of it. In her eyes, Jacqueline Lee Bouvier, Queen Deb of the 1947 to 1948 season, was destined for a far greater union than marriage to a struggling writer of middling means—and no matter how happy Jack and I might be, Mummy would consider it one of the biggest disappointments of her life. So no, I hadn't mentioned Jack to anyone at home, for to expose him to the salt air of their scrutiny would only tarnish him—tarnish us—and prematurely, before there was anything to shine.

We hadn't made any promises. But I knew the way he felt about me, and I was pretty sure he knew I felt the same. Jack was my refuge, my encouragement, my bright future. Together we would create a new home far from the critical eyes of our parents, and it would be filled with ideas, and laughter, and mutual respect. I would never find someone who understood me better, or cared for me more deeply. I only had to say yes.

Spring that year of 1950 proved coquettish, teasing us with brilliant flashes of sun and blue skies that flipped suddenly to gushing rain and pelting hail. I had been waiting for the trees to blossom into great exuberant ruffles of pink and white, but as soon as a sunny hour or two coaxed a flower bud to unfurl its tender petals, a tempest would sweep in and crush them. The parks were a wasteland of battered plants and wide, placid puddles the color of milky coffee. Parisians tramped around with long faces and muddy shoes, stabbing at the ground with the umbrellas we carried everywhere.

It was the type of weather that made you want to stay inside, which was probably why it took me a few weeks to notice how strangely Jack was acting whenever we went out. Looking back, I see it began when I returned from Spain. But I distinctly remember the evening in mid-April when it struck me that something was off.

We had planned to meet at the cinema to see *Orphée* again, having failed the first time to grasp Jean Cocteau's strange and sinister film about the underworld. Jack was late, unusually for him, and so I waited under the bright marquee, lighting a cigarette to pass the time. I had barely taken a puff when he came up behind me as if he'd been keeping watch from the shadows.

"Were you hiding?" I teased.

He touched his cheeks to mine—once, twice—so that I smelled the fresh pine scent of his shaving lotion. "From you? Never." At his voice, as playful as always, I began to smile.

"Are you ready to descend into the abyss?"

"After last time, I came prepared with refreshments." From behind his back, he revealed a diamond-shaped tin in gold and white, printed with the words LE ROY RÉMI. "They're calissons—almond sweetmeats I bought down south," he explained.

I clapped my gloved hands together. "I adore almonds!"

"I remember." He smiled at my enthusiasm. "They go well with this." Unbuttoning his coat, he showed me the silver flask tucked in his inside pocket.

"Is that marc?"

"Cognac."

"Golly, I hope I don't get tipsy."

"With this film, it could only help." He gestured at the entrance. "Shall we?"

I led the way inside, heading to the front of the cinema, where our seats were assigned. I was picking my way across the row, halfway to the center, when his fingers touched my elbow. "On second thought, sweetheart, how about we sit up there?" He jerked his head to the back.

"What about our tickets?"

"They won't care." He nodded at the usher, who was lolling against the wall, picking his nails. "Come on, we'll have more space in the back."

The theater was half empty. *Orphée* had come out a few months ago and most people had already seen it. But when Jack patted his coat pocket and winked at me conspiratorially, I thought I understood. "All right," I said, and we turned to exit the row, forcing a pair of spidery ladies to rise anew so that we could pass back the other way. "Oh, *je m'excuse*, madame!" I apologized as my heel trod on a bony foot.

"Do you not have the impression that you're disturbing everyone?" the owner of the foot said, her tone, as sweet as birdsong, belying the sarcasm of her words.

"Old cow," Jack muttered when we had escaped to the back of the theater, installing ourselves in the very last row. "Sorry, sweetheart, but I get so aggravated by the way these people have to adorn every last insult with a little bow. Nothing is ever straightforward in this country—you ever notice that? I'd rather be punched in the nose than stabbed by their sly mockery."

"The straightforward honesty of good old American rudeness." I shot him a teasing glance.

"That's right." He grinned. "What you see is what you get." He leaned back in his seat, stretching his long legs into the aisle.

The lights began to dim. I opened the tin of calissons and extracted one, finding the confection stickier and more cloying than I'd expected. I offered them to Jack, but he declined, and I tucked the box into my pocketbook, intending to give them to Mary Ann, who had a notorious sweet tooth.

"Wash it down with this," Jack whispered, handing me the flask. I took a sip, feeling the liquor's warmth spread through my chest, all the way to my fingers and toes. We passed the flask between us a couple of times as the newsreel played, Jack stowing it back in his pocket once the film began rippling across the screen.

Try as I might to absorb myself in Cocteau's mysterious dream sequences, his retelling of the Orpheus myth failed once again to capture me. At times the acting seemed overwrought, almost farcical, and I wondered if it was inadvertent, or another example of what Jack had been grousing about—French criticism cloaked in irony. Beside me, Jack seemed restless, crossing and uncrossing his arms, and craning his head to watch as the usher showed a straggler down the aisle to his seat.

Suddenly Jack's mouth was at my ear. "What do you say we get out of here?" he said in a low voice.

We were almost at the end of the film, when Orpheus looks back in the mirror and sees his wife, the one scene that had startled me in my previous viewing. "There's only a few minutes left," I whispered.

"I'm feeling light-headed," he said urgently.

"Are you all right?" I touched my palm to his forehead, which felt clammy.

"I need some fresh air." He gripped my hand, not letting go as I fumbled for my coat and pocketbook.

We slipped out the side door and into the night. It had just finished showering and the pavement was shiny under the yellow streetlights. Jack was quiet, seeming to concentrate on taking deep, even breaths. I snuck little glances at his face, hoping some color would return to his cheeks. "Is this helping? Are you feeling any better?" I asked as we moved briskly down the wide boulevard, turning onto a small side street.

"I just want to walk." He spoke faintly, but his hand clutched my fingers.

"How about something to eat—would that help? Oh, maybe a"—I extracted the tin of sweets from my pocketbook—"calisson? They say a bit of sugar can—"

"For chrissakes, Jacqueline, stop fussing!" he barked, and I fell back, stung. He had never spoken to me so sharply. Anger and hurt prickled at the back of my throat, but I forced my expression into blankness, smoothing a polite smile upon my lips.

"Sweetheart, wait." He pulled me into the darkened doorway of a flower shop. "I shouldn't have snapped at you, I'm sorry. It's just work getting to me, that's all."

"Have you been feeling poorly for a while?" I searched his face for clues. "If you need a good doctor, there's a list at Reid Hall that I could—"

"No, no, it's nothing like that." He frowned, gazing past my shoulder. "It's nothing a brisk walk won't cure," he added after a moment.

As if trying to convince himself, we began walking again, circling the quartier in sharp twists and turns, until the blood ran high in our veins. We must have walked for three quarters of an hour without stopping, but when we finally came to the Rose Rouge, Jack's pace slowed. The door to the basement club was closed, but a tangle of notes poured through the cracks.

"How about a drink?" he asked, and I agreed, relieved to see a spark of animation return to his features.

We entered to a rush of heat and sound. On this Wednesday night, the club was busy but not swamped, and we quickly spotted Jimmy, George, and some of Jack's other expat writer friends grouped around a couple of tables. They waved at us, moving chairs to make room, and by the time the barman brought a round of whiskeys, the hunted look creasing Jack's brow had softened. Someone passed him a drink, and he pulled it close, swirling the amber liquid, smelling it, lifting the glass and meeting my eye in a toast. When he finally drank, I sensed the relief coursing through him. It reminded me of the way my horse, Danseuse, would roll around in the dirt the second she was turned out of her stall.

I sipped from my own glass but scarcely tasted a thing. For I had seen someone else look at a drink that way: Daddy.

After that day I began watching Jack more carefully, and I found plenty to observe. There was the afternoon we had lunch at a well-known soufflé restaurant, when he excused himself between the main course and dessert to make a quick phone call. "I just need to reschedule a meeting, sweetheart," he said, dropping a kiss on my head and dashing out the door.

"Perhaps it is different in *Amérique*, mademoiselle," said our waiter when he delivered the quivering mounds of whipped egg and sugar to our table. "But here in France we wait for the soufflé; the soufflé does not wait for us." He cast a pointed look at the empty chair across from me.

When Jack finally returned, he was brimming with apologies, saying he'd had to walk ten blocks to find a working pay phone. But he seized the complimentary bottle of Grand Marnier and doused his deflated soufflé so thoroughly that I wondered.

There was the morning in the Louvre when he dragged me from a marvelous exhibit of Renaissance paintings to the collection of ancient armor, leading me in circles, up the stairs, down the elevator, and back up a different flight of stairs, insisting he knew a shortcut, refusing to ask for directions when it became clear we were lost. The gallery of Roman antiquities happened to be near the exit, which happened to be close to one of Jack's favorite cafés.

"Let's stop for an *apéro* before lunch, all right, sweetheart?" he said. Before I knew it, we had ducked inside and Jack was ordering small glasses of pineau, a sweet apéritif wine. I had just taken a sip when I heard someone exclaim, "Hey, Jacques!" and there was Charlie—Jack's friend from the communist bookshop; Claude's pal from school—sitting at a little marble-topped table with a glass of beer before him.

"What are you doing *here*?" Jack asked, once we had all kissed each other hello. He had gulped half his glass of wine already, the pinched look fading from his face. "I didn't know you were an art maven."

"I'm meeting my mother to see the Ingres exhibit," Charlie explained. "I'm afraid she still hasn't shed all her bourgeois tastes."

Jack's grin told me this was a joke. Still, as we sat, I found myself listening to Charlie with extra care, attempting to reconcile my ingrained prejudices with a new effort to be open-minded.

"How was the bookshop last night?" Jack asked.

"You didn't miss a thing," Charlie assured him.

"Did you see Vladimir?"

"Only for a bit. He had to leave early."

"Who's Vladimir?" I asked.

"An exchange student from Moscow," said Charlie.

"That's what he *says*." Jack raised an eyebrow.

"Aw, come on, Vlad's harmless. We've had some terrific talks about Russian literature. He loves books, that's all."

"Yeah, but he also loves Stalin," Jack declared.

Charlie rolled his eyes, but with affection. "You should have heard him and Olivier last night, going on and on again about dialectical materialism. Even Vlad got fed up. He called Olivier an old windbag."

Jack chuckled. "Tell her about the trick you played." He produced a packet of cigarettes from his coat pocket and offered them round.

Charlie launched into the tale—something about a

hole in Olivier's coat lining, hidden bits of muenster cheese, and a terrible smell. "Boy, was he steamed when he figured it out!" His eyes danced. "I guess he's still real mad. Would you believe he had the nerve to ask Geneviève to dance last night? Right in front of me!"

"You *dance* there too?" I said before I could stop myself.

"Well, sure," said Charlie. "We don't just sit around singing the 'Internationale' and writing manifestos."

"Charlie is a Lindy Hop champ," Jack said. "He's won several competitions."

"Aww." Charlie ducked his head. "Just two!"

"You should take Geneviève to the *guinguette*," Jack suggested. "Dazzle her with your dance moves."

"I tried," he said glumly. "She says it's bourgeois." He ran his fingers through his hair. "I just wish I knew how she felt about me. It's driving me crazy! Did I tell you she stood me up at the cinema last week? I didn't hear from her until two days later, and then she called and wanted to meet right away . . ."

As Charlie described the confusing behavior of his inamorata, it occurred to me that maybe I'd been wrong about Le Compagnon de voyage in at least one way: I had imagined it a dour and humorless den of iniquity, but it sounded more like a lively social center for lefty intellectuals and poets, complete with petty rivalries, silly pranks, and hopeless crushes.

"I was thinking of asking her to the anti-colonialism march," Charlie was saying. "Do you think she'd say yes?"

"There's one way to find out," I encouraged him, glancing at Jack.

But Jack was signaling to the waiter for another drink. "What anti-colonialism march?" he said.

"There's one next weekend," said Charlie. "Didn't Vlad tell you? He said he did."

"He did not." Jack flicked his cigarette between his fingers, flakes of ash flying into the air. The waiter delivered his wine and he seized the glass without thanking him. "When is it? And where?"

"It's Saturday . . . place de la République. We're meeting at nine—Oh!" He started up from his chair. "There's my mother. I have to run. I'll see you tomorrow at the shop. We can talk about it then, all right, Jacques?"

"Sure," Jack said, but he spoke coolly, and there was a set to his jaw that I knew too well.

"What a sweet kid," I said, once Charlie had dashed off. "I hope his heart doesn't get crushed."

"They all seem sweet at first," Jack said grimly. "But

in the end you realize they have no sense of humor." He drained his glass and raised his hand to order another.

And then there was the Sunday afternoon we were in Jack's apartment, when he went to answer the ringing telephone in his study. Before I could second-guess myself, I darted to the polished wood cabinet where he kept the liquor, inspecting the few bottles within—cognac, calvados, gin, and some clear liquid that smelled of herbs and pure spirits—all of it almost full or unopened. Jack's step nearby made me start, and, looking up, I saw he was in the doorway. "Wrong number," he said, touching the door of the liquor cabinet with a question in his eyes.

"I was . . . thinking of pouring a drink." I attempted to hide my fluster behind a vague smile.

"Sure, help yourself," he said easily, though it was not yet three o'clock and we were about to go for a walk.

"Care to join me?"

"I won't, thanks. I have to work on some revisions later."

I didn't much feel like it either but didn't know how to get out of it. Just as I was reaching reluctantly for the gin bottle, the phone began to ring again.

"There's tonic water in the kitchen," Jack called over his shoulder as he went to answer it.

I listened to his footsteps receding down the hall,

then the creak of the study door opening. *"Allô? Allô?"* he repeated, as I stared into the cabinet. I wasn't sure what I'd been expecting, but it wasn't this collection of dusty bottles. Perhaps he kept a secret stash somewhere else, but after my experience with Daddy, who arranged his bar cart in shining rows of military precision, I doubted it. *"J'ÉCOUTE! Qui est à l'appareil?* Who's calling, please?" Jack barked from the other room. I guessed there was no response, for he slammed down the receiver and stalked back into the *salon*.

"Wrong number again?"

"I guess so." He eyed the bottle of gin in my hand. "You know, I think I will have that drink." I poured him a neat measure and he swallowed it in a gulp, holding up his glass. I poured him another, and he downed that one too. Before I could pour a third, the phone began to ring once more. Jack went out into the hall and came back with our coats. "Let's go for a walk."

"But what about the phone?"

He waved a hand toward the incessant noise. "It can ring." His complexion looked pale and clammy—from the gin, I supposed—or maybe from the insistent trill of the phone ringing and ringing. I felt it vibrating in my skull.

Outside, the sky was dark and heavy, the clouds almost low enough to touch. The air held the ominous, expectant calm that precedes a storm, and I knew we had chosen exactly the wrong moment to take a walk. Indeed, we had scarcely gone ten steps when the rain began, little flecks growing to fat drops, which quickly transformed into a deluge. Everyone scattered from the streets, dashing into buildings, huddling beneath porticos and awnings. My hair was soaked, despite the umbrella, my shoes sodden beyond salvation, yet Jack kept walking, and so did I. And as we walked I was surprised to sense the unease of the last few minutes, hours, days, weeks, lifting, as if the downpour was washing it away. Jack's step became light, his shoulders dropped, his brow smoothed. He tucked my arm through his, and together we walked along the boulevard, sauntering to and fro on the empty sidewalk. When he turned to grin at me, his face looked almost euphoric.

I didn't like to confide in anyone, and so I kept my concerns to myself. It was difficult, however, because my thoughts were constantly preoccupied by Jack's erratic behavior. There were moments when I felt so sure he had a problem with drink that I could have abandoned him on the street, turned on my heel, and walked away forever. Most of the time, I wasn't so certain. Everyone drank an awful lot back then, at all hours of the day or night—wine with meals, a glass of red to warm up a cold afternoon, cognac accompanying coffee like salt with pepper. We drank to celebrate and commiserate and to simply pass the time, and I found it hard to determine how much was excessive.

I knew Jack was perceptive enough—and observant enough—to notice me watching him. But he didn't say anything, and his behavior toward me never changed. Most of the time he was as playful and lighthearted as ever, and my heart soared to be with him. But in scattered moments something sent him spiraling, some demon chasing him that could be shaken off only by a long walk and a stiff pour. Try as I might, I couldn't predict what would upset him. Eventually I came to believe his moods were rooted in his work—the relentless cycle of elation, self-criticism, and doubt that writers endure—and I trusted that once his novel was sold to a publisher, his sunny, even-tempered disposition would return.

In the meantime, I watched and brooded, all to the detriment of my studies. Madame Saleil sighed when she saw me now, and one morning as I passed her in the corridor at Reid Hall, she called me into her office.

"What has happened to you, Jacqueline?" she scolded. "A brilliant girl like you—I had high hopes you'd become a stellar academic. But you must throw yourself into the intellectual life! I sense your heart is elsewhere."

Indeed it was, though I didn't like to admit it after all she'd done for me. Instead, I promised to work harder and rushed off to skim the text for my next small group discussion, which was starting in half an hour.

With my thoughts so muddled, my future felt suspended—yet life crept steadily forward. Easter came and went with the familiar rituals of high Mass and roasted leg of lamb, and unfamiliar ones like chocolate bells instead of eggs. Madame taught us how to eat white asparagus, holding a plump spear between our fingers, dragging it through a puddle of hollandaise, and savoring the tang of lemon against the grassy, delicate crunch. Often I came home to find Ghislaine bent over a pile of new peas, or hulling strawberries. She had never been very keen on cooking, but lately she had been helping in the kitchen more and more.

In fact, she was around the apartment more and more, I realized one Saturday when I left her pinning up her hair in the morning and found her, hours later, still with curlers on her head. Lately she came straight home from the office instead of meeting friends after work, and she no longer went to lunch or the cinema on the weekends. I overheard her tell Mary Ann that she was saving money for a summer holiday in Spain, but then she started paying the *bonne*, Marie, to take Christian to the park on Sunday afternoons. When she did go out with us, it was only to the café around the corner—a quick drink or bite to eat—and she fidgeted all the while, bouncing her leg so that the plates rattled on the table.

Even Ghislaine's temperament seemed different. Whereas before she had been perpetually exhausted, now she whirled from room to room, scrubbing floors, patching the knees of Christian's trousers, cooking watery soups and burned biscuits, leaving a trail of shining surfaces in her wake. The change made me curious.

"Has Ghislaine seemed different lately?" I asked Claude one afternoon. We had ducked into the Bon Marché to avoid a sudden rain shower and found ourselves in a world of color, fragrance, and light—gleaming glass counters, opulent fabrics, and cinch-waisted dresses with voluminous skirts, not to mention the new spring hats, which were arrayed on silver stands and lit from above like works of fine art.

"What do you mean by different?"

I hesitated. "She seems . . . restless." It was more than that, though. It was a constant, furtive agitation, as if she was afraid something might happen if she stopped moving. "Remember how she took me to the coiffeuse near her office last week? We were on the métro coming home—not really chatting, just sitting next to each other, you know? Well, the train stopped at Concorde and all of a sudden she jumped off. Didn't say a single word, just rushed off right as the doors were closing. When she caught up to me at Jasmin, she said she'd lost track of the stations."

Claude frowned, smoothing the fingers of her gloves. "It's funny because something similar happened to me last Saturday," she said slowly. "We were having lunch at the *crêperie*—you know, the one around the corner? We'd just sat down and were looking at the menu, when she leaped up and insisted on switching tables. It was a bit of a fuss because the waiter claimed everything was reserved—even though the restaurant was practically empty. There was only this little old man eating his sad *galette jambon fromage* alone by the window and studiously ignoring us. Finally the waiter let us have a table by the kitchen—and then, would you believe it? Ghislaine said she wasn't hungry anymore. And she left! I had to apologize profusely and slink out. I don't know if I can show my face there again."

"Could she be having problems at work?" I suggested, attempting to gauge how much she knew about her sister's clandestine activities.

"As a secretary? I doubt it."

I pretended to admire a row of bejeweled satin turbans, trying to collect my thoughts. I gathered she didn't know about Ghislaine's spying, which didn't surprise me, but it meant I needed to tread carefully, for the secret wasn't mine to divulge. "What if you asked her?" I suggested.

"She'd only shout at me." Claude sighed. "She has a lot on her mind, but . . ." She straightened a straw cloche on its stand, her expression troubled.

"But?"

She turned to face me. "Remember when I told you about Maman and what happened to her during the war?"

"Of course."

"What I didn't tell you was that Ghislaine was active too. She was a radio operator, sending coded messages—the most nerve-racking, dangerous job of them all. She used our *chambre de bonne* as one of her safe houses; it was empty since our housemaid went back to Brittany at the start of the Occupation. That's why they sent me away. The Germans had learned how to triangulate the signal, you see, which meant the Gestapo was always just a couple of seconds behind her. She could never relax—she was always on the run, living on her nerves. The equipment was dreadfully heavy and she was hauling it between safe houses in a suitcase. She was basically a teenager, and that was part of her cover, because she looked so young."

Her hand came up to clutch the strap of her pocketbook, pulling it tight across her shoulder. I held my breath, afraid to interrupt.

"Most radio operators only lasted about six weeks," she continued. "But Ghislaine was successful for a good long while, at least eighteen months. And then . . ." She pressed her lips together.

"What—what happened?"

"She got caught. They took her to Fresnes. She escaped—that much I know. But nothing more. She doesn't discuss it, and she doesn't like people to know about it. We never talk about it. But the prison at Fresnes—that's where the Germans took their worst enemies: resistants and foreign spies and they—they punished them. It was a barbaric place, the most horrific, the cruelest . . ." Her gaze slid from mine. "I can't imagine what she had to do to get out of there."

I couldn't speak. I lowered my eyes and stared at the brim of a slim cartwheel hat, the tight weave of straw, the fall of its grosgrain ribbon, conscious of how each graceful detail contrasted with the ugliness of Claude's words. I was stunned by Ghislaine's history, half admiring and half horrified by the bold bloody nerve of

her. And yet, it also explained her air of veiled shrewd-
ness. It occurred to me that Ghislaine's absentminded-
ness, her elusiveness, was not merely the weariness of
a single working mother but a way for her to dodge
and deflect painful memories, to maintain her privacy.
Of course, the disadvantage to keeping people at arm's
length was that no one understood who you really were.
I knew that better than almost anyone.

"Oh, Claude," I said sadly. "This should be such a
happy time for you." It was what I had expected to find
in France: extravagant, buoyant happiness—not this
fragile, broken society that slept with one eye open.

She shrugged. "How can I complain? We survived
when many others did not. Unfortunately, it comes
with a price. Ghislaine seems fine most of the time, but
she . . . she takes things too far. She sees threats everywhere, but she flies into a rage if you dare suggest it's
in her head. Honestly, sometimes I've wondered if she
wants that feeling of danger—she mentions it so often,
it's almost like it comforts her, as bizarre as that sounds.
And she has nightmares. They can be quite intense. I
know Maman worries she'll wake you girls up."

I hadn't forgotten that voice in the night, that desperate, pleading voice blending with the howling wind:
"Please, please, please. Help me." It was a relief, in a
way, to have an explanation, to know I hadn't imagined

it. "Don't worry," I said. "I think I understand a little better now."

"You mustn't breathe a word of this to anyone. Promise me." Claude's eyes didn't leave my face. "Ghislaine would be dreadfully angry if she knew I'd said anything."

"I won't. Cross my heart." I touched a hand to my chest. "I'm glad you told me, though. At least it helps explain her moods a little better—and they're less alarming once you know the reasons behind them."

"Yes, I suppose you're right." She had moved so that her back was against the window, making her expression hard to read. "But I have to say, Jacqueline, I've never seen her like this before."

Chapter Fourteen

Jack checked his watch and flashed me a guilty smile when he saw I'd noticed. The lecture hall was filling rapidly, the chatter of voices blending into an indistinct clamor, the heat of our packed bodies causing sweat to prickle at my temples. I had tried to save seats for Madame and Ghislaine, but two birdlike women had plucked them away, hopping over our legs and settling in with their knitting while waiting for the program to begin.

Twisting in my chair, I scanned the audience, spotting Claude's beau, Bernard, sitting a few rows behind us. He returned my wave with a nod, friendly but grave. Susan and Mary Ann stood at the back, and I saw several of Claude's classmates from Sciences Po scattered through the crowd, including Charlie, who acknowledged me with a wink.

"See?" I nudged Jack. "Charlie's here. Aren't you glad you came after all?"

"I'm just happy I'm not the only fellow." Jack spoke near my ear, causing the fine hairs along my neck to stand on end.

"Are you implying that men don't support the Union des femmes françaises?"

"Not at all! I'm saying that more of us should," he said smoothly. "I didn't realize you were such a feminist yourself."

"Me? I'm only here to support Claude."

He raised an eyebrow, but before I could say anything else, the audience broke into scattered applause and the panel of four took the stage. Claude looked especially small and young beside the three other academics and writers, each woman chosen to represent a different stage of life.

They began discussing the question "What are the fundamental rights of women?" and talked about how life had changed since 1939, when France entered the war. They talked about the new roles and responsibilities thrust upon French women during the Occupation, when some were forced to survive on their own, their husbands and brothers taken as prisoners of war, herded into work camps, or killed. They talked about Simone de Beauvoir's book *Le Deuxième sexe*, which had been published last year, and which examined the reasons women were considered secondary to men despite being half the human race. They talked about the right to vote and serve on juries, which had been granted to French women in 1944, and about the new postwar emphasis on higher education and employment.

"My friends and I do feel more economic necessity than ever before." Claude spoke with her precise diction. "And of course we also have a greater chance of ending up as spinsters. At least with a university degree, we can hope for a better-paying job."

Her words surprised me, for I had supposed that Claude would marry Bernard soon after she graduated from Sciences Po. They weren't engaged, but they had an understanding, and I had imagined her dabbling in local politics while tending to a growing brood of children, just as I might one day scribble children's books and short stories while tending to mine. (Though I had vowed to never become a housewife, I knew that housewifery was ultimately the fate of all well-brought-up young ladies.)

But now, as Claude spoke of her desire to work in government, I found myself considering my own future. What if I didn't marry right after college but found a job—a job that expanded my world beyond Mummy's sphere, a job that could give me opportunity to write, and meet interesting people, and travel? Not a forever job—not a career—but something breezy and buzzy that I could spin into cocktail chatter for the rest of my life. Claude was right—a college degree would open many doors—and with the help of Jack, and Madame Saleil, and the de Rentys, and possibly Mummy's network of old battleaxes, I felt confident I'd find something to bring me back to Paris. I smiled a little, imagining the possibilities.

"Like most girls, my dearest dream has always been to *fonder un foyer*—get married, create a home, raise a family," Claude was saying. "But I believe meaningful work is also possible for women in this New France." She concluded to an energetic round of applause.

Afterward, we joined the crowd in the courtyard, where long tables had been set against a wall that was covered with wisteria blossoms. Waiters circled with trays of champagne and little lacquered canapés, and for once the sky was a delicate, effervescent blue, rippling with fish-scale clouds that were lit from below by the late-day sun. Around us, French voices rose and fell in a lilting cadence, my ears picking up bits of conversation like a radio tuning its reception.

I turned and saw Claude surrounded by admirers,

gesturing with her hands, talking in her clear, declarative way. Bernard broke into the circle, handed her a glass of champagne, and then retreated to gaze at her with unabashed admiration. He was a few years older than us—a lawyer who had joined Général Leclerc's army in Africa during the war—possessed of a shy, thoughtful nature that paired well with Claude's serious determination. If I had to speculate about their future, I guessed they'd be very happy together.

"Cigarette?" Jack offered me his case and I took one, leaning close to him, breathing in his fresh juniper scent before he lit it. He gave me a smile, his regard steady upon mine.

"I should find Madame and Ghislaine," I said, tipping the last bright drops of champagne onto my tongue.

"Ah. After all these months, am I finally to meet the mysterious Ghislaine?" He tapped his cigarette onto the cobblestone paving, bits of ash scattering like crumbs. "If I didn't know better, I'd suspect she's been avoiding me this whole time."

"Maybe *you* are avoiding *her*," I suggested. "Or maybe you're the same person and that's why you're never in the same place."

Jack grinned, then flagged down a waiter to refill our glasses. "I should say hello to Charlie, but I want to stay and hear this intriguing tale of deception."

"Go on." I released him with a wink. "I'll tell you more later."

I found Madame and Ghislaine by the bar, looking a bit flushed. Madame was serenely admiring the wisteria, while Ghislaine gulped champagne.

"Wasn't Claude wonderful up there?" I said, kissing them hello.

"She wasn't bad," said Madame, fiddling with her necklace.

"Not bad? She was magnificent! So articulate, thoughtful, intelligent . . ."

"Maman is being bourgeois," teased Ghislaine, tossing a handful of mixed nuts in her mouth. "Inside she's simply bursting."

"I've been trying to congratulate her, but she's swamped with admirers." I glanced around, trying to see if Claude was free, and instead spotted Susan and Mary Ann, who came rushing over.

"Madame!" Mary Ann exclaimed with such pure American exuberance that half a dozen heads turned to stare. "Oh my goodness, you must be so proud! I could hardly believe it was the same timid little Claude!"

"She was absolutely marvelous," Susan said warmly. "An inspiration for all women, young or old, French or American."

"Oh, you girls are too kind," Madame protested, but she was pleased, I could tell.

"This is a bit like being at my own funeral," said a familiar voice, and there was Claude, peeping past Mary Ann with a grin. Bernard stood by her side, holding her school satchel along with his briefcase.

"Claude!" Mary Ann swooped in to hug her. "Congratulations!" And with cries of *"Bravo!"* and *"Félicitations!"* we kissed her cheeks, patted her shoulders, and raised our drinks, toasting her success.

As soon as our glasses were empty, Jack appeared. "Hey, there she is! The woman of the hour!" he called, kissing Claude's cheeks. A waiter circled round with a chilled bottle, and I took a sip of fresh champagne, cold and tart and tingly, feeling it travel straight from my stomach to my head. I was drifting on sparkling wine, and sunset-stained clouds, and the scent of spring blossoms, and perhaps this was why I wasn't paying attention when Jack began greeting everyone, only remembering my manners when I saw him hesitate before Ghislaine with a puzzled smile.

"Bonsoir . . ." he began.

"Oh, sorry, allow me to introduce you." I stepped in. "Ghislaine, this is Jack, who you've heard me talk about so much. Jack, this is Ghislaine, Claude's sister . . ."

The words died on my lips when I saw her face, bleached of color, her eyes fixed upon his, dark and frozen. I looked at Jack, hoping to glean an explanation, but he had retreated behind a pleasant half smile, although I thought I saw a muscle move in his cheek.

"*Enchanté*," he said.

Ghislaine brought her glass to her lips, found it empty, and lowered it. "Excuse me," she said. "I must go powder my drink, er, refill my nose . . . Oh Christ, you know what I mean."

But before she could step away, a young man came bounding toward us. It was Charlie, a smile splitting his face, moving so quickly his dark wavy hair blew back in the breeze. He skidded to a stop and threw his arms around Ghislaine.

"Geneviève!" he cried. "What are you doing here?"

Looking back, I see that this was the moment when everything began to unravel. I didn't know it at the time, of course. At the time, I was busy connecting the dots: Geneviève must be Ghislaine's alias, and if Charlie knew it, she had surely been spying on him. Of course she had. Was he not a communist youth leader, active at the university? I was surprised it hadn't occurred to me before.

Charlie must have felt Ghislaine go rigid, for he pulled back and looked her in the eye. "I didn't know you'd be in town tonight," he said with a confused smile. "I wish you'd have told me."

"I wasn't—er—I—" Her eyes darted wildly around the group. We were all listening, Madame and Jack looking at the ground, but the others staring with expressions of varying degrees of bewilderment.

Charlie followed Ghislaine's gaze, catching sight of me. "Jacqueline? You know Geneviève? And . . . Jack? And you two"—he swiveled to Susan and Mary Ann—"weren't you at that party?"

"*Excusez-moi*, but you're confusing me with someone else," Mary Ann announced. "I wasn't at any party with you. As for her"—she jerked her head—"her name's Ghislaine, not Geneviève."

He fell back a step, his eyes continuing to move around the circle. "Claude?" he said in disbelief, his features pinched. Suddenly he flushed. "Oh," he gasped. "I've been an ass." He clamped his mouth shut, as if afraid he'd blurt out something more, throwing another glance at Claude. "A complete ass."

Claude's eyes were narrowed and I could almost hear the pieces clicking together in her brain—the missing address book, and proofreading our essays, and circumspect behavior—all of it adding up to confirm what she might have suspected for months. She hadn't known about her sister before, but she knew now.

"I thought we were friends," Charlie said to her, his voice rough. "How—how could you?"

Claude's face, which had been so alight with joy on this evening of triumph, crumpled. "Charlie," she said in an urgent whisper. "Please believe me: *I didn't know.*"

He spun away, searching out Jack, looking at him with anguish in his eyes. "Did you know?"

Jack shook his head. "Just goes to show, you can't trust anyone."

Charlie flattened his mouth—in rage, I thought, before realizing he was suppressing tears. My heart turned in my chest, for he seemed so very young and idealistic.

"Hey, old chap. It's all right." Jack put a hand on his friend's shoulder with the same steady calm he'd offered me on the night I'd discovered Ghislaine's espionage. "Come on. Let's—let's go get a drink."

Charlie flinched at his touch, his whole body tense. Jack withdrew his hand and waited, with an earnest furrow to his brow. A moment passed, and another, and finally Charlie relented, his posture softening. *"D'accord,"* he agreed. As they moved off together, I saw Jack patting his coat pocket and caught the flash of his flask, shining in the last light of day.

My legs were shaking. I reached into my pocketbook for a cigarette and eventually managed to light it.

"What just happened?" Mary Ann said, loudly enough to be heard in the next arrondissement.

Susan elbowed her. "I'll tell you later," she muttered.

"Who was that kid?" Mary Ann demanded. "Why on earth was he calling Ghislaine Geneviève? And where'd she go, anyway?"

I looked around me with surprise. Indeed, Ghislaine had vanished.

The next day I stepped through the massive doors of Reid Hall and found Jack smoking a cigarette. "Jacqueline!" He waved.

"Hello, stranger." I greeted him with a cool smile and kept on walking. He had disappeared last night, even though we were supposed to go on to dinner after the event, he and Charlie vanishing without a word of warning. I had searched for him everywhere, in all the corners of the courtyard and lecture hall, even slipping a busboy a few *sous* to make sure he hadn't taken ill in the W.C. Eventually, I invented a headache and told Madame and the others I was feeling too poorly for dinner. By the time I got back to the apartment, it was no longer a fabrication.

"Listen, I know you're sore about last night. Can I

buy you lunch and explain?" Jack jogged a step to catch up to me.

"Is that all? An explanation?"

"And an apology," he added. "Please, sweetheart, at least can you slow down? I can barely keep up."

"Hmmph," I scoffed, for Jack had the strength and speed of an antelope, as I knew from the past few weeks. Nevertheless, I slackened my pace slightly. "Very well. You may buy me a sandwich. No—" I said, when he began to protest. "I have studying to do at the library. It's a quick sandwich eaten beside the Seine, or nothing."

"As you wish." He bowed his head.

A few minutes later we were sitting on the hard stone bank of the river, our feet dangling over the edge. It was a gray day, but warm, the sun's heat trapped in the clouds like in a glasshouse. Jack handed me a length of baguette filled with ham and butter, and I placed it in my lap, my appetite diminished by pique.

"Listen," Jack began, "I shouldn't have left you high and dry last night, especially without any warning. Charlie was devastated and he's been such a good friend—I needed to help him, you know? But that's not an excuse. I was a heel, and I'm sorry."

"You could have at least told me you were leaving."

I lit a cigarette, inhaling sharply. "I felt like a fool looking all over for you."

He rubbed his face with his hands. "I'm sorry, Jacqueline. I just—I guess I panicked. Charlie was so spooked by Ghislaine, I was afraid he was going to—to do something reckless."

"You mean hurt her?" I said in alarm, momentarily forgetting my vexation.

"No, no, he wouldn't do anything like that. We talked, and it's fine now. Don't worry." He looked down at the sandwich in his lap, fingering the wax paper wrapping. "That was quite a night, huh?"

"Indeed," I said crisply. But my annoyance was fading. The events of last night had left me too jittery to freeze Jack out now. I needed to talk to him—needed him to reassure me that this was all a tempest in a teapot. "Had you—I suppose you'd met Ghislaine before?"

He lit a cigarette, throwing the match into the water below. "At the bookshop, yes. She said she worked at one of the porcelain stores around Les Halles—told us she lived with her parents and commuted in from the suburbs. Charlie fell for her hook, line, and sinker. He's just a kid, you know. He thought Geneviève was this beautiful, glamorous woman hanging on his every word."

"Hmm. And yet she swore to Claude that she wasn't stringing him along."

"Is that right?" He flicked ash across the cobblestones. "What else happened when you got home last night?"

I thought back to the dimmed apartment, all six of us creeping about in socked feet, hissing at each other in low voices for fear of waking Christian. Ghislaine had come home shortly after us and passed immediately into the bathroom—although it wasn't her night for a bath—insisting that Claude help her wash her hair. The two of them were in there for ages, fragments of their conversation rising above the roar of running water.

"How could you . . ."

". . . swear on the head of my son! I didn't lead him on."

". . . why Charlie? He'd never take orders from Moscow! Never!"

"Why can't you understand? You can't trust any of them!"

I reported all of this to Jack, though it wasn't much. "I don't know how long they were in there, but eventually Madame made them unlock the door and come out. This morning Claude ate breakfast in the kitchen and left without saying a word. Ghislaine and Madame acted like nothing had happened."

"How about the other girls—Mary Ann and Sue? They say anything?"

I fiddled with the edge of my sleeve. "Sue must've put the fear of the devil into Mary Ann because she's stopped asking questions."

"If that's all it takes, you girls should've invented an anti-communist spy ring months ago."

Despite myself, I smiled. Of course Jack noticed, and his expression turned pleading. "Listen, sweetheart, I know things seemed turbulent last night—and it didn't help that I behaved like a cad. But in the grand scheme of things, all of this—Ghislaine and Charlie, the spying—it'll blow over soon. It's—it's just a tempest in a teapot."

There they were at last, the exact words I had been hoping to hear. And yes, I knew they were cliché, but still they brought me comfort, for weren't clichés rooted in truth? For the first time since last night, I allowed myself to relax. Jack had offered a reasonable explanation and a sincere apology—more than that, he was here to soothe me with his steady reassurance. This time when he looked at me with his heart on his face, I allowed my hand to brush his arm.

"Oh, sweetheart." He seized my fingers. "I knew how upset you must have been last night, and I've been sick about it. I'm so sorry. Truly."

I watched his thumb trace a path across my palm, gently, ever so gently, my hand looking delicate nestled within his. "It's all right," I said in a soft little voice. "Just don't let it happen again."

"Never again," he promised.

When I returned to avenue Mozart that evening, the apartment was stifling, the dense, gray-sky heat clinging to my skin and making it prickle. It was around five o'clock and usually Madame was home by now, starting dinner with the wireless on low. Today, however, there was no greeting, no clattering of pans, no friendly face popping out of the kitchen doorway. I went around opening windows, trying to dispel the heavy air blanketing the rooms like a bad mood. In the front hallway, I kicked off my shoes and carried them to my bedroom, nudging the door open with my foot.

"*Bonsoir, Jacqueline,*" came a voice behind me.

I turned with my hand on my heart. "Ghislaine! Golly, you startled me. Have you been here this whole time?"

"Yes," she said with a pleasant smile. "I need to speak with you."

I had been feeling steadier after my talk with Jack, but now a jittery clatter began rattling through my chest again. "I have some schoolwork I need to finish.

Can it wait until later?" I asked, knowing I'd feel more comfortable with the others around.

"No," she said, her expression unchanging. "It can't."

"Very well." I moved out of the doorway, offering her the chair in my room and seating myself on the edge of the bed.

She regarded me with a canny spark in her dark eyes. "You know about my special work."

I withdrew my cigarette case from my pocketbook and took time to select and light a smoke, trying to gather my thoughts. But what was the point in fibbing? "Yes," I said.

"You stopped keeping your letters in the bottom desk drawer. That's how I knew. All those long letters from your friends in America, your poor lonely papa, your mother—she gives terrible advice, by the way; you should ignore her. And then one day—poof! They all disappeared, and I thought, *Ah, Jacqueline is cleverer than she lets on.* None of the others had an inkling, you see, not even my own sister. I quite admired you, actually. But then I thought—" She tilted her head. "*Jacqueline is so sheltered.* You Americans didn't live through the Occupation. You don't have the same scars as us, nor the same experiences or suspicions. Could you really have figured it out all by yourself?"

"What—what do you mean?" Surely she hadn't guessed I'd overheard her and Madame that day in the bath.

"I wondered," she continued in the same musing tone, "could there be someone feeding Jacqueline ideas? And then last night the answer became obvious—Jack."

"Jack!" In my shock, I dropped the cigarette on the floor, hastily snatching it up before it could burn the carpet. "I don't know what you're implying," I said, crushing it into the ashtray. "I think for myself."

"Oh, Jacqueline." Ghislaine sighed. "Jack is a communist, can't you see?"

"He's *what*? That's absurd. I know you've seen him at that bookshop, but—"

"He's a regular at Le Compagnon de voyage. He's friends with Charlie and loads of other people in the student groups. He spends time at the shop like it's his living room—he was at the youth party congress in Marseille—"

"For his *research*. He writes about French politics for the American press."

"A journalist." She snorted.

"I've seen his articles!"

"He can be a journalist and a communist at the same time!"

We regarded each other for a moment, our mouths

set firm, each of us cemented in our conviction yet determined to persuade the other.

"Look," I said. "Say he's a communist. Say he's feeding me ideas, as you suggest. Why would he tell me you're a spy?"

"He was trying to learn more about me."

"Why?"

"Why do you think? I've been watching him!" she cried. "Didn't you ever wonder why I was never home when he came to pick you up? Ever since I read that book of his—"

"You read his manuscript?"

"You left it lying in the middle of the *salon*! The entire apartment has probably read it."

I drew a sharp breath. None of this was worse than I'd suspected, but to have it confirmed was like being thrown from a horse—broken trust, wounded pride and all.

"Listen," Ghislaine said more gently, "you read his novel. Don't you think it's awfully . . . sympathetic to Lenin?"

"That's the genius of it," I insisted. "He's managed to humanize a monster."

She opened her mouth and closed it again, glanced at the cigarette case on the bed. "May I?" she asked. I lit one for her, and another for myself, soothed by the ritual click of the lighter, the crackle and hiss of the paper as it caught flame.

"Jacqueline," she said softly, and her tone was almost pleading, "he was there, at the youth party congress in Marseille. Of course I knew him from the bookshop, but I never expected to find him at some poky meeting of pimply-faced Marxists. Why would a prominent American magazine send a journalist to cover an event that's barely even mentioned in the French press? It makes no sense." She blew out a little smoke. "But there he was, buying rounds of drinks, tossing out cigarettes like handfuls of confetti . . ."

"You're suspicious because he's generous?"

"No, of course not. There is something . . . strange about him. I can't put my finger on it. But there is a feeling I get—that big smile, those white teeth, so shiny. So affable."

"You mean he's *American*? Ghislaine, honestly. These are all stereotypes. Too generous. Too gregarious. I'm surprised you didn't say he's too loud."

"He is."

"You're allowing your prejudices to cloud your judgment. Jack swears he's not a communist, and I believe him."

She brought her cigarette to her lips, inhaling deeply. But I had caught a glimmer of doubt and pressed forward. "If he was what you think, I would know. We spend too much time together for him to hide." I fixed my gaze upon her until she blinked. "Have you found any actual evidence?"

"Well, I haven't uncovered any Soviet connections, but—"

"You see? This is all pure conjecture."

"Perhaps." She shrugged. I guessed from her reticence that she didn't agree, nor could she prove me wrong.

Ghislaine reached toward the ashtray, balancing her cigarette against the edge. Her lipstick had left a mark on one end, a smudge of cerise on white paper. I stared at the bright stain, then focused on the ember, smoldering dark and disintegrating rapidly into dust. She picked up the cigarette again, and when our eyes met, hers were troubled. "You must be more careful, Jacqueline," she warned. "Politically, things are not stable here in France. Paris these days, it is a nest of spies—everybody coming through on stolen passports. You must be careful of who you choose to trust."

Like you? I was tempted to say, but I held my tongue. What was the point of throwing her mistakes in her face? "Tempest in a teapot": Jack's words echoed in my mind. "This'll blow over."

"I will," I said, softly. I was about to add that I

appreciated her concern, but at that moment the phone began to ring.

"I'll go," said Ghislaine, rising from the desk and moving into the hallway.

It occurred to me that I had held my own in our discussion, presented my arguments clearly, and convinced her that I was right. It wasn't the first time I had won a debate by employing wit instead of wile, but it was rare enough for me to feel a rush. I lit a fresh cigarette off the end of the last, drawing smoke into my lungs and exhaling with relish. Mummy abhorred chain-smoking—"So terribly vulgar!"—never mind that she did it herself when she thought no one was looking.

Ghislaine's call must have been cut off, for the telephone started ringing again and she picked it up right away. I assumed it was Madame, phoning from a callbox, asking one of us to fetch the baguettes for dinner. Moving to the window, I tried to see if there was a line forming out the door of the *boulangerie*. Yes, it looked like there was a queue already . . .

Ghislaine's step sounded behind me, and I half turned. "Do we need bread?" I asked.

"No, it's the phone—" But before she could continue, it began ringing again.

"I'll get it," I said, marching to the front hall, snatching up the receiver on the fourth or fifth ring.

"Oui, allô?" Silence. *"Allô? Allô?"* I repeated. *"Je vous écoute!"* No response. "Must be a wrong number," I said, and I hung up. Almost immediately it began ringing. Again, I answered; again, there was no response. "How very peculiar," I said. "Has this happened before?"

"Yes," she said slowly. "It used to happen all the time during"—the phone began to ring—"THE WAR," she said, raising her voice above the din.

Eight rings. Nine. Ten. Seventeen. Twenty. Finally I eased the receiver off the stand. *"Allô? Bonjour? Allô? J'écoute!"* Silence. I set it down.

Ghislaine eyed the telephone like it was a sleeping cobra. Suddenly, she snatched the receiver and left it off the hook.

"You know, it's funny," I said. "This exact same thing happened the other day when I was—" I broke off, the memory traveling through me like an electric jolt. "Why during the war?" I said instead, managing to keep my voice steady despite the buzz of nerves.

"The Gestapo." She reached for a sheaf of loose papers and began straightening them on the telephone desk. "They used to harass us, calling and calling on the phone, but when we picked up there was nothing. Just a dead, ominous silence. Shortly after that Maman and Papa were deported." She attempted to screw the cap onto a fountain pen, but her fingers were trembling so much it fell to the floor.

I stared at her in horror. "You think someone's threatening you? Are—are you certain? Maybe it's a loose wire somewhere. Or—?"

"I'm afraid not, *chérie*. No, there's only one logical explanation: Somebody is sending me a message." She paused her tidying, giving me a shrewd look. "Did you say this happened to you the other day?"

Heat rose in my face with throbbing pressure, pounding along the ridge of my neck, the top of my scalp. "Not me," I admitted, because I was afraid—really and truly afraid—panicked, and heedless of what I was saying. "To Jack."

Chapter Fifteen

I wanted to call Jack, go to him, walk to his apartment if necessary and demand answers. But I knew better than to tell a man how I felt about him. Emotions were volatile, and revealing them made you vulnerable. Instead, I did what I'd learned as a little girl hiding in the closet while my parents raged at each other: I opened a book and retreated within its pages. In the fantasy world of fiction, conflict and drama had purpose—things happened for a reason, unlike in real life, which so often seemed disconnected from a greater wisdom.

By the time I saw Jack again two days had passed—two days during which I slept in snatches, subsisted on cigarettes, and vowed a hundred times to drop him without an explanation. Lee always said it was Mummy's cruel influence that made me excise some people from my social circle with the cool precision of a surgeon—my sister preferred stormy denouncements and fiery renunciations—but the truth was, if someone had hurt me, or dismissed me, or betrayed my trust, I could no longer bear to let them see any part of me, least of all my ire. I felt safest when no one knew what I really thought.

So when Jack and I met that sunny spring morning at the Gare de l'Est, I greeted him with a smile and an embrace, allowing him to take my hand as we ran to catch our train. It was May Day, the first of May, which in France was *la fête de travaille*—Labor Day—the workers' holiday. Jack and I were spending it in Reims, taking in the high Gothic grace of the cathedral, lunching at a bistro he knew in town, perhaps touring the cellar of a storied champagne house.

Our train shot out of Paris and its suburbs, plunging straight into rolling farmland. Here in the countryside, spring had already burst to full force, with sumptuous green pastures, blossoming fruit orchards, and newborn lambs bounding up little hills. Sunlight splashed everywhere, transforming the landscape into a Corot painting, all hazy sky and clipped shadows, so enchanting I found it difficult to tear my eyes away— which provided a convenient excuse to avoid talking to Jack.

We descended the train at Reims and walked a few short blocks to the cathedral. My heels clicked a rhythm upon the sidewalk, a steady beat that said *Now, now, now, ask him now.* I knew what I should do. I ought simply to turn to him and ask, Jack, are you a communist? And he would laugh in astonishment, and say, Sweetheart, no! Nothing could be further from the truth. And then we could continue on with this morning, this day, this life together, my trust in him undiminished.

But I didn't ask. I didn't ask because I was afraid to know the answer. Instead, I found myself brooding as we walked through the cathedral, breathing in the ritual scents of incense and burning candles. Perhaps the problem was me, my own naïveté, for I'd believed Jack when he said he cared for me, just as I believed Ghislaine when she said I shouldn't trust him. Or perhaps the problem was that there were many truths, everyone with their own version, and I accepted too easily that one of them was real.

Jack kept up a cheerful patter, reading bits aloud from his guidebook, pointing out the thirteenth-century stained glass radiating color from the rose window, admiring the fine worn sculptures of France's ancient kings on the cathedral's exterior façade. At lunch, he talked about a Carson McCullers novel he'd just read, which had recently opened as a play on Broadway. "Maybe we can see it this summer if we're in the city together," he suggested, as I picked at a green salad. I made the appropriate responses, smiled at the right moments, asked the right questions to keep him talking, but inside I was scrutinizing his behavior, changing my opinion of him every half second until I wanted to scream.

"Let's go for a walk," I said after we had drained the last drops of coffee from our cups and stubbed out our cigarettes.

"Good idea," he said cheerfully.

Several minutes later we were strolling in the vineyards that came right up to the edge of town. The plants were carefully tended, their rows as precise as military ranks, the pruned branches starting to leaf with glossy little shoots.

"I suppose they have the day off," Jack observed.

"Hm? Oh, the vineyard workers, you mean. Well, it is Labor Day."

"It's not an easy job, you know. Most of them work under terrible conditions. Long hours, low wages, very little employee protection—"

I turned to face him. "Tell me something, Jack. Are you a communist?"

If he was surprised by my question, he didn't show

it. A crease appeared on his brow, a pained, puzzled furrow that deepened as the silence grew between us. "Is that what's been bothering you all day?"

"Perhaps." I crossed my arms.

"After all these weeks—all this time we've spent together—you think I'm some sort of—of secret pinko? Surely you know me better than that by now."

"That's not a denial."

"Are you serious?"

I lifted my chin. "Completely."

"Why would I hide something like that from you? You know I'm friends with Charlie and those folks because of my work. You—you've read my articles. You know my opinions. You—" He broke off, his eyes narrowing. "Does this have something to do with Ghislaine?"

I shook my head. "You know, at first, I thought you were just anxious about your book being out on submission. All those long walks, the drinking—golly, the drinking! The way you needed to down half a flask of cognac just to sit through a film. I assumed it was nerves. But then it occurred to me that maybe you thought someone was following you. That makes more sense, doesn't it? That would explain why, whenever we take a walk, you lead us round and round in circles. Or why you dragged me out of the Hôtel Continental with half a bottle of champagne still on the table. Or why you insisted we leave the cinema before the film had even ended. Were you trying to lose your minder?"

"I wasn't *feeling* well, I told you."

"Is that why your phone was ringing off the hook?"

A muscle moved in his cheek. "What does that have to do with anything?"

"Ghislaine told me the same thing happened during the war. Apparently their line used to ring all the time when they were under Nazi surveillance. As a warning."

He blinked. At this point in the day, the sun was just slightly over the zenith, the light so harsh and bright it leached the color from his face. A breeze rustled through the vines, causing the leaves to hiss and whisper. Jack stared down at his shoes, which were dusted with chalky soil, then out across the vineyards running down the slope in orderly lines. Finally he turned to me. "I'm not a communist," he said softly. "But I don't know what I can say or do to convince you to believe me."

"You could start by telling me the truth."

He drew a sharp breath, pressing his mouth tight, but said nothing. We watched two white butterflies chasing each other through the air, circling in a swift bobbing dance. "What if I've taken an oath not to reveal it?" he finally said.

"What the devil does that mean?"

He raised his eyebrows, his expression rueful, and that was what tipped me off in the end: the aura of regret surrounding him, his genuine sadness that he'd needed to keep this secret from me for so long. Suddenly I guessed what he couldn't tell me. "It's the CIA, isn't it?" I said quietly. "You're working for them? No, hold on, you probably can't answer that. How about . . . I'll tell you what I think, and if I'm wrong you can interrupt me."

He remained silent, which I interpreted as consent.

I said: "You must've been recruited at Harvard because I've heard they go to all the Ivies and Seven Sisters looking for the cleverest folks." I shot him a glance, but his face remained impassive. "They offered to send you to Paris, and you thought it sounded like a terrific way to get back to France, have an adventure, and maybe . . . it appealed to your sense of duty too? A serviceman like yourself." I bit my bottom lip. "And the writing . . . the writing was just a cover. A useful excuse to nose around left-wing circles. But—but you enjoyed it more than you thought and decided to give it a go—"

"Cigarette?" He held out his case.

"Ah, okay. I got that last bit wrong." I selected one, holding it between my fingers. "You always dreamed of being a writer. That part's true. But this helps you stay afloat." His lighter clicked and I leaned into the flame, breathing in the smoke. "It all makes so much sense now," I said, exhaling in little puffs. "The enormous apartment. The secret office. The secret telephone in the secret office. The . . ." I paused, fingering my cigarette, flicking ash from the tip. "It's them, isn't it? You're being followed. By Soviets."

"Don't worry about that. It's nothing." He bent to pick up a twig and began breaking it into little pieces, tossing them into the dirt. "Jacqueline, this isn't . . ." His eyes scanned mine with an anxious expression. "I never planned on doing this forever. Back in the States, I had this feeling that . . . life wasn't making sense. I was always waiting for something: for the war to end, for college to end, for a promotion at work, for my book to sell. I thought moving to Paris would make things happen—stir things up—but even after I got here there was still this dissatisfaction gnawing at me." He hesitated, shoving his hands in his pockets. "But then I met this—this bright, beautiful young woman who loves talking about books and ideas and, well, honestly, it seemed like a miracle."

I studied him closely, unable to speak. I sensed that I was seeing Jack for the very first time—all the ambition, doubt, and hesitation that lay beneath the polish and charm—and that I needed to tread carefully.

"I've hated keeping secrets from you," he said in a low voice. "For months now, it's been eating me up inside. I just—" He closed his eyes for a brief moment. "I hope this doesn't change things between us."

"How can it not?" I said unhappily, for I was grappling with an all-too-familiar sense of betrayal. And while it wasn't as terrible as I had feared—thank heavens he wasn't a communist—still he had deceived me, and with that deception came the sting of humiliation. "Everything we talked about—all our plans for the future . . ." My voice dipped and disappeared. I brought the cigarette to my lips, inhaling until the ember flared.

"No," he said sharply. "That was true, all of it. Sometimes"—he swallowed hard—"sometimes I think that's the truest thing I've ever felt."

"How did I not see it? All this time, it was right in front of my face." Tears stung my eyes, and I blinked, willing them to disappear. "I wish I didn't feel like such a damned fool."

"Sweetheart, please." Jack's brow crumpled. "I've wanted to tell you a thousand times—you have to believe me. Honestly, this work is—it's horribly nerve-racking and unpleasant. I loathe all the deception that comes with it. Mostly because of you. But also Charlie and a few of the others have become real friends—they've invited me home to meet their parents, given me Sunday lunch, taught me more about France than I could have learned in a hundred years on my own. They're real people— honest, good-hearted people, not some ruthless, faceless Soviet menace, and I—I don't know how much longer I can lie to them and still live with myself."

His shoulders sagged and I realized that it hadn't been just the espionage work, or worry about whether his novel would find a publisher that had been bothering him these past few weeks. Jack was at a crossroads, his sense of patriotic duty wrestling with his personal morality. And he hadn't been able to tell a soul.

Witnessing him like this, my feelings of hurt and embarrassment began to fade. I understood that he needed me, to talk with him, and listen to him, and care for him in the same ways he cared for me. Yes, he had lied, but his falsehoods weren't like others I had known: not like Daddy, who lied to cover up his drinking and then grew defensive when I challenged him; not like Mummy, whose entire marriage was a lie, a twisted manipulation to maintain the lifestyle she desired. Jack had lied to me, clumsily, and now I wondered if it was because he'd been so desperate to unburden himself— that he wanted to be caught. When I reached for his hand, I knew I could forgive him.

We had saved time to visit a champagne *cave*, but of

course they were all closed for the holiday. But before we left Reims, we stopped at a café near the station and Jack charmed the owner into letting him buy two glass coupes and a bottle of chilled Veuve Clicquot, which we drank on the train. Like most things consumed illicitly, it was exceptionally delicious, the effervescence going straight to my head, leaving me flushed and dreamy. Jack too seemed more relaxed than he had in weeks, and a comfortable silence stretched between us. As I leaned against his shoulder, watching the farms give way to the Paris suburbs, it occurred to me that I had never felt so close to anyone.

Almost overnight, or so it seemed, Paris burst into bloom, transforming from a soggy, spattered bog into a frilly pink and white fairyland. In the afternoons after class, I liked to go to a café across from the jardin du Luxembourg, sitting on the *terrasse* to read and smoke, and watch the blossoms sway against the deep blue sky. It was, I decided, my favorite springtime café, breezy and splashed with dappled light—unlike my favorite winter café (drenched in sun), or my favorite autumn café (long banquettes and thick hot chocolate), or my favorite summer café (cooled by the tall shadow of Saint-Sulpice).

On days like these, when the trees were flowering,

and the sky shimmering, and the sun shining on every crevice of Haussmannian architecture, the thought of leaving Paris made my heart split in two. I'd sip my demitasse of coffee, lean my chin on my hand, and pretend I lived around the corner. Maybe I was a junior editor at a fashion magazine, scribbling stories in the window of my attic loft. Maybe I was married to Jack, with an apartment on the Left Bank and a country house in Normandy, one baby at the crèche and another on the way. Maybe the miracle of daily life in Paris was enough to diminish the importance of things I'd been taught my whole life to esteem, things like prestige, and power, and privilege.

I hoped so. Ever since I'd discovered the true source of Jack's income, I'd known that beginning our life together would be more complicated than I'd anticipated. Either he continued despite the stress and risk, or he gave it up for a leaner life than I'd expected, at least for a while. It made me anxious at first, until I stopped to consider the past several months I'd spent at avenue Mozart with the de Rentys: I had never lived more simply, and I had never been happier. Truly, the pure pleasures of Paris made ordinary life extraordinary.

I still remember one day in early May, walking home from the Sorbonne along the Seine. Though I'd taken this route a hundred times, I found myself captivated by the river's curve, the little bridges that swept across it, each with their own personality, the bits of blue sky glinting through the lacework of the Eiffel Tower. Living in Paris was like a love affair, each encounter revealing a new and seductive facet. By the time I reached home, I was half drunk on its beauty.

I was humming a little as I turned my key in the lock and stepped into the apartment. "Maman? Is that you?" called a voice from the *salon*. The sight of Ghislaine, slumped on the sofa, her face set and white, brought me quickly to my senses. She was cradling her right arm, which was scraped and bleeding, and bent at a strange angle.

I gasped. "Are you all right? What happened?" I dropped my schoolbag and rushed to her side.

"I fell . . ." She winced.

"Hold on," I told her. "I'll help you."

In the kitchen, I chipped some ice and wrapped it in a towel, found a tray and laid it with a pitcher of water and a glass, the aspirin bottle, and a flask of calvados that I grabbed from the dining room. Back in the *salon*, I placed the ice pack on Ghislaine's forearm. "Do you think it's broken?" I asked as she grimaced.

"*Mon dieu*, I hope not." But when she reached for the calvados, her cheeks blanched three shades whiter. "Those bastards!" she hissed.

"What? Who? Should I call an ambulance?"

"No. I'll be fine. Can you . . . ?" She raised her chin toward the calvados. I poured her a measure and she drank. When the glass was empty, she held it up, and I poured her another.

"How did this happen? Did you trip?" I asked, after a sliver of tension had eased from her face.

"Not exactly." She shot me a look, and my heart began racing, though I didn't understand why. "You know that narrow little street behind our building? Rue de la Cure? Well, I was taking a shortcut home from the *épicerie* and all of a sudden I heard this awful racket, and then this *deux chevaux* came roaring round the corner practically on two wheels, barreling straight toward me. It came so close I could see the faces of the three boys inside. I scrambled to get out of the way, but slipped and fell, and skidded on the pavement, which is how my arm got all scraped up."

"How awful! Did they stop and help you at least?"

"Help me?" She let out a bitter laugh. "No, *chérie*, they didn't help me. Frankly, I'm lucky the driver swerved and missed me."

"You mean—" I swallowed against a lump in my throat. "He did it on purpose?"

"I'm afraid so," she said grimly.

"But *why*?"

Ghislaine looked down at her injured arm, which was swelling rapidly. Despite her outward calm, her mouth was trembling, and the mascara smeared under her eyes hinted at tears. "That's the thing—I don't know. Was it Charlie and his gang? Or someone from the Partisans of Peace? André was trying to tell me something a few weeks ago, but he's always so damned alarmist about everything . . ." She seemed almost to be talking to herself. "It couldn't be," she muttered. "It just couldn't be. I haven't found anything compromising on *them* . . ."

I stared at her in horror. "You think this is related to your—your work?"

With some effort, she raised her eyes to mine, twin pools, dark and glassy. "Yes . . . If I had to guess, I'd say someone was giving me . . . another warning . . ." she said weakly, before her lids fluttered shut.

I waited for her to explain, but when she didn't speak for several moments, I saw that she had fainted dead away.

Ghislaine's arm was broken. She had a displaced fracture that required a cast for at least six weeks, perhaps longer. "So clumsy of me," she told the other girls that evening after Madame had brought her home from the hospital. "I was in such a rush to fetch

Christian from the crèche, I wasn't looking where I was going. I tripped over a rough patch of pavement and landed flat on the ground with the groceries scattered all around me—can you imagine? Half a dozen eggs smashed to smithereens."

"You're lucky it wasn't your neck," said Madame briskly, plumping a cushion and positioning it under her daughter's arm.

"True," said Ghislaine. "At least with a broken arm, I can still go to work."

"Work!" Madame was appalled. "That's absolutely out of the question. You have an *arrêt maladie* signed by your doctor."

"But, Maman! We're swamped at the office—I can't just abandon my colleagues."

"They'll understand," said Madame, with a steely glint in her eye. "Even if I have to call on your *chef* myself."

Across the room I caught an expression of relief flicker across Claude's face.

For the next few days, Ghislaine moped around the apartment. With her broken arm, she couldn't help with household chores or even enjoy a walk outside, and so, every morning after depositing Christian at the crèche, she installed herself in the *salon* with a pile of the day's newspapers, reading carefully through each one. Sometimes she'd snort at an editorial or clip out an article, but mostly she tossed the crumpled pages to the ground with a scowl. At least she could read in peace now that the telephone had quieted, its endless ringing silenced as if by magic.

One Thursday morning, Ghislaine and I were alone in the apartment when there came a rap on the front door. Before I could rise from my desk to answer it, I heard Ghislaine's leaden step, and then her greeting as she admitted the visitor. "What a surprise!" Kiss, kiss. "It's so kind of you to drop by. Let's go in the salon—we can talk quietly there." I made sure they were at the far end of the hall before peeping out to see a woman's slender figure, dressed in a black swing coat, a pillbox hat pinned over her blond chignon. Just before she reached the sitting room, she turned her head and I found myself gazing into the fine-boned features of Marie-Madeleine Fourcade. She looked at me with a steady, unblinking stare before following Ghislaine into the salon, closing the doors firmly behind her.

Less than ten minutes later they emerged. "Don't fret, chérie." Marie-Madeleine's voice floated across the apartment. "After a good long rest, you'll be back before you know it, stronger and sharper than ever." They paused by the front door. "I'll come see you again." Kiss, kiss. "And don't forget, you must be absolutely discreet about *everything* until you hear from me. That is *essential*. Can you promise me that?"

"Yes, Marie-Madeleine," Ghislaine said dully.

"Good girl." The front door creaked open. "Now, I must fly, but I'll speak to you soon. Don't forget—you promised!" With a bang, she departed.

Twenty seconds passed and then something crashed against the wall. *"Putain de merde!"* screamed Ghislaine.

I found her sitting on the floor, slouched by the front closet. Her face was red and shiny, and the boot she'd just thrown was lying against the opposite wall, a thick black smudge above it. Silently I offered her my hand, and after a moment of hesitation she grasped it.

"What happened?" I asked, once she had struggled to her feet.

"Je suis limogée," she said shortly.

"What?"

"Sacked," she explained. "Fired. Dismissed. Terminated. My services no longer needed."

I drew a sharp breath. "For what reason?"

"Why do you think? I've been compromised. I bet it was Charlie, that dirty bastard."

My heart gave an unexpected thump. "Sorry?"

"Charlie. He must have blown my cover," she said bitterly. "He probably wanted revenge because he thought I was leading him on. What a little baby."

"Hold on, you think Charlie? Really? I mean, I suppose it's possible, but . . ." Charlie seemed too young and earnest to act so maliciously.

"Who else could it be, Jacqueline?" she snapped. "He'd better watch out." She clenched her uninjured fist, and a ballooning fear made my breath stop short in my chest.

"But, Ghislaine," I protested. "Surely you wouldn't— you're not thinking of—" Didn't Marie-Madeleine just tell her to disappear for a while? How could she disobey?

"I'm going to find out what happened," she declared, her eyes blazing. "And whoever it was will be sorry."

After Ghislaine had returned to the sitting room, slamming the doors behind her, there was nothing for me to do but leave for the Sorbonne. With the end of the year approaching, I couldn't afford to miss any more lectures—and yet I felt so agitated, I had half a mind to skip class and go straight to Jack. He could help me discern fact from speculation—he would know what to do. By the time I reached my métro stop, I had decided to walk to his apartment. I turned to cross the street in his direction, but before I stepped off the curb, a delivery truck swept in front of me, knocking me off balance.

"Jeepers!" I gasped, grasping at a lamppost and managing to right myself.

"Crazy fool," muttered the woman next to me. "He's going to kill someone if he's not careful."

I stared at the truck as it barreled down the boulevard toward Jack's building, and my skin began to tingle. The incident had been eerily similar to Ghislaine's accident. Although I was sure this driver had no malicious intent, I suddenly knew that as much as I wanted Jack—his steady smile and sound advice, the solid warmth of his arm around my back—I couldn't be certain how he would interpret Ghislaine's situation, or what information he would pass along to his colleagues. Drawing a deep breath, I reoriented myself in the direction of the Sorbonne. I would have to navigate this situation by myself.

For once, I was early to class. I bought a copy of *Le Monde* from the newsagent on the corner and found a seat in the enormous *grand amphithéâtre*, lighting a cigarette and unfolding the afternoon paper, forcing myself to focus on every article on the front page until my heart slowed. The lecture hall began to fill, students drifting in and finding seats. I opened the newspaper and there, on page three, I saw a headline that made my blood run cold.

THREE FRENCH STUDENTS CHARGED WITH SPYING FOR SOVIETS

MARSEILLE. Following a series of raids, three students of the Institut d'études politiques de Paris (known as Sciences Po) were arrested and accused today of sabotage and spying in a ring the Government declares was led by Soviet Russia.

The suspects, Léon Dubois, 24, of Nanterre, Pierre Lefebvre, 21, of Le Havre, and Jean Pepin, 20, of Sisteron, were arrested on conspiracy charges of overseeing a spy network that provided classified information on French economic and military affairs to Moscow in a spying operation that appeared to begin in 1948, prosecutors said. The three also turned over names of French Communist Party members so the Soviet Union could try to recruit them.

For six days the three men evaded police in a manhunt that began in Paris and continued across several *départements* to the south of France. They were arrested yesterday in Aix-en-Provence while attempting to escape police in their vehicle, a black Citroën *deux chevaux* . . .

"*Salut!*" said a voice, and Martha slid into the seat beside me.

I rustled the paper shut and instinctively inhaled on my cigarette. The ash had grown so long it threatened to break off under its own weight.

"You all right?" she said, pulling out her notebook. "You look like you've just seen a ghost."

"Fine. I'm fine." I bent over my bag, searching for a pencil, taking an extra long time so she wouldn't be able to inspect my face.

"I guess you saw the news?" She nodded at the paper on my desk. "Three Sciences Po students were arrested for spying. Everyone at Reid Hall is talking about it."

"Oh, really? What are they saying?" I said as casually as possible.

"Mostly they're just shocked to think this was all happening right under our noses." She gave a little shiver. "Apparently they've been hiding in the cellar of a candy shop, can you believe it?"

I crushed the cigarette under the toe of my shoe. "Do you have a pencil I can borrow?"

She looked at me a little strangely. "Sure."

Our professor came striding into the hall, coattails flying wide behind him. "Let's begin," he said and, to my relief, launched into his lecture without further preamble.

Martha dutifully began scribbling notes, but I found it impossible to concentrate on the philosophy of aesthetic judgment. Instead, I kept trying to match the details of Ghislaine's accident with what I'd read in the paper. There were three boys in the car, she'd said, and there were three students named in the article. They were in a *deux chevaux*, she'd said—a black one, according to the article.

It had to be the same trio. Didn't it?

Chapter Sixteen

It was the only thing anyone wanted to talk about. In the *grand amphithéâtre* of the Sorbonne. In small group seminars at Sciences Po. In the *cantine* at Reid Hall. In the cafés that lined the boulevard Saint-Michel. In the libraries, and bookstores, and jazz clubs, and stationery shops, and all the other places we frequented, you could hear a steady stream of hissing voices repeating the same words over and over: The Sciences Po spy ring. The Sciences Po trio. The student spies. *Les espions étudiants.*

There were all sorts of rumors, many of them distasteful: The three were hopeless drunks. They were brilliant linguists. They were scholarship students. They were immigrants from North Africa. They were whatever would mark them out as different, because the truth—that they were ordinary young Frenchmen swept up in the idealism of Soviet Marxism-Leninism—was too frightening to accept.

"I heard one of them worked at the chocolate shop over the summer," I told Jack. "It's owned by his uncle."

"Hm?" He looked up from his book.

"The chocolate shop. Where they were hiding in the cellar. You know, the Sciences Po spies," I explained, in response to his puzzled smile. "Martha's host mother's sister lives in Aix and she heard that one of them—the youngest, I think?—is the owner's nephew. Apparently he worked at the shop over the summer and never gave back his key."

"Is that so?" Jack lit a cigarette.

"Martha thinks they could've stayed there for weeks, maybe even months—can you imagine?"

"I can." He nodded, puffing smoke.

I waited eagerly for him to share his expert knowledge of secret hideouts, and getaway cars, and false identities. Instead, he shot me a lopsided grin. "Evidently, they must've been home *sweet* home." He nudged me with his elbow. "Get it?"

I groaned but couldn't help laughing. "Look at you with the *bonbon mot*," I shot back.

At this he guffawed, his smile lighting up his entire face. Suddenly he grabbed my hand. "Let's run away together," he said with a sparkle in his eye. "You, me, the express train to the south of France. What do you say, sweetheart? We could be in Nice by teatime, married by cocktail hour, and spend the summer honeymooning on a Mediterranean beach."

"Why, Monsieur Marquand." I blinked at him coquettishly. "You flatter me. But surely you know I'm not the kind of girl who can get married without a retinue of courtiers and a feast of sugared almonds."

"Silly me!" He slapped a palm against his forehead. "And here I was congratulating myself on arranging the troubadours and jousting matches." His tone was jovial, but to my surprise I saw his smile slip, if only for an instant.

"Tell you what." I squeezed his hand. "I'll think about it. As long as you remember the troubadours, of course."

"Of course." He winked and returned to his book.

I picked up my magazine and stared at the page, but the words scrambled together until I found myself reading the same sentence over and over again. "Let's run away together," he had said. Did he mean elope? I examined the idea. Married. In the south of France. To Jack. Jack's wife. Mrs. John Marquand Jr. It sounded shocking, and madcap, and scandalous—and most of all like enormous fun.

Of course, none of this was serious. Jack had been joking. Hadn't he?

When I returned home that evening, Ghislaine dragged me into the dining room, keen to show me the articles she'd ripped from the day's papers. Through convenience or circumstance, I had somehow become her confidante—probably because Madame disapproved thoroughly of the entire situation, Claude was cramming for her graduating exams, and Ghislaine didn't know the other girls well enough to trust their discretion. I did not relish this role, but I tolerated it because Ghislaine still seemed so distrait about the accident, focusing all her energy on uncovering the truth of what had really happened. If I suspected she was trying to replace the rush and thrill of her spy work, I knew better than to suggest it.

"Did you hear anything today?" she asked me. We were surrounded by a sheaf of thumbed newspapers, late-day sunshine spilling across the dining table, even though it was nearly eight o'clock. I never stopped marveling at the daylight hours of summer in Europe, the way their brilliance lengthened until the nights ceased almost to exist.

I told her what I'd learned from Martha about the chocolate shop owner, information that she greeted with a dissatisfied grunt. It had been four days since the arrest of the Sciences Po trio, and news of them had started to fade from the papers.

"I simply don't understand it," Ghislaine said for the hundredth time. She reached for a clipping that featured smudged mug shots of each suspect. "I'm absolutely certain it was them. This one"—she jabbed a finger at the heavy-browed Léon Dubois—"was driving the car that nearly ran me over. I still see that face in my nightmares. But . . ." Her eyes narrowed, examining the pictures. "Why come after *me*?"

"They probably think you turned them in."

"Well, yes, *obviously.*" She snatched a cigarette from her case and lit it. "But why? Before last week I'd never set eyes on any of them. Nor did I have an inkling about their activities. The only thing I can possibly think of is that they noticed me at the Partisans of Peace congress in Marseille."

"Were they there?"

"I have no idea. But they were caught in Aix."

I frowned, confused.

"Aix is close to Marseille," she explained. "It's only twenty minutes by train."

This seemed like the flimsiest of all possible connections, but I nodded like it could be meaningful.

"But even if they saw me in Marseille, what on earth would give them the idea I was onto them?" She tapped her cigarette over the ashtray with her index finger—clumsily, because her injured arm meant she had to use her left hand. Tap, tap, tap. I tried not to stare at the little flecks of ash flying across the tablecloth. "It just doesn't make sense," she muttered. As she returned to the newspapers I saw her face twitch, and not for the first time I wondered if she could be on the brink of a breakdown.

The next morning I woke early and met Paul de Ganay in the bois de Boulogne to go riding. My horse, a palomino named Fantôme, gave a soft nicker when he saw me, nudging his nose into my palm, hoping for one of the sugar cubes he knew I stashed in my pockets. "Who's a clever boy?" I crooned, stroking the velvet nap of his forelock. "How I'll miss you, my darling." He didn't respond, but then again, he was a horse. He didn't understand longing, or nostalgia, or the bittersweet uncertainty of not knowing what came next.

Paul and I mounted and began trotting along the

park's wooded trails, passing man-made lakes and waterfalls, the sun casting dappled shadows through the trees. I tried to concentrate on the rhythm of the horse, but everywhere my eye was caught by changes to the landscape, beds of tulips that had been mulch a few months earlier, ordinary trees now flamboyant with blossoms. It had been autumn when I first came here, the leaves vivid upon the ground; then winter, with its cold-cheeked gallops and bare branches bristling overhead; and soon summer would arrive, the trees and lawns thick and green. I would miss it, for no matter what happened, this was to be our last ride together in the bois de Boulogne for quite some time. In a few weeks Paul would depart for the army base at Poitiers, where he would begin his mandatory military service.

We reached an unbroken stretch of *allée*, and Paul turned a little in his saddle. "Ready?" he asked with a smile. We urged our mounts into a canter, jogging past slim trees and low brush, losing ourselves in the speed and smells of warm horse and damp earth, the clatter of hoofbeats. By the time we returned to the stables, I was flushed and disheveled, my heart pumping in my chest with a steady strength that made me feel invincible.

I said goodbye to Fantôme, lavishing him with pats,

and, after tidying myself up, walked over to the little café in the park where Paul was waiting on the *terrasse*. "I ordered you a *noisette*," he said, indicating a demitasse cup filled with coffee, a whisper of milk turning it the rich, warm color of hazelnuts.

"You're an angel." I lit a cigarette and tipped my face up to the sun. "Isn't this heaven?"

"This coffee?" He pulled a face.

"This coffee, yes! Bitter and bold, not like the dirty old dishwater we have back home. This café with its proper glasses and white tablecloths right in the middle of a park! This—this—this!" I flung out my hands at the graceful wrought-iron chairs, the striped awning, the ladies preening in their fine spring dresses, the men sipping small glasses of beer that glowed amber in the morning sun, the curly-haired little dog tucked in his mistress's lap nibbling a biscuit like it was his princely right. It was a scene from a hundred years ago, or a hundred years from now; it was completely ordinary, and totally seductive, and all I could ever want from Paris. "I wish I didn't have to leave," I said impulsively.

He shot me a rueful smile. "Do you have to?"

"Yes. No. I don't know. I'd like to finish my degree," I said, surprising myself, for until this moment I hadn't known it to be true. "But I don't think I can face going back to poky old Poughkeepsie."

"Why not transfer?" he suggested. "You could finish at the Sorbonne."

"I just might." But even as I said it, I knew I wouldn't. Things were changing in Paris, the gang shifting—Paul leaving, Claude graduating, the others getting engaged; in a year or two they'd be married, starting homes and families. Even Madame was preparing for her new lodgers, writing letters to their mothers to assure them of her attentive care. A few months from now, everything would be different, no matter how much I wished things would stay the same for a little while longer.

"You'll write to me at Poitiers?" Paul said, and I caught a wistful note in his voice. He would be lonely down there, I suspected, although he must be lonely here in Paris, ever since Henri had moved to Sweden with Sonia, joining her family's bank.

"I'll come visit," I promised, waving a little smoke away. "I'd like to motor down to the Côte d'Azur, and Poitiers is on the way, n'est-ce pas?"

He lifted an eyebrow. "Depends on who you're asking. According to the Sciences Po trio, yes."

"Golly, did they stop in Poitiers?" I laughed, for truly they were inescapable, on everyone's mind, appearing in every conversation.

"I heard their route was Paris to Poitiers, Poitiers

to Saint-Etienne, to Aix-en-Provence . . ." He ticked off the towns, and I made a mental note so I could tell Ghislaine later. "Ending, of course, at the infamous sweet shop."

"A chocolate shop, can you believe the hypocrisy? Could there be a more profound symbol of our disgusting bourgeois capitalism?" I wagged a finger in mock disapproval. "If they had any principles at all, they'd reject it as exploitative and imperialistic. Tsk, tsk. Marxists these days."

He grinned. "I suppose when you're on the lam you really can't be too picky. But evidently the shop doesn't sell chocolate, so I guess they're not complete phonies."

"Even more suspicious! What kind of candy shop doesn't sell chocolate?"

"They specialize in traditional Provençal sweetmeats made from ground almonds and candied fruit—it's some medieval Italian recipe that's rather sickly. Calissons."

"Bless you."

He laughed. "No, that's what they're called—calissons. The shop was already famous for them, but I bet this Sciences Po story isn't hurting business."

Without warning, a fly buzzed close to my ear and

I jumped. Something that Paul said was bothering me, but I couldn't put my finger on it. "What's it called? The shop?" I said carelessly.

"Hm? Oh, Le Roy Rémi. They sell these beautiful tins, all white and shiny gold, but then you open them up and . . ." He grimaced.

My lips curved automatically into a smile, the kind I'd practiced in my deb days. A high-pitched whine began buzzing about my head again, but I couldn't tell if it was the housefly or something else. I drew a deep breath, thinking furiously. Suddenly I started, and it had nothing to do with the fly.

"Before I forget . . ." Paul hadn't seemed to notice my distraction. "I brought you a little present. Nothing fancy. Just something to remember us."

I managed to make the appropriate responses, forced my trembling fingers to tear open the wrapping paper, gazed dumbly at the framed photo within, the group of us posed on the steps of Ledoyen the night of Paul's twenty-first birthday ball.

"It's the only shot I could find of us all together," he explained. "But perhaps it's not the right one . . ."

I wrenched my attention to the photograph, noting our coltish limbs and tousled hair, our crumpled gowns of chiffon and satin and crooked black bowties, our broad goofy grins brimming with innocence and high spirits. Already it seemed like a thousand years ago, a souvenir of a lost era. "It's perfect." I touched his arm. "I shall treasure it," I said, and I meant it.

I'd always hated farewells and this one was no different. How could I possibly thank Paul for all he'd given me this year—the horse rides, and country weekends, and introductions, and French instruction, and everything else? Perhaps he hated them too, for he quickly kissed my cheeks and said he'd let me know his address in Poitiers. *"A bientôt,"* he said, "see you soon." It was only after I watched him amble away alone that I realized he hadn't said goodbye.

Once he had disappeared around the corner, I grabbed the strap of my pocketbook and headed to the métro with my head down, moving like a New Yorker. When walking seemed too slow, I ran.

This time I didn't hesitate. I went home to wash and change my clothes and then I headed right back out again. After all these months, my feet traced the familiar trajectory by themselves and I made my way to the Left Bank with no conscious memory of the journey. It was a little before noon, and I knew exactly where to look.

Sure enough, when I went to the café and peered through the plate-glass window, there, right between

the painted lines of script that read CAFÉ—VINS—
SPIRITUEUX ET LIQUEURS, was a familiar figure standing at the bar, arms crossed, a small glass of something
winking on the counter. I rapped on the window and
Jack turned, his face breaking into a smile of surprise
and delight. "Come in," he mouthed, pointing at his
drink. But I shook my head and gestured at him to
come out, which he did, after draining his glass and
settling the bill.

"I was just passing by and saw you in the window,"
I said once he had emerged.

"I'm glad you did." He slid an arm around my
shoulders and squeezed, then lowered his head to mine.
At the last second a gust of wind blew a speck of dust
in my eye, forcing me to turn away. The kiss landed
somewhere near my left ear.

I extracted a handkerchief from my pocketbook and
dabbed at my eye. "Let's go for a walk, it's such a beautiful day. Do you have time?"

"For you? I have nothing but time." For once I knew
his words to be completely true.

We set off toward the park, but when I saw the trees
stretching above the gold-tipped fence of the jardin du
Luxembourg, their branches swaying gracefully, something inside me balked. Instead, I veered left, leading
him around corners, down narrow streets, past build-

ings of pale stone caked with soot and dirt, past the Neo-Classic columns of the Panthéon, past a *place* lined with café tables set for midday, all while Jack laughingly protested. "Go easy, sweetheart, a fellow hasn't had lunch yet." And: "Hey, where're we headed anyway?" And finally: "Is everything all right?"

"Sure," I said. "Everything's fine."

We turned onto the rue Monge and drew to a stop. There, between a restaurant and a hotel, was a doorway cut into the wall, so plain you'd miss it if you didn't know where to look. I guessed Jack hadn't been here before, because he didn't utter a word as we walked through it, entering a short tunnel that gave way to a large, sun-washed circle of dirt edged by stone barriers.

He lifted a hand to shade his eyes from the light reflecting off the dusty pale surfaces. "What is this place?"

"A Roman arena. Les arènes de Lutèce, they call it, after the ancient name for Paris."

"Les arènes de Lutèce . . . of course. I've seen this place on the map but had no idea it looked like this . . ." He spun around slowly, taking it in. "By golly, I thought those were walls, but they're benches—in tiers! Tiered seating! I wonder how many people it—"

"Fifteen thousand," I said crisply. I hadn't brought

him here to discuss the wonders of these ruins, architectural treasure though they were.

"There must've been gladiator battles here," he said as we climbed the stands and sat in the middle, halfway between the top area relegated to slaves and women, and the lower portion reserved for Roman male citizens.

"Oh, yes, mortal combat." I crossed my ankles demurely and reached into my pocketbook for a cigarette. "To the death." I clicked my lighter and drew a grateful breath of smoke into my lungs.

In the arena below, two boys fought a duel with sticks, hamming it up for their imaginary audience, the wind standing in for the roar of the crowd. Their shouts echoed off the walls and empty stone bleachers, reverberating faint and ghostly.

"You know, I heard the funniest thing this morning," I said, staring at the cigarette between my fingers.

"What's that?" Jack leaned back on his elbows, stretching his legs before him.

"Remember that candy shop in Aix? The one where they caught the Sciences Po trio?"

"Oh, sweetheart." He frowned, patting his pockets, retrieving a cigarette. "You're not still worrying about *them*, are you? They've been caught and will be duly punished."

"It doesn't sell chocolate." I turned away in a cloud of smoke. "Can you imagine?"

He chuckled a little. "Leave it to the French, eh? They have a specialty shop for every darn thing. The other day I walked past a store that only sells light bulbs."

"Yes, this sweet shop in Aix is exactly like that, specializing in just a few things. Recipes from the Middle Ages—isn't that charming? Like a piece of edible history."

He lowered his head to light his cigarette, striking three matches before one finally caught.

"You know what they sell? Nougats. And you know what else?" I turned to look at him, noting the way his mouth had tightened at the corners. "Calissons."

He coughed and waved away a little smoke. "You mean those little almond candies? Why, I gave you a tin of those, didn't I? They sell them everywhere in Marseille."

"Is that right?"

"Sure. Great big stacks of them at all the tourist shops. They're a popular souvenir."

I sat still for an instant, perfectly still, absorbing the sun on the crown of my head, the ruffle of the breeze, the solid presence of Jack by my side. "It's funny you should mention that," I said. "Because I heard this shop sells a particular kind that's not available anywhere else. What's it called? Oh, yes, Le Roy Rémi."

He shrugged. "You must've heard wrong. You've never been to Marseille, have you?"

"I haven't," I admitted. "But I read it here." Reaching into my pocketbook, I pulled out the glossy gold and white tin of calissons that he had given me a few weeks ago. I'd unearthed it from a pile of clothes in my room, having neglected to give it to Mary Ann after all. On the lid the words LE ROY RÉMI were emblazoned in red Gothic script, and inside the sweets were lined up with precision, their shoulders clinging stickily together.

Jack shifted his weight, sitting up. "Does this really matter, sweetheart? I'm having a hard time understanding why this is so important to you."

I ignored him, fishing out a promotional pamphlet from the tin, and began to read aloud. "In 1919, in the heart of Aix-en-Provence, renowned nougat expert Ernest Pepin opened a boutique to sell the traditional confection popular since the Middle Ages. In 1947, his son Rémi, trained at his father's knee, took over the shop and introduced a new sweetmeat, an ancient specialty of the Kingdom of Provence called the calisson, which means little hug in the Provençal language. Today our boutique in Aix-en-Provence is the only purveyor of Le Roy Rémi calissons, which are based on the original recipe of medieval nobility, with high-quality ingredients produced in our sunny region. If it's not Le Roy Rémi, it's not royal!"

"Gosh." Jack leaned forward. "That's laying it on a bit thick, isn't it? You'd think they'd never had a revolution in this country."

"You know what I think?" I said in a musing tone. "I think you know more about the Sciences Po trio than you've been letting on."

"Aw, sweetheart, you flatter me, but—"

"I think you've spent an awful lot of time with them. I think this operation has been going on for months, maybe even longer—certainly long enough for them to take you to Le Roy Rémi on your trip to Marseille. Their arrest must be a real triumph for you. But you're not allowed to breathe a word about it to anyone."

He spread his hands but remained silent.

"You made a mistake giving me the calissons. But then I thought their hideout was a chocolate shop, and you went along with it. Because you're still under-cover, right? So it's imperative that no one knows you were involved, not even me. But obviously *someone* suspected you—because you were being followed—" Something stuck in my throat, and I swallowed hard.

Instinctively Jack glanced behind him, but there was

no one. Aside from the two boys playing in the ring below, we were alone, which was why I had chosen to come here.

"Things started heating up," I continued, my pulse pounding along my temples. "Constant surveillance. Incessant phone calls. You were getting nervous— *really* nervous—that you'd been compromised. But you couldn't give up the case, right? Not after all that hard work, all that time. Certainly not after the arrest warrants had been issued and the trio was *so close* to being caught. Besides"—I looked at him carefully— "if your handlers ever suspected you'd been exposed, they'd yank you straight out of Paris, isn't that right? So you—you found a solution. You—" I blinked under the intensity of his gaze. "You planted a rumor that *Ghislaine* was the secret informant—that *she* was the one investigating the trio. Once everyone thought *she* was the spy, they stopped suspecting you."

Jack's eyes dropped from my face.

"I'm not sure who you told," I said. "One of the trio? Or was it Charlie? He was already pretty angry with her, after all. I think it was someone else, though. Someone more influential. And it worked, didn't it? You stopped getting tailed. The trio was caught. And you're still squeaky clean."

"Sweetheart . . ." He flicked the end of his cigarette, once, twice, three times. "I'm not really sure what to say."

"You don't have to say anything." My cigarette had burned to a nub, but still I brought it to my lips, inhaling the last shred of tobacco. "I bet you think this all turned out peachy, right? But I want you to know something." I dropped the butt to the ground and crushed it with my heel. "Last week, in the middle of the day, Ghislaine nearly got mowed down by a car outside the *épicerie*." I had started shaking, my voice, my hands, my limbs. *"Because of you."*

"Holy hell!" Jack stared at me. "Is she all right?"

"She has a broken arm. But she was lucky—it could have been much worse."

"Those bastards. Those Goddamn little bastards." His jaw tightened. "I can't believe they would attack a woman like that, right on the street, in broad daylight no less."

Heat flashed through me. "You can't *believe* it? Are you serious? They're ruthless, Jack. Isn't that what you told me about the Soviets? They—they send people to the gulag. They interrogate, and torture, and when they finally extract a confession—or even if they don't!—they kill you point-blank, just like that, bam! Why does any of this surprise you? Ghislaine could be *dead* right now."

He scrubbed his face with his hands. "Look, I agree, sweetheart, this is all extremely disquieting. But let's keep things in perspective: Ghislaine is fine—I mean, she must be pretty shaken up—but she's alive. The Sciences Po trio has been unmasked and arrested, and God willing they'll spend the rest of their lives rotting in some French prison. I'm not saying what, er, happened was right—in fact, I see now that it definitely was not—but all's well that ends well. What matters most is that Ghislaine is safe—and the bastards got caught. Surely you can see that?"

His dark blue eyes were pleading, reminding me of the stakes at hand. Despite my anger, I felt myself relenting. For of course I understood the jeopardy we faced, the real threat of the Soviet Union, and the importance of his work. Unmasking a spy ring was an enormous coup. But I couldn't help feeling that his success had come at a price. I darted a glance at him. "You told me the other day . . ." I hesitated, twisting my fingers together. "You said you didn't know how much longer you could do this."

He nodded slowly. "I remember."

"Would you ever . . . stop?"

He hunched over, elbows on knees. "I've thought about it. I've thought about it a million times, marching in there and telling them I can't be part of the gang anymore. Especially after they said I should start investigating some of my American friends—Jimmy and some of the other fellows at the club. Well, I told them flat out no and they backed down. But who knows how long that'll stick?" He drew a deep breath. "The problem is, I make so little from my writing . . . how could I take care of you?"

"I'm tougher than I look," I assured him, but his words were sobering.

"There's something else," he said slowly. "Something I've been wanting to tell you. We're starting up a magazine here in Paris—me and my pal Doc Humes, and a friend from the *Lampoon* called George Plimpton. Also this fellow Peter—Peter Matthiessen's coming over from New York; he's a Yale man, but not a bad sort. We've got funding for at least five years, salaries and everything. It'll be a literary magazine, you know, the real deal, despite its origins—fiction by young writers."

I sat up a little straighter. "But, darling, this is wonderful, don't you see? You can finally quit! Surely this magazine will sustain you for a while, until your novel becomes a huge success. Because I know it will. I just know it—Hold on." I bit back my enthusiasm.

Something he'd said was pricking my senses. "What do you mean, 'it'll be the real deal, despite its origins'? What are its 'origins'?"

He looked at me helplessly.

I crossed my arms. "Who's backing this literary magazine?"

"I don't—" His voice turned ragged. "I don't know how to answer that."

"It's a cover," I said quietly and held my breath, waiting for him to contradict me. But the silence between us stretched until finally he turned to look at me in mute appeal. "You're not quitting," I said, with a flash of illumination. "You're using this magazine as your new and improved cover. In fact, you have no intention of quitting—not now, and maybe not ever."

"Sweetheart, please, try to understand. I want to be a writer, yes. But I don't come from family money—I don't have a generous father paying my way, or—or a trust fund when I turn thirty. I have to be practical— don't you see? If I give up this work, it would mean a cold-water *chambre de bonne* and beans out of a can for supper every night. You don't want to live that way, do you?"

"I don't want to live *this* way! The lies, and the deception—and the *work*, yes, I *know*, Jack. It's *important*. But what about the duplicity?" Tears trembled beneath my eyelashes, threatening to spill down my cheeks, but I bit the inside of my lip and forced them back.

His face turned cold. "I thought you'd at least see what a boon this magazine is to me. I've been asked to start a literary journal that *actually pays well*. Only a fool would turn this down."

"Only a fool would take *them* at face value! They're calling it a literary magazine now, but I bet it turns into propaganda."

"Are you questioning my judgment?"

"No, I'm *questioning* your integrity." My heart was hammering in my chest, overpowering my senses. I had thought Jack a man of honor, but now here he was, steadily continuing with this work he only half believed in, while steadily ignoring the terrible price of secrecy and betrayal. Suddenly, I couldn't bear to look at him, couldn't bear to see his face—so familiar, so beloved—shadowed by his weakness. I couldn't bear it—but I couldn't ignore it.

"Jacqueline, sweetheart, please." Jack placed a hand on my arm. "I don't want to quarrel. I should've asked you about the magazine first, instead of jumping right in like that. Please let's not let this put a wedge between us."

But things between us had changed. Between us

now was Ghislaine, and his underhandedness, and all the reasons he had used to justify it. Between us now were his doubts, and denials, and concessions to a life of convenience. I had fallen in love with Jack's talent and ambition, his purpose and determination and character; but now I had glimpsed his frailty, and all my esteem and admiration were slipping away. I tried to grasp at it, tried to hold it close, but it was dissolving into a mist too fine to contain.

"I'm sorry, Jack," I said in the clear, precise way he loved so well. "I'm so sorry—I can't." My voice shook as tears began falling down my cheeks.

To his credit, he didn't argue, or plead his case, or ask why. He understood. "Oh, Jacqueline," he said, his voice so low it broke. "I was always afraid this was too good to be true."

It seemed impossible that we could say goodbye right here, on this bright, breathtaking spring day, that we were embracing for the last time—me brushing my cheek against his coat lapel, inhaling his juniper scent— walking to the métro together, taking trains in opposite directions. I was too stunned to cry, too stunned to do anything but sit and stare out the train window as the black tunnel walls became white tiled stations and back again, dark, light, dark, light, all the way home.

Upstairs, I found the apartment empty. Ghislaine

was at a doctor's appointment, and the others were at their usual midday activities, and so I shut the door to my room, and I shut the chintz curtains against the relentless light, and I shut my eyes and allowed myself to cry. The tears were hot and savage. I wept for my dreams, and hopes, and plans, which, I saw now, had been but mere fantasy. I wept for Jack, caught in the age-old trap of art and existence. I wept for myself too, for the loneliness that had been my constant companion since childhood, the solitude I had learned to embrace, and cultivate, and sometimes resent. I wept because I was alone, again, and feared I always would be. I wept because I loved Jack, still, despite everything, and because I knew with absolute certainty that we could never make each other happy.

I wept until my head ached, and my jaw ached, and the space behind my eyes ached. I wept until the church bells chimed two o'clock, and then I got up and washed my face because people would be coming home and I couldn't be seen like this, not by anyone. I slid a cardigan around my shoulders, and a pair of sunglasses on my face, and I slipped out the front door and into the brilliance of a glorious spring day in Paris. I walked, numb behind my dark glasses, but soon I began noticing things, despite myself, little flashes of beauty: the extravagant loops and swirls of black wrought-iron railings, the clouds like candy floss suspended in great cottony tufts, the sky reflected in the Seine all blue and white and shimmery. Masses of peonies crammed the flower shops, and an array of candy-colored drinks paraded upon the café tables, and golden light glowed on the cobblestones. And it was all so beautiful, so very, very beautiful, I felt it in my heart like a burn, like a balm, the sorrow, and the solace, and the constant. Paris.

PART IV

L'été

Chapter Seventeen

There came an afternoon at the end of June when I began packing my trunk and valise, dividing my clothes between the two. I had survived my final exams, somehow, and now I was the only Smith girl still at avenue Mozart. Susan and Mary Ann had departed two weeks ago to spend the summer hosteling across Europe before sailing home, and soon I too would bid farewell to this drafty, creaky-floored apartment and the family who made it so dear.

"Goodness, the room looks so empty without your books and pictures."

I turned to see Madame in the doorway. She wore a light cotton dress in her favorite shade of leafy green, the full skirt stirring in the breeze drifting in from the open window.

"I wish they could stay," I said. "And me too."

She smiled a little wistfully. "Wouldn't that be lovely? But life moves on, *chérie*. Even when we think we're standing still, things keep changing." She stepped into the room. "I have something for you. A little souvenir."

She placed in my hands a small odd-shaped parcel wrapped in brown paper and string. I opened it carefully, finding inside a porcelain saucer with a border of green and gold, a long-tailed brown bird painted in its center. I drew a sharp breath. "Is this—Surely this isn't Sèvres porcelain? Oh, Madame, I couldn't possibly— it's simply too precious—"

"I found it at the flea market." She shrugged. "The dealer thought it was just a fussy bit of old china—he couldn't wait to be rid of it. There's an ugly chip, you see, right there on the rim. But I thought you might like it for your own *cabinet de curiosités* one day."

"If I ever have one," I said, more ruefully than intended.

"Of course you will." Her dark eyes narrowed. "Even if it's in the home you create for yourself. These happy times, they're what keep us hopeful. Don't forget—a museum of comfort."

I stood to kiss her cheeks. "How can I thank you for everything this year?"

"Oh, my dear. It's been a pleasure to share it with

you." The affection in her voice was so sincere it was almost too much for me. She had lost so much, suffered so deeply, and yet here she was, utterly unafraid to give of herself.

I longed to tell her how much I admired her. But before I could find the right words, she was brushing away my emotion with a pat of my shoulder, murmuring something about starting dinner. She stepped into the hallway, leaving behind a faint flowery perfume that would always remind me of her. Even now, when I smell dried lavender, I think of the Comtesse de Renty.

If I had learned anything at all this year, it was because of Madame: her courage, and restraint, and strength; her curiosity, and eye for antiquity, and heightened awareness of beauty; her dignity in the face of tragedy. I learned it all from her.

At first it felt strange to be traveling south without Jack. We had talked about it so often, made so many plans, I couldn't see a sign for Toulouse or Montpellier on the highway without feeling a pang. I kept glancing over to make funny little jokes and observations, only to find Claude sitting in the passenger's seat beside me. Still, as we drove south from Lyon, I sensed the light growing sharper, the air warmer and dryer, the fields fading from lush and sodden to dry and bronzed, and with the changing landscape my spirits began to lift.

Ghislaine had generously lent us her faithful old Panhard Dyna, a rattletrap round-topped car painted a chic shade of forest green. "After all, *I'm* not going anywhere for a while," she'd said, indicating her arm, which was still in a sling. And so Claude and I set out on a three-week road trip across France. There was scarcely any traffic because scarcely anyone owned a car, and we wandered at our own pace, zigzagging north and south as our fancy struck, no château too remote for a detour, no de Renty cousin too long lost for a visit. We saw little villages radiating from stone churches, and fields of wheat tilled by farmers in smocks and clogs, and barefoot kids chasing herds of sheep across open meadows. We dressed in shorts and sundresses and canvas jute sandals, not a hat or glove or pair of stockings in sight. We ate picnics of fresh goat's cheese, coarse rounds of peasant bread, and dried *saucisson* sliced with a folding pocketknife that Claude kept in the glove box, and with this simple food we drank rough red wine bought at roadside stands.

We snapped a thousand photos that I've since lost—perhaps Claude still has copies—but I don't need them to recall the rugged, ridged terrain of the Massif Central, our little car straining up the hills before coasting down to valleys split by trickling streams. I can still picture Claude behind the wheel, shouting *"Pauvre con!"* at some poor man she had nearly run down in the street of some town as I clung to the passenger door handle and howled with laughter.

We took turns driving, stopping to chat with whomever we pleased, farm wives, and goatherds, and children up in trees picking cherries. We inspected Roman ruins, and toured decaying castles, and dipped our feet in rivers, and ponds, and ancient washing pools. And bit by bit the vise on my heart began to loosen, the blood flowing again to my cheeks, and my limbs, and my soul, and eventually there were entire hours and even days when I didn't think about Jack at all.

"Are you ready to go back to New York?" Claude asked me one afternoon. We were sunning ourselves beside a stream, our bare legs stretched out upon the grassy bank.

"I suppose I'll never really be ready." I twirled a piece of straw between my fingers. "But I've resigned myself to it. Especially after . . . these past few weeks." I didn't mention Jack, and she didn't ask, but she knew what I meant. "I've decided not to return to Vassar next year," I told her.

"Oh, really? No more poky old Poughkeepsie for you?"

"I've applied for a transfer to the George Washington University. If it comes through, I'll live at Merry-wood with Mummy and Uncle Hugh."

She raised an eyebrow. "Is that what you want?"

"It's only for a school year. After I graduate, maybe I'll move back to France. We'll see. Of course, Mummy's desperately hoping I'll meet some brilliant Washington politician who'll snap me up off the market."

Claude reached for the bottle of wine and refilled our wooden cups. "Just remember that you're brilliant too, Jacqueline Lee Bouvier," she declared. "Whoever he is, this lucky man who marries you, he'd better appreciate how brilliant you are."

After a couple of weeks of wandering, we met up with Yusha, my darling stepbrother, joining him at a château near Saint-Jean-de-Luz, where he was vacationing with some school friends. And then the days really started flying by, with trips to the beach at Biarritz, sightings of wild Basque ponies, and evenings fizzing with the dry sparkle of txakoli, the local wine. Here in Basque country, the food was sun-warmed and savory with aged sheep's cheeses, dry-cured hams, and buttery pastry crusts filled with cherry jam. Of course, every region in France had a different cuisine to sample, a different type of wine to taste, each one a precise reflection of its place in the world.

Suddenly time was slipping through my fingers. We were in Bordeaux. The Loire Valley. Back in Paris for a night. The next day Yusha and I would take an overnight ferry from Cherbourg to Dublin and, after motoring around Ireland, cross over to inspect the moors and monuments of Scotland before heading south to England. We would set sail from Le Havre on August 17, bound for New York on the *Liberté*.

Our departure for Ireland marked the end of my year in France. The ferryboat left Cherbourg in the thick fog of early morning, and I stayed on deck as we pulled out of port, hanging over the railing to glimpse every last crag and hollow of the French coast vanishing into the mist. One second it was there, rough and jagged, and then there was only a blur of gray sky and sea. It happened more quickly than I thought, leaving me with wet cheeks and the taste of salt on my lips. It was over, this unforgettable, transformative, sometimes difficult year. It was over, and I wondered if I would ever stop missing Paris, if I could ever stop aching for its smells, and states, and splendors. Perhaps *this* was the great first love of my life: not a man—not Jack; but France, real France—*la France profonde*—not the fairyland of ancient aristocracy I imagined as a child, but a flawed and beautiful place that I had discovered for myself.

I never did stop missing it.

I thought about returning the following year. By then I had graduated from the George Washington University and I was at a loose end, one broken engagement under my belt and Mummy harping at me to find another fiancé—"And for heaven's sake, make it stick this time." She let me know quite clearly that unless I was betrothed, I needed to find a job.

When the CIA came to campus, I put in an application like many of my classmates. What can I say? I was young and idealistic, and the Korean War had broken out a few months earlier, leaving me with a sinking pit of doom in my stomach. Working for the agency seemed like a concrete way of fighting against communism, particularly if I could use my French-language skills investigating conflicts in Algeria and Indochina. (And it wasn't just me: Decades later I discovered that several of my Smith in Paris classmates had joined the French desk after graduation, including dear old clever Martha, whose oath of secrecy meant I didn't learn about her job until more than twenty-five years after she quit.) It was serious, steady, worthwhile work—but in the end the men in suits reminded me too much of Jack, all easy charm and eyes that never quite settled. I wanted to forge my own path, not follow him around like some sort of track pony.

In October, I entered *Vogue* magazine's Prix de Paris,

not really thinking I had a chance, and not even sure I really wanted it. The winner would work for six months at the *Vogue* office in Paris, followed by six months at Condé Nast in New York—a marvelous opportunity if you wanted to become an editor, which I wasn't certain I did. All my life, I had dreamed of *writing* stories, not refining someone else's, and so I dithered as I worked on my application, motivated mainly by the prospect of living in Paris again. I had nothing to lose, and perhaps this was what allowed me to pour my heart into the contest's essays and short fiction, revealing and inventing myself in the same stroke of the pen. No one was more astonished than I when I actually won.

I begged Mummy to let me accept the award. "It's *ideal* for me, don't you see? It fits in with all the things I'm interested in—art, and fashion, and books. Oh, *please*, Mummy."

But she said no and refused to change her mind. She didn't want me living with Daddy in New York, and she certainly didn't want me going back to Paris. "What if you become involved with some—some *foreigner*?" she said, her voice low with horror. "Absolutely not, Jackie. I want you home in the Washington D.C. area." *Vogue* was infamous for paying its girls mere pin money, and without Mummy and Hughdie's support I had no choice but to turn down the prize.

I suppose it was for the best. I lived at Merrywood with Mummy, Uncle Hugh, and my siblings, took a job as the inquiring camera girl for the *Washington Times-Herald*, and allowed the District of Columbia to become my destiny. But alongside my public life, which everyone thinks they know so well, I have nurtured a private passion, and it is France. I've never stopped dreaming of it, never stopped reading French history and novels, watching French films, or devouring French culture—art and fashion and food—never stopped turning to it for inspiration and refuge. In so many ways, it has sustained me.

In 1951, Lee and I went on a madcap summer tour of Europe, driving across the continent in a leased Hillman Minx. Mummy must have been feeling guilty about the *Vogue* prize, for she granted us a generous allowance and wrote letters of introduction to the kind of people she loved to mingle with in Washington: ambassadors and heiresses and captains of industry. We spent half our time in skirts and hats and white gloves, bobbing our heads at cocktail receptions, and the other half wearing shorts or strapless sundresses, flirting with boys we met at nightclubs. It was wonderful fun, but I still regret that our stop in Paris was too brief to see the de Rentys, and our room at the Hôtel Continental too luxurious for me to re-create the ambience of my swaddled student days.

Things changed rather swiftly after that—not just for me, but for the others as well. Claude and Bernard wed in 1951 and soon welcomed the first of five children. It's no surprise to me that she has managed everything so beautifully, becoming an elected official, high-ranking civil servant, and advocate for the memory of those deported from France during the Resistance. We have tried to keep the spirit of our Franco-American sisterhood alive, sending our daughters to each other during the summer holidays.

A year or two later, Ghislaine remarried, moving with Christian to her new husband's home in Geneva. I was pleased she had found love again with a successful, warmhearted businessman who treated Christian as his own. I only hoped the ghosts of the past would settle for her, especially after the Sciences Po trio had been found guilty and sentenced to life imprisonment.

Jack and I exchanged letters sometimes, and even met for lunch once or twice when he was passing through Washington. Our conversations were as fun and flirtatious as ever, filled with chat about the latest books and films. He never mentioned his romantic life (except to tease that he was still pining for me), which was why I was surprised to hear that he and Susan Coward married in 1953, right before the debut issue of the literary magazine he'd helped launch, the *Paris Review*. It took a good long gallop for me to get over this news, but in the end I acknowledged that Sue was pretty and sensible and a thoughtful fellow boarder at avenue Mozart. I felt certain she would care for Jack far better than I ever could.

Sometimes during that first winter home from Paris I found myself in the parlor at Merrywood, arms bare, feet unslippered, face blazing from the cloying central heat. I would recall the icy discomfort of avenue Mozart—the drafty thin-paned windows and the pure northern light falling through them—and a pang would shoot through me, so sharp it left me breathless. In moments like these, I would sometimes scrawl a postcard to my dear friends, because I needed them to know how much I missed them. And I needed to prove to myself that they existed—that the year had not been a dream.

Chères Madame, Ghislaine, *et* Claude,
I have a horrible homesickness today for 78 avenue Mozart.

Je vous embrasse,
Jacqueline

Chapter Eighteen

They told me it was inconvenient to pass through the Latin Quarter, a sentimental detour that took too much time—and time was the last thing we had, programmed as we were to the last second. But it had been more than a decade since I'd lived in Paris and I longed for a glimpse of the old neighborhood. When I pointed out it would be a poignant reminder of my student years, the men in gray suits relented. From the airport, we entered the city at the porte d'Orléans, sweeping through the 14th arrondissement, up the boulevard Saint-Michel, and all of a sudden my heart was in my throat as I caught sight of all the beloved places: the jardin du Luxembourg, its trees in full leaf behind wrought-iron gates; the Panthéon's dome peeping over rooftops; the quai des Grands Augustins, lined with dark green *bouquiniste* stalls. Unlike New York, which seemed to shed its skin every season, Paris looked exactly as I remembered it, exactly as I had imagined it for so long. I wanted to leap from the car and wander the little streets, gaze at shop windows, absorb the rise and fall of French voices, allow the language to emerge from my throat like a song.

I hadn't counted on the people, though. They were lining the streets in a thin perimeter—not a dense crowd, but a visible one—waving at our motorcade as we passed, clapping and cheering.

"Listen." I placed a hand on my husband's arm. "They're calling for you." I squared my shoulders and aimed a smile out the window. I knew all about the crowds that admired and adored and claimed my husband for their own. They followed us everywhere, even to our front doorstep, until I felt like I couldn't do anything, say anything, laugh, cry, or even speak, without inciting criticism or political gossip.

"Gosh, isn't that nice?" He waved at them, our car slipping westward along the Seine, following a route I had walked a hundred times. As the shouts grew louder, his brow creased. "You know something?" he said. "I don't think it's . . ." He cocked his head, concentrating for a moment. Finally, he turned to me, his eyes dancing. "I think it's for *you*."

"Oh, darling, please." I laughed. "They don't know who I am."

"Are you kidding? After all those interviews you gave in perfect French in the run-up to this trip?" He motioned toward the window. "Trust me, they know exactly who you are. Listen to them!" We fell silent for a second. "Jack-ie! Jack-ie! Jack-ie!" He tapped the rhythm on my leg.

Now I could discern it too, incredible though it was. There was my name being chanted in a strong, steady beat. "JACK-IE! JACK-IE! JACK-IE!"

When I raised my hand, to my utter astonishment, they erupted into a roar.

It was the last day of May 1961, and my husband and I had come to France on a state visit as president and first lady of the United States of America. He had been in office for a little more than four months, and I had almost accepted that my time—my home, my privacy—were no longer my own. By now, I was used to observing everyone around me, watching them as closely as they watched me. By now, the press had developed their own narrative of who they thought I was, scrutinizing everything I ate and wore and bought. By now, I knew the truth about my husband and our relationship, and I had learned how to conceal my pain.

Ours was not an easy marriage, but I must admit my husband always recognized the best of me. From our very first meeting at a Georgetown dinner party, when we sparred over eighteenth-century French and English history, he let me know that he admired intelligence as much as beauty. I spent some of the happiest days of our engagement translating and summarizing a pile of French books on Indochina, helping him prepare for his first major foreign policy speech as a senator. As his political career bounded forward, he relied on my advice about many things, but in particular French language and culture. It was at his request that I helped plan the official schedule of our three-day state visit to Paris.

At first it felt funny, in all those meetings with White House and State Department officials, to redirect their suggestions. I had to tread lightly because, after all, they were the experts on foreign policy and protocol and all the personalities involved. But I quickly realized *I* was the expert on France. I knew French history and saw how we could honor it in our program of events. Most high-level visits focused on policy speeches and lists of political and economic points read aloud in conference rooms. But ours would incorporate museums and theater and receptions in some of the grandest spaces Paris had to offer—the salle des Fêtes of the Hôtel de Ville, the galerie des Glaces at Versailles—and I knew these choices would underscore America's admiration of French culture, our respect for the French people, our appreciation of our friendship. France was forever our first ally, *malgré tout*—despite everything.

In the weeks before the trip, my husband was jittery and snappish, his nerves worn thin by the Bay of Pigs debacle, which had occurred in mid-April. The French newspapers, especially on the intellectual left, had been enraged by the CIA-supported attack on Fidel Castro, and he told me to expect anti-American sentiment in Paris. "Better brace yourself for a chilly reception," he warned. "I know you adore the French, but they can be vicious."

"It can't be worse than anything I encountered as a student," I said, thinking of the yellow posters that used to plaster the walls near the Sorbonne, screaming about L'OCCUPATION AMÉRICAIN! and LES AMÉRICAINS EN AMÉRIQUE!; remembering all the critical essays, and street protests, and spiteful sly remarks that could cut you to the core if you weren't thick-skinned enough, the embarrassment when the criticism was justified, the sadness when our two governments disagreed, because the relationship meant so much to me.

In the eleven years since I'd returned home from Paris, the Marshall Plan had succeeded, France had flourished, America and Europe had become cultural and economic powerhouses. But it was all still there, hanging thick in the air—the same old tensions between America and France, the left and right, communists and conservatives, the Soviets and their hunger. How could any of us have known back then, as we shivered in the parlor at avenue Mozart, that we were witnessing the battle lines being drawn for a conflict that would define the politics of our adult lives?

From the minute we landed in Paris, it was a whirl of interviews and speeches, meeting men I'd idolized as a teen—André Malraux, Charles de Gaulle—heroes of the Resistance, now leaders of the République. There were champagne toasts in gilt-tipped reception rooms—a dinner at the Élysée Palace, where I dismissed my official interpreter and conversed with Président de Gaulle directly—a gala banquet at Versailles that concluded with a ballet performance in an antique theater lit with flaming torches as spotlights. There was the trunk full of exquisite clothes—gowns and suits and pillbox hats—as carefully considered as costumes for a theatrical production. There was the speech in which my husband, bemused and slightly awestruck, declared himself the man who had accompanied his wife to Paris.

There was splendor and ceremony and lavish beauty—and with each unfolding moment I felt more and more conscious that I was living through history, shadowed by my Bouvier ancestors who had left this country, and me, the twenty-year-old American who had returned to claim it. France was entwined with my soul, perhaps because I had willed it so, and if I had attained any success in life, it was rooted in my experiences here, in my love for French language and literature, and especially in the French friends who had opened their world to me.

I had provided a list of names to the men in gray suits, not entirely certain if they would follow through with invitations. But at the Hôtel de Ville, I spotted them, and at the sight of their familiar faces, my eyes stung. I stole a moment to chat with each of them, pressing my cheeks to theirs—Claude, Bernard, and Madame of course, Paul de Ganay and his parents, and dear Madame Saleil, who had recently returned to Reid Hall for the academic year. "This is the woman who taught me to love France more than anything," I told André Malraux when I introduced her. He bowed his head over her hand, and she nearly fainted at such attention from the minister of culture.

I think Madame Saleil thought it was a flimsy bit of politesse on my part, but I sincerely meant it—about her, and all of them—my professors and classmates and the friends I had come to think of as my French family. They had taught me to love France in all its glorious, messy, rigid formality, and in doing so they taught me about myself, and what it meant to be an American in the world. Such was the priceless gift of a year spent studying abroad: the awareness of new possibilities and other points of view, the sparking of a love of travel, the confidence born of relying on my own resourcefulness. Such was the significance of my year in Paris that I forever considered it the high point of my life, even as other events of triumph and tragedy played out upon a grand stage. I would always take refuge in my memories of Paris—and France would remain that corner of the world where I was young and happy and free.

Author's Note

This is a work of fiction, but it is based on the real lives of Jacqueline Bouvier, John Marquand Jr., the de Renty family, and other people who lived in Paris after the war. As such, it was important to me to portray their stories as accurately as possible, based on information found in the historical record. Jacqueline Bouvier Kennedy Onassis was famously private and guarded, and her personal papers are largely unavailable to the public. Much of what we know about her comes from the memories of others—friends, family, and foes. In this book, I have attempted to explore her emotional life, especially as it related to the events of the era, while still remaining faithful to the facts.

In the winter of 2019, I went to Paris to retrace the footsteps of Jacqueline Bouvier for a travel story in the *New York Times*. I knew she had studied there from 1949 to 1950, which she called "the high point in my life, my happiest and most carefree year," and from those words I foolishly assumed postwar Paris was a place of optimism, beauty, and joy. But I hadn't counted on the grief, still raw after the Occupation, or the damage—bullet holes, dirt, and neglect still scarring the city—or the fragile state of France and, indeed, all of Europe, before the Marshall Plan took hold. As I read more about postwar France's political instability, I realized this was a complicated period, and that the tale of Jacqueline's year abroad reached far beyond the scope of a travel story.

For my article I had the privilege of interviewing Claude du Granrut (née de Renty), Jacqueline's host sister, in her sunny apartment near the Palais Royal. A former deputy mayor of Senlis, a small town in northern France, she remains an active member of UNADIF, an organization that honors those deported, detained, and lost in the Resistance, and their families. In 2020, she was awarded the Légion d'honneur by the French government.

Over demitasses of coffee and squares of dark chocolate, Claude du Granrut described a young woman determined to embrace her experience in France. "She was always called Jacqueline. Never Jackie," she said.

"And I never spoke a word of English to her. Ever." She talked about the earmuffs, scarves, and gloves that Jacqueline wore to ward off the bitter cold of the apartment at avenue Mozart, and of the genuine affection between Jacqueline and her mother, the Comtesse de Renty. Later, reading du Granrut's memoir, *Le Piano et le violoncelle,* I learned more of her parents' story, their work in the Resistance spy ring Alliance, their suffering in German slave-labor camps, the death of her father, and the strength of her mother. For the rest of her life, the Comtesse de Renty remained a passionate advocate of women who had been deported from France because of their work in the Resistance, lobbying the French government for the same rights and recognition received by their male counterparts.

Ghislaine de Renty and her son, Christian, were indeed part of the household at avenue Mozart, although details of this period of her life are not publicly known. In fact, Ghislaine is a composite character, her history combined with that of an older de Renty sister, Christiane, who had married and left home by 1949. Like her parents, Christiane was part of Alliance during the war, and she was awarded the Légion d'honneur for her work. She is buried at Père Lachaise Cemetery beside her husband, Gilbert Beaujolin, another Alliance member and Resistance hero.

Ghislaine's second marriage, to businessman Jean-Pierre Marchal, was long and happy, and by 1991 she was a wealthy widow dividing her time between Geneva and Mougins, a village in the hills above the Côte d'Azur. When she mysteriously missed two consecutive lunch dates, the police went to her villa and discovered her corpse in the cellar, struck brutally on the head and body, and covered in blood. The only significant clue was two messages on the cellar doors, both reading *"Omar m'a tuer"*—Omar killed me—scrawled in blood and, nearly as distressing to French journalists, grievously misspelled. How could a woman of Ghislaine Marchal's education and social stature make such a rudimentary spelling error, confusing the past participle *tué* with the infinitive *tuer*? Was it the addled mistake of a dying woman? Or was it all a setup?

The Omar of the messages referred to Omar Raddad, Ghislaine's part-time gardener, a young Moroccan immigrant who spoke broken French, and who had been described by his other employers as pleasant, helpful, and practically illiterate. Raddad swore he was innocent, and evidence against him was scarce, but the news reports were laced with speculation and thinly veiled racism. "L'affaire Omar Raddad," as the case became known, gripped the country, provoking a public debate on anti-Muslim discrimination, racial profiling, and inequality in France. Raddad was convicted by French courts and sentenced to eighteen years in prison, but in 1996 he was partially pardoned by French president Jacques Chirac and his sentence reduced. As I write this, more than thirty years after the crime, a report has emerged with DNA evidence that could clear Raddad's name, should the case be reopened in court. Ghislaine's murder remains unsolved.

Jacqueline stayed friends with Paul de Ganay for the rest of her life. He died in 2009, never married, and while his private life remains private, he was described to me as "a confirmed bachelor." A renowned polo player on the international circuit, he helped maintain the tradition of the sport at his family's estate, the Château de Courances.

John P. Marquand Jr. was an editor, contributor, and founding member of the *Paris Review*—but aside from a few novels published under his pen name, John Phillips, and his marriage to Jacqueline's former roommate Susan Coward (who died in 1977), not much is known about his work or life. Did he and Jacqueline have a Paris romance? It seems likely, given that several biographies of Jacqueline discuss their relationship, some in salacious detail. When I checked the endnotes, it appeared to me that at least a few of the sources might have had an axe to grind.

I based Jack Marquand's character loosely on one of his contemporaries, the writer Peter Matthiessen, who also lived in Paris during the early 1950s and who also helped start the *Paris Review*. In 1951, Matthiessen and his wife, Patsy, were young parents and writers living on the Left Bank—but they had another source of income. While at Yale, Matthiessen had been recruited by the CIA, which sent him to Paris after graduation to keep an eye on communist activity. When it was determined that his cover as an unpublished novelist was too flimsy, he proposed the idea of a literary journal, joining forces with Harold L. "Doc" Humes, George Plimpton—and, presumably, Jack Marquand. But Matthiessen soon found that befriending French leftists had made him sympathetic to their beliefs and disillusioned with the CIA. He left Paris, quitting the agency and the magazine—and the period remained a source of embarrassment for the rest of his life.

I relied on a few sources to understand Matthiessen's history, including the articles "Peter Matthiessen's Lifelong Quest for Peace," by Ron Rosenbaum (*Smithsonian* magazine, May 2014); "A Writer's Controversial Past That Will Not Die," by Jeff Wheelwright (*New York Times*, February 2, 2018); and the book *Finks: How the CIA Tricked the World's Best Writers*, by Joel Whitney, which also discusses the provocative question of how the CIA funded literary magazines in Europe as a form of soft-power propaganda.

For details on Jacqueline's life, especially her childhood, I consulted many sources, including *America's Queen*, by Sarah Bradford; *Jacqueline Bouvier: An Intimate Memoir*, by John H. Davis; *Jackie as Editor*, by Greg Lawrence; *As We Remember Her*, by Carl Sferrazza Anthony; *Cooking for Madam*, by Marta Sgubin; *The Best Loved Poems of Jacqueline Kennedy Onassis*, by Caroline Kennedy; *All Too Human*, by Edward Klein; *Jackie, Janet, and Lee*, by J. Randy Taraborrelli; *Jacqueline Bouvier Kennedy Onassis: The Untold Story*, by Barbara Leaming; *The Fabulous Bouvier Sisters*, by Sam Kashner and Nancy Schoenberger; and *Jacqueline Bouvier Kennedy Onassis: A Life*, by Donald Spoto. The illustrated scrapbook created by Jacqueline and her sister, Lee Radziwill, during their 1951 trip to Europe—published in 1974 under the title *One Special Summer*—provided a tantalizing glimpse of their cleverness and wit. To obtain a sense of Jacqueline's French fluency—which was much lauded, and not exaggerated—I watched and listened to her interviews on French television and radio, which were recorded before the state visit of 1961 and are archived at the Bibliothèque Nationale de France.

To re-create the political atmosphere of postwar

France, as well as other details of Paris from 1949 to 1950, I relied on several books, including *Paris Journal 1944–1955*, by Janet Flanner (Genêt); *Paris in the Fifties*, by Stanley Karnow; *My Life in France*, by Julia Child with Alex Prud'homme; *Les Parisiennes*, by Anne Sebba; and *Paris after the Liberation 1944–1949*, by Antony Beevor and Artemis Cooper, which was one of the last books Jacqueline worked on as an editor. My understanding of America during the early days of the Cold War was informed by sources such as *Ethel Rosenberg: An American Tragedy*, by Anne Sebba; and a declassified State Department paper from December 1949 titled "The Soviet 'Peace' Offensive." I learned more about Marie-Madeleine Fourcade and the Alliance spy ring from *Madame Fourcade's Secret War*, by Lynne Olson. The article "Jacqueline Kennedy, Frenchness, and French-American Relations in the 1950s and Early 1960s," by Whitney Walton (*French Politics, Culture & Society*, vol. 31, no. 2, Summer 2013), provided insights into Jacqueline's influence in foreign policy during the Kennedy administration.

I am indebted to two sources that allowed me to imagine Jacqueline as an American student in Paris in 1949. The first is Alice Kaplan's biography *Dreaming in French: The Paris Years of Jacqueline Bouvier Kennedy, Susan Sontag, and Angela Davis*, which is impeccably researched and tremendously insightful. From descriptions of the de Rentys' apartment, to interviews with Jacqueline's friend Martha Rusk, to unearthing Jacqueline's Smith in Paris transcripts, the author left no stone unturned, and I heartily recommend her book if you are interested in reading more about this subject.

The second is the collection of letters, diaries, and memories from the Smith in Paris group of 1950 to 1951, just one year after Jacqueline's. In 2000, some of the group met in Paris for their fiftieth reunion, and from this gathering grew a photocopied, spiral-bound compilation called *Coming of Age in Paris*, edited by alumna Mary Allison Kirschner. Reading about their everyday experiences—their horror of Turkish toilets, meals of worm-riddled roasted veal, and panic over examinations—left me laughing, crying, and filled with admiration. Studying abroad in 1950 required grit, with polio lurking in boardinghouses, letters from home taking weeks to arrive, and food often scarce on the table. These young women navigated their adventures with great aplomb, and, like Jacqueline, many of them considered their year in Paris the high point of their lives. I feel fortunate to have had their words to guide my story. I am also grateful to Smith in Paris alumna Lois Grjebine, who spoke to me about the cold feet, fluttering nuns' robes, and beautiful grimy buildings she experienced in 1950s Paris. She told me about the fistfight she once witnessed between two audience members during the intermission of *Waiting for Godot*. "I thought: *Culture is alive!*" she said.

There have been enough books written about Jacqueline Bouvier Kennedy Onassis to fill a specialty bookshop. Most of them gloss over her time in Paris, dismissing it as a brief, insignificant period in a life filled with great historical moments. But I believe that this year—the academic year of 1949 to 1950—was when she was able to be her most genuine self. Far from the security and expectations of her family, before her tumultuous marriage, or motherhood, or the relentless glare of international fame, she was able to determine what she truly loved in life, and set out to achieve it. France would forever be her guiding compass, influencing her greatest accomplishments, and French language and culture would remain her intellectual refuge for the rest of her life.

—Ann Mah
Hanoi, Vietnam

Acknowledgments

Thanks to my agent Deborah Schneider for her unwavering support and encouragement, and to the team at Gelfman Schneider/ICM Partners and Curtis Brown UK for their dynamic work—Penelope Burns, Enrichetta Frezzato, Cathy Gleason, and Claire Nozieres.

At HarperCollins/Mariner Books, thanks to Katherine Nintzel, for her expert guidance and perceptive editing that helped shape this story. Thanks also to Liate Stehlik, Jennifer Hart, Kelly Rudolph, Molly Gendell, Brittani Hilles, David Palmer, Kerry Rubenstein, and Amelia Wood for their support and enthusiasm.

A travel article I wrote for the *New York Times* inspired this book, and I am grateful to my editors Lynda Richardson and Amy Virshup for the opportunity.

In Paris, Jacob Cigainero, Andrea Field, and Erin Reeser were invaluable resources. For information on Smith in Paris and the history of Reid Hall, I am grateful to Brunhilde Biebuyck, Marie-Madeleine Charlier, and Meredith Levin. Thanks to Smith alumna Lois Grjebine who shared her memories of studying in Paris from 1950 to 1951.

Heartfelt thanks and gratitude to my early readers for their sharp and intelligent suggestions: Meg Bortin, Juliette Fay, Allison Larkin, and Hilary Reyl. Thanks also to Jérôme Avenas for help with French history, punctuation, manners, and much more.

My love and thanks to Chris, who helped me analyze these characters with Freudian finesse, and who remains my favorite foreign exchange student. And to Lucy, who inspires me.